THE VISITORS

KAREN WOODS

First published in 2012

EMPIRE PUBLICATIONS
1 Newton Street, Manchester M1 1HW
© Karen Woods 2012

ISBN 1901746 984 – 9781901746983

Printed in Great Britain.

ACKNOWLEDGEMENTS

As always thanks to all my readers, and facebook and twitter friends. With each book I've written my fan base has grown. Thanks to all my family and friends, and my children Ashley, Blake, Declan and Darcy.

Thanks to John Ireland and Ashley Shaw at Empire, without their belief in my writing I would have never have started. Also a big thanks to Darren Tipple for his help.

Also a big thanks to James and my parents Alan and Margaret for all their support. Also big kisses to my brothers Alan and Darren – keep smiling lads.

As always I try to keep my books real and tell it how it is, I will always write raw gritty storylines and try to keep my readers happy. At the moment I'm working on my seventh novel "Sleepless in Manchester" so watch out for it.

All my readers can reach me on my website www. karenwoods.net or on twitter @karenwoods69

My last thanks is to my son Dale, goodnight god bless son.

*In Memory of Billy Hayes (Dad), Billy Hayes (son),
Jean Hayes - gone but not forgotten.*

CHAPTER ONE

SUSIE JONES SAT CHEWING on her pink glossed fingernails as the judge passed sentence on her man. Her life would never be the same now and she knew she'd have to pull her finger out to help him all she could. Looking at the dock she tried to keep her eyes dry but she was struggling. Tim was led by the guard through the side door inside the court. He turned his head quickly as they removed him and raised a smile towards his girlfriend. Bringing his large hand up towards his mouth he placed a kiss on his fingertips and blew it towards her. He was gone.

The courtroom was filled with noise and no one seemed to care that her world was falling apart right in front of their eyes. Grabbing her expensive Jimmy Choo handbag, Susie hooked it over her shoulder and left the courtroom. Tim's solicitor now came to her side and expressed his regret. He approached her with caution as he could see she was upset. Susie was a fiery woman and he knew from the past she was like a ticking bomb. "Sorry Susie. You knew he was going to get time anyway, didn't you?" he patted the middle of her arm. "I just thought the judge might have been a bit more lenient." He glanced around and made sure no one could hear him. His voice became low "He's a harsh fucker Judge Prescott. If it would have been any other judge we could have got at least a year knocked off his sentence."

Susie slid her tongue across her top teeth. She was angry and the grip on her handbag told him she was ready to explode. "Can't we appeal against it? I mean three years for punching someone to protect yourself. It's a fucking joke."

The solicitor scowled and shot a look at her. "Susie it wasn't just a punch though, was it? Tim nearly killed the man."

Huffing she looked down at her expensive shoes. "Well he never died, did he, so they should have just seen it for what it was." Her hands stroked the side of her face as she became defensive. "It was a fight between two drunken men, that's all." The solicitor knew he was fighting a losing battle and shrugged his shoulders. He just stood now and let her have her say. Susie called him a shit solicitor and told him point-blank she wouldn't be using him again. They stayed talking for a few more minutes and the legal representative looked stressed as he wiped small droplets of sweat from his forehead. Susie eventually walked away from him shouting "you're a fucking waste of space" over her shoulder at him.

The Mancunian weather was typically depressing. Dark clouds hung from the sky and looked like they were nearly touching the floor. Each one told a story of depression and life living on the breadline. Susie pulled her grey coat tighter around her body and ran towards the car park. Once sat inside her car she searched through her handbag looking for her mobile. Quickly dialling a number she checked her face in the rear view mirror. "Hiya love it's me. He got slammed for three years." You could hear the voice of someone else on the phone and it sounded like they were laughing. "Right okay, I'll be there in ten minutes. See you soon." She threw her phone on the passenger seat. Pulling the seat belt round her she clicked it inside the socket.

Susie and her boyfriend Tim had been together for over four years. It wasn't the best of relationships and the love they once shared had disappeared years before. Susie never left her partner because he gave her all the material things she needed in life. Tim was a grafter and always earned a good crust. Susie lived in Harpurhey, Manchester in a close knit community. Her home on the council estate had everything she could have wished for.

Driving her silver X5 BMW she weaved in and out of the traffic. Her heart was aching inside, but that was for the money she'd miss out on, and not for her boyfriend Tim.

Susie had been having an affair with Tim's best mate for the last few years. She'd fallen for him big time but hid it well. Pulling up in the car park she could see her lover's black car in the distance. Checking her face in the mirror for the last time she quickly scanned the area. That's all she needed was for some nosey bastard telling Tim she was shagging the brains out of his best mate Ashley.

"Come here you dirty bitch," Ashley laughed. He grabbed her by the waist and twisted her thin figure into the air.

"Put me down nob-head," she giggled.

"What's up with you? Tim's inside now so we don't have to hide anymore do we?" He waited for a reply with a serious face. Susie panicked, she'd filled Ashley's head with so much shit in the past and he really thought she had no feelings for her boyfriend. She'd told him they were like brother and sister and that they rarely had sex together. What a lying slut she was.

"Yeah Ash, you're right, but I don't want everyone knowing about us just yet. Tim's just got three years rammed up his arse, and I need to let him down slowly don't I?"

Ashley sneered at her and tilted his head to the side. "Well as long as he's told, I'm not arsed. I've waited long enough for you, so a few more months won't make any difference. Anyway where we off to? Do ya fancy a few beers?"

Susie straightened her clothes and headed to his car. She looked anxious. "Erm... not really Ash. My head's all over the place at the moment, I just need to chill for a bit. Shall we go to yours?" Ash started to walk to his car. He was swinging the car keys round his fingers. He stared at her for a bit longer than he should have and Susie knew she'd rattled his cage.

Sitting in his car he reached over and sunk his lips on hers. She wasn't in the mood for him and quickly shrugged him away. "For fuck's sake Ashley. Someone might see us."

His face turned red with anger as he shoved her body back to her seat with a fierce push. "Fucking stop being hormonal, will you. I'm only showing you a bit of affection." Susie looked in a world of her own as she gazed through the rain splashed window. She had so much to take care of now, her head was up her arse. The brothel Tim ran was now her responsibility. Usually she would just call in the gaff to see him, but now he was rotting in jail she had to step up to the mark and make sure the money kept rolling in.

The brasses in the brothel hated Susie with a passion, and she knew they would make her life a misery. There was one woman in particular who she was dreading facing. Her name was Joan and she held nothing back from Susie. Every time she'd visited the brothel in the past she was always there, waiting to have a pop at her.

Joan was a hard fucker as well. The scars on her cheeks told Susie she wouldn't think twice about pummelling her fist deep into her face, if she ever got on the wrong side of her.

The car pulled up outside Ashley's apartment. He lived near the city centre in and like Tim he was into loads of hooky deals. Susie had fancied Ashley as soon as she met him and it was obvious that he'd had the hots for her too.

Ashley Taylor was a grafter and always had cash. He had the best of everything. Tim had even told Susie in the past that his mate was a womaniser, but that never deterred her. His six foot body frame was rippling with muscles. His dark hair was always styled neatly and he always wore designer clothes. Sometimes it pissed Susie off that he was such a posing bastard. In the past he'd laughed at her Primark label sticking from her dress and said she needed to up her game if she wanted to be his woman.

After locking the car up, they both ran to the front door. The rain was falling hard and Susie lifted her handbag over her head to protect her neatly styled locks. The front door now opened and they both entered. Ashley dragged her straight up the stairs into the bedroom. It was obvious his cock was throbbing for her. He was eager to get her kit off and at one point he was yanking at her blouse because he couldn't undo the buttons. "Fucking get stripped off then, these bollocks need emptying." Scooping his nuts in his hands he displayed them like a proud peacock. Susie looked pissed off as she rolled her black lacy knickers down her firm thighs. Her underwear had just about hit the floor and he mounted her with a frenzied look.

Lay on top of her he inserted his throbbing member.

"I'm not gonna be long Susie, so don't be expecting any big long love session. My balls have been aching for you all day." Susie looked at him crouched on top of her. He was good-looking, and looked so sexy. Her own problems seemed to drift away.

The two of them lay entwined in each other's bodies and every jerk he gave made her moan with pleasure. Rolling on top of the red silk bedding he bit onto her bottom lip as he shot his load. Susie looked hot and as he ejaculated, she let out a groan of enjoyment. "Fuck me harder Ash, fuck me." His body struggled to finish her off but within seconds they'd both found heaven.

Lying on the bed he rolled to her side. His hand gripped hers, and he kissed her fingertips. "That was alright our kid," he sniggered.

Softly punching his waist she chuckled. "You're a cheeky fucker you are Ash," Susie loved his cocky attitude. Two naked bodies lay staring at the ceiling. Susie knew he would have something to say now as his constant deep breaths told her he was planning a speech. She wasn't wrong, her eyes rolled to the back of her head as he began. "Right Susie, you can come and move in with me. I could do with a woman's touch around the place anyway." Her head turned quickly towards him, her face was red.

"Ay I'm no fucking cleaner. Tim pays someone to clean our house, so I suggest you get that fucking daft thought right out of your head." She blew a hard breath. "Me...a cleaner. Get a grip man. You're so fucking funny you are. You need to take your head from out of your arse and smell the coffee, mate."

Ashley loved her bluntness and leant into her face. She could feel his warm breath tickling her cheeks. "You're mine now love, so you need to start giving a little bit back to this relationship," his nostrils flared as he ran his fingers through his hair. "Fucking hell, I've waited long enough for you, so you owe me big-time."

She retaliated, and bolted up from his side. "Yeah you've waited for me there's no denying that, but never in a million years will I be your skivvy."

His head wobbled as he started to laugh. "What about a sex slave then?" he rolled on the bed laughing as if he had a feather up his arse.

Susie held a stern look on her face and spoke with sarcasm. "Yeah I can do that, but any rubber gloves you have bought for me can be shoved right up your arse." Ashley backpedalled. He loved this woman with all his heart and would have done anything to make her happy.

"Susie you know I wouldn't have you cleaning and all that shit. I'm joking with you, Muppet. I just want us to be happy, and if that means getting a cleaner in, so be it." He looked at her with puppy dog eyes. He was so sincere.

"I know that Ashley. That's why I'm here with you. We've got a special bond me and you and I'd hate for you to spoil it." She raised her eyebrows and gave a cunning look. She knew she could wrap him around her little finger and played the game of a besotted woman. She stroked her finger across his bottom lip. "I just need time to sort all this shit out. I mean, I've got to manage the brass gaff now," she fell back onto the bed and shook her head. "Imagine me doing that Ash, I'm dreading it."

His face remained frozen. You could tell he was thinking. "Let me run it then. I know all the shit and how it works, so I'll just do it for you." Susie didn't trust Ashley where money was concerned. He would have robbed a blind man to earn a quick few quid. Susie jerked up from the bed and she searched for her knickers.

"Nar love. I can do it by myself. I don't want us being connected in anyway just yet. You know what people are like round here, they would put two and two together straight away." Pulling her body, he cradled her in his grip. She looked like she was suffocating with his love and pulled away struggling. "Right drop me off. I've got to go and see Tim's family. They'll be going off their heads when they know their golden balls son got slammed for three long uns." Ashley removed his hands from her body and sat watching her as she started to get ready. He loved her so much and his pain was written all across his face. He would have killed for this woman.

"Right come on, take me to get my car." Ashley dragged his tracksuit bottoms on and grabbed his white vest top from the floor. He looked sexy as he slipped his vest over his tanned toned body. Susie located his car keys from the bedside cabinet and passed them to him. She knew what was coming next and planned her speech ready to reply to him. "So are you coming round here later on then, or what?" Susie looked anxious; she gripped his face in her hands.

"Orr I wish I could babes, I've just got so much to do, and once I get to Tim's mam's she'll have me there all night, moaning," she pointed her finger into his face. "So don't be phoning me ay." Ashley growled at her as she walked away from him.

"It does my head in you know. You're my woman now, and the sooner everyone knows it, the better." He rammed his feet inside his trainers.

"It all comes to those who wait," Susie giggled. She was trying to make light of the conversation. He wasn't amused.

Ashley dropped Susie off near Tim's parent's house. Her own car wasn't far from there. A quick kiss on his cheek and she left his side. "Fucking stalker," she whispered under her breath as she watched him drive off. Susie trudged towards Tim's parent's house. She just hoped his sister wasn't there visiting. Helen was a right interfering cow and she'd clashed with her, on one or more occasions.

The sound of a letter box rapping could be heard. A face now came to the window and Susie could see Tim's sister squashing her face up against the glass. She placed her finger up against the glass and mouthed "One minute."

Sighing, Susie took in a deep breath. "Here goes," she mumbled. The front door swung open and Tim's mother and sister stood there urging her to come inside. Once the door was closed Helen started to talk.

"Where's our Tim?" Susie shook her head and covered her face trying to look upset. She was a brilliant actress and deserved an Oscar for this performance.

"He's in prison. He got three years," she flung her body against the wall and looked like her legs were melting. "What am I going to do without him?" Arms were flung around her body from Tim's mother as she sobbed. Helen just stood watching the drama with a curious look on her face. She hated Susie with a passion and knew now her brother was behind bars she would have to watch her like a hawk.

"Put the kettle on Helen. Do Susie a sweet cup of tea. She's a nervous wreck," Tim's mother said. Helen blew a hard breath and trudged into the kitchen. Twisting her head back over her shoulder she watched the drama queen still performing for her mother. She didn't trust her one little bit.

Susie pulled off the heartbroken girlfriend well. A box of tissues was now placed at her side. Patting the white tissue paper under her eyes she squeezed a few teardrops out. "I'm just so lost without him. He's my world, what am I going to do without him?"

Tim's mother came to her side. She rested her flat palm on her lap as she spoke. "We're all here for you love. You're not on your own. Don't ever think that, we're your family." Helen returned carrying three cups hooked around her fingers. She was a big girl and looked like she'd not stopped eating for months. Her short cropped hair sat on her head like a river of grease. Banging the cups down on the table she parked her arse on the sofa. She shot a look at Susie, there was no way she was pulling the wool over her eyes. Helen was listening to her every word.

Helen secretly blamed Susie for her brother's imprisonment. Tim had been involved in a fight in the local pub months before and as always Susie was in the middle of it. Helen was there and she watched Susie flirting with all the men in the pub as usual. It was inevitable that before the night was over her brother was going to chin someone. Tim was well-known for having a short fuse and everyone knew not to fuck with him. Helen tried to hold her brother back when the fight first started. He'd seen a man touching Susie's arse. He was too strong for her to restrain, he was like a caged animal. Helen had to watch him waste the man; there was nothing she could do. She covered her face as he stamped all over man's head with incredible force, he was ruthless.

Susie was watching the fight too and Helen could see her laughing as the other man fell to the floor for the eighth time. Tim left him in a bad way and the victim was lucky to be alive. The landlord phoned the police instantly and Tim was arrested shortly after that.

Helen reached for her brew and dunked her chocolate biscuit inside it. With one bite the biscuit was gone. The chocolate was visible at the sides of her mouth. She was such a scruffy cow. Helen smirked at Susie, "I'm going to be helping you anyway love. Tim's told me already, that if he got time I was to help you out." Susie looked shocked. That was all she needed, his sister on her case. Helen was like Miss Marple and she knew she'd uncover her secret if she was with her twenty four seven. Susie held her head high and replied.

"Thanks Helen, but I can manage. It's just a shock at the moment. I'll be sorted in a few weeks."

Helen wasn't giving up that easy and continued. "I'm helping you and that's the end of it. Do you hear me?"

Susie backed down and agreed as she watched Tim's mother nodding her head with approval. "Okay I'll shout you if I need you."

Helen looked at her mother and nodded her head. "Our kid doesn't have to worry about fuck all while he's in jail. We can sort everything." Tim's mother Mary looked pleased and sat back in her chair. She knew all about her son running a brothel, everyone did. Mary turned a blind eye to all his antics.

Helen's son toddled into the front room. His wet nappy was dangling between his legs like a ton of bricks were held inside it. Green snot hung from his nose and his attempt to wipe it had caused it to spread all across his face. Susie screwed up her face as she clocked him. Helen clutched at her son's anorexic arms. "Eww... come here you scruff. Look at the state of your snozzle." The young child tried to fight her off as she used the end of her sleeve to wipe his nose. Susie shook her head and heaved. Helen was a minger. Once the child was free, he walked to Susie's side. She squirmed as he ran his tiny fingers over her pants. These were her best River Island trousers and no way in this world was this kid going to ruin them. The family's eyes were on her watching her every movement. She tried to move him away without being nasty. Her face raised a struggled smile. Sniffing hard she smelt a pongy aroma. Her nostrils flared as she looked at the child and located the stench.

"I think he's dropped a load Helen."

Huffing, Helen pulled her fat arse up from the chair. "Fucking hell Matthew, that's your third turd today. What the fucks up with your arse?" Reaching inside a white plastic bag at the side of the chair she pulled out a new nappy and some baby wipes. The kid was squealing as she captured him in her grip. Lying his body flat on her legs she pulled the stinking nappy from his body. His two legs were now held in her hand as she yanked his arse up in the air. "Oh you dirty bleeder. Your arse is rancid. Oh my god this shit looks like King Kong's finger," she giggled. Susie yanked her shirt up to cover her nose. She was retching. Helen was using the old nappy to wipe the shit from his bum cheeks. He was caked in it. Everyone watched as Matthew screamed at the top of his lungs. His arse looked red raw and small blisters could now be seen all over his private area. Once he was clean, Helen flicked his frail body back onto the floor. "Shut up moaning, you mard arse, you're done now." The child ran to his nana for comfort. "Come here son," she said with open arms.

Helen lived not far from her mother's house with her long- term boyfriend. She had three children with him.

Her partner was a lazy fucker and just the word 'Work' made him sweat like a paedophile at a child's party. Helen claimed benefits she wasn't entitled to, and lived life from hand to mouth every day. She was so different from her brother Tim. Susie felt sickened to think she was even part of his life.

The three women sat for a while discussing Tim's sentence. Susie knew she would have to be two steps in front and one behind Helen to keep her out of her business. Yeah, she had just the thing for her if she ever tried interfering in her life. Susie held a cunning look on her face as she stood up to leave. "Right I'm going home. I better get used to being alone hadn't I?" She was searching for some sympathy and it wasn't long before she found it.

Tim's mother was by her side instantly, wrapping her two loving arms around her. Helen watched with jealousy in her eyes as her mother spoke. "We're here for you love. Like I said, anything you need, just give us a shout." Susie gave her an endearing smile and walked towards the front door. Helen was behind her edging to speak.

"As soon as the kids are in bed tonight I'll call round and see you. It's a bit of company for you isn't it?"

Susie panicked. "Orr.. not tonight Helen. My heads in bits I just want an early night. Maybe tomorrow ay?" Helen looked like she wanted to jaw her there and then. You could see her clenched fist hung at the side of her legs.

"Right no worries. I'll just phone you instead for a chat. I know what it's like when you're upset. A problem shared is a problem halved, isn't it?"

Susie stood open mouthed, she was eager to get away. "Thanks you two, I don't know what I'd do without you!"

"Orr bless," Mary whispered.

Susie walked to the car. She could feel Helen's eyes burning into the back of her head as she opened the door. "Fat interfering slag," she muttered under her breath.

The time was ticking on and Susie knew she'd have to go and see Joan who ran the brothel. She was dreading seeing her and prepared herself for a load of abuse. Joan had always run things for Tim over the years. Susie knew she fancied the arse off her man and laughed at her sometimes, thinking Tim would ever look at her in a million years, she was an old hag. Pulling up at the house Susie searched for her mobile phone to tell Joan she was outside. She could hear a ringing tone. "Joan it's me Susie, I'm outside your house. Are you in or what?" There was a muffled reply and Susie quickly ended the call. Checking her face in the wing mirror she left the car.

Joan stood at her front door with a fag hanging from the corner of her mouth. Last night's make up was still visible around her eyes, she looked rough. Susie tried to raise a smile but they both knew they hated each other's guts.

Joan was dressed in a long t-shirt that barely covered her arse cheeks. False tan could be seen smeared across her plump legs. She looked orange. Standing at the front door Susie waited for Joan to invite her inside. The woman stood with a cocky look on her face and it was Susie who had to make the first move. "Any chance I can come in for a minute love. We have a few things to sort out about work and that?" Joan flicked her cig into the front garden and trudged inside leaving the door open for Susie to follow. A strong smell of cat piss was in the air, Susie's nostrils flared as she lifted her hand over her mouth.

Joan plonked herself onto the grey sofa and kept her eyes focused on the TV. She was a right ignorant bitch, Susie looked pissed off. Placing one hand on her hip she began to speak. "Tim's in prison. So I'll be managing Delia's from now on."

Joan sneered and looked directly at her. "You couldn't manage a piss up in a brewery, never mind manage the girls love." Susie bit hard on her bottom lip. This woman was taking the piss out of her and she knew she'd have to stand up to her once and for all. Susie was shaking inside and her voice trembled as she continued.

"Listen Joan, things are going to be hard enough without you adding to it all. I know I don't know how everything works, but I'm gonna have to fucking learn aren't I?"

Joan's eyes pierced into Susie as she stuttered. "Well I'm not going to lie to you. The girls can't stand you, so how do you plan to run things. Once they know you're the new boss I'm sure the girls will fuck off."

Susie held her own and raised her voice. "If that's the way they feel, then let them go. And if you have any problems working for me, you can do the same."

Joan looked uneasy. Sitting upright in her seat she tugged at her t-shirt pulling it over her knees. You could tell she needed the job more than anything and started to backpedal. "You can rely on me love," she cracked her knuckles. "I won't give you any trouble. I can talk to the girls for you. They listen to me. I'm just saying there are a few of the girls you've upset in the past and it's going be a hard battle to get them back onside. But I'll do my best."

Susie looked confident when she answered her. "Well it's my way or the highway. I've got to do my best while

Tim's in the clink, and if anyone, and I mean anyone," Susie paused and stared at Joan a bit longer than she should have, "stands in my way or starts trying to fuck with my head, they'll be out the front door as fast as lightning. So make sure you tell them that."

Joan lit another cig; she looked frustrated as she flicked her lighter more than once to get a light. Lifting her head, she replied. "Yeah I'll have a word with them. Like I said before, I can't promise they'll listen."

Susie stood tall and flicked her hair round her shoulder. "Right," she paused and looked at her watch. "Tell the girls I'll be there tonight about half eleven."

Joan screwed her face up, "Yeah no worries."

Susie walked towards the front door and turned back slowly as if she'd forgotten something. Taking a deep breath she shouted into Joan. "Make sure all the girls are free to see me when I get there. You're the manager, so let's see you manage." There was no reply from Joan as Susie slammed the door behind her looking pleased with herself.

CHAPTER TWO

Susie looked at the clock ticking away on the wall. It was nearly eleven. Slipping her shoes back onto her slender feet she stood to check her hair in the nearby mirror. Joan had already rung her to say the girls were expecting her. She sounded nervous when Susie spoke to her minutes before and she knew her visit was going to shake some heads.

The house felt eerie. She was used to Tim being sat at home playing on his Play- station, but tonight she felt lonely. Her mobile phone started to ring and she glanced at the screen. It was Joan's name flashing again. "You can fucking wait. You shag bag," she shouted at the phone. Gripping it from the side she tossed it into her bag. With a quick squirt of her "Armani Diamond" perfume she was ready to leave.

The night air was cold as it trickled around her body as she walked to her car. Opening the car door she heard a familiar voice shouting her name in the distance. "Susie, its Helen, wait up." The sound of stamping footsteps could be heard drawing nearer. Susie looked pissed off as she shook her head in disbelief. Was this bitch watching her every movement from afar? Susie scanned the area. Nobody else was about. Helen was most definitely spying on her.

"What are you doing out at this time?" Susie asked with a cocky face. She rolled her sleeve up to check the time.

"I was just going to check you were okay. Good job I caught you innit?" Helen said.

Susie stood waiting for her to speak again. She wanted to rip her head off. "Where you off to then?" Helen queried.

Susie huffed, and opened the car door ready to get inside. "I'm going to meet the girls at Delia's. I've a few things to sort out, why?"

Helen sniggered and hurried to the passenger side and opened the car door. "Well I'll come with you. Bit of back up, and all that." She jumped into the car before Susie could get her words out. It was too late; Helen was now sat in the vehicle pulling her seat belt round her fat round body. Susie was livid and slammed her door shut letting her know she wasn't welcome.

Helen sat smiling and knew she'd rattled her cage.

Susie sniffed up loudly. She could smell something strange. She followed her nose and it led her straight to Helen. "What's that fucking smell?" she asked, as her face creased with sickness.

Helen giggled as she waved her hand near her crotch. "Orr sorry about that. It's my guts. I had a curry for my tea and now I'm paying the price. I can't stop farting yanno. I'm like a walking gas bag."

Susie quickly pressed the button to open the window. She hated this woman with a passion. "Dirty cow," she mumbled.

They drove to Delia's in silence. Helen was rooting about in the glove compartment and Susie told her straight. "Stop being fucking nosey and close it back up". She was bugging her big time and she was losing her patience. Helen closed it back up and sat sulking. "I was only looking, for God's sake, take a chill pill."

The traffic was quiet and they were soon there. Helen was dressed in grey tracksuit bottoms and a long discoloured white t-shirt. The food she'd eaten throughout the day was still visible all over the front of it. She was a scruffy cow without a shadow of a doubt.

Pulling up into the car park Susie turned the car engine off. "You can wait here. I'm not going to be long and I don't want it to seem as if I've brought you along for back up."

Helen sat thinking for a second and nodded her head. "Yeah I see what you mean. Well, I'll sit here for ten minutes and if you're not back I'll come inside," Helen's face was serious. "I know what these girls are like yanno. They wouldn't think twice about slicing you up."

Susie screwed her face up and spoke in a sarcastic tone. "Slice me up, get a grip will you." Susie was more than capable of kicking some arse. She'd fought with Tim in the past and she knew some kick arse moves. Helen was so dramatic and Susie had to bite her lip to stop herself from telling her to shut the fuck up. She stepped out of the car and headed towards the entrance.

The night was cold and the area was pitch black except for one lonely lamp post that gave off very little light. She started to jog to the front door of "Delia's". The sound of her heels clicking on the concrete pavement could be heard. Pressing the small silver button on the intercom with her long pink nails, she shivered as she waited for someone to answer. A voice could now be heard, Susie spoke quickly into it with her mouth almost inside the speaker. "It's me. Susie. Can you let me in or what? I'm freezing my tits off out here." The sound of a buzzing noise could be heard. The door opened.

Facing Susie was a flight of stairs. The lighting was soft and you could just about make out each stair. Holding the wooden banister she trudged towards the top of the staircase. Susie could smell damp. As the light got clearer she could see the red carpet on the top of the stairs. It looked hanging. Dirt was visible all over the floor covering and it made the place look cheap and nasty. A black door now stood facing her. Taking a deep breath she opened it with caution.

The room was bright, and she could see a reception desk and a few leather sofas scattered about the area. Joan now came into sight looking flustered. "Oh right you're here. Just let me go and get the girls for you." Susie knew by her face she was in a bad mood. "I hope you're not going to keep them long, because they have a job to do yanno," she moaned.

Susie parked her arse on the sofa giving Joan a stale

look. As she left the room, a few girls now came to join her. Each of them looked spaced out. They wore silk housecoats that hung from their frail bodies. Tim had told Susie that brasses were hard to come by these days, and judging by the girls in front of her, he was right. These women were the dregs of the brothel chain.

Joan now came back to join her. She looked on edge. She was flexing her fingers that hung by her side. "Right it's just Pippa we're waiting for now, she said she won't be long she's just with a punter. I popped my head inside her room and the guy's arse was like a fiddler's elbow so she'll be with us soon." Susie raised a smile. She could feel eyes burning into her from every direction. The prostitutes looked as hard as nails and you could see Susie swallowing hard as they all gathered round her.

A man now walked past them all tucking his shirt into his black nylon pants. He hung his head low, and you could tell he felt ashamed of his guilty pleasure. "Bye," Joan shouted to him, but he never replied and hurried through the exit like a rat leaving a sinking ship.

Pippa now came to join them. Susie lifted her head up and looked at her in more detail. Tim hadn't mentioned he had a new girl working for him. She was gorgeous and she had a figure to die for. Flicking her long blonde hair round her shoulders she placed one of her long slender legs on the table. Pippa pulled out her fags from her stockings and stuck one into her mouth. "Anyone got a light?" she asked. One of the girls hurried to pass her a lighter. She was treated like royalty amongst them. Flicking the flame she dipped her head to light her cigarette. Taking a long deep drag she sat next to Susie blowing the smoke into her face with a malicious look in her eyes.

Susie looked uncomfortable; she sat forward cupping

her knees in her hands. Her fingers waved about near her face as the smoke hit it hard. She coughed slightly and shot a look towards Pippa that could have killed. Susie could see Joan smiling from the corner of her eye and knew this new girl was big trouble. She swallowed hard and coughed to clear her throat.

"Right ladies, I'm not going to keep you long. As you all know Tim has just got three years in prison, so I'm going to be running things until he gets out." Susie could hear giggling at the side of her and quickly spun her head to see the culprit. Her face looked on fire. "What's so fucking funny love?"

The woman smirked. Looking at the other girls she gasped and spoke to them all shaking her head. "How the fuck can you run this gaff. You don't know the first thing about it!"

Susie stopped her dead in her tracks. She bolted to her feet and made sure all the women could see her face. She was fuming. "Girls you don't seem to be fucking listening to me. I said I'm running things now. This isn't a fucking interview for you all. I'm the boss okay."

The brasses all seemed to be looking at Pippa for support. As they watched her she stumped her cig out in the ashtray and sat back swinging her legs out in front of her. Pippa gasped and everyone was hanging onto her every word. They wanted her to bring Susie down to earth with a bang.

Pippa became cocky as she stroked her calves slowly. "Listen Mrs up your own arse. We girls have been in this game for a long time and we don't need no wannabe Madam starting to try and change things. Why fix what's not broken?"

Susie stood her ground. She gripped her fingers

tightly and knew she would have to defend herself. Who did this hooker think she was speaking to? "Ay fucking baggy fanny. Don't you ever talk to me like that; otherwise you'll be out of that door before you know what's hit you. Do you get me or what?"

Pippa looked anxious. She fidgeted around and knew she would have to back down. She'd heard from the girls that Susie was a loudmouth and quickly tried to make a joke out of it all. "Ay, less of the baggy fanny. I've probably got the tightest motty in here." The girls all joined in the debate now and laughter could be heard. Susie looked relieved as Pippa sat back down. She reckoned she could take her out, but there was something about this woman that told her to be careful.

The women were listening to Susie now as she took control again. "As I was saying, I'm going to be your new boss. A few things will be changed in this place but only the decor. It looks like a shit tip," she shot her eyes at the entrance. "The carpets stinks, when was the last time this place had a lick of paint."

Pippa jumped in again holding her sides laughing. "We're the only thing that's had a lick in this place, never mind the fucking walls." Susie broke a smile. This woman had a wicked sense of humour. Everyone laughed with her. Susie felt like she'd made her mark on the hussies and started to relax. She could see Joan sneering at the side of her. Susie could see by her face she wasn't happy that the girls hadn't kicked off.

At that moment the entrance door swung open and nearly came off its hinges. Helen stood looking flustered. Pippa growled at her and looked her up and down. She was just about to give her some abuse when Susie introduced her. "Everyone this is Helen, Tim's sister". A few of the girls already knew her and nodded their heads. Helen seemed in pain and held her stomach area as if she was going to keel over. Her knees were knocking together and she was swaying about. "Where's the shitter? I'm gonna shit my kecks if I don't get on the toilet soon." Joan showed her the way and she wobbled past them all as if she was squeezing a penny between the cheeks of her arse. Small droplets of sweat could be seen on her forehead. She didn't look well at all. Susie was spitting feathers. She looked annoyed as she watched Helen go past. What an embarrassment she was.

A few of the girls now left as punters came through the door. It was obvious the men had been before because they knew Joan. Susie watched as the girls led the two customers to the bedrooms.

Pippa still sat on the sofa looking her new boss up and down. Susie was intrigued by her and wanted to know a bit more about her past. Falling back into her seat she began the conversation. "So how long have you been working here? Tim's never mentioned you before."

The woman grinned and licked her bottom lip. "I've been here for about six months now," she held her head back and chuckled. "I can't believe Tim has never mentioned me though. He's a top lad, yanno."

Susie urged her to continue. What the fuck was she on about Tim was a top lad. How did she know? She delved deeper. "So was it Tim who found you or Joan?"

Pippa gasped and giggled sarcastically. She knew she was winding her new boss up and loved every minute of it. Twiddling her hair between her fingers she smirked. "Nobody found me love. I agreed to work here when Tim told me what kind of business he ran. I was on my arse, and he had this place, so it all made sense if you know what I mean?" Susie watched the brass as she spoke about Tim. She seemed to melt in the chair at the sound of his name. Her eyelashes fluttered as she continued. "I met Tim in a nightclub. I was a dancer there. The money was alright but I had trouble with the management."

"No fucking wonder. You're a gobby cunt," Susie mumbled under her breath.

"Tim was like my knight in shining armour I suppose. He didn't like the way the boss spoke to me and told him straight that I was leaving."

Susie jumped in. Her face was red and her mouth was dry. "What do you mean 'your knight in fucking shining armour?' Are you saying you've been sleeping with my man?"

Pippa shook her head slowly. She knew what she was doing. "Nar am I eck. I'm just saying he's a good man, and for you to look after him. He's a good catch for any woman you know."

Susie wanted to jump on her and scratch her eyeballs from their sockets but the sound of someone moaning in the room made her turn her head. Helen was stood at the doorframe with one hand resting on it. Wiping her forehead she spoke to Susie. "I'm not a well woman love. Are we going to be long or what, because I feel like I could shit for England?" Susie located her handbag and quickly had a few words with Joan. Before she left, she shot a look at Pippa who was still sitting on the sofa looking like the cat that had got the cream. Susie looked puzzled but had a gut feeling that Tim had been sleeping with her. Gritting her teeth she nodded her head towards Pippa as she left.

Helen was still moaning as they went down the stairs. "Will you shut the fuck up?" Susie snapped, "You're doing my bastard head in. I said for you to stay in the car didn't I?"

Helen's face looked blank and she spoke to her with an apologetic tone. "I was touching cloth. I would have shit all over the car if I didn't get to a toilet fast." Susie blew her breath. "Well you should have squatted outside or summit. I bet the girls think I'm a right shit bag now having you waiting in the car." Susie yanked the door open with force. She was raging now and let Helen have it. Standing with one hand on her hip she let rip. "Let's get one thing straight. You don't need to look out for me. I'm big enough and strong enough to sort out anything or anyone that stands in my way." She froze in her step and Helen turned her head to look at her. "Including you, Helen."

Helen stood gawping. Who the fuck did she think she was, talking to her like that? She tried to calm her. "Stop fucking stressing will you? And what do you mean including me. I'm your family and I'm here to make sure you're okay, but if you want to ride it solo sweetheart, feel fucking free." Susie carried on walking towards the car as Helen carried on moaning behind her. She'd seen her arse and wasn't shutting up for love nor money. "I mean I do someone a favour and this is how I get treated. Well fuck you Susie; I know when I'm not wanted." Susie slid the key into the car door. Jumping inside she waited for Helen to get in. She wanted to leave her there but she knew that would have been over the top behaviour, she snarled as she watched her click her seat belt on.

All the way home Helen held her stomach and Susie felt quite bad for her previous rant. It was obvious this woman was in pain, and she tried to show some concern. It was hard for Susie to be nice to her because she really hated Helen with a passion but she played the part well of a concerned friend. "You need to go to the doctor's love. I mean to have a smell like that coming from your arse; your guts must be rotting away."

Helen was forgiving and spoke straight away. "I've been loads of time love, but they just say it's indigestion. Tablet after tablet they give me but nowt seems to work."

Susie thought about Helen's size and spoke aloud without thinking. "Your weight won't help though will it? I mean come on, you must be touching on twenty stone."

Helen nearly choked and waved her hands in the air. "Am I fuck twenty stone you muppet, I'm about nineteen. It's just that I look bigger because I wear baggy clothes and all that," she dragged at her clothes lifting them up from her stale sweaty body.

"Yeah right," Susie laughed.

"Nar honest, I've lost pure weight, ask my mam. I've been on that 'Slim Fast' stuff."

"Well you don't look any different to me," Susie smirked.

"I could murder a kebab. I've shit all that curry out from before and now my stomach's empty," she gripped Susie's arm and pleaded with her. "Any chance we can stop at Pizza Lane or summit?" Susie sighed at the beached whale at the side of her. She had to laugh though because Helen was just so funny in her own way.

Helen ran into the takeaway as if her life depended on it. She came out shortly after with a Kebab wrapped in white paper. She was holding onto it for dear life. It looked like a roll of five by four carpet slid under her arm as she got back into the car. Helen ripped her food open and squashed the Nan bread together at the end. Her hands were shaking as she took her first bite. The smell filtered Susie's nostrils. She was starving too. She hadn't had a bite to eat all day; she was looking at the food and licking her lips.

"Orr will you go back in Helen and get me one?" Helen was ripping her Kebab apart in her teeth like a feeding lioness. Meat and salad was dangling from her mouth. She agreed with a nodding head. Susie searched her bag for her purse as her mobile phone started ringing. Quickly glancing at the flashing screen she could see Ashley's name. Ignoring the ring tone she passed Helen a crisp ten pound note.

"Get me one of them what you're eating," she pointed on Helen's lap. "Get some hot chilli sauce on it please." Helen still held her half eaten food in her hands as she took the money from Susie. She left the car and could be seen still munching her food through the shop window.

Quickly redialling the number Susie held the phone to her ear as she kept one eye still focused on Tim's sister. Her voice was low as she spoke. "I'm with Helen, Ash. You'll have to ring me back later when I've got rid of her. I'm on my way home soon," she paused and rolled her eyes. "Fucking hell I've been to see the girls at Delia's, stop stressing will you? Right, right, speak soon bye." Quickly chucking her phone back in her handbag she watched her food being prepared through the large glass window. Her mouth was watering.

Both the women sat eating their scran in the car. Helen had finished eating long before Susie; she could feel her eyes watching her like a dog waiting for some food to be flung her way. Susie had never been a big eater but tonight she felt like she could eat a scabby horse much to Helen's disappointment. Susie left just a few strands of

Doner meat and a bit of fallen lettuce, she got ready to fold the white paper and throw the remains away.

"Wait up there, don't throw it. I'll finish it," Helen gasped.

"Greedy bitch" Susie mumbled as she handed her the remains of her feast. Helen was eating like she'd never been fed. No wonder she was so big.

Susie headed home she was exhausted. She dropped Helen off first and was glad to see the back of her. As she drove off she could hear her shouting that she would see her the following day. Susie ignored her and watched her waddle into her house as she left. "You won't be seeing me tomorrow lard arse," she giggled.

The phone was ringing again. Turning the music up Susie ignored it. After all, it could only be Ashley wanting to know where she was. He was becoming a nuisance and she hated his desperation. It was late as Susie entered her house. She looked quickly over her shoulder making sure nobody was watching her as she pushed the key into the lock. She looked uneasy and quickly bolted the door once she was inside. Her eyes were tired and she was ready to drop.

Walking into the living room she noticed her cigs. "Fucking hell, that's where I'd left them," she said to herself. Susie had been gasping for one earlier and thought she'd lost them. Dragging a fag from the gold Benson and Hedges packet on the table, she hung it from her mouth searching for her lighter. Flicking the end of her finger over the lighter she stuck her head towards the flame. Sucking noises could be heard as she inhaled her first blast of nicotine.

Kicking her shoes off, Susie grabbed the remote control for the telly. Scrolling through the channels she looked for something to watch. Every time she pressed a TV station it was the same as the last. "Fucking babe-station," she laughed. "Ten minute teaser, what the fuck is this world coming too with all these porn channels?" Susie tilted her head to the side as she watched a blonde woman on the screen stretching her body out across the bed. The woman was sucking on her finger slowly and ordering the viewers to phone the number at the bottom of the screen for more adult fun. "What a fucking joke," she moaned. Susie knew Tim had stayed up late into the night to watch these programmes. She'd had endless arguments with him the past, calling him a dirty pervert. She knew without a shadow of a doubt that he'd phoned these sex lines, the numbers had been on her phone bill. Tim had denied it of course, but she knew deep down inside that her partner was one of them sad male wankers who got off on talking dirty to some horny slut down the phone.

The phone started ringing again. "For fucks sake Ashley you're doing my head in now," she growled. Pressing the green button on the phone she spoke in an angry manner. "What's up now?" She held the phone from her ear as she listened to Ashley going ballistic at her. Smiling to herself she tapped her fingernail on her front tooth. "Just chill ya beans, will ya. I told you where I was. It's not as if I'm bouncing around in someone's bed is it?" Laughing to herself you could hear Ashley getting angry. Susie had finished playing with him now and spoke to him with a giggle in her voice. "Listen, just shut up for one minute you crank. Are you coming over or what? I need a back warmer for tonight its freezing?" she was holding her hand over her mouth to disguise her amusement. "Right, alright come through the back way.

I'll turn the sensor lights off. See you soon, hurry up I'm knackered." Susie threw her phone on the table at the side of her.

Turning all the downstairs lights off, Susie crept to the back door waiting for her lover to come. Peeping out into the back garden she checked the area for nosey neighbours. Nothing but a cat could be seen. As she watched the animal sneak along the back fence she smirked. The cat's mannerisms were as devious as her own. Watching it balance along the wooden fence it seemed oblivious of her.

Suddenly she heard shuffling noises. A dark figure blocked out the light from the nearby lamp- post. A large body frame now crept up her garden path. The crunching sound of gravel could be heard. "Sssh," she whispered with one finger held up towards her mouth. You could just about see Ashley's eyes. He was dressed like a Ninja, all in black. Gripping hold of his black padded jacket she pulled him inside. "What the fuck are you dressed as? Hurry up and get in before someone clocks you." Her eyes were dancing as his head dropped down to check out his clothes. Running his hands up and down the black material he sneered. He knew he was overdressed but somehow it seemed the right thing to wear at the time. He wiped the sweat from his forehead.

"What do you mean? You cheeky cow. Did you want me dressed in fucking bright rainbow colours or summit? I just thought I would blend into the night if I wore black."

"You're such a nob," she chuckled. Susie quickly locked the back door and turned to see Ashley peeling his coat off. He was struggling. Touching his body with her index finger she could feel the wetness of his sweaty skin. He was so sexy, there was no denying it. Her body craved his touch. Stroking her hand over his arms she felt the ripples of muscles. He knew she liked what she saw and flexed them harder.

"Do you want a drink or owt before we go up to bed?" she asked.

Ashley shook his head. "Nar, I'm sweet." He seemed eager to get to the bedroom. Grabbing at his crotch he winked at Susie.

"Come on then, take me to your love nest."

Ashley had been up the stairs in the past, but that was only to use the toilet. Of course he'd looked in the bedroom where she slept with Tim, but it had always made him feel sick knowing his woman was sharing a bed with another man.

Flicking the small light on, the lovers went upstairs. Susie's feminine touch was written all over the bedroom. Jumping on the king-size bed she patted the space next to her. "Come on then, get your kit off." Ashley blushed and stood fidgeting. He didn't think it would have bothered him but as he parked his arse on the bed he felt strange. This was his mate's bed and he knew he'd overstepped the mark. Falling down onto the crisp white bedding he locked his hands over his head. He lay staring for a moment until Susie kicked at his legs.

"What's up with your face now, mard arse?"

Rolling onto his stomach he dragged his t-shirt over his head and flung it on the floor. Lifting his head up, he gripped her chin in his hand.

"It doesn't feel right this yanno."

Susie shook her head; she knew exactly what he was talking about. It was written all across his guilty looking face. "What the fuck are you going on about?" she said.

He could see she was getting ready to explode and sat up as if boiling water had been poured all over him.

"I can smell Tim on the bed that's all," he wiped his hand over the sheets with a flat palm and held it up to his nose smelling it. Passing his hand over to Susie he insisted she smelt her boyfriend's body scent. She pushed his hand away with force.

"Fuck off, will you," she hissed. Why would she want to smell the sins she was committing. "You need to sort it out Ash; you rather get in the bed or fuck off home. It's up to you." She peeled the bedclothes back from the bed and yanked her clothes off. He knew she was pissed off and quickly made the decision to join her in bed. "I'm just saying that's all; don't go all moody on me now."

Lying beside her he stared into her closed eyes. Her eyelashes were flickering. She could feel his eyes burning into her but kept them shut. He'd been a dick-head and now she was making him pay. He was getting the silent treatment.

Ashley blew his warm breath onto her face with an endearing look held in his eyes. "Orr don't be mad babes, wake up; I know you're not asleep." Susie pulled the blanket up and covered her mouth, she was dying to laugh. She was playing with his emotions like a cat played with a mouse's tail. Sinking his warm lips onto hers he could see she was responding. Her eyes slowly peeled opened and she looked lost in his big blue eyes. Their mouths connected and the kiss they shared was intense. The sound of groans filled the bedroom and within minutes you could see his body on top of hers thrusting between the sheets.

Susie felt satisfied with Ashley's sex. Her eyes were struggling to stay open as she dipped her head into her lover's chest. Tomorrow was another day and she knew she would have to sort her shit out and get everything in order. Tim was gone for now and she was the one in control. She felt important and planned for her future.

"Goodnight babes" Ashley whispered. Gripping his hand she lifted it to her mouth and kissed his fingertips.

"Goodnight love" Susie whispered with a cunning look in her eye.

CHAPTER THREE

The phone was ringing constantly. Susie hid her head under the pillow hoping to drown out its piercing tone. Ashley was awake and draped his arm heavily over her body. "Will you answer that fucking phone, or better still unplug the fucker. It's doing my head in."

Susie's arm now came out from the covers and searched for the phone. Fumbling with the receiver she dragged the phone to her ear under the covers. "Hello," she mumbled. Her body bolted up from the bed. Her leg kicked at Ashley's. Once his head appeared from under the sheets she screwed her face up, and placed one finger up to her lips looking nervous. "Hiya babes. Yeah I'm still in bed. It's not that late is it?" Holding the phone from her ear she rammed two fingers into the ear piece with a screwed up face. Tim was pissing her off.

Ashley held a mischievous look as he disappeared under the covers. Susie was now explaining what had happened with the girls at the brothel to Tim. She couldn't wait to mention Pippa's name to see how he reacted. "Yeah, it went well. You didn't tell me you had a new girl working for you. That Pippa is a right cocky cow. I nearly punched her lights out the way she was talking to me." Susie sucked her lips together as Tim tried to tell her about Pippa. She could feel it in her gut by the way he was speaking that he'd definitely been sleeping with her. The conversation went on and Susie was organising a prison visit to come and see him. Grabbing a small piece of paper from her bedside cabinet she grabbed her handbag to search for a pen. Rummaging around in it she finally found one, much to her relief. Ashley's head could be seen between her legs munching into her lady garden. Giggling she lifted up the sheets. Her eyes burned into him as a warning for him to stop. Ashley ignored her and continued to seduce her even more. Susie was struggling to control her pleasure as she started to write down the things Tim was demanding. "Right, yeah I've wrote it all down. Socks, boxers, t-shirts, trainers, and trackie-bottoms." Nodding into the phone she looked like Tim was boring her, she yawned. "Right Tim I will. I'll book the reception visit for about two o'clock. Yeah I love you too, see ya."

Placing the phone down Susie lifted the sheets up. Ashley was laughing his head off. "It's not funny ya dick-head," she scowled. "He a paranoid cunt to start with, so any changes he hears in me; he'll be on me like a ton of bricks."

Ashley yanked the sheets from his body. His temper was boiling. "What the fuck are you arsed for? You're going to tell him about us soon anyway, aren't ya?" he hissed. "Why are you giving a fuck what that tosser thinks?"

Susie flung herself onto the bed. "Not this again," she whispered under her breath. It was only ten o'clock in the morning and he was already giving her a hard time. Ashley would have to go if he carried on like this; he was doing her head in big time.

Reaching for a cig she gasped a deep breath. Tim was

in HMP Strangeways and wanted a visit from her today. He'd reeled off his list of demands and now it was up to Susie to get everything he needed. Tim wanted her to go into town to get him some sneaks. Why did he want new trainers when he wasn't going anywhere? Slippers would have been the better option surely. Staring around the bedroom she inhaled deeply on her cig. From the corner of her eyes she could see Ashley putting his clothes on at the side of her. He seemed angry and in a strop.

"I've got to book a reception visit for the nick today. Tim wants me to get him some new trainers. He said you would sort me some cash out." Tim had never said such a thing, but she wasn't using her money to kit him out. After all Ashley was his wingman wasn't he? He looked at her with a disgusted look on his face. The unwritten rule on the outside was if your mates were in nick you helped them out. You had to make sure they didn't want for anything. Any other time Ashley wouldn't have minded but Tim was his enemy now and he wanted him out of his life as soon as possible so he could enjoy his woman to the full. Ashley marched about the bedroom shaking his head.

"Well Tim can take a fucking run and a jump if he thinks I'm buying him any trainers. Why does he think that I'll sort him out? Ask Judd or Malc. It's about time they did something for him." Malc and Judd were grafters too, but they weren't as close to Tim as Ashley was.

Susie looked stressed and dragged her fingers through her hair. Ashley wasn't parting with any cash and she knew she'd be the one buying all the stuff for her convicted boyfriend. Sitting in silence for a minute she flicked the TV on. Her favourite TV programme was on. Jeremy Kyle was one funny man; he made her laugh as he shouted at the guests on his show. The storyline was about a mother who'd disowned her kids and now they were there on national TV asking her why she'd given up on them for a life of beer and drugs. Susie folded her pillow under her head to get comfy. She was shouting out at the guest on the show. Ashley was still angry and never spoke a word; he had a face of thunder.

Susie reached for the phone and listened to the ring tone. After about ten minutes of waiting on hold she finally got through to the booking centre for Strangeways. She told the woman whom she wanted to visit and what clothes she was bringing in for the inmate. The woman told her the only visit she had left for today was at twelve o'clock. Quickly checking the clock that hung on the bedroom wall, she agreed she could make the visit. The visit was booked.

Slamming the phone down, she rooted in her wardrobe for something to wear. Ashley was sat on the end of the bed smoking. Susie grabbing a faded pair of jeans and a bright pink top out of her wardrobe as Ashley began to speak. "What are you getting all dressed up for?"

Susie stood twisting her hands as she faced him. "What the fuck are you going on about now?" Ashley sprung from the bed like boiling water had been poured on him and growled into her face. His eyes looked wild and she didn't like the way he was making her feel. She looked scared.

"I'm going on about these." He snatched the clothing from the edge of the bed and flung them at her with full force right into her chest. "You can see ya tits through this top and ya know how sexy your arse looks in these jeans. Are you doing it to wind me up or what?"

Susie stood thinking for a minute. She was scared of him at this moment, but there was no way in this world was she backing down from him. "Listen nob rash. Since when have you been my Lord and master? Don't even start to think that you can start telling me what to wear, because I won't have any of it ya prick. Do you hear me?"

His fist pummelled into her ribs, she was on the floor now and could feel a burning pain in her stomach. Opening her eyes she could feel Ashley's breath in her face screaming. "Slag! Keep it fucking shut. I've just about had enough of your shit. Now you're my woman there's a few ground rules to start getting used to. Do you understand?" She screamed out in pain but he was using her as a punch bag and wasn't stopping for love nor money. Her body shook as the last punch hit her hard. Her knees came up to her chest and she struggled to breathe.

Ashley left her lying on the floor and sat on the edge of the bed. It was the steroids that were making him act like this. Ever since he'd started injecting them into his arse cheeks, he knew he had a problem with the rage he felt inside. He was a ticking bomb and now that he'd exploded there was no going back. Ashley looked like a man of steel, and you could see the purple vein in his neck pumping with adrenaline.

"Get up from the floor," he ranted. Susie was weak but as he shouted again she knew she would have to obey him. She stayed silent, wary of what he was going to do next. His eyes looked filled with madness and he looked like he'd lost the plot. Susie was holding her stomach and Ashley could see he'd hurt her. Susie fell onto the bed as she tried to stand up, she was weak. She'd always been a fighter in the past and although she knew he would wipe the floor with her, she couldn't just sit and take this from him. Who the fuck did he think he was? Susie stood up shaking like a leaf.

There was a gun under the bed. Tim had always kept it there for emergencies. She knew how to use it as well. Her boyfriend had shown her. Should she make a run for it, she hesitated. Her heart thumped in her ears. Watching Ashley she knew she had to put up some kind of fight. Standing tall she blew a hard laboured breath. "You daft twat. Get out of here now, before I have you removed. Who the fuck do you think you are, doing this to me?" Pulling her top up Susie revealed her red beaten body. Each rib looked like it was on fire. "Look what you've done to me," she screamed.

Ashley had calmed down, and you could see he was sorry. He stood up and leant his head down to kiss Susie's cheek, she moved away. "You're a fucking crank. I want you out of here now!" Tears were forming in the corner of her eyes. She didn't want to cry because that was a sign of weakness and she could never be seen to be weak. She repeated herself with a piercing voice and this time Ashley responded.

"I'm sorry love. It's these steroids, they've fucking me up big time yanno. I just lose the plot for no reason."

Susie was livid. "Well you've lost me now, that's for sure. I want you gone, do you hear me? Gone!" Her voice was still loud as she snarled at him. Ashley slipped his trainers on and walked back to where she stood and wrapped his arms around her, hoping he could win her trust back.

"Please Susie. I'm sorry. I just snapped." Digging deep

inside his pocket he pulled out a wad of cash. There must have been at least five hundred pounds there. Throwing it on the bed he spoke to her with a desperate voice. "Go and get yourself something new. I'll buy you something later on too. Please don't end it Susie; I love you more than anything." Her eyes shot to the cash. She licked her lips slowly and inhaled, you could see her chest rising. Susie had him just where she wanted him; she knew he would have given anything at that moment for her forgiveness. Money was her world and with that she stared into his eyes. He was waiting on her every word. Holding her two hands he squeezed them gently. "Forgive me Susie, I swear I'll never, ever hurt you again."

She didn't believe a word he said, but the money was staring back at her. She needed it more than ever. "Right, I have to get ready. Phone me later." Ashley looked at her with endearing eyes. He looked relieved she'd forgiven him. Holding the bedroom door open she let him know she wanted him gone. With a quick kiss on her cheek Ashley left under protest. She shouted down to him as she heard him pounding down the stairs. "Go out the back way. Helen's on the prowl so be careful." The sound of the back door slamming could be heard. Lifting the blinds up from the window she watched him go out of the back gate. "Good riddance prick," she muttered.

Ashley was a crank and the sooner he was out of her life the better. How dare he think he could hurt her like that? Tim had given her a slap in the past but nothing like that. Looking around the bedroom she located her pink top and jeans. Her body was on fire and the pain she felt could be seen in her face. She found it hard to get dressed; every move she made caused her to howl out in pain. Checking the time, she knew she'd have to hurry. She had so much to do, before the visit.

Susie had been to Strangeways before, but that was years ago and Tim had been with her when they'd visited his mate. Today was a different story though, she was alone. Susie felt apprehensive.

HMP Manchester, known locally as Strangeways, was notorious. It held some of the world's most dangerous criminals. Murderers, rapists and armed robbers among them. The red bricks stood from the prison walls like each of them had a story to tell. The large tower was a local landmark and it looked like it held mystical, ominous powers. Looking up at it Susie wondered if anyone had ever been imprisoned up there in the past. It was like a tower in the "Disney" movie where a princess was trapped inside by an evil witch. Susie imagined Prince Charming climbing up it with haste, to free his true love. She loved a happy ending.

Walking into the visitors' centre, Susie dragged the bag that contained Tim's property with her. She looked strained. Her boyfriend had only been in nick five minutes and the demands had started already. Tim's trainers cost her £150. She could have spent that on the dress she'd seen in "Miss Selfridges" instead of wasting it on his sorry arse. Susie had thought about going to Bury New Road where snide trainers cost around forty quid, but she'd quickly changed her mind because she knew Tim would have been able to spot a fake trainer from a mile off. Tim was a poser and always wanted the best of everything. Bury New Road was well known for snide goods and she'd been there in the past with Tim to grab a few bargains. She never told any of her friends that she wore counterfeit goods. She had an image to maintain. Susie looked around the centre. Lots of other people were sat there too, waiting for their visits.

Placing the heavy bag of property onto the counter, Susie stood waiting for the female screw to come from behind the hatch to help her. Did she think she had all day? Because as Susie watched her, she could see she was just sat chatting with another officer without a care in the world. "Excuse me," Susie shouted as she tapped her fingernails on the side window.

The warden turned her head and snarled at her angrily. "Will you just wait a moment, I'm talking? I'll be with you in a minute."

She shot a look to Susie that would have killed. It was clear now that she'd have to wait until the warden had finished her conversation. Susie stood blowing; she stared at the other visitors. Her eyes rose towards the ceiling. "It's a fucking joke this is. I mean you would think we're the prisoners the way we get treated." A few people in the visitors' centre nodded their heads. They all knew the hard- knock life of being a prison visitor without her saying anything.

The officer appeared at the window. Her face was cocky and she could see she'd pissed Susie off. "Who have you come to see?" she demanded, looking at Susie as if she was a piece of shit on the bottom of her shoe. Susie was in two minds whether to tell her to shove the visit up her fat arse but chewing down on her bottom lip she knew she had to hold her tongue.

"Tim Marshall".

She wanted all the visitors to hear every word she said. No one was taking the piss out of her today. She'd just about had enough. The woman pencilled his name onto a large white book in front of her.

"Are you bringing any property?" They stared at each other. Their eyes were fighting with the will to win. Susie dragged the trainers up to the counter along with his other stuff. The warden examined every inch of the trainers as if her life depended on it. Once she sealed the clothing into a large transparent bag she spoke.

"Right take a seat. I will call you when it's time to go over to the prison." Susie saw a table not far from her and waited. The centre was so depressing. All the people who sat there had doom and gloom written across their faces. Susie didn't think she belonged there and screwed her face up as she looked down her nose at the other visitors. Looking at the man at the side of her she ear- wigged as he spoke to his mate in a broad Mancunian accent. Susie was from Manchester too, but she never spoke like that. Well at least she didn't think so.

The women in the room sat looking like they were going out for a night on the tiles. They wore skirts up their arses and had make-up plastered all over their faces. They looked cheap with their Primark labels sticking out from their clothing. Even their false tan was streaky and looked orange.

Kids ran about the visitors' centre without a care in the world. There was nothing to keep them occupied except a few toys scattered in the corner of the room. Wheels were missing from the cars and the jigsaws were battered and chewed. Nobody seemed to care about the children who visited the centre.

A mother chased her toddler about the room looking stressed. Yanking her red mini skirt up, she tried to run in her black stilettos. "Get here you little bastard," she whispered, as she screwed her face up at her child. Dragging him by the arm she gripped the back of his jumper and plonked him back on his seat. The kid was struggling and launching his fists into her legs. "You naughty boy," she moaned. "Just wait until you get home." Raising a smile to everyone nearby she tried to laugh it off. "I'm gonna waste the fucker when he gets out of here. It's every time we come to this place. He's always the same."

Her face dropped into her hands as she watched him break free again. He was like a cannonball, running round the place like a whippet. Looking at his mother the boy shouted in an angry voice. "Fuck off, fuck off." The kid was only about three years of age and his mother just sat there shaking her head at him, she couldn't cope. Susie watched the kid with shock. Her mouth was moving but her words were stuck. She wanted to grab the young woman by the hair and rag her about on the floor. It was her fault the boy was acting like this. You only had to look at her to know where he got his foul mouth from.

The sound of a phone ringing could be heard. The visitors all seemed to know what was coming next. Susie watched as they all stood up. The foul mouthed woman was now trying to coax her son back to where she stood. "Come on son. We're gonna see ya dad now. If you're good, I won't tell him you've been messing about in here." The child rolled on the floor and his mother yanked him to her side. "Little bastard," she muttered.

The screw started to shout out the prisoner's names. "Visits for Hayes, Johnson, Woods, Marshall." Susie grabbed her money before she locked her bag inside one of the large grey lockers situated near the back of the room. She'd already been told that she could only bring £20 onto the visit. She double checked she had the right amount of money in her hands and clutched at it with a tight grip.

The people filed out of the centre and headed to the main entrance of the prison. They all walked in single file, like ducklings walking behind their mother. Kids crying and people arguing could now be heard. This was all so stressful for Susie. She shook her head as she watched the people in front of her heading towards the main prison.

Walking inside the entrance her eyes gawped at the next procedure. Clocking the woman in front of her, she began to take her shoes off too. Were these security checks really necessary? For crying out loud, they were only going to see their loved ones? Peeling her coat off her shoulder she put it on the conveyor belt to be checked. Looking around, Susie waited for further instructions. She was now urged to go towards a female guard who stood looking at her wearing white plastic gloves. Susie was being searched. Standing on a large box she felt the female guard running her hands all over her body. Bet she loved the power she felt over everyone as she searched them, Susie thought. You could see by the screws face that she loved her job.

"Lift your feet up love," the woman asked. Susie obeyed her and one at time she scraped her feet up from the floor.

"What the fuck could you hide under your feet," Susie whispered under her breath, she was at breaking point. She stood waiting to collect her belongings as they came through the security check. Some kind of stamp was now put on the back of her hand.

Now waiting, Susie watched the man behind her getting searched. She could see how distressed he looked. His eyelids were flickering rapidly and he was chewing on his lips constantly. It was obvious to Susie that he was concealing something on his body.

Another visitor now joined her as they all walked up the stairs towards the next landing. She could hear him whispering to the male at the side of him. "Hope that fucking dog isn't here today. What fucking day is it?"

His mate laughed as he answered him. "It was here this time last week, so it might be here again today."

"For fucks sake," the man moaned, "well if it comes near me, it's getting my foot right up its sweaty ring piece." They chuckled as they sat on some chairs facing another big desk. Susie wanted to stay near them both. If they were smuggling drugs inside the prison and getting away with it, she could need them in future. Fluttering her eyes at them both, she smiled letting them know she was onto their little secret.

The guards now started to call their names out. A male guard opened the turnstile for the visitors to come through. The personal checks were still far from over. Once they were through the next door, each of them was told to stand on a thick yellow line. Each line was painted on the concrete floor and a distance away from one another. The warden spoke to the visitors. His voice was loud and full of authority. "Don't touch the dog please. He's just going to walk past you, nothing to worry about." Susie stood with her hands held down by her side. She kept her head still and watched the brown and white Springer Spaniel filter through them all. The dog's tail was swinging rapidly. Susie turned her head once it had passed her. The man behind her could be seen with his eyes closed. He looked like he was whispering something under his breath.

All the visitors were now free to leave. Susie looked at the man again. He was by her side fidgeting. Checking no one was listening she prodded him in the waist with her finger. "You did well. I thought that hound was definitely gonna get onto you." The visitor gave her a triumphant look. The first piece of his mission was now completed. All he had to do now was get the drugs to the inmate, and then the job was done. Susie giggled as they waited at the top of the stairs for the electronic door to open.

Susie could already see the inmates sat at small tables waiting for their loved ones. People were squeezing their faces up against the glass, eager to get inside. The door now opened, and the visitors walked inside, scanning the area for their loved ones.

Susie stood for a moment. "Where the fuck is he?" she mumbled. She couldn't see him anywhere. About forty prisoners were sat at the tables and they all were wearing red bibs over their clothes. They all looked the same. An arm could now be seen waving in the air. Squeezing her eyes together Susie looked towards it struggling to make out if it was Tim or not. Walking slowly she smiled. It was him.

"What a fucking joke it is to get in here. I've been outside for ages. It's like fucking Fort Knox in here. I can tell you," she sat down as she continued. "Every two minutes you're getting searched." Tim was eager to talk.

"Shut the fuck up moaning, and give me a kiss," Tim chuckled. His eyes were all over her like a rash. Susie leant over the table and puckered up. You could see Tim inhaling her fragrance as their lips connected. The inmate pulled her closer but she yelled in pain. "What's up with you," he snarled. Susie realised what she'd done and had to think quick.

"Erm .. I fell down the stairs before." Kicking her leg up at the side of the table she showed him her large heels.

"It was these heels that done it. I just lost my balance. You know what I'm like. I'm a clumsy fucker." He believed every word and kissed her hands as he held them both across the table.

"You look sexy, babes". He wanted to shag her brains out. You could see it in his eyes. Tim's hand was now tugging at his crotch. "Fucking hell love. My cocks throbbing like fuck." Susie leant over the table slightly as he raised his arse from the chair to show her his manhood beneath his jeans. "Touch it," he smirked. You could see the shape of his trouser snake.

"You horny fucker," she giggled. Susie could see the full outline of his penis in his jeans and her face blushed slightly hoping nobody else could see it.

"Unshackle the beast," he giggled.

Susie blushed. There was no way in this world she was tossing him off on a visit. She'd heard stories from her friends about what happened on prison visits and she wanted no part of it. Tim didn't turn her on one little bit, and there was no way she was yanking his tackle on this visit or any visits in the future. He could go and take a running jump.

"Go and get me some scran then, I'm fucking starving. The food in this place is crap. Get me a butty, a brew and some chocolate." People were queuing up at the serving hatch; Susie could see two women serving behind the counter.

"Yeah, hang on then. I'm not queuing up yet. It's fucking hammered. Look at the queue," she shot her eyes to the long line of people stood waiting to be served. He looked at the queue and he agreed with her nodding his head.

"Yeah best wait a few minutes until it calms down."

Looking at his girlfriend in more detail he studied her face. Susie was such a self-centred cow and he knew his time in prison would be hard with her as his woman. She cared about nothing but herself. Susie was a gold-digging bitch and he knew only too well she didn't love him anymore.

Susie sat back in her seat. Tilting her head to the side she couldn't wait to ask about Pippa. She'd been on her mind all day, and now she wanted him to tell her the facts about her. Hanging a finger from her mouth she began. "So how come you know Pippa?"

Tim blanched, he was fidgeting. "I don't really know her; I just gave her a job that's all."

Susie pounced. Her face was over the table and she was looking him directly in the eyes. "What do you mean? You just gave her a job," her teeth were clenched together. "So are you telling me, she just knocked on Delia's and said 'can I have a job?"

Tim swallowed hard. "Yeah summat like that. Fucking hell Susie what's up with that? Do you think I've been banging her or summit?"

She looked angry. The guilt on his face was there for everyone to see, she paused for a second. "Well how did you meet her then?"

Tim sighed and fed her a story that was nothing like the one Pippa had told her. He was such a lying bastard. Trying to change the subject he asked her to go and get some food. Susie huffed as she stood up. Grabbing the money from the table, she left him on tenterhooks. Tim was running his fingers through his hair. He looked relieved.

Susie stood waiting to get served. The man from earlier was now sat near her. He was visiting an older man

who looked a couple of butties short of a picnic. Susie
wondered if he'd passed the drugs over yet and kept her
eyes focused on his every move. She couldn't see anything.
"Yes love," the woman said.

Susie stuck her head over the counter and looked
at what food they had to offer. "What a load of shit,"
she huffed. "Erm… can I have two coffees and a…" she
paused as she scanned the sandwiches in front of her. "A
tuna mayonnaise sandwich please." The assistant began
making the brews. Susie's eyes now scanned the chocolate
selection. She was hormonal and was craving a sugar fix.
"Can I have a Wispa and a packet of Rolos as well love?"
The woman passed her the two hot drinks with caution.
Placing them on a red plastic tray Susie handed her the
money. Gripping the tray with difficulty she made her
way back to Tim.

Tim was smiling as she placed the food onto the table.
She shot him a look and he knew she wasn't happy. A
male guard was now at her side. His walk was slow and
he seemed to be checking her out. He was a dish and
Susie loved the attention he was giving her. The screw
was bulging with muscles and you could see his biceps
through his crisp white shirt. Susie wanted him to rip
her knickers off there and then. He was sex on legs. With
one last glance he walked past the table. Tim was snarling
at him. "Nosey twat. What the fuck is Jenkins snooping
at?"

Susie didn't hear a word Tim was saying and carried
on watching the screw with drooling eyes. "He could
sort me out anytime," she sniggered, as she felt a wave of
excitement ride through her body.

"Dirty cow," her boyfriend hissed. Tim checked the
area and started to whisper in a low voice. He made sure

Susie was paying him full attention, his hand covered his mouth. "I need some gear in here. I have to make some money fast."

Susie stared at him before she spoke. "How the fuck do you expect me to do that, I'm not bringing fuck all in?"

Tim looked angry. "Will you shut the fuck up and listen ya nob. I'm not saying for you to bring anything in. I mean, I need a visit from someone who will."

Sighing, Susie looked relieved. Tim rubbed at his arms as he racked his brains for a drugs mule. "Get Ashley on it, he knows some proper dirty bitches who'd do owt for a quick few quid."

"Who the fuck does he know?" Susie snapped.

Tim looked at her and could see how angry she was, he chuckled. "Ashley's a player. He's got loads of women out there who'd die for him."

"I thought he had a girlfriend?"

"Yeah he says he has, but come on love, he'd shag anything with a pulse."

Susie had to control herself. She wanted to tell Tim straight that Ashley had been sleeping with her for years; she took a deep breath and spoke like she didn't care about his mate's love life. "Yeah I'll see if he can sort a visit out. What stuff are you talking about anyway?"

Tim's eyes danced about and he spoke in a firm voice. He scanned the area to make sure nobody was listening. "Some brown and sniff. I can earn a right few quid from it in here. The smackheads will do owt for a quick toot."

Susie sucked her lips. As long as she wasn't involved Tim could do whatever he wanted. "I need you to get some money out of the bank for it. About five ton will do for now."

Susie nearly fell from her chair. "Get a grip, will you? Five hundred pounds for drugs. My arse."

He dragged her arms over towards him and pressed his fingers deep into her skin. "Listen don't start with all that shit." His warm breath was in her face and she could tell he meant every word he said. "Just get the money together and give it to Ashley. He'll do the rest."

Panicking she agreed. Pulling away from him. "Okay, okay," she whispered.

The visit was coming to an end. Inmates could be seen standing and kissing their visitors. Susie watched the woman from earlier and she could see her boyfriend's hand disappearing up her short skirt. Her kid was still running about the room and she didn't give a shit as long as she was getting a bit of slap and tickle.

"Come on then, give us a kiss." Tim sunk his dry lips onto hers. His breath smelt of camel shit and she pulled her face from his.

"Your breath stinks, you need to brush your teeth," she said. Tim didn't listen to her and carried on getting his quick fix of love, Susie didn't respond as he carried on regardless.

Susie got up and wiped her mouth on her sleeve. She could still taste Tim's stale breath on her lips. Turning her head before she left the room she gave a half-hearted wave to him as he sat at his table. All the visitors stood together waiting for the screw to let them out. As her eyes followed a guard coming towards her, she realised it was the sexy one from earlier. Each person in turn was let out of the door. As Susie's turn came Jenkins spoke to her. His voice was low and he made sure no one else could hear him. "You shouldn't be coming to places like this love."

Susie smirked. Her heart was beating quickly.

Struggling for words she spoke. "I know. I'm meant for better things me, aren't I?" The screw nodded his head and winked at her. You could tell he was flirting, and Susie knew it too. With one last glance at each other Susie left. She could feel his eyes burning into her as she walked away. She started to strut her stuff. Standing tall, she pulled her shoulders back and gave a walk Claudia Schiffer would have been proud of.

People were now going down the stairs as if there was a fire. Susie held the rail at the side of her and tried to regain her balance. "What's the fucking rush," she cursed to the crowd. No one listened to her and they carried on barging past.

Through the exit door and fresh air hit Susie's face. She inhaled deeply and her nostrils flared. Her body was craving a cigarette and she hurried back to the visitors' centre to get them from her locker. The woman with the child from earlier was now at her side. The kid was still crying and being naughty. Susie couldn't hold her tongue. "He's a fucking handful him, how do you cope?"

The woman laughed out loud. "I know, I need a taser gun for the brat don't I?"

Susie chuckled. "Yeah that would sort him right out." They walked together to get their belongings. The woman introduced herself as Vicky. Susie was a nosey person and wanted to know the ins and outs of a cat's arse hole.

"So is it your boyfriend who's in nick or what?"

Vicky nodded as she tried to keep hold of her son's hand who was now trying to break free. "Yeah he got slammed last month for six years."

"Six years! What the fuck did he do?" Susie gasped.

Vicky giggled. "Oh just a bit of drug dealing. He was one of the foot soldiers who ended up getting caught."

Susie looked gob-smacked. "Well that's a long time just for selling drugs. There must be more to it."

Vicky became defensive. She screwed her face up and didn't like the way the conversation was going. "What do ya mean, more to it?" Vicky was staring at her now and waiting for an answer.

Susie knew she'd overstepped the mark. "No love, I'm just saying that's a long time for selling drugs."

Vicky grabbed her son's arm as she entered the visiting centre. You could tell that Susie had pissed her off. Vicky left Susie's side and could be seen bending down to get her belongings from her locker.

Sat in the car Susie lit up a fag. It looked like each drag was calming her nerves. The stress seemed to disappear from her face. This was her life now and she hated every minute of it. She had to change it somehow, someway.

CHAPTER FOUR

Vicky Dixon looked knackered as she walked down the busy road towards the bus stop. Her son was still being naughty and she looked like she was on the verge of leaving him on his own.

Sat on the cold plastic seat inside the bus shelter, she could see her son swinging around a lamp- post near the main road. Her body looked deflated and it was only when a car honked its horn at the toddler that she decided to stand up and get him. Her legs looked weary as she trudged to get him.

Vicky's face was on fire with temper and this time she let her child have it. He'd been a nightmare all day. Grabbing him by his coat she launched her flat palm right across his arse. With every swing the little boy howled out in pain. She was frothing at the mouth as she yelled into his face. "All day you've been asking for this. You little twat." Vicky swung her hands at him. She was beating him hard. The child was dragged back inside the bus shelter crying his eyes out. Looking at him she plonked back down on her seat. "Cry, you'll piss less," she sniggered.

Vicky watched her son rubbing at the back of his pants. "I hate you," he moaned. Her face looked cocky.

"Do you want to borrow my mobile phone?" she asked in a sarcastic manner, reaching her phone out to him.

The child thought about her words and looked confused. "Why, who am I going to phone?"

Her laughter could be heard now as she covered her mouth to try and keep a serious face. "Someone who gives a fuck, because I don't."

The boy stamped his feet on the floor and made another attempt to go back to the lamp- post. This time his mother made no mistake about showing him who was the boss. She leathered him. The boy now sat next to her crying his eyes out. He tried to break free again but after a forceful dead- leg from his mother he knew she meant business. He was sobbing out loud as snot hung from his nose.

A car now passed, honking its horn. Vicky screwed her eyes together as she watched the woman from the prison visit wave her hand at her. "What the fuck does she want?" she mumbled. Grabbing her son's hand she yanked him towards the BMW X5. The passenger door now opened. "Where you going to? Do you want a lift?" Susie looked friendly and smiled at Vicky with her eyes wide open. The kid was already climbing inside the car. Vicky pulled at him but it was too late he was already inside sitting on the back seat.

Vicky hitched her legs up and struggled to get inside. This car was mint and she felt proud to be inside it. Her own boyfriend drove a Fiat Panda – 'The Rust Bucket' she'd called it in the past. Turning her head to her son in the back of the car she told him to get his feet down from the leather trim. Susie was watching him like a hawk and regretting even giving them a lift in the first place. Pulling her seat belt across her body Susie started to speak. "Where do you live?"

Vicky cleared her throat and spoke in her best voice. "Just in Blackley love, Andrew Road. Do you know where that is?"

"Yeah I know where Blackley is, so you can tell me whereabouts when I get nearer." Vicky inhaled deeply. This woman smelt so fresh and clean. The smell was a million miles away from the Impulse deodorant she'd sprayed on herself earlier. Vicky looked over at Susie's hands as she pulled out onto the main road. Her fingers were long and slender and her nails looked in tip-top condition. She hid her own hands by her side. Her own nails were chewed, they looked like she'd picked a thousand potatoes.

"I'm sorry if I offended you before love. I just don't think before I speak."

Vicky smiled as she turned her head to see her son sitting in the back. "No worries. I've just had a shit day that's all. I mean coming to this place once a week is enough to stress anyone out innit?"

"Tell me about it," Susie nodded, "I've never felt so intimidated in my whole life. The screws think we're criminals too. Did you hear the way they speak to people?"

Vicky was up in arms. She knew exactly what she

meant, Susie continued. "Cheeky fuckers they are. They know we need to get into the nick, so they just take liberties," she chuckled. Vicky looked about twenty two years of age but she seemed a lot older in the head.

"Mam can we have McDonalds, I'm hungry."

Vicky blushed, the toddler knew she didn't have any money, he'd asked her earlier for some sweets. Her purse was empty and she didn't have a pot to piss in until the following day when her benefit would be paid into her account. Trying to remain calm she spoke in an animated voice. "Mummy will make you something nice when we get in. McDonalds is for special occasions." That was it, the kid was bawling again. Vicky looked at her wits end. She wanted to jump in the back of the car and throttle the little bastard to death. Forcing herself to calm down she said, "Declan, please don't start again. I just can't cope with it anymore."

Susie could see the pain in her face. It was obvious she didn't have any money. "Tell you what," Susie smiled, "if you're good all the way home I'll get you a McDonalds. What do you say about that?"

Declan was cheering and clapping his hands together. The little brat was happy now. "Can I have chicken nuggets and a strawberry milk shake?" Vicky was going under. The embarrassment was written all across her face. Susie spoke to her with a soft voice. "That's if it's alright with your mummy?"

Vicky grinned. "I would have got it him myself but I'm skint. These prison visits cost me an arm and a leg. I never have a spare penny." Susie agreed as she turned the music up. The Script played "The man who can't be moved." Susie sung along with the words. Vicky looked at her with a grin across her face. She was definitely a mad head. Vicky felt some of her depression lifting. At least she had saved her bus fare now and could buy some cigs. Susie had saved her life, without her nicotine fix she was a right moody cow. Without this lift home she would have had to go into her corner shop and beg for credit to see her through until the next day. Vicky had done it before in the past and hated sucking up to her local shopkeeper. She was living on the bread line and some days she didn't have enough food to feed herself and her child.

Susie looked at Vicky from the corner of her eyes. She was a pretty little thing and she had a fabulous figure. Tapping her fingertips on the steering wheel, the traffic came to a standstill. Susie wanted to know more about this girl. She held a cunning look on her face before she started the conversation. "So who do you live with then? Is it just you and Declan?"

Vicky turned her head to the back seat and looked at her son. "Yeah it's just me and this fucking nuisance in the back." She pulled at her son's leg and smiled. "Well it is now his dad's in nick."

Susie dug deeper, wanting to know more, she was a right nosey bitch. "It's a long time to wait love. Are you going to be faithful?" Vicky took a moment and made sure her son wasn't listening in the back of the car. He was playing with some gadget he'd found on the seat. "I'm going to try. But who knows what's around the corner. Like you said it's a long time to wait innit?"

Susie giggled. "Yeah you're a woman with needs aren't you?" Vicky covered her broken tooth as she nearly choked with laughter. Susie was so straight talking and she made her piss laughing with her bluntness.

Declan was jumping up and down on the back seat. He could see the McDonalds and his eyes were on fire with excitement. "We're going to McDonalds," he sang at the top of his voice. Vicky held the bottom of her stomach, it was rumbling. She could hear her own body's call for food. The aroma of the fast food could be smelt filtering through the small gap in the window. Vicky inhaled deeply and you could see her nostrils flaring.

Susie pulled into the drive- through. Two cars were in front of them and Declan kept on repeating to Susie what his order was. He was doing her head in, but she kept her calm. "Do you want something to eat love?" Vicky could feel her face going red as Susie looked directly at her. Her tongue was sliding over her bottom lip. She looked starving as she held onto her knees. Susie repeated herself as she neared the intercom to make their order. "It's my treat," Susie smirked. Vicky nodded and concentrated on the menu board at the side of her.

Once the food was ordered they drove to the next window to pay for their food. Vicky watched as Susie pulled her 'Paul's Boutique' purse out from her bag. She'd wanted one of those purses for ages, and she examined every inch of it. Opening the window Susie grabbed the food from the assistant. Passing Declan his Happy Meal in the back she drove to the car park situated at the side of them. Once the engine was turned off they all sat munching their grub. Declan had never been so quiet.

Vicky was eating so fast that sparks came off her fingers. Susie could tell she was more than hungry. "Fucking shame," Susie thought as she watched her devour her Big Mac meal. Susie wasn't really good at making friends but this girl seemed to like her. Vicky was passing Declan a small white napkin to wipe his hands. They both watched him clean his hands, and Susie was glad he wasn't making a mess of her back seats.

Susie looked full and patted her stomach. "I needed that I can tell you. I haven't had a bite to eat all day. It's just been rush, rush, rush. I've no time to fart these days, never mind anything else."

"I know what you mean,"Vicky replied as she finished the last bite of her burger. Declan was now playing with the small toy he'd got inside his Happy Meal, he looked content.

"Come on then. Let's get you home" Susie giggled.

On the way, Susie was itching to get to know more about this young mother. "So Vicky, do you go out on the piss or what?"

"I wish, I'm always skint,"Vicky moaned. "Plus I don't have anyone to babysit. My mam has fuck all to do with me anymore."

Susie was hanging on her every word as she pumped her for more information. "Why, don't you get on with your parents love?"

"Nar she's a piss head. She's only seen Declan a few times since he's been born. My family are a waste of space. I still talk to one of my sisters though."

Susie watched Vicky's face change and knew she was upset. She felt motherly towards her and reached her hand over, to the passenger seat and patted her leg. "Same here love. My family are just the same. The only time I see them is when they want something. We're a pair together aren't we?" They agreed as they drove up Rochdale Road towards Blackley.

Vicky gave Susie directions. Turning off Rochdale Road Vicky led her to a council estate. Motorbikes were flying up and down the road with youths hanging from them without any helmets on. Thick scarves hung around their faces covering their identity. Vicky sat tall in the car;

she looked like she wanted someone to see her as she scanned the area for any familiar faces. For crying out loud, here she was sat in a BMW X5 and nobody was about to see her in this smart car.

Susie drove past some houses. Lots of them had the windows boarded up and the gardens looked overgrown with weeds. "Anywhere here love," Vicky said. The brakes slammed on the car and they came to a halt. Words were few between them now and Vicky thanked her for the lift home and the food. Declan was starting to act up again and was refusing to get out of the car. You could see Vicky felt embarrassed. "Come on son. You can watch a film when we get in. You can watch your 'Cars' DVD if you want." The child seemed to be thinking it over, and he quickly scrambled over the seats to get to his mother. "Thanks again," Vicky said with an endearing look. Susie smiled and watched her enter the house.

"Poor fucker," Susie whispered as she watched her chase her son down the path before he broke free. Declan was definitely a handful. Her mobile went off. Susie grabbed it from the dashboard. It was Ashley's name flashing. Taking a deep breath she threw the phone back in her bag. "He can fuck right off," she ranted. Susie felt tired. She'd not even bothered washing her hair today. There was just no time. Her body was still aching and all she wanted to do was to go home and get a nice warm bath. She'd bought some new bath oils that she wanted to try, and tonight she planned to use them.

Music was playing as she drove home. Usually she would have had her tunes pumping out from the speaker, but today she couldn't be arsed. As she pulled up near her house she could see Ashley's car, parked outside it. "What do you want, you toss pot?" she cursed.

Ashley's face was hidden by a big bouquet of flowers as he trudged towards her. He was holding a big white fluffy teddy in his other hand. Susie stood at her garden fence with one hand on her hip with a cocky look on her face. She hated flowers. She would have much rather have had a bottle of perfume or something. Flowers were a waste of money in her eyes, and they reminded her of death. "Here you go my sweetheart," Ashley giggled as he passed her the massive bunch of flowers. He looked chuffed as he hung on her every word. Taking them from him she tucked the flowers under her arm and headed down the garden path towards the front door. He stood frozen as he swung the teddy by its arm. He looked gutted and you could see he was ready to snap. Once the front door was opened he marched inside after her.

"Is that it? Are you not gonna say thanks or fuck all for the flowers. I felt a right cunt buying them as well. The woman must have thought I was a right soft arse." Her eyes kept focused on the kitchen sink as she pulled the flowers from the cellophane. She placed them in a glass vase from underneath the sink.

"Yeah, give me a fucking chance. I'm not going to throw my arms around you in the street am I? Ya muppet." He was smiling now. Susie turned round to face him and held her arms out. There was no way she was walking to him. If he wanted any loving he would have to come to her for it. Ashley went straight in for the kiss. As their lips connected he kissed her with passion. Susie looked like she enjoyed the kiss, and looking down at Ashley's crotch he was enjoying it too. His penis was now visible. It looked swelled as if it was ready to burst through his tracksuit bottoms. Susie ended the kiss. Flicking the switch on the kettle, she handed him the vase and told him to park his arse in the living room. Dragging his coat from his body he obeyed her and left the kitchen.

The kettle boiled away and the bubbling noise from it made her put the coffee into the cups. Kicking her shoes off Susie looked so much smaller. Carrying two cups into the living room she could hear someone knocking at the front door. Ashley was now at the window gawping at the visitor. "Who is it?" Susie snarled as she placed the two brews on the glass table nearby.

"It's Helen, I think."

"Oh, for fuck sake. That's all I need. Did she see you?" Ashley nodded. Huffing noises could be heard.

Susie opened the front door. Helen didn't wait for an invite inside and just barged past her. "Ignorant bitch," Susie mumbled.

"How was our kid? Was he alright?" she shouted as she went straight into the front room. Susie didn't reply. She was finding it hard to control her temper and stayed in the lobby for a few minutes to try and calm herself down.

Helen met Ashley's eyes. Her face seemed to change as she looked at the two brews on the table. "Alright chub rub," Ashley giggled nervously. He'd always had banter with Helen in the past and today was no different.

"Cheeky cunt, you are," she sniggered. "Are you still shagging anything with a pulse?" Ashley went white in the face. Susie heard her accusations and stood at the door waiting for him to reply.

"Nar am I eck. I've got myself a real woman now. Slappers are a thing of the past." He fidgeted about. Helen seemed to be watching Susie's reaction. She could see Ashley looking at her brother's woman and wondered why he'd changed his tune all of a sudden. Usually he would tell her about some dirt bag he'd been shagging but today he was holding back. She continued probing him.

"Come off it Ash. You always have some dirty little bint on the go." He looked uncomfortable and tugged at his grey t-shirt. His mouth looked dry as he licked his bottom lip.

"Straight up love, I'm loved up now, honest."

Helen laughed out loud. "Well that's a fucking first. I don't believe that for one minute. Do you think I was born yesterday?"

Ashley sat down looking anxious. He looked like he was blushing. Helen eyed the brews on the table and turned her head to Susie who was just about to sit down.

"I'll have a brew, love."

Susie couldn't hide her feelings any longer. She screwed her face up as she plonked her arse in her seat. "Well you know where the kitchen is. Go and make one."

Helen huffed and looked at Ashley. "Oh no brew for me, but she's done one for you I see."

Her eyes shot to the two cups on the table. Ashley smiled. He could see Susie was looking at him for support. "I made the brews Helen. Susie is done in from the visit. Look at her she's knackered."

Helen jumped up from the chair in a mood. "Well I hope she's got some nice choccy biscuits in, because I love to dunk my biscuits?" Helen disappeared into the kitchen.

Susie rammed two fingers into the air and directed them towards the door. "I fucking hate her with a passion. She pisses me right off." Ashley reached for his brew and blew the hot drink as he slurped his first mouthful.

Sitting back in his chair he winked at Susie. "Calm down love," he whispered.

Helen came back to join them with a packet of Susie's favourite biscuits. The pair watched Helen as she sank her brown stumpy teeth into the seal to break the packet open. Helen lifted her head up and looked gobsmacked as her eyes focused on the dining table.

"Who's the flowers from?" Susie swallowed hard and she struggling to find an answer. Ashley stepped in. "Oh I got them for her. Tim said to get Susie something to cheer her up," he chuckled. "So I used my imagination and got her a bunch of flowers."

Helen was like a detective. She stood up from her seat and walked to the table where the flowers were. Bending her head down, she inhaled hard at the bouquet. "Flowers remind me of death yanno."

Ashley raised his eyes to the ceiling and watched her pick the teddy up. "Orr this is cute." Holding the cuddly toy close to her body, she squeezed at it with all her might. You could see the teddy's eyes nearly popping out. She was such a heavy-handed bitch. Helen sat back down. She was eager to eat as many biscuits as she could. Ashley and Susie watched her devour the biscuits and you could see by their faces they were sickened by her eating habits.

"So how was he then?" Helen asked as she spoke with a mouthful of biscuit. She looked like a horse chewing on an apple.

Susie pulled her legs onto the chair and folded them at the side of her. "He was alright. He never stopped moaning though. Bring me this, bring me that. Do this, do that."

Helen looked anxious as she spoke. "Well he needs stuff doesn't he? The man's in jail, for Christ sake. What do you expect?"

"If you think it's easy, Mrs fucking know it all. You sort the fucking visits out."

Helen stared at her. The smile on her face was there to wind Susie up. Taking a minute to think about her reply, she leant forward in her seat and spoke directly to Susie. Ashley was watching them both and he was getting ready to split them up. He could see they were both getting ready for a fight. Helen let rip. "Do you know what Susie? If you carry on talking to me like a daft prick, I'm gonna give you a piece of my mind. I've held back for long enough now because you've been upset, but if you carry on with this attitude I'll show you what I'm all about. Do you get me?"

"Now, now, ladies," Ashley smirked. He could see Susie's fist clenching together and he knew she was ready to dive on Helen.

Susie was livid as she bolted up from her chair. "Who the fuck, do you think you're talking to ya fat slag! Get a grip will you. And if you think you can twist me up," she laughed sarcastically, "bring it on." Ashley was bouncing about the front room now. His two long arms were waving about in front of his face. Susie was growling into Helen's face pointing her fingers near her nose. Ashley tried to calm them down but Susie grabbed at Helen's arm.

"Come on. Get the fuck out of my house. Thinking you can come round here, and chat shit to me." Helen struggled to get up from the chair. Her cheeks were red with temper. Pulling her t-shirt over her gut she made a grab for Susie.

The two women were at war but Ashley managed to

keep them apart. "Will you just go home?" he shouted at Helen, "Susie's got enough on her plate without you stressing her out as well."

Tim's sister bounced about the living room as she tried to grip Susie, "Fuck off Ash, she's a horrible bitch and I'm sick it. She's always the fucking victim. Poor little Susie!" she said sarcastically. Helen made her way to the front door as Ashley struggled to keep Susie from jumping on her. Helen laughed nervously. "You'll come to earth with a bang one day, you cocky bitch. And I for one, hope I'm there to watch you fall flat on your sorry arse."

"Just go, for fucks sake," Ashley yelled.

Susie was trying to break free. "Fat bastard, get out of my house," Susie snarled. The sound of the front door slamming could be heard. Helen nearly took the door from its hinges. The house shook. Susie dragged at her clothes, she was angry. "Why did you hold me back? I would have battered her all over the place. I'm no shit bag, yanno. She's a fat blubbering whale."

Ashley sighed as he shook his head. "Fucking women." Reaching into his pocket he pulled out two cigs. "Here, get a fag down ya neck. You're a fucking stress head."

Susie's hand was shaking as she pulled the cigarette from his grip. Dipping her head into the lighter flame she inhaled deeply. Smoke rings now came from her mouth as her jaw clicked slowly. "I swear Ash; she's just one of them people who wind me up big time. I've never got on with her. She's an interfering slut." Ashley smoked his cig and just nodded his head, anything for a bit of peace.

"So how was the jailbird then?" Ashley asked in a calm voice.

Susie was sat next to him on the sofa. She could feel his warm breath on her face. "Yeah he was okay. He wants you to sort a visit out to get some gear in."

"Nar, not a fucking prayer am I taking any drugs into the 'Ways. It's on top to fuck," he moaned. Susie continued as he stubbed his cig out in the ashtray.

"Well he said for you to get some bird to do it for him. His actual words were," her eyes were wide open, "'You know loads of slappers who'd do out to earn a few extra quid'."

Ashley laughed out loud and looked cocky. "Yeah I do. Mouldy Marie from the Two Hundred estate, she'd do owt for some quick cash!"

Susie sniggered. "Who the fuck is mouldy Marie?"

"She's just some junkie who's game for anything. All the young lads go to her for a suck. She only charges a fiver a blow."

Susie screwed her face up and spoke in disbelief. "A fiver for a gobble. No way. You're lying?"

"On my life love." Ashley held his flat palms out in front of him as he swore on his mother's life. "She sucked two of them off at once. Honest to God."

Susie held the bottom of her stomach as she broke into fits of laughter. "Ewww, what a dirty slapper."

Ashley sat staring to the floor, and it was obvious something was lying heavy on his mind. His voice was low as he turned to face her. "Did you tell him about us then?"

Slowly Susie shook her head. She was wary of him. "Not yet. But I will soon. I promise."

Ashley dragged her to his side and cradled her in his grip. "Shall we just get in bed and watch a DVD? You need to rest don't you?" For once he was right. Susie looked drained and the beating he'd given her earlier didn't help. She melted like butter in his arms. Susie needed some love and didn't care where it came from. Blowing from her mouth she gasped.

"Orr what about 'Delia's'. The girls will be expecting to see me?"

Ashley kissed the top of her head and inhaled the fragrance from her hair. "I'll nip round now, and check things are alright. You run the bath and get yourself sorted. I won't be long," he squeezed her arse cheeks. "Then we can have a night away from it all. What do you say?"

"Tell them I'll be there tomorrow night. I'll be fresh as a daisy then wont I?"

Ashley stroked the side of her face. His eyes looked so full of love for her. Dipping his head he quickly pecked a kiss on her cheek and stood up to leave. "Right you go and get in the bath and I'll sort the rest out. I'll park my car out of the way when I come back. You know what the nosey bastards are like round here don't you?" Susie yawned and stretched her arms over her head. With another quick kiss he was gone.

The stair that faced her looked depressing. Every inch of her body was aching. Holding the banister she trudged up towards the bathroom. Susie peeled her clothes from her body. You could see every bruise now in its full glory. Some of them looked red, but as you looked closer to the skin you could see the yellow and black colours beginning to form. Her body submerged beneath the bubbles. Holding her head back she relaxed. What the hell was she going do to keep everything running while Tim was in the clink, she thought.

Blowing a big pile of bubbles in front of her mouth she chuckled out loud as she looked at herself in the mirror. "You'll do whatever it takes. Won't you Susie girl?" Her face looked cunning as her head disappeared under the bathwater.

CHAPTER FIVE

Vicky Farrell sat in her front room. The television was on loud, but she seemed to be staring at the screen without even watching the programme. What a depressing place it was. Toys were scattered all over the floor and the bin at the side of her was heaving with rubbish. Vicky was normally house proud but since her boyfriend had been imprisoned, cleaning was the last thing on her mind. Her son Declan was rolling about on the floor with one of his cars making some screeching noises. She looked at him and shook her head. "Noisy fucker, shut up will you?" Declan was a naughty kid and there was no getting away from that fact. She'd been to the doctor's with him on one or more occasions telling him that she thought he had a behaviour disorder, but he just told her Declan was a boisterous little boy and he would settle down in time. Her doctor never ever gave her a satisfactory consultation. Her only chance of sleep was dosing the kid up with Calpol. She was sure he was immune to it these days because he very rarely slept a full night.

Months before, Vicky had terminated a pregnancy. She'd only told Blake's sister and everyone in the world now seemed to know her business. It was the best thing she'd ever done; she knew another child would have pushed her over the edge. Her boyfriend had just been imprisoned for six years, and even the thought of mothering another child crucified her. Vicky was at her wits end.

Blake was her boyfriend of five years. He was her life, her everything. He provided for her and helped her with their troublesome son. Her boyfriend was all she had in life and she missed him so much. Blake was a drug dealer when he was on the out, he was known as a bit of a hard case. He'd promised Vicky he would only sell drugs until they got the things they wanted in life. That day never came and he just got deeper and deeper into the drug world, dragging her down with him. Her man was a foot soldier for the big guys and he never really earned a carrot from any deals. She was sure he'd dabbled in taking drugs too, but she could never prove it. Her only hope was that he'd win his appeal and be a free man again. She wasn't getting her hopes up though.

Today Vicky was up in court. She'd still been cashing Blake's giros while he was in jail. He'd told her to. He said there wouldn't be any comebacks. Yeah right… A jealous neighbour must have grassed her up, how else would they have found out about the extra cash she was getting? Her neighbourhood was well known for people grassing each other up, nobody was safe. As soon as your back was turned they'd stick the knife in. They loved to see people fall flat on their faces. Vicky had her suspicions who the snitch was and knew in time she'd pay the culprit back in full. Blake had bribed his younger brother to sign on for him at the job centre. He looked the spitting image of him anyway, and people always thought they were twins. He'd promised to treat him for his part in the fraudulent claim and that was good enough for his younger brother to make him carry out the task.

The giros were only for £130 each fortnight, but the money made a big difference to Vicky's life, so she just kept on doing it. Just two giros she'd cashed, and she got caught for the both of them, just her luck. People she knew had done it loads of times and got away with it. She was just an unlucky person.

Declan was going to her sisters while she went to court. Even though she didn't get on with her very well, she didn't have any option, because there was no one else to mind the brat. All her friends had left her months ago, and it was very rare she saw any of them. She did have one friend called Jayne, but she lived miles away, and it wasn't very often that she saw her.

Since Vicky had met Blake he was her world and she closed the door to everyone else in her life, including her family. He was all she needed or so she thought.

"Right son come on let's get ready. We're going to Auntie Michelle's soon. You're staying there for a bit while I nip out on an errand." His voice went through her as he kicked his legs rapidly on the laminated floor.

"No, I wanna come with you. I hate it there. She's nasty to me." Vicky sighed.

"Well hard fucking luck. You're still going, come on move it." Declan's screams pierced her eardrums as he let rip. "Shut the fuck up," she yelled into his face. She looked like she was losing control. Vicky wanted to kick the living daylights out of him and had to hold her breath as she walked away from him. She was shaking from head to toe and looked white in the face. Her bottom lip was trembling.

Declan was shouting behind her at the top of his voice. "She's a bitch. Fuck off, fuck off," he ranted.

Looking in her wardrobe Vicky blew a hard, laboured breath. Her clothes were tattered. She needed to look respectable for her court appearance and nothing in her wardrobe came close to what she required. Dragging an old woollen dress from the back of the wardrobe she held it up in front of her and dusted it down. Tears streamed from her eyes as she held the black dress to her face. She smelt it.

Life had taken Vicky to some dark places in the last few months, and she didn't know if she was coming or going. Declan stood at her bedroom door staring at her. The blue blanket he'd had since being a baby was held close to his face for comfort. He was slowly rubbing it on his red cheeks. The furry cloth looked like it needed a good wash. Dirt and food was visible all over it. Snot hung from the child's nose, and he sniffed hard trying to remove it.

Vicky shot a look at him and hated that she couldn't cope. She'd always promised herself that she would be a good parent to her child, but it was so hard. Feeling the moment, she stretched her two arms out towards him. "Come here for a love." Declan trudged to her side with a scowled look across his face. Squeezing him tightly in her arms she sobbed her heart out. "Things are gonna get better son. I promise you. I don't know how, and I don't know when, but they will. I promise." Declan didn't understand what she was going on about and was more interested in the toy he'd seen on the floor. He pulled away from her with force. Vicky sat looking at him playing with his Buzz Light Year.

Looking in the mirror she pulled the fluff away from her dress. Her black boots had seen better days. They were once her favourites, but now they needed heeling and scuff marks were visible at the front of them. Wetting her finger she tried to remove the patches of dirt.

Standing tall, she gripped her hair in her hands and placed it in a pony tail. Her locks looked greasy, and if you looked closer to her hair you could see that her roots were several shades lighter than the rest. Spraying some deodorant across her body she tried to hide the stale smell of cigarettes. Patting her cheeks for a bit of colour she turned to see Declan at the side of her. Chocolate was visible all over his face. "For crying out loud. I've just got you fucking ready. Go and get a cloth while I try and sort you out. You scruffy little bastard." Declan pulled a face and remained in the same spot. Yanking at his clothes she flung him to the floor. "Do I look like I need you playing up again? I'm putting you in care if you carry on." The kid just lay on the floor. He knew exactly how to wind his mother up and screamed from the top of his lungs. Vicky bent down towards him and rubbed a wet flannel all over his face. Her flat palm rubbed vigorously, and even though she knew it was wrong she couldn't help but squeeze at his nose with the flannel to stop his breathing for a few seconds. He was clean again.

Vicky looked at the pine clock on the wall in the kitchen. She was running late. Dragging Declan's arm with force she pulled his grey parka coat from the nearby banister. "Come on we better get a move on. Move ya arse." Declan moaned as they left the house. He hadn't even had any breakfast. Vicky was skint again and nothing but a stale piece of bread was left in her kitchen cupboards. She was hoping her sister would feed him when he got there; after all it was still early. They walked at speed down Rochdale Road towards the Vine Estate where her sister lived.

The morning was wet and windy. It was typical Manchester weather. Everyone was rushing about and held their heads down as the wind picked up. Declan's hands looked purple as he clenched them together for warmth. Watching the buses pass she wished she'd had the fare to make her journey quicker. Vicky's legs were freezing. They looked like bottles of milk. Dipping her head, she dragged at the moaning child at the side of her to pick up speed.

Vicky rapped at the letter box. She could hear shouting from inside the house. A girl now opened the door. She only looked about nine years of age. She looked at Vicky like a piece of shit. It was Michelle's daughter Darcy. "Mam its Vicky and Declan."

"Well, tell her to come in then. Don't leave her waiting at the door." Michelle's voice was loud. The girl opened the door fully and went back inside as Vicky followed her. Darcy didn't really know Vicky and they'd only spoken on the odd occasion, but it was obvious her mother had told her all about her otherwise why else would she be acting like a complete bitch.

Declan bolted into the front room like shit from a shovel. His voice was loud and Vicky could see her sister eyes lifting towards the ceiling. Puffing on a cig she looked Vicky up and down. Why did she always make her feel so small? Vicky was younger than her and she let her know on more than one occasion that she was older and a lot wiser.

Declan was diving all over the place messing all the cushions up on the couch. Vicky growled at him much to Darcy's delight, because he'd gripped one of her dolls and was throwing it in the air. "Turn it in Declan," Michelle shouted. He turned to face her and smiled, but carried on regardless. Darcy looked distraught. It was her favourite Baby Annabel doll. She'd just got it for Christmas and there was no way he was destroying it. Walking up to him, Darcy gritted her teeth together. Unfolding his fingers from around her doll's neck she made him squeal like a pig. Her mother looked as proud as punch that her daughter had taken control.

"How would you like someone squeezing your neck ay?" Darcy's hands cupped round her cousin's fat neck. Her face looked evil as she leant over him. "See how you like it." Her bony fingers strangled round his throat and he was struggling to breathe. His face was going purple and Vicky was just about to step in when Darcy let him go.

"Bitch, bastard" he yelled after her. All eyes were now on Vicky to chastise her son for his foul mouth. Vicky looked weak as she smacked his arse at ten to a dozen. She didn't really want to do it but her sister had left her no option. Declan ran around the house and searched for a hiding place. Ramming his body behind the sofa he hid away licking his wounds.

Vicky asked the time as she looked about the room for a clock. She needed to make a move to Manchester Magistrates courts. She asked if she was okay to leave her son. Michelle loved the power she held over her sister and took her time in replying. "Yeah, how long you gonna be though, because I can't be doing with him all day." Her eyes focused at the legs she could see sticking out from behind the couch.

"Hopefully, not long. I should only get a fine or summit shouldn't I?"

Michelle blew a hard breath. Shaking her head she started her long overdue lecture. "You're such a daft cow in the first place. Fancy thinking you could still get Blake's money when he's in nick."

Vicky looked at her for a second. "Interfering know it all," she whispered under her breath. Twisting her body she told her she would have to leave. Vicky hovered about the room and thought about kissing her son goodbye.

Best leave, she thought and walked to the front door. "See you later, hopefully," she shouted with a giggle in her voice.

Vicky picked up her stride as she neared the courts. She felt calm now Declan wasn't by her side. It was bliss. No screaming kid and no pulling at his coat to make him hurry up. She could get used to this life she thought as she entered the building.

Making her way to the TV screens spread across a large wall she scanned at them all, trying to find her name. Once she'd located it, she realised she was in courtroom four. Her body was craving nicotine and she felt irritable. She'd not had a cig for hours. Her teeth looked like they were grinded together as she jogged up the stairs to meet her solicitor.

Vicky sat down and twiddled her hair. She looked anxious as she looked at the characters surrounding her. Each of them looked like they'd lost the plot. The man at the side of her stank of stale beer and her face screwed up as she inhaled his mouldy body odours. She could see her representative at the other end of the corridor.

Standing in the dock Vicky could feel her legs shaking. All eyes were on her as the charges were read out. She'd already pleaded guilty to the offences on a previous court appearance. Vicky placed her hands in her pockets to keep warm. She looked like she was shivering. The judge peered over his round glasses at her. He looked a right miserable cunt. He had a face like thunder as he coughed to clear his throat. As predicted he gave Vicky a fine. His lecture about fraud went on a bit longer than necessary and even the prosecution were raising their eyes in boredom. Mike, her solicitor, smiled over at her and gave her a cheeky wink. He knew she wasn't going to get time and a slap on the wrist was all he expected her to encounter.

Vicky walked away from the courtroom. Fucking three hundred pound fine, she thought, was the judge having a laugh, or what? She didn't have two pennies to rub together, never mind three hundred quid. Her brief was at her side rubbing his hands together. Patting her shoulder he looked proud of the result. "I think that went rather well," he boasted. Vicky strained her face to smile. Her solicitor was in her face and his breath stank of garlic. Creasing her cheeks she pulled away from him.

"Yeah it's alright if you've got that sort of money innit? How the fuck am I gonna pay the fine?" The solicitor looked shocked and turned his nose up. He could see tears forming in the corner of her eyes and kept schtum.

Vicky left the Magistrates courts with a black cloud of desperation hanging over her head. Looking up at the tall buildings in the city centre she wondered if she would have the courage to jump from one. She inhaled deeply through her nose. She could smell tobacco. Watching a man at the bus stop, she could see him puffing quickly at his fag before he got on the waiting bus. The cig end now lay near her feet. Quickly scanning the area she looked like she was thinking of her next move. Her head swivelled around like an owl as she bent down to the ground.

The burning cig was now in her grip. The grey smoke from it blew up towards her face. Standing to her feet she began walking with speed. Sucking on the half smoked cig, she could feel the rush of nicotine riding through her body. She felt a bit dizzy and had to take a minute to regain her balance.

Vicky walked through Manchester City Centre looking inside each shop window. Stopping at 'Miss Selfridges' her eyes focused on a red pair of shoes. She loved the colour red and sighed as she saw the price tag on them. "Fifty five fucking pound," she huffed. Trudging away from the shop she slowly came to terms with the fact that she would never own them. Clicking her heels together she closed her eyes. "There's no place like home. There's no place like home," she whispered. The Wizard of Oz was one of her favourite films and she giggled as she looked at the action of her feet. If only she had magic shoes. She looked happy as she was imagined the adventure and wealth brought from the red shoes she'd saw in the shop window.

Rochdale Road was busy. Cars sped past her and didn't give a shit that she was freezing her tits off. Holding her hand in front of her she looked at the one thing of value left in her life. Blake had said it was an engagement ring but she knew he'd being given it from some drug addict for a bag of smack. "That's it," she huffed. "It's this fucking ring that's giving me all this bad luck. Bet it was some smackhead that had nicked it from someone." Dipping her finger into her mouth her teeth pulled at the rim of the ring, it looked swollen as she dragged it over her knuckle.

'Mays' was a well known Pawnbroker in Manchester. If you ever needed any money fast this was the place to go to trade your jewellery in for cash. Pulling the shop's door open, she joined the queue of desperate looking people. Each of them looked eager for some cash. Vicky had pawned stuff in the past and knew it was a never-ending cycle. One minute you had your precious gold and the next thing it was sitting in the window of Mays ready to be sold. That was the thing about pawning stuff. It was alright getting the cash, but when the time came to get it back out, most items were lost due to the fact that you didn't have a pot to piss in.

Vicky stepped up to the glass window and shoved her gold ring under the counter. A man now picked it up and examined it with his eyepiece. "How much are you looking for?" he never looked at her directly.

"Erm... whatever you think is the best price." Rolling the ring around on his index finger he shot her a look that meant it wouldn't be a lot.

"Twenty pound is the best that I can do. I mean it's pretty bent isn't it?" Vicky agreed. She'd thrown the ring at her boyfriend so many times in the past and even tried chewing it in her mouth to show him that she meant business.

"Yeah that will have to do, won't it," she sighed. These bastards knew how desperate she was and took advantage of her situation. Watching the man type out her pawn ticket she pulled her birth certificate from her purse and squeezed it under the counter. No one was allowed to pawn stuff without any ID.

Vicky held the twenty pound note in her hands. She looked chuffed. She was rubbing at her finger for the missing ring and looked bare without it. Stepping outside she went into the shop next door. Goblets off license sold everything. Cigs were the first thing on her list, she was gasping. As she stood waiting to get served she looked like a junkie waiting to get a fix. "Ten Bensons and Hedges please," she mumbled. The shopkeeper turned his back and found the brand of cigs she wanted. Handing him the twenty pound note she looked happy that she had some money in her pocket for a change. As he was handing her the change her eyes shot to a cheap bottle of vodka. Licking her dry lips she hovered in the same position debating her next move. She'd had a hard day after all and she deserved a little drink didn't she? Eyes looking at the cash in her palm she made her decision. "Sorry, can I have a bottle of that vodka as well. Her finger was now wafting in front of her pointing to the alcohol on the shelf. The Asian shop keeper looked at her in disgust. It was only twelve-thirty, what did she expect? The shopkeeper was so used to all the alkies coming into the shop for ale and passed her the drink with a disapproving look on his face.

The bottle was cold as she placed it in her coat pocket. If the truth was known she wanted to sit on some bench somewhere and swig the lot of it down her throat in one gulp. At least then she would feel numb and not give a fuck that her life was going downhill at record speed. Vicky continued walking. Declan was on her mind and she decided when he was in bed later on in the evening she would drink the lot of it and get wrecked.

The money she had left was jingling about in her pocket. It was all she had to feed her son. Vicky needed a miracle to help save her. She looked up to the grey skies and her mouth was moving slowly. She looked like she was praying to God for help.

CHAPTER SIX

Susie put the final touches to her make up as she stood in front of the mirror in the bedroom. It was an expensive mirror too. You could tell by the gold details all around the edge of the frame. Tim had bought it months before from a top retail store. It was no cheap shit. It was the dog's bollocks.

With her mouth open wide her hand tilted at an angle as she applied the black mascara brush over her not so long eyelashes. She'd always complained about her tiny lashes in the past and today was no different. "Little bushy bristles," she huffed as she looked at the end result closer in the mirror.

Tonight Susie was off to the brothel to spend the night there. She had to see how things worked if she was ever going to run it and after all it was her bread and butter and the only income she had at the moment. Susie planned to show all those dirty bitches that she was no pushover. It wasn't rocket science really was it? And it was good to show the girls she was getting involved and showing them some interest.

Susie knew Joan was fiddling the books. Tim had told her in the past and the sluts days were numbered now she was on the case. Ashley lay on the bed watching her every movement. "What time are you going again?"

He knew exactly what time she was going out, and Susie hated she had to repeat herself yet again. "I told you before, deaf lugs. I'm sure you're a bit mutton jeff." One hand was now held on her hip as she leant in towards his face. "Fucking nine o'clock." Her head nodded up and down slowly as she said it again with a slow voice. Susie looked like she was talking to a deaf person. Her words were so exaggerated. She smiled and Ashley looked pissed off at her attempt at humour.

"I didn't hear you dick-head! So that's why I was asking again."

"Well I'm making sure you hear me this time that's all," she chuckled nervously. Her face looked mischievous and he knew she was taking the piss.

"Well I'll come with you for a bit if that's alright. I wanna see how that paint has dried anyway." Ashley and a few of his mates had taken on the task of painting the hallway at the brothel and that was the only excuse he had to go with his lover. She scowled. He was like a fart lingering around her twenty four seven. Whenever she looked over her shoulder he was there like a bad smell. Ashley was bugging her big time. Susie's disappointment was there for him to see and he examined her face to make sure he wasn't seeing things. His nostrils flared. She could see his knuckles turning white as he clenched his fist at his side. His voice was sarcastic. He'd been looking for a reason to belt her all night. "Why, you don't mind me coming with you, do ya?" his voice was shaking. Susie held her breath and combed her hair. Her lips were moving but no sound was coming out. She was cursing under her breath. He was by her side now pulling her face into view. "If I'm not wanted, just fucking say so, instead of hiding it." Susie pulled from his tight grip with a struggle. She could see him shaking and knew she was in big trouble if she didn't back down.

"Fucking hell Ashley, don't be going on one. For fucks sake," she blew a frustrated breath. "I haven't said I don't want you to come have I?" She was playing with him now and he didn't know how to react. He looked confused. He wanted her to argue with him so he could have kicked her head all over the place. His temper was boiling with the steroids racing through his veins. Rage was written all over his face and a purple vein at the side of his neck could be seen pumping at speed looking like it was going to burst.

Ashley was like a ticking bomb and she had to think quickly. Susie defused him instantly. She was a clever cow. Singing her head off, she slipped her black dress over her head. She could feel his eyes watching her as her dress rolled down her slender body. She'd learnt how to deal with him now and there was no way in the world she was giving him any reason to beat her within an inch of her life. "I want you to come with me sweetheart. Why are you going all snide?" Walking towards him she draped her arms around his neck, and planted a sloppy kiss on his cheeks. "Mard arse," she huffed. Ashley stood tall. She'd apologised and that was enough for him. He was her Lord and master again. Susie was learning fast that he liked the control he felt over her. He looked pleased as he flexed his muscles at the side of her.

Ashley was following Susie in his car. She could see him driving up her arse in the rear- view mirror. Turning the music up, she felt happy for a change. Rhianna's tune 'Complicated' now played at full pelt. The speakers were pumping as she sang along to the tune.

Pulling into the seedy car park at the back of Delia's, Susie turned her engine off. She could see Ashley parking up, and he looked eager to get to her side. As she opened her car door he was already there. Bending over the passenger seat she grabbed her handbag. Her 'Jimmy Choo' bag now looked old and ragged. "Come on stop fucking about, I'm freezing my bollocks off out here," he moaned. Susie growled at him and chewed on her bottom lip. You could see his two nipples fully erect underneath his grey fitted top.

"I'm coming, hold ya horses, will ya?" she pleaded. Her long legs could be seen coming out of the car. Ashley clocked them with lust in his eyes. He was a horny fucker. His sex drive was massive; all day long he was looking for a hole to fill.

They walked to the entrance. A few drunken men seemed to be debating whether they were going inside the brass gaff. Susie could see them counting their money as they staggered about trying to hold each other up. Pressing the intercom Susie shivered. Ashley gripped her and kissed the top of her head. "Get off me ya muppet. The fucking CCTV." He looked dazed as he looked around for the cameras. She spoke in an angry voice. "The girls can see everything that's going on outside here, ya tosser." He knew she was right and backed away with a deflated look on his face. A buzzing noise could be heard.

The door opened. With a desperate grip Susie pulled at it hard to gain access. The smell of fresh painted was in the air. Susie cast her eyes up towards the top of the stairs. The place looked half decent now, and she felt proud that she'd already made changes in the joint. Pulling the last door open, she could see the reception. Susie scanned the area as Ashley parked his arse on a nearby sofa.

Pippa came into view like she owned the gaff. Her walk was tall and every curl in her hair looked in tip-top condition. Susie gawped at her. There was no getting away from it. This girl was hot stuff.

Susie went behind the reception desk and her eyes focused on the books. She needed to be two steps in front of Joan if she was to catch the thieving cow in action. "Is it busy tonight?" Susie asked. There was no reply and she may as well have been talking to a brick wall. Her head lifted and she shot a look at Pippa who was sat next to Ashley flirting. She repeated herself again as she watched the brass making a play for him. Susie looked stern and she held her head to the side with her eyes wide- open. Ashley clocked her gaze and nudged the prostitute in the waist.

"What you saying?" Pippa answered with a cocky face. Susie's nostrils flared and Pippa walked to the front of the desk. Her face told Ashley she was on to him and he looked like a small child who'd been caught with his hand in the biscuit tin.

"I said, if you can stop throwing yourself at Ashley for a minute, you would have heard me."

Pippa shrugged her shoulders and turned to Ashley. She looked him up and down. He was fair game. Why was Susie bothered? Pippa reached for the cigs that she'd left on the coffee table in front of her. Tapping the box at the end one cig came out. Susie was losing patience.

"Where's Joan?"

Pippa lit her cig and blew the smoke from her mouth with force. "In the toilet I think?"

"You think? She's supposed to be managing this place, not sat on the shitter all fucking night."

Pippa held her head back and laughed. "The woman has to piss yanno."

"Has it been busy?" Pippa shrugged her shoulders. "I have, I don't know about the rest of the girls. You'll have to ask Joan."

A buzzing noise could now be heard. Pippa nodded at Susie with instructions. "Just press that button on top of the counter. Some punters are at the door." Susie located the button. Looking at the CCTV she froze, peering at the screen she looked closer. Susie was biting her nails; a large smile appeared over her face. Pippa urged her to let the punters in. "Will you hurry up before they fuck off. I've got a living to make yanno." Susie pressed the button and a buzzing noise could be heard. She left Ashley sat on the sofa and made herself scarce.

Susie hid in a small office at the side of the reception; she could see two men entering. Joan came through the other door and greeted them. Watching the two men sit down Susie peered through the gap in the door. Was her mind playing tricks on her, or was it him. Watching the man she examined every inch of his face. Her lips curled up at the side. She smiled and nodded her head. "Gotcha Jenkins ya bastard," she muttered.

Joan sorted the men out with the girls they desired. Pippa stood slowly and looked the punters up and down. She grabbed the good-looking one by his hand and led him through the door to her place of work. "Fuck shagging the minger," she whispered to the other girl who'd copped for the ugly guy. Once the other male had gone through the doors, Susie came out of hiding and told Joan she wouldn't be a minute. She held a devious look on her face. Creeping down the corridor she came to Pippa's love nest. A small glass panel was in the door and she could see the punter taking his clothes off. Susie dipped her head back out of sight. She looked like she was thinking about her next move. Fingers tapping on her teeth she looked fidgety. Digging deep into her coat pocket she searched for her mobile phone, it was one of the latest ones out and the camera on it was top of the range.

Two bodies could be seen lying on the bed. Pippa was sucking her client off. Without any hesitation Susie brought her phone to the glass window and started to take pictures of the two of them. Her finger was moving rapidly trying to capture the shot. She needed these photographs more than anything if her plan was to work.

Minutes passed and Pippa was straddled over her guest. You could just see his face. He looked pissed as a fart. Susie angled her hand at the door and made sure she got more evidence of the goings-on. Nodding her head slowly she left the side of the door with a cunning grin spread across her face. Shoving the phone back inside her pocket she headed back to see Joan. The shit was about to hit the fan.

Joan looked wrecked. Dark circles were visible around her eyes. She looked tired. Susie knew her manager had dabbled with crack in the past and by looking at her face tonight she'd been on it again. Joan looked uneasy as Susie came bouncing back into the room.

"Where have you been?" Ashley moaned.

"Just checking a few things out, that's all. Why did you miss me?" Susie giggled with a cocky face. His head sank back into the 'Playboy' magazine that he'd picked up from the table. Tugging at his crotch it was obvious he was getting aroused. He continued to look at the pussy shots holding the magazine up to his face to get the best view. Joan looked hot and uncomfortable. Small droplets of sweat were visible on her forehead, and she was constantly licking at her lips.

Drugs were a big part of brothel life and Susie knew that more than anyone. After all these women were having sex with anything that moved, so they needed something to help numb the pain didn't they? Susie was in Joan's face. Their noses were nearly touching. You could see Susie was making her feel uncomfortable and she looked like she loved every minute of it. Head tilted to the side, Susie looked directly into Joan's eyes. "You've been smoking crack again haven't you?"

Joan became defensive and waved her hand about in front of her face. "Get a grip woman. Those days are long gone now. I don't touch the stuff no more. I haven't for months."

"Lying twat," Susie thought. Joan's pupils looked like saucers and she looked on another planet. Joan's words were shaky. She tried to change the conversation. She hoped Susie would back down and not be onto her seedy little secret.

"This place looks miles better now that it's had a lick of paint, doesn't it?" Susie was looking at the books again. Standing up straight she cast her eyes over each figure. Heavy breathing noises could be heard. Susie scraped her long fingernail down the white piece of paper. She could feel Joan at the side of her breathing down her neck. Her breath stank of alcohol. "You'll find all the books are in order love. There's nothing for you to worry about."

Susie lifted her head up and stared at her. "I hope so love, for your sake."

Cupping her hands together Joan offered them both a drink. She wanted Susie away from the books as soon as possible. She needed a drink to calm her nerves down, she was on edge. Ashley ears pricked up, he looked like a dog waiting for its owner to return. He was ready for a drink and stood up, bouncing about. "Where's the beers then?"

Joan liked Ashley and smiled at him anxiously. He was a man's man and she'd had a laugh with him and his mates when they were in days before, painting the brothel. Ashley was a rum fucker. Joan clapped her hands like a seal at the Zoo. She loved a drink and always made sure she always had a stash of Stella and vodka on the go. "Follow me then," she said with a giggle in her voice as she looked at Susie still concentrating on the figures. Ashley now pulled her away from the books.

"Come on Susie. Get a drink down ya neck to chill you out. You looked stressed."

Walking down the corridor, Pippa's door opened. Susie hid in the shadows and kept her head low, she didn't want Jenkins to spot her. Pippa was holding the man up, escorting him to the exit. She could be seen winking at

Ashley as she passed him. The man looked in a world of his own and his eyes were nearly closed as he tried to focus down the dimly lit corridor.

Joan's office was a mess. Lots of empty cups were all over the place. The bin was heaving with finished bottles of vodka. Susie sniffed hard and her nostrils flared slightly. "Fucking hell, it smells like someone's died in here. Can't you open a window or summit?" Ashley agreed as his face squirmed. "You need a plug-in air freshener in here Joan. It smells of arse." Joan giggled and stretched her bony body up to open the small window at the side of her. She stood on a chair to open it. A slight breeze now entered the room. Susie rubbed at her arms. Goose pimples were now visible on her skin.

A red sofa was positioned at the back wall of the office. It had seen much better days and was ready for the skip. It stank of cat piss. Susie plonked herself down on it and she didn't look pleased as she wiped the fluff from her clothes.

Ashley swigged rapidly at his can of Stella, he could see Susie wasn't happy. Her face looked red and he knew something was wrong. "What's up with your mush?" he said finally when Joan nipped out to greet a punter.

"She's ripping us off big time, the tart."

"Who is?" he asked with an absent look on his face. Ashley could be so thick at times. She kept her voice low and whispered as her eyes kept focused on the door.

"Fucking yo-yo knickers that's who."

Chewing on his lips his eyebrows rose to the top of his head. "You mean Joan?" he asked.

"Yeah, ya dizzy bastard. Who else would I mean? She's bang at it." The door opened and Joan came back into the room with a cig hanging from her mouth. Reaching for her beer she swigged a long refreshing gulp. Wiping the spillage from her lips with a quick swipe, she made a loud burp. "Sorry," she giggled.

Susie paced the room looking like all hell was about to break loose. Turning her head slowly she spoke with a suspicious tone. "Has it been busy tonight?"

Joan swallowed hard. She'd caught her off-guard. "Erm… It's been a bit quiet. It doesn't start picking up until later on. Why what's up?" Joan was pulling at her clothes looking agitated.

"Nowt, just asking that's all." Silence filled the room. You could have heard a pin drop. Ashley was in his comfort zone and necked one beer after another. He wanted to be out partying and looked like he had something to say. Coughing to clear his throat he got Susie's attention.

"Do ya fancy coming out for a bit. I'm in the mood now for a few beers?" Susie nodded her head slowly as her eyes pierced into Joan's face. She was pissed off, and wanted a well deserved night on the tiles.

"Yeah fuck it, why not." Joan blew a laboured breath. Her hand covered her face trying to hide her relief. She wanted Susie gone from there as soon as possible. She was pissing on her parade big time. "Right Joan, I might call back later if that's alright?" Walking back to the reception Joan replied "Yeah love whatever." in a matter-of- fact voice. As they came through the door into the waiting area Susie could see another four men waiting. Each of them held that guilty look of infidelity on their faces. One man was around sixty-five and Susie wondered if he might have a heart attack on the job.

Pippa was leaning on the counter. Her shimmering legs could be seen sticking out from beneath her red silken housecoat. The punters were eager to have sex with her and the oldest man had already decided he was the one who was going first. He looked edgy waiting for the brass to look at him. Pippa's eyes were all over Ashley like a rash. Flicking her hair across her shoulders she grinned at him. Ashley made sure Susie couldn't see him and smiled back.

"Are you going already, babes?" she asked in a seductive voice. Ashley went red in the face and nodded. Susie was by his side now protecting her man.

"Yeah he is going, what do you want?" Pippa held no fear for Susie, unlike Joan who was running about like a blue arsed fly. She reached for Ashley's arm and stroked it invitingly.

"I just wanted to see if you fancied coming back later on to pick me up, that's all." Ashley was going under. He was crumbling. You could tell by his face he wanted to ram his cock deep into Pippa, but how could he say yes, when Susie was by his side. He chuckled with nerves. Dragging his fingers through his hair he replied.

"I can't tonight chick. I've got too much on. Maybe some other time, ay."

"Your loss," Pippa huffed.

Susie walked to the exit gritting her teeth. Waving her hand above her head she said goodbye to them all without turning her head. Walking down the staircase Susie froze and turned back to face Ashley. She clenched her fist and dug it into his waist. "Do you think you're smart?"

"What?" he said holding his hands up in the air to pledge his innocence.

"You know exactly what I'm going on about. Don't play the fucking innocent with me because it won't wash." His face held a smirk as she carried on down the stairs. Once outside she marched to her car in a full blown strop.

Ashley had already told Susie where they would meet. She had to go home first and drop her car off. Starting the engine she watched Ashley drive off with speed from the car park. His tunes were pumping and she knew it was going to be a long night. Ashley and Susie both sniffed Cocaine on a regular basis. Her body was already craving it as she drove to the junction. Indicator on, you could hear the clicking noise of it. Susie sat forward in the driver's seat. As she pulled out into the main road, her head was turning left then right waiting for a gap in the traffic. She looked like she was watching a tennis match. Susie paused. There was a gap in the traffic and she should have pulled out but she found herself staring at a man swaying down the road. Screwing her eyes up she realised it was Jenkins again, the screw from Strangeways prison. Crawling out onto the road she watched his movements as he tried to walk. The man seemed to be taking two steps forward and ten steps back. Pulling up out of sight, she lit a cig.

Susie was late. She'd watched the screw for over half an hour. She looked relieved when she saw him entering a house. She could see him struggling to find his front door keys and watched him fall into the nearby bushes on a few times. The man disappeared from view as he finally unlocked the door. Susie clocked the address and quickly typed it into her phone. Nodding her head, she smiled like the cat that had got the cream; Jenkins was going to pay through his front teeth for his infidelity. Now it was party time. Pulling back onto the road, she headed home at speed. Cocaine was calling her and she was excited at the thought of feeling the white dust filtering through her body.

CHAPTER SEVEN

Tim lay in his cell tapping his fingers to the 'NDUBZ' tune that was playing on the radio. "How do ya find the words to say that it's over?" His voice was low as he sang along to the track with a dull tone. His bitch of a girlfriend had left his sorry arse to rot in jail; there was no two ways about it. Two months had passed and he'd only seen her twice. Susie had told him straight she was no letter writer and his mail and visits would be few.

The cell was his home now and as he looked around the four grey depressing walls he wanted his life to end. A window in the middle of the room was his only contact with the outside world. Tim spent hours looking out from it hoping he would see a familiar face. He never did. His cell faced Bury New Road and he could always see members of the public trotting about. He would have given his left eye to be free at the moment.

His pad mate was lay asleep at the side of him. He was an alright lad and they seemed to get along fine. He was in for drug dealing and had already kicked the arse out of his seven year sentence. Snoring could be heard. It was pissing Tim off big time. He placed his hands over his ears to try and dismiss the grunts from his pad mate. Launching his shoe at him with full force he yelled "Will you shut the fuck up snoring. You're doing my bastard head in?"

The body in the bed near him stirred. The man looked in his early forties. Peter kicked his sheets from his bed and looked angry. "You nob-head. What have you woke me up for?"

Tim ran to his side. He was in his face now, teeth gritted. "I'm sick of it. Every day and every night it's always the fucking same." Heads were touching as they both pushed harder at each other with their foreheads. They looked like two bulls with their horns locked. None of them seemed to be backing down and they looked ready to fight.

The cell door flew open just in time to stop them fighting. A screw stood there with a stern face. They both backed away from each other cautiously. "What's going on here?" the officer asked. He could tell they were both upset and sniggered as he entered the pad. His eyes were all over the place.

A few more screws joined him now, and they could be seen putting white plastic gloves on. One warden escorted the two prisoners outside. It was a cell raid. Mattresses were being tossed up in the air and you could see the prison officers searching every nook and cranny for illegal items. "Fuck all," one of them shouted as he searched the small bedside cabinet. Tim and Peter were stood outside with their backs held up against the wall. They looked like they were shitting their pants. Tim prayed they didn't find the last bit of sniff he was storing. He was having a crap day, and this was all he needed, a nicking for drugs. There was nothing the convicts could do to stop their cell being turned over. They tried causing a scene at first, but they didn't stand a chance because the screws were pinning them up against the wall not listening to a word they had to say. This was an everyday occurrence in prison life.

Mr Pollit had been a screw for over five years, and he was used to the goings on inside Strangeways prison.

He knew some stories that would have made your toes curl. He often told the younger officers about his dealings with inmates. Prison life was hard, and he knew he would always have to watch his back as he walked the prison landings. The inmates inside there wouldn't have thought twice about slicing him up the moment his back was turned. He was a wise old soul.

Mr Politt's colleague's seemed to be taking instructions from him as they searched every inch of the cell. Twenty minutes passed and nothing was found. The screws left the pad empty handed much to their disappointment. Throwing the inmates back inside the room they spoke to them as if they were pieces of shit. "We're on to you two, don't worry. Next time we'll have ya." The screw nodded his head at Tim and shot him a look. Tim pushed past him. His shoulder skimmed Jenkins' chest as their eyes met. His blood was boiling and he could have easy pummelled his fist into the cocky bastard's face.

The two men now started to clean the mess up. Peter flung his mattress back on the bed and quickly turned to Tim. "That was a close shave, wannit?"

Tim nodded. "Sorry about before mate. I'm so stressed out over Susie. She's doing my fucking head in big time."

Peter knew exactly what he meant and accepted his apology. His own girlfriend was the same. Once he'd been slammed his woman seemed to change too, it seemed like she didn't give a flying fuck about him anymore. "Women ay mate. The best thing to do is to not let her bother you. My Mrs is exactly the same. She's never in when I phone. And when I do speak to her, she seems in a rush to get rid of me." Tim was hanging on Peter's every word. The man was talking sense. Susie was just the same as his girlfriend. Every time he spoke to the bitch, she was always just going somewhere or just doing something. Tim stood from his bed and checked the screws were gone. Placing his ear to the door he couldn't hear a thing. He walked back to his bed and grabbed a nearby trainer. Lifting it up in his hands his fingers yanked at the sole of it. Tugging hard, his face looked strained and his fingers were going red. Eventually he pulled enough of it away to grab the small plastic bag concealed inside it. "They didn't get this baby though, did they the wankers!" Tim swung the drugs about in his fingertips as if he was holding a dead mouse's tail.

Peter was checking outside the door. He didn't feel safe and his eyes were all over the place. The screws knew they were hiding something and he looked at his pad mate with concerned eyes. "They must have had a tip off. Why else are they onto us?"

"It's that bastard Jenkins. He's got it in for me, I know he has. Have you seen the way he looks at me? The man's pure evil."

Peter knew Tim was right; the screw he was talking about was always on his pad mate's back. He was making his life a misery. "I wonder what his problem is." Peter whispered.

"Dunno mate. I think he's after shagging my arse or summit. The gay fucker."

Peter laughed out loud as Tim chopped them each a line of sniff. He didn't have that much left and wanted to get rid of it as soon as possible.

Two white lines now lay on the small mirror in Tim's hand. The men took turns in snorting the lines of Charlie with a small rolled up piece of paper. Tim's body looked fierce as the whiff took effect. Every muscle in his arms seemed to be pumping. He looked invincible.

Both of them lay on their beds. Peter was pouring his heart out and holding nothing back. The drug had unleashed his emotions. "Women can't be trusted mate. I caught my Angela at it before I got slammed. She was fucking the brains out of my best mate, yanno."

Tim bolted up from his bed and was hanging on his every word. He was dragging his fingers through his hair in disbelief. "What she shagged your best mate? How did you find out?"

Peter started to make a roll-up. Sprinkling the tobacco into the Rizla paper he looked sad and shook his head slowly. "I think I knew summat was going down. Every time they were together they were always laughing and joking." Popping the thin roll-up into his mouth he flicked the lighter. The flame struggled and he quickly sucked at it to get a light. "I wasted her mate, when I caught her." Tim looked shocked as he continued, "I came in one night earlier than I should have and knew something didn't feel right. She'd got rid of the kids and the house was in complete darkness. I could hear noises coming from upstairs and at first I thought we were being robbed." He passed Tim half of the cig. Tim's cheeks sunk in at each side as he struggled to get a drag of it. Peter lay down on his bed. Folding the pillow underneath his head, his eyes stared at the ceiling as if he was remembering every sordid moment. "I crept up every single stair. My baseball bat was in my hands and I was getting ready to whack the thieving fuckers heads right off. Opening the bedroom door was the worst thing I could have done."

Tim was gripped. "Why mate, what happened?"

Peter rolled on his side and stared at Tim. His face looked white and he sighed as he clenched his fist. His knuckles were turning white. "He was banging my missus wasn't he?"

"Who?" Tim urged with an angry voice eager for him to continue.

"Jona. My best mate," he said as he spat in the bin at the side of him.

"No way," Tim gasped. He sprang from the bed. Cocaine was filtering through his veins and he looked stressed. "The cheeky bastard. I hope you wasted him?"

Peter chuckled. His voice was menacing. "Oh don't you worry Tim. He was dealt with good and proper. I let him have it royal. My baseball bat whacked him to fuck, all over his body. She was screaming her head off for me to stop."

Tim nodded his head; anger was all over his face. "Fucking hell man. How did you cope with that?"

"I didn't mate. It still haunts me every fucking day. I should have really have fucked her off but I couldn't. I don't know why."

Tim huffed as he cracked his fingers. "I couldn't have done it mate. Fucking hell. Shagging your best mate. That's lower than a snake's belly that is, she must have more front than Blackpool."

Peter threw a pillow over at him laughing. "I've shagged most of her mates anyway. So I suppose it was payback. Plus I gave her Chlamydia, so I think we're equal now."

Tim relaxed. "You're a right fanny magnet aren't you?"

Peter sat looking proud. He gave Tim a cocky glance and nodded his head slowly. "Yeah man, I could never be faithful. These birds are too hot to miss out on. I swear I'm like a dog on heat when I'm on the out."

Tim jumped on his bed. His head seemed to be doing overtime. The drugs he'd taken weren't helping him and he was becoming paranoid. Stroking the photograph of Susie on his wall he spoke to her as if she could hear him. "You better not start any of that shit love, because trust me, I'll do you and your lover boy right in. Do you hear me?" his voice was chilling.

Peter giggled. He was adding fuel to the fire and loved winding his pad mate up. "Women are all the same. The minute your back's turned their knickers are down and they don't give a fuck about you."

Tim screwed his face up. His Susie was a lot of things but she was never a slag. He tried to defend her. "Well maybe the women you know are mate, but my Susie will stick by me no matter what."

"Yeah, yeah," Peter laughed. "We'll see."

It was soon time for all the prisoners on the landing to have their social time. It was the best part of prison life. One hour talking and chatting to each other and feeling free. The inmates could be seen flying out from their cells like they were suffocating. A lot of them had been banged up all day and this was the only time they could get out to stretch their legs. Loud noises of people shouting and laughing could be heard. Tim headed for the phone.

Four lads stood in the queue waiting to make a call. Tim watched eagerly for each prisoner to finish. Shouting could be heard. "You silly bitch. You carry on being smart and I'll have someone come round there, and shave ya fucking hair off. Do you hear me?" The inmate cursed down the phone. He was frothing at the mouth as his clenched fist smashed against the receiver. Another convict grabbed the phone from his hand. "Ay, what do ya think ya doing? Don't be wrecking the phone. We all need to fucking use it." He gripped the phone from the distraught prisoner and looked for back up from the other inmates.

The prisoner was wild and he knew he couldn't tackle him on his own. Tim's chest expanded in his t-shirt and you could see his nostrils flaring. The tips of his ears seemed to be going red as he stepped forward. The phone was now dropped from the convict's hand. He was kicking at the prison walls and at one stage his head was banging at it with speed. He'd definitely lost the plot. "Fucking lying bitch," he ranted.

Tim waited for the phone. Every phone call before him seemed to be the same. The prisoners were paranoid about their women on the out. The convicts all seemed to be lovey-dovey one minute and the next they were like animals swearing and cursing down the receiver. Tim sighed as he dialled Susie's phone number. Listening to the ring tone he prayed she would answer. He seemed weak inside and needed some reassurance that she would always be there for him no matter what.

"Yo, Susie. It's me Tim." His face looked white as he slowly kicked his foot against the wall in front of him. "What do you mean you're just on ya way out? Fucking hell Susie I've waited all day to phone you. Can't you just wait five minutes?" His smile dropped completely from his face now. His ear pressed hard against the phone. He was listening. "Who the fuck is that shouting in the background?" he yelled. Susie paused. He repeated himself. "What the fuck is Ashley doing there?" He was growling at the phone now and he was eager for her to reply.

Slamming the phone down Tim stamped his feet and dragged at his clothing in temper. He couldn't let the other inmates see him like this. Head dipped he trudged to the toilets. "Fucking slag," he mumbled under his breath.

The toilet area was empty and he kicked at the cubicle door nearly taking it off its hinges. Stood behind the door his body folded up in desperation. Elbows placed on his knees his hands gripped at his face as he tried to hold back the tears. It was no good, a river of sadness now started to fall. The stench from the toilets was sickening. His eyes focused on the floor and he could see all the splashes of piss near where he was sat. One hand holding the wall he dragged his body up to stand tall. He could hear someone coming in the toilets and covered his mouth to hide his torment.

Tim joined Peter for the last ten minutes of social time. His mind was doing overtime and no matter how much he tried, he couldn't get the thought from his head. "The bitch is shagging around," he whispered to Peter who was bent over the pool table getting ready to take his shot.

Peter lifted his eyes and turned his head to Tim. "Nowt ya can do mate. You just have to take it on the chin. There is fuck all ya can do in here, is there?"

Tim was chewing on his bottom lip. His eyes were flickering at speed. His words were fast and furious. "I'm taking fuck all on the chin mate. You watch and learn." Peter looked at him and shook his head. Tim looked fucked in the head and he knew he was planning something evil for his girlfriend.

Lying in his bed, Tim's fingers touched Susie's glossy photo on the wall. He would have usually kissed her goodnight but tonight, his fingernail scraped at her photo, right across her eyes ripping some of the snapshot away. She was due to visit him the next day and he planned exactly what he was going to say to her in his head. Peter was snoring yet again and Tim pulled the blankets over his body. Tonight he felt lonely.

CHAPTER EIGHT

Susie dragged herself up from the bed. Even lifting the quilt from her body seemed like an effort. She was hungover. Last night had been a long one, and the signs of all the late evenings she'd been having recently were written all over her face. She looked haggard. Ashley was asleep next to her. You could just see the top of his head sticking out from the covers. "Where's the cigs?" she asked. Her hand pushed at his body next to her. Moaning could be heard. Pushing harder at him he pulled his head from underneath the blankets. His hair was stuck up all over the place and he was sucking at his dry lips. "Get us a drink will ya? My mouth's drier than a camel's arse."

Struggling to get up from the bed, she wobbled as she tried to regain her balance. Her eyes were small and one of her false eyelashes was hanging on by a drop of glue at the corner of her eye. "Find the cigs then," she moaned as she left the room to get a drink. Ashley stretched from the bed and located his jeans on the floor. With a struggle he yanked them onto the bed and searched the pockets. Susie could be heard going downstairs.

"Fucking hell, I spent a right few bob last night." His hands held a wad of cash fanned out in front of his face.

"Well you will buy everyone drinks won't you, Rockefeller?" her face frowned. Passing him the orange juice she watched as he gulped the liquid down in one go. He was more than thirsty. Wiping his mouth, he pulled her towards him. "Do ya wanna play hide the sausage?"

She giggled as he tickled her. Her body was weak and she couldn't be arsed with his love gestures. "Orr fuck off will ya, I had enough of that last night. My fanny's red raw." He grabbed at his cock and waved it around in front of her. She wasn't interested.

Susie found the cigs from the side of the bed and popped one in her mouth. She peeled the drooping black eyelash from her eyes. She sat examining it. "Fucking hell, no wonder I couldn't see properly with this fucker hanging over my eye. I thought I'd had a stroke or summat," she chuckled.

"Give us a cig then," he pleaded as he sat up in the bed waiting for his nicotine fix. Searching his jeans he found the remains of the cocaine from the night before. Holding it towards the light he sighed. "Fuck me; we tanned some sniff last night." Her eyes gazed at the transparent bag in front of her.

"Don't you mean you did? Every time I looked at you, you were like a fucking hoover." His finger was pointing in her face as he spoke in a sarcastic tone.

"Yeah, and every time I was at it, you were beside me, so don't come all the innocent with me, you coke whore."

She smiled at him as she took a long drag of her cig. "Well I'm not gonna sit there with you all straight headed am I?" He coughed loudly as he shoved the white powder back in his pocket. Ashley's chest crackled, he sounded like he smoked a hundred cigs a day.

"Did you sort that visit out with Mouldy Marie for Tim? I'm going to see him in a bit, and he'll go sick if it's not sorted?"

Ashley tutted, "Nar I'll go and see her in a bit. I hope he doesn't expect me to pay for it all. She charges two ton to do a visit, yanno?" His face was like thunder. Susie shook her head and fell back onto the bed sighing. Her legs were hanging from the bed. What the fuck was she going to do now? Everything was costing so much money and her income had fallen already without paying people to take drugs in prison.

"Well just get it sorted. I'll have to find the money from somewhere won't I?" She replied nastily. Ashley wasn't happy and dragged the covers back over his body. He'd proper spat his dummy out.

"Fucking leave the nob-head to rot, we owe him fuck all." She knew by his tone not to argue back.

Later, when Ashley had gone home and Susie was putting the final touches to her make-up, the postman shoved a letter through the door. As she stuck her head up to the window she could see the postman leaving her garden. Wrapping the towel around her body she ran down the stairs. Two white envelopes lay staring at her on the floor. Holding her bath towel with one hand she bent down to pick them up. Looking at the handwriting she could tell they were prison letters.

Perched on the bed she shoved her finger inside the envelope to open it. She could see it was a long letter as all the writing stood from the four pages. Snatching a cig from the side, she lit it as she started to read the bullshit Tim had written. Her face looked worried and at one point she threw the letter on the bed making a v sign at it. Susie stared around the bedroom. She looked anxious. Grabbing the letter again she continued to read it. Helen must have been writing to Tim, she thought, because he knew all about the flowers Ashley had bought her. Gritting her teeth she flung the letter to the floor. "Right you fat bitch, you wanna play with the big girls do ya?"

Susie could be heard running down the stairs. She came back into the bedroom and dropped the big Yellow

Pages directory on the bed. She flicked through the pages until she found what she was looking for. Susie giggled like a witch who was getting ready to cast a spell. Reaching for the phone she placed her thumb and a finger at the side of her nose. She was getting ready to squeeze it. "Hello, I would like to report someone for committing benefit fraud please." Her voice sounded odd and she sounded like she had a severe case of the flu. Susie could now be heard giving all the details she knew about Helen and her partner. She was a right grassing bitch and told them that Helen had a man living with her even though she was claiming single person's benefit. "No love, I don't want to give my name. I just don't like people who take advantage of the system." She sounded concerned and played the part well. After a few more minutes Susie put the phone down. Rubbing her hands together she rammed her fist into the air and looked happy at her revenge. "Let's see who's laughing now you fat interfering cow," her laughter shook the walls as she continued getting ready.

Looking at the clock on the wall, Susie finished writing her letter. Instead of putting it in an envelope she shoved it in her back pocket and patted at it with a smile on her face – the name Jenkins was written on the front of it. One last look in the mirror and she was ready to go. Susie left the house and set off on her journey to the prison.

The familiar sight of Strangeways prison looked at Susie as she went to park her car. Her mind was working overtime and she looked stressed. Today she looked scruffy. Her hair was just shoved back in a ponytail. She'd promised herself a trip to the hairdressers but she never found the time anymore. Her mobile phone started ringing. "Hello," she yelled down the line. "Orr, stop lying, no way. Why won't Marie do it? Did you tell her she'd earn two hundred quid from it?" Her voice was frantic. You could hear Ashley shouting down the phone at her and she ended the call. Her head sank on the steering wheel and she looked close to tears. "What the fuck am I gonna do now?" she gasped.

The weather was pleasant for a change. The sun was shining and a cool breeze filled the air. Susie could see Vicky walking towards the visitor's centre. She quickly grabbed her stuff from the car and shouted over to her. "Oi..Vicky," The girl turned her head and smiled. She had no kid with her today and looked relaxed for a change. Susie hurried to her side. "You should have said you were on a visit, and I would have come and picked you up."

Vicky looked embarrassed. "I didn't know I was coming. I was gonna fuck the visit off but changed my mind at the last minute."

Susie nodded her head. "I know what you mean love." They both trudged to the depressing visitors' centre. "Where's ya lad?" Susie asked with a giggle in her voice.

"He's at school, thank fuck." Vicky smiled and let out her emotions as if she'd known Susie for years. "Peace and quiet, I wish they had a night school too, because he'd be in it, let me tell you."

Susie smiled. The poor girl looked at her wits end. It was obvious she'd tried to make the effort to look nice for the visit, but her black leggings were a wash away from the bin as were the rest of her clothes. Vicky looked tatty and like she needed a good bath. Susie looked at her in more detail as they queued up at the desk. She was pretty underneath her tattered look. Her eyes held so much sadness and they looked like a sea of desperation.

Sitting at the table Susie looked about at the visitors.

It looked like the setting for "Shameless" the TV series.

Every kind of low life was sat there. Junkie's stood out like a sore thumb as they spoke out loudly and argued with each other. There were some nice people sat there too, but like Susie they sat away from the crowd and away from the down and outs.

Vicky looked troubled and Susie was dying to get to the bottom of it. "Do you want a drink?" she asked but Vicky declined. As usual she didn't have a pot to piss in and Susie could detect that just by looking at her face. Susie went to the hatch without asking anymore questions. "Watch my bag," she shouted back to Vicky. She'd clocked the two smackheads watching her queue up. Susie shot a look at them, and let them know she was onto them. "Scumbags," she muttered under her breath.

Vicky looked Susie up and down. Playing with her greasy hair you could see the jealousy in her eyes. Life had dealt her a crap hand of cards, and her life was on the road to nowhere at record speed. Susie walked back holding two plastic cups. "There you go love." She placed the two cup of coffee on the table and pulled a Mars bar out of her pocket to accompany it. Vicky was smiling. If the truth was known she hadn't had a bite to eat all day. Thanking Susie, she started to eat the chocolate bar. Susie sat down and watched her every move. This girl was desperate and you could Susie's face getting ready to interrogate her. Vicky slurped at her drink as she munched on her chocolate bar.

"So Vicky, tell me more about yourself. Do you work or owt?" Vicky dipped her head in embarrassment. The last job she'd had was her paper round when she was fifteen, and there was no way she telling her that. She shook her head and remained silent.

Susie was plotting and knew she would have to act fast. She made sure no one could hear her. Moving her head closer, she looked straight into Vicky's eyes. "It must be hard not ever having any money?" Vicky chewed on her lips and looked ready to burst out crying. Susie placed her warm hand on top of Vicky's as she continued. "If you ever want to earn some quick cash, just give me a shout."

Vicky looked puzzled. Why was this woman helping her and what the fuck was she going on about? She was desperate to earn extra cash and asked her straight out. "How can I earn some extra money?"

Susie was excited. She sniggered as she whispered into Vicky's ear. "You can earn one hundred pound today if you want?" Susie knew the usual fee should have been two hundred, but she was eager to save some money knowing this girl was desperate.

Vicky was nodding and her eyes were alive with excitement. One hundred pounds would sort her right out. She could go shopping, buy cigs and maybe even get herself a new outfit. "What do I have to do?" Susie kept her face straight and explained that she could take some drugs into the prison and pass them to her boyfriend Blake.

Vicky blew a frustrated breath. "Why would I take them in for Blake?" Susie tutted.

"Ya dickhead. The drugs are for my fella. Blake will have to pass them to Tim once there inside the jail."

"Fuck off," Vicky replied. People heard her and she covered her mouth knowing she was bringing attention to herself. Susie snarled as Vicky continued. "Blake would go sick at me. I mean just to go on a visit without any warning and pass him drugs. He'd go mad."

"Well you don't have to take them in today. Have a word with ya boyfriend and see what he thinks. I mean he's got to know how hard it is for you out here hasn't he?" Susie preached. Vicky chewed her fingernails at speed. She needed money fast; there was no doubt about it. Once she'd explained to Blake that she was getting paid for it he would understand, surely. She looked anxious. Susie was drinking her coffee and watched her from the corner of her eyes with an evil glance.

"Right I'll do it today," she whispered. Susie looked devious and asked Vicky to follow her to the toilets. Too many people were about now, and she wanted to make sure everything went to plan. Once inside the toilets, Susie stood behind the door to make sure no one else could come inside. With one foot holding the door shut she bent down inside her bag rummaging about. Vicky was stood at the sink watching her. Holding a bag of cocaine out in front of her she grinned. "Here it is love. Simple, just shove it in your bra, and when you get on the visit give it to Blake." Vicky was listening to her every word. Susie was right, how hard could it be? Taking it from her hand she studied the white powder. There were some small tablets in the bag as well, she pressed at them with her fingers. Susie saw her concern and jumped in. "Oh they're just some steroids. The lads go mad for them in prison. It makes them look macho without even going to the gym I think." She walked to Vicky's side and placed her arm over her shoulder. She could see the fear in Vicky's eyes and knew she would have to do some quick talking to get her onside. "I would take them in myself, but the screws are onto me. They never stop looking at me," Susie lied.

"So what will happen if I get caught," Vicky said with

a worried face.

Susie chuckled. "Nar you look sweet. Just look at your innocent face." She turned her around and made her look into the mirror.

Vicky stood staring at herself, Susie was right. "Plus that money can help you with your son and that, can't it?" Susie was nearly there and knew with a bit more persuasion she would have the young girl by the short and curlies.

The drugs were concealed in Vicky's bra. Susie helped place them out of sight and stood looking at her new drugs mule. "There you go chick. You can't see a fucking thing." She patted Vicky's breast down one last time and straightened her top. Susie knew she would have to give her some more encouragement as she could see she wasn't sure. Opening the toilet door she smiled and looked at Vicky. "Come on love, we'll be going over to the prison soon." Vicky swallowed hard and walked slowly from the toilets. She looked white in the face. "When we come out from the visit, I'll go to the bank and get you some money out. I mean, you'll want to go on a spending spree won't you?" Vicky nodded slowly.

Susie looked relieved when the names for the visits were called out. She helped Vicky up from her seat and tried to take her mind from the drugs sitting in her bra. "If you fancy it tonight, we can go out for a drink?"

Vicky looked shocked. This woman was class, and she didn't think in a million years she would ever mix with her sort. Remembering her son she held a sour look on her face. "I can't, I haven't got anyone to mind Declan."

Susie looked in deep thought. With her fingers on her lips she giggled. "Well I'll come to your house then. That's if you don't mind?" Vicky was over the moon and wanted to hug Susie but refrained. As they walked to the prison's entrance the drugs concealed in her bra didn't seem to matter anymore. Vicky had a new friend, or so she thought.

The screws seemed to be looking at Vicky longer than necessary. Her mouth looked dry as the female guard rubbed her hands up and down over her body. Susie was watching from a distance and twisted her fingers repeatedly. Vicky had passed the first test. Now it was time to go upstairs to the next level. Vicky prayed the sniffer dog wasn't there. As if she just realised what she was doing, she turned and was getting ready to go back down the stairs. Susie gripped her arm and hissed into her face. "Where the fuck are you going. Just get ya arse back here. You're nearly in now." Vicky looked scared. Susie was at her side and the look in her eyes told her she meant business.

Stood waiting outside the main visiting door, Vicky looked like she'd shit her knickers. There was no dog there today and she looked relieved as the screw opened the door. Susie was behind her and pushed her in the back to move forward. You could see the in-mates waiting at their tables. Susie held back now and seemed to be waiting for something. As all the visitors went inside she watched the screw lock the door behind them. Walking slowly back to him she waved Vicky on without her.

Susie stood facing Jenkins. He smiled at her and remembered her from the last visit. "Hello Miss. Can I help you?" His voice was sweet and he certainly knew how to flirt with the ladies. Susie looked at him and held her head to the side. Licking the front of her teeth in a sexual manner the screw thought he was on a winner.

"I hope you can help me sir." Her voice was low as

she dug her hands in the small pocket of her jeans. The security check hadn't located it, and she knew her plan was getting ready to step up to the next level. Keeping the small white folded paper out of sight she held it in her grip. She offered a handshake to the screw and watched his face as he felt something in his palm. The officer smiled. This woman was good. She was giving him her phone number and making sure nobody else could see it. Without looking at the note he placed it into his black pants and watched the sexy young woman leave his side. His mouth was watering as his eyes watched her arse swing away in the distance. Placing his hand on his crotch he tried to control the urge of his manhood trying to stand tall in his trousers.

Susie sat with Tim and he was asking her why she was talking to Jenkins. "Oh just asking what you have to do, to bring you some clothes in that's all. He said you need to make an application in the jail or summat," she lied. Tim didn't need to know her cunning plan yet until the ball was in motion.

Tim nodded. "Yeah I know that," he looked angry. His eyes were screwed up small. He hadn't even asked for any food from the canteen yet and Susie knew something was on his mind. Trying to keep calm she leant over and kissed his cheek. He scowled and pushed her back down. "What's fucking up with you," she moaned. His teeth were showing and his face looked hot. Sweat was visible on his head as he jerked forward.

"What's up with me? I'll tell you what's up with me, you dirty tramp. Why is Ashley buying you fucking flowers and all that?" He grabbed her hand over the table and you could see her skin turning white where he was applying pressure. She dragged her hand away and sat back down, so he couldn't grip her anymore.

Moving her hair from her face, she spat over the table at him. Her face looked serious as she rammed her finger over the table at him. "Ashley got me some flowers because I was upset. Not that you give a flying fuck about how I feel, do you?" Tim was not having none of it, you could see his nostrils flaring and the vein in his neck pumping with rage. He waited for her to continue. Susie knew she would have to pull a good act out of her bag, and forced a few tears from her eyes. As they fell onto her cheeks she spoke in a dramatic voice. "I was crying all the time Tim and I felt really, really down. Ashley just tried to cheer me up. Is that a sin?"

Tim held his head back in the chair and stared at the ceiling. Looking back at her he still seemed angry. "Why fucking flowers. He's never bought a bird flowers before."

"I don't know," she sobbed. People were looking at them now and a screw walked over and stood near the table letting his presence be felt. Tim grabbed her hands and dropped his head onto the table. The warden walked away looking happy that nothing serious was going on.

Tim opened his heart hoping she could put his mind at rest. "It's just being in here, everything just seems twice as bad. I know Ashley never meant anything by the flowers, but you have to understand where I'm coming from. My head's up my arse and I'm thinking loads of different shit about you."

Susie agreed and looked at the canteen. She needed to get away for a minute and get her story straight. "Do you want a drink?" Tim nodded; Susie was soon at the canteen window.

"Are you off your fucking head, bringing drugs in

jail," Blake snapped. He was livid and at one stage, he was nearly getting up from his seat to leave the visit. Vicky looked a nervous wreck.

"Just take them this one time, that's all I'm asking." Her voice was desperate and she knew she'd made a mistake by bringing the drugs into prison.

"Who's the guy I have to give it to?" he said with a pissed off voice. Vicky could see Susie at the canteen. She discretely told Blake who she was and to watch her back to her seat, to see the inmate she was visiting. "How the fuck have you ended up doing this, you crank. You could get years if ya get caught ya muppet," he was stressing. Blake sat back and shook his head. It was his fault she was in this position and he knew it more than anyone. He'd let his woman down big time and he could see what she had to do to make ends meet. Vicky looked defenceless as he scanned every inch of her body. Susie walked past and Vicky pierced her eyes at Blake.

"That's her, watch were she sits," Vicky whispered. Blake's eyes followed the woman's every movement and he sat out of his seat a little to watch where she was heading. Vicky froze and her hands were shaking. Her chest seemed to be rising as her hand gripped around her neck. "Blake, I'm shitting it now. Should I just take the drugs back out with me and give them back to her?" Blake never replied, he looked in deep thought. If he was bringing drugs into the prison, surely he must benefit too. He leant over the table. Scanning her blouse, he tried to see if he could see the drugs. There were no traces to be seen.

"Right at the end of the visit I'll grab it from you." Vicky's face looked relieved. "I'm never doing it again, honest." Blake smiled. He never thought she had it in her to do anything like this, and he grabbed her closer for a kiss. The two of them looked lost in the moment and you could see the love they shared was true. Well at least for now.

Susie explained to Tim what was going on and he looked happy now that he was getting a parcel inside the jail. He shot a look over at Blake and the men exchanged a nod. Tim looked at Vicky in more detail. The girl was pretty, a bit scruffy, but with a bit of work she could be a darling. He winked at Vicky.

Susie had talked her way out of the mess she was in and Tim seemed to have bought her bullshit. His mind was now focussed on the drugs and he was eager to meet Blake to get the drop from him. Susie had done well and he kissed her hand softly. They spoke about the brothel and she told him that Joan was definitely on the fiddle. Tim didn't seem too bothered and told her to do whatever she needed to do.

The visit came to an end. You could see all the inmates kissing their loved ones goodbye. Tim looked over at Vicky and smiled at her. Her heart was in her mouth. He was drop-dead gorgeous and she liked the attention she was getting from him, she flicked her head back and straightened her clothes. Susie had always seemed like she wasn't interested in Tim anyway, and if that was the case, it was time for Vicky to strut her stuff. Tim could change her life and she smiled back at him, letting the guy know she was more than interested.

Blake's hand was rummaging in Vicky's bra. He was quick and nobody saw anything. The drugs were now in his grip and he sat back down at the table trying to shove the drugs up his arsehole. Nobody was watching him, they were all saying goodbye to their loved ones. He got the drugs out of sight before his body search.

Susie waved her hand in the air to Tim. She blew a kiss and watched Vicky heading towards her. She would have to pay the daft bitch now she thought; she hated parting with any cash. Vicky looked happy for a change. In fact it was the happiest Susie had ever seen her. They both walked to the exit with the other visitors.

Jenkins stood at the door letting people out. Vicky looked at Susie. The officer never took his eyes from her and he held a peculiar look in his eyes as he watched them pass. Susie smirked at him and walked past him with a wiggle in her walk.

"Fucking hell, what's, his problem?" Vicky asked.

"Dunno love. Probably needs a good shag or summit," Susie giggled.

The colour was back in Vicky's face and she looked like a weight had been lifted from her shoulders. She whispered as she leant into Susie's ear. "I'm never doing that again. My heart was in my mouth all the way through the visit. I fucking shit myself, yanno." Susie was walking at speed. All she wanted to do was to get out of the place. Tim was doing her head in and she was thinking of sending him a "Dear John" letter telling him it was all over. Vicky could see the change in her and asked if she was okay. Susie never replied.

Once they'd collected their belongings from the visitors' centre, Susie told Vicky she would give her a lift home. Susie was quiet for a change. Vicky looked concerned as she spoke to her. "Are you okay love? You just look sad." Susie carried on walking and headed for the car. She did need someone to talk to without a shadow of doubt and Vicky wasn't in her circle of friends, so what was the harm in telling her what was playing on her mind?

Susie looked serious as they sat in the car. Lighting a cig she passed Vicky one. The poor girl never had any fags and she took the cig from her with a smile on her face. Susie rested her hands on the steering wheel as she inhaled deeply on her cigarette. Her head looked out of the window as she started talking. Vicky was listening eagerly. "I'm so pissed off with it all Vicky. You don't know the half of it." Her head turned to Vicky and looked away again. She looked like she didn't want her to see her face as she confessed her sins.

Vicky was hanging on her every word. "A problem shared and all that," she coaxed.

Susie rotated her head back to her and looked at her for a few seconds. It looked like she was debating whether she could be trusted. Her fingernail rested on her teeth. After a few seconds Susie began. "I've been seeing Ashley, Tim's best friend. I have been for some time now." Vicky's mouth dropped and her eyes opened fully. Tim was gorgeous, why the fuck was she cheating on him? If he was her man she would have been more than happy. This woman wouldn't know a good thing if it hit her in the face. Susie continued, her face looked red and she looked embarrassed.

Vicky knew she couldn't show any signs of the way she felt and giggled. "Good on you girl, as long as you're happy."

Susie screwed up her face and sighed. "I was happy to start with, but I just seemed to have jumped out of the frying pan into the fire. If you know what I mean?" Vicky nodded. "It was all exciting at first and Ashley was everything I ever wanted," she paused and looked like she was going to cry. Vicky reached over and patted her leg.

Susie pushed her hand away. She wasn't a soft arse and didn't need any comfort. Susie wanted people to see her as strong and by breaking down in front of this young girl, she was doing herself no favours. Vicky backed off and sat waiting for her to continue. "Ashley wants me to tell Tim about us. I mean, come on, the man's in fucking nick for crying out loud. Even I'm not that ruthless to do that to him while he's serving a sentence."

Vicky loved the gossip. Nothing exciting ever happened in her life, and this was like her own personal Jeremy Kyle show. She agreed with Susie. "Nar you can't finish with him when he's in jail that would be proper tight. This guy Ashley should know that. Just tell him straight love, he should understand."

Susie couldn't hold back the tears and no matter how much she tried they just ran from her eyes. This time she accepted the comfort from her new friend. Vicky held her close as she sobbed. She inhaled her fragrance and closed her eyes. Susie smelt fresh and clean and she wished she was the one leading her life.

After Susie had visited the bank Vicky held the cash in her hands and felt alive. She sniffed the money and held it to her chest. Susie had left her now and she was debating what to spend the money on. With a spring in her step she headed for 'Cash Generator' in Harpurhey. Months before she'd pawned her laptop, and now was her chance to get it back out. Facebook was her only chance of any company and the thought of speaking to all her long lost friends put a smile back on her face.

Vicky queued up in the shop. Pulling the crumpled ticket from her bag she tried to straighten it out. Lots of people were in the shop and she could see the look of desperation on their faces. They had televisions, CD players and phones to trade in for cash. Vicky had only pawned her laptop for thirty quid and now she was at the front of the queue she was debating whether or not she could afford to get it back. Passing the ticket underneath the counter she smiled at the shop assistant. "Can I get that out please?" The woman read the ticket and left the window. Once she returned Vicky smiled and passed her the cash.

Susie went straight home feeling depressed. Everything looked to be getting on top of her. Throwing her bag on the table she plonked herself into a chair and kicked her shoes off. She loved the time she was spending on her own and reached for the TV remote. There it was, just what she needed. A chick flick, 'P.S. I Love You' was one of her favourite films and she snuggled down on the sofa to enjoy every minute of it. Susie looked upset as she watched the storyline on the telly. Her arms were wrapped around her body as she watched the main character crying on screen. The sound of her mobile ringing could be heard. "Fuck off," she screamed at it, as she placed a pillow over it to drown out its tone. Standing to her feet she headed for the kitchen. Opening the fridge she cast her eyes over the food inside. Grabbing a half eaten bar of chocolate she looked content.

Susie's phone rang again. "For fucks sake." Pulling the cushion from it she stared at the screen. It wasn't a number she knew. "Hello," she answered in a low voice. Her face turned white, it was Tim. "How have you got a phone in nick?" Susie said. Tim told her he'd picked up a Blackberry phone in jail. He said it had cost him over two hundred quid. He was buzzing with it. Tim had done well with the drugs he'd got in on the visit and already he was trading with the prisoners for drugs. Tim asked Susie to get him a top-up for the phone. Her face was angry, but she agreed to it. He was gone.

Susie stored Tim's prison phone number in her mobile. That was all she needed – him phoning her all the time. Gripping her phone in her hand she looked like she was going to launch it at the wall. Lying flat on the sofa she pulled a soft cream fur throw over her. The film was kicking in now and she promised herself she would watch it to the end. Susie switched her phone off. Sucking on the chocolate bar she cuddled up and turned the volume higher.

Vicky sat on her sofa dusting her laptop off. Declan was watching a DVD and was being quiet for a change. Plugging her computer in she sat upright in her chair and prepared herself to log into Facebook.

Vicky felt alive again. All her old friends were there to see. Pressing the chat button she watched all her friends pop up eager to talk with her. Vicky had over twenty two friend requests. Clicking the blue box to reveal the names, she sat hypnotised by the screen. Most of the people wanting her friendship were men. Chewing her fingernail she clicked on each new friend. The men were dishy and she giggled as she accepted their requests.

Susie said she'd call at Vicky's tonight about nine o'clock to have a drink with her. She was looking forward to some company for a change instead of being sat on her own. Scrolling down on the screen she typed Susie's name in the search engine. She was hoping that she had enough information to find her. Eyes piercing into the computer, a list of all the Susie's from Manchester came up. Vicky leant forward and checked out each profile picture. After a few minutes she found her. Clicking on her full profile she could see her there in her full glory. She was a right posing bitch. Vicky's eyes scanned her picture albums. Tim was there on them too and she could see his second name was Marshall because he'd been tagged in some snapshots.

Vicky looked about the front room, her fingers were tapping on the keyboard and she had an urge to try and find Tim on the social network. After a few minutes she located him. There he was, his full profile looking back at her. Vicky hid her face with her hands. She looked excited. He was so sexy. Pressing the 'friend request' button she asked for his friendship. She knew he was in prison but when he got out surely he would look at his facebook and accept her as one of his friends; after all she'd brought drugs into the prison for him.

Vicky carried on talking to her friends. Suddenly a red alert message came to the top of her screen. She clicked on it. Rubbing her hands together she blew a deep breath. Tim Marshall had accepted her friend request. "How the fuck has he done that," she mumbled. Then she remembered that Blake had told her about some of the inmates getting mobile phones in the nick. Staring at the screen she looked on the live chat. This was somewhere you could speak to people directly. Tim's name was there in the list of friends and her fingers were twitching to write him a message. Lighting a cigarette she just sat staring at the screen. A blue box now appeared at the bottom of her facebook page with Tim's name spread across it. Slowly clicking on it, she could see the full message he'd wrote. "Hi sexy," he'd written, with a kiss at the end of it. Vicky's heart was pounding in her chest and she dragged at her hair as she read the message over and over again. Another message appeared. "Don't tell Susie you've been talking to me. Let's keep this our secret." Vicky felt sick and her face was on fire. Quickly without thinking she typed a message back to him. "Hi Tim, glad you got your stuff in. If you need me again, just ask. And don't worry I won't tell Susie we've been talking." She pressed the send button and sat back in the chair waiting for his reply. He was back in a flash. Declan was at her side now and she quickly moved him away from her computer. "Go and get a biscuit, I'm busy." The kid was moaning but she used her leg to move him from her side. She was on a roll now and nobody was going to spoil it. Vicky felt alive and kept bursting into fits of laughter. Her fingers were tapping at the keyboard constantly.

As time passed, Tim said goodbye to Vicky on facebook. He was so sexy and he made her heart skip a beat. Looking at the time she quickly pulled Declan up from the floor. He was half asleep now and he moaned as she took him upstairs to bed. Susie was due any time soon, and she wanted to make sure he was fast asleep before she got there.

Running a quick bath Vicky decided to make an effort to look nice for when Susie got there. Peeling her clothes from her body she stood shivering in the bathroom. Quickly submerging her body into the tub, she swilled the hot water all over her skin. Looking down at her scrawny body she realised how much she'd let herself go. Her pubic mound was like an overgrown bush, and black hairs were growing all over her inner thighs. Grabbing an old razor blade from the side she tried to trim her lady-garden into a nice neat pattern. The razor was gliding frantically over her crotch. Within minutes she was laughing her head off. She'd gone way over the top and all that was left of her bush was something the size of Adolf Hitler's moustache.

Vicky was just pulling her skinny jeans on, when she heard someone at the front door. Pulling the net curtain back from the window she peeped outside hoping it wasn't the loan man. She hadn't paid him for a month and he was calling at all hours of the night trying to catch her. Vicky tapped on the bedroom window when she saw it was Susie. "One minute," she shouted as she placed one finger to the window. Susie looked pissed off.

"Hiya come in," Vicky said as she opened the front door to her. Susie walked inside and you could see her pulling her face. It was obvious she didn't really want to be there. Taking her into the front room Vicky looked embarrassed. She'd tried to straighten the house up, but it still looked scruffy. "Get some glasses love. I'm dying for a drink. I need it after the day I've had," Susie moaned. Vicky started to head into the kitchen and Susie was still shouting to her. "That nob-head has only got a phone now. He's already been on to me giving me more orders."

Vicky froze as she reached into the cupboards to get the glasses. "How's he got a phone in prison?" she answered back.

"You can get owt in jail love, if you have the money. The fucker's got a Blackberry phone, so he can even see what I'm doing on facebook now."

Vicky held the glasses in her hand and started to make her way back into the living room. She was blushing. Susie kicked her shoes off and curled her feet up on the sofa. Grabbing a tall glass she twisted the lid from the vodka. Reaching into her bag she pulled out some lemonade. "Here, get a glass of this down ya neck." Vicky held her empty glass over to Susie; she half-filled it with vodka, and only added a drop of lemonade.

Music was playing in the background and Susie was

mouthing the words to some song that was playing on the radio. She was pissed out of her head. "Can I just use your toilet love?" Susie asked as she struggled to stand up.

"Yeah straight upstairs and second on the right," Vicky said. "Fucking hell Susie you're wrecked." Susie turned her head and smiled as she kept one hand on the wall near the door frame.

"I know love, but ay, who gives a fuck."

Vicky chuckled. "Go on; get to the toilet before you piss ya knickers." Susie was gone.

Vicky could see Susie's shoes staring at her. They were from River Island she could see the label inside the shoe. With one ear held at the door, she listened carefully. Susie could be heard being sick upstairs. Slowly Vicky gripped the shoe in her hand, and held it up in front of her. Feeling like Cinderella, she slid her narrow foot inside the multi-coloured shoe. It fitted perfectly. Grabbing the other one, she walked round the living room in Susie's heels. She looked confident as she made her way to the mirror that hung on the wall. Dipping her face nearer she smiled at herself with a cunning grin. "This is the life," she whispered.

"What the fuck are ya doing with my shoes on," Susie ranted. Vicky deflated and sat back down dragging them off her feet as if they were on fire.

"Orrr I'm sorry, I just love them and wanted to see what I would look like wearing them." The shoes were placed back next to Susie.

With a smile on her face Susie stared at Vicky. Reaching down to the shoes she picked them up and dangled them in her hands. "You can have them love. I've got loads of shoes anyway."

Vicky shook her head. "Nar fuck off. I was only trying

them on. They belong to you."

Susie held her head back and laughed. Throwing the shoes over to Vicky she slurred, "I can get a new pair any time I want. Ashley will buy them for me. You need them more than me, you've got fuck all."

Vicky snarled. "Cheeky bitch," she mumbled, but she knew she was right. Holding the shoes in her hands she kicked her flip-flops off and slid them over to Susie. "Here then, you'll need something to go home in." Susie's eyes looked tired. Her phone started ringing. Flopping over into her handbag she pulled her mobile phone out from it. Her eyes were screwed up as she focused on the screen. Jerking her head back she blew a breath from the side of her mouth.

"Here he is now, my prince charming." Pressing the green button on the phone she fell back onto the sofa. "Hello sexy." Vicky stood up and walked across the front room with her new shoes on. She was twisting her legs one way and then the other. Vicky listened as Susie asked Ashley to come and pick her up. She threw her phone back inside her bag. Vicky knew she didn't have long and wanted to get into her for information about Tim. Necking a big mouthful of vodka, she lit a cig and sat forward looking directly at Susie.

"So tell me love, you don't want to be with Tim anymore, because you love Ashley. Is that right?" Susie stared at her as if she was gathering her thoughts. Coughing to clear her throat she sat back in her chair and twisted her hair around her finger.

"Me and Tim have outgrown each other. If I'm being honest with you, I've never really loved him. He just had everything I needed, and I knew I could have a better life with him. Come on," she paused. Her hands were held out in front of her now as she cradled her knees. "I'm from a council estate and men like Tim are much sought after. Who wants a boyfriend with fuck all?"

Vicky was nodding. "Yeah I know what you're saying." Vicky listened carefully and she fully understood what Susie had done to get by in life. Money did buy happiness and as soon as Vicky got a taste of it, there was no way she was ever letting go. A plan seemed to be hatching in her mind.

A car was honking its horn outside, Susie stood to her feet. "Here's Ash," she giggled. Gripping Vicky in her arms, she pecked her on the cheek. "Listen I've had a good night and you've cheered me up, God knows I needed it. We'll have to go out next time instead of sitting in this shit-tip."

Vicky saw red and opened fire, who did this stuck-up cow think she was, calling her humble abode. "Ay Lady fucking muck, less of the shit-tip. This is my home and I do my best, alright. I'm not like you dripping in cash."

Susie shook her head. "Orr I'm sorry love. You know I don't mean it like that. I just mean it would be good to get you out and about for a change, instead of being sat in here staring at four walls, that's all."

Vicky let her off the hook and led her to the front door. Ashley's tunes could be heard pumping outside and she could see him looking over at her. Vicky waved slowly. Fucking hell Susie had the lot, men dropping at her feet and more cash than sense. What a lucky bitch she was! Vicky wanted her life. Waving at the front door she watched them drive off.

Sat alone with the music still playing, she felt lonely. Vicky looked down at her new shoes and loved them. Reaching down the side of the sofa she lifted her laptop up to the arm of the chair. Quickly logging onto facebook she searched for any of her friends that might be online. Vicky was pissed and she was struggling to keep her eyes opened. Tim's name now popped up. "What you up to honey," the message read. Vicky didn't think twice about replying and before she knew it they were talking non-stop for over an hour. Tim had told her to come and visit on her own, so they could get to know each other better. He told her Susie rarely came to see him anymore, so she would never need to know. Vicky thought about her own boyfriend Blake. Tim was right, no one would ever know. With that in mind she typed back her reply telling him she would come and see him in prison.

Vicky flicked the computer off and headed upstairs to bed. Her eyes were nearly closing as her head fell onto her double bed. With the shoes still on her feet she pulled the blankets over her and snuggled down to get some shut-eye. Life was worth living after all, she thought as she drifted off to sleep.

CHAPTER NINE

Helen sat reading the white piece of paper in front of her over and over again, she looked a mess. Her mother was trying to console her but she was still upset. "Mam, what the fuck am I going to do? Why, are the benefits people coming to see me regarding some information they have received?"

"Well someone must have grassed you up that's all I can think of," her mother huffed, "you just need to see it through and deny any accusations they throw at you." Grabbing the letter from Helen's hand she read it through again. "So it's at two today they're coming then?"

Helen fidgeted about and looked white in the face. "Yeah fucking two o'clock. I'm shitting my knickers." Her partner Mike came into the front room and Helen snarled at him. He looked like a beanpole compared to her "Aren't you ready yet? You know the Social are coming soon. So you need to fuck off out of here before they see you."

Mike sighed. He was such an easy going guy and hated the life he was living with Helen. She was a control freak. "I'm going, fucking hell give me chance will you. You moaning twat."

Helen bolted up from her chair and ran at him. "If you was fucking working we wouldn't be in this position would we, ya clampet?"

Mike backed down from her straight away. He knew she wouldn't think twice about punching his lights out. Grabbing his coat from the side of the sofa, he looked at his partner's mother. "Right I'm off to the job centre." He raised his eyes to the ceiling and left. The sound of the front door being slammed could be heard.

Helen sank back into her chair and lit another cig. She'd been chain-smoking all morning. With her head in her hands, she shook it from side to side. "Have you got all his stuff out of the wardrobe and out of the house, because they'll be looking for signs of a man living here, yanno. So get rid of everything?" Tim's mother said.

Helen panicked. "Fuck off mam, they won't go that far will they." Her mother rolled her eyes.

"Well they did with my friend Chelsea. They checked everywhere in the bastard house, even the bathroom looking for razors and that."

Helen jerked up from the chair. "Oh, for crying out loud! Mam you better watch the kids while I go upstairs and cart all Mike's stuff." Helen's two small children were lying on the floor watching the telly. "Go on then get a move on they'll be here soon." Helen went into the kitchen and came back with a roll of black bin liners. "Right I won't be long," she moaned as she left the room.

Helen was like a woman possessed. Grabbing all Mike's clothes from the wardrobe she sank them deep inside the black bag. He didn't have a lot of stuff so it didn't take her long. Heading into the bathroom she grabbed his razor from the sink. Her eyes scanned around the bathroom as she reached for the 'Lynx' deodorant on the side. Her body was sweating and two large wet patches appeared underneath her arms. She was a right sweaty bitch. Wiping her head with the side of her arm she carried on trying to locate any more signs that a man was living with her.

Helen sat clock watching, she looked nervous as she chewed on her fingernails. Her mother had taken the kids out; she didn't trust them mentioning their dad's name in front of the fraud investigators. Peeping out of the window constantly Helen was stood smoking. She could see a blue car pulling up outside her house. Stubbing her cig out in the ashtray she ran for the air-freshener to spray about the living room. Taking deep breaths she looked like she was going to pass out. There was a knock on the front door.

Helen slowly walked to the door. She could see the shadow of two people stood there. One looked like a man. Her fingers gripped the lock and she slowly opened it. Looking at the man and woman she tried to raise a smile. "Hello Helen Marshall, we have an appointment booked with you regarding your claim for benefit."

Helen nodded as she invited them both inside the house. Walking into the hallway the two fraud investigators were already looking all over the place. "Nosey twats," Helen whispered.

"Do you want a brew or owt?" Helen asked with an animated smile on her face. They both declined. The woman sat on the sofa and reached into her black briefcase. Helen plonked on the chair facing her and held her hands under her chin. "So why are you here?" Helen piped up. The woman introduced herself and her colleague.

"Right Helen, my name is Carol Smith and my colleague is James Harrison. I'm just going to read something out to you before we start the interview. Is that alright?"

Helen sighed. "Yes no worries." James looked at her with a stern face, and she knew he was going to be hard work. Carol read out some legal documents and then once she was finished, she held her white writing pad in her hands and tapped her blue pen on her teeth.

"Helen we have received a phone call reporting that you are living with your partner Mike Skerrit. You are claiming single parent benefit you know."

Helen was up in arms. She'd promised herself she would try not to lose control but it was too late, she'd lost the plot. "Am I fuck, living with anyone. Who's said that?"

Carol shook her head. "The person made the accusations anonymously, so we don't have any names just the information they've given us."

Helen gritted her teeth. "Yeah that's fucking typical. Do you know what? I've got fuck all. I could understand if I was rolling in money and all that, but honestly, I've got nowt. Not a pot to piss in to be exact."

Carol started to give her some of the information that they'd received. "Is Mike the father of your children?"

Helen swallowed hard. Looking the woman straight in the face she answered her. "Yeah he is, but there is no way I'm having any kind of relationship with him. The man's a tosser."

Carol looked at her workmate. "Is he registered as the father on your children's birth certificates?"

Helen hunched her shoulders and sat back in her chair as she chuckled. "Course he is. He's their dad."

Carol sat back and James, her workmate took over. He was champing at the bit and eager to get involved. "Well we have documents here that say Mike has his giro sent to this address." He held a piece of paper up towards Helen.

Licking her dry lips Helen looked agitated. "Yeah he does have his mail sent here. It's just a postal address that's all. And anyway, the guys a shirt-lifter."

Carol and John looked at each other in shock. "What do you mean Helen?"

Helen held a mischievous grin on her face. Grabbing a cig from her packet she walked about the front room as she stood with her back to them looking out of the window. "Mike is gay. I caught him in bed with a man."

Coughing could be heard and James looked uncomfortable. Carol spoke again. "So if he's gay how come you have children with him? Has he always been gay?"

Helen turned slowly; she could see them hanging onto her every word. "No not always. It must have been something that has always been in him. I mean being gay doesn't happen overnight, does it?"

James scowled, he wasn't having any of it and he

knew she was lying. "Helen no matter if he's gay or not. We've still had reports that's he's living here with you and your children."

Helen forced some tears from her eyes and hugged herself as she fell back into her chair. She could feel their eyes on her and played the part of the leading lady in her own show. Snivelling, she continued. "Do you know how much it hurts me to say that the man I loved is gay?" Carol was caught up in the moment and was edging to the side of her chair; she looked like she wanted to comfort the woman in front of her. Helen continued. "Mike was my everything, yanno? When I caught him in the arms of another man my world collapsed around me. I mean, come on." Helen wiped the crocodile tears from her eyes. "You can compete with another woman can't you, but another man. It's a different ballgame." Carol told Helen to take a minute to calm down before they carried on.

Helen stood up from the chair and grabbed another cig. "I'm just going in the garden. I won't be a minute." Helen left the fraud investigators and walked through the kitchen to the back door. Hands held over her mouth she struggled to keep the laughter inside. Her belly was wobbling as she chuckled to herself.

Helen sat back down in the living room. Carol had more questions to ask her and began straight away. "Can we have a quick look around Helen?"

She nodded and acted daft. "Yeah, what are you looking for?"

James shot her a look and spoke in a sarcastic tone. "We're just checking for any signs of a man living here. It's just procedure. No doubt we won't find anything."

Helen sank her head. The bastard was onto her.

Waving her hand towards them she guided them upstairs. "Yeah, feel free. Do what you have to do."

The sound of cupboards doors opening and closing could be heard upstairs. Helen held her ears to the ceiling and listened carefully. They were coming downstairs now. Sitting straight in her seat she watched the door eagerly. Carol smiled at her as she came into the living room. "Right Helen we're nearly finished now, just the last few questions."

"Yeah, no problem," Helen muttered.

James was on her like a rash. Reading from his notes he reeled off a few more questions. Helen kept her cool and answered them in a confident manner. They had fuck all on her. She began to relax and made it quite obvious that she wanted them both out of her house as soon as possible. Watching them both stand, Helen stood up beside them. Looking at Carol she shook her head. "Can you not give me any information of the grassing bastard who phoned you, because when I find out who's been chatting shit about me they're gonna get a piece of my mind. The interfering, jealous cunts."

Carol shook her head. "As I said before Helen, it was an anonymous phone call. We don't hold any information, we just investigate the calls."

Helen walked behind them to the front door. "So is that it. What happens now?"

James turned to face her and interrupted Carol. "We will look at the evidence we have, and then we'll get back to you if we need to know any more information."

Helen raised her eyes to the ceiling and huffed. James was arrogant and if he wasn't there investigating her, she would have given him a piece of her mind. Helen watched them leave. Stood at the front doorstep she could she her mother approaching with the kids.

The car drove off and Helen sighed. "Thank fuck for that," she mumbled.

Her mother was coming up the garden path. Her face looked strained as she pushed the pram. "Have they gone now or what?"

"Yeah come on, get inside, and wait until I tell you what I've had to say."

Her mother grinned. "Orr what have you done now. You little bleeder?" Helen dragged the pram into the house. Yanking her kid with one arm from the pushchair she led him into the front room.

Helen covered her face as she began to speak. Her mother parked her arse on the sofa and sat opened-mouthed as her daughter began to tell her what she'd said to the benefit agency. "Orr Mike's gonna go mad mam, but I had no other option. I just sat there with a poker face and said Mike was gay." Her mother covered her mouth and you couldn't tell if she was angry or if she was about to break into fits of laughter. Helen continued. "I told them I caught him in bed with another man."

Laughter filled the room; Helen's mother was rolling about the sofa. "Orr Helen I'm gonna piss myself. No way did you tell em that?"

Helen chuckled. "Yeah Mam, I had to, they were like the fucking Gestapo."

"What's Mike gonna say? Are you going to tell him what you've said or what?"

Helen struggled for breath as she tried to get her words out. "Yeah course I am. It's his punishment for being a lazy fucker."

"He's going to go berserk, Helen!"

"I'm not arsed," she giggled.

Helen sat up straight, pulling at her t-shirt, she huffed. "Someone grassed me up, yanno. The woman told me."

"Who would do something like that?"

Helen looked serious and gritted her teeth. "Fucking Susie, that's who mother. It's just got her stamp all over it. Remember last year when we had words and she said she was going to grass me up to the social."

Helen's mother shook her head. "No love, she wouldn't do owt like that. She's not that low."

Helen nodded her head slowly. "Mam, it's her alright and I'll make sure I pay her back in full, just watch this space."

CHAPTER TEN

Susie stood in the brothel. She was on her mobile phone and looked like she didn't want anyone to hear the conversation she was having. She was stood huddled in the shadows at the corner of the room out of sight. "Yeah that's all I want Jenkins," she whispered. "I know where you live, so don't be playing any games with me." Susie listened on the phone for a minute and finished the call. She looked relieved as she headed back to the reception area.

Pippa was sat in the waiting area looking her up and down. Susie lifted her head up and shot her a look "What are you gawping at?"

Pippa licked her top teeth. "I don't know, but it's looking back, love."

Susie made her way to the front of the room. Stood with one arm on her hip she opened fire. "Listen Pippa, I'm not in the mood for any of your games tonight. So say what you've got to say and get it off ya chest."

The whore jerked her head back and laughed. "Take a chill pill will ya. If I've got anything to say, you'll be the first to know about it."

Susie's nostrils flared. Her eyes were burning into the tart and you could see her fist clenched at the side of her. Susie walked back behind the reception desk. She could feel Pippa's eyes on her. Dipping her head she started counting the money from the takings the night before. She looked confused. The cash wasn't adding up.

"Where's Ashley?" Pippa piped up again, "Is he not making a show tonight or what?"

"Why, what's it to you?" Susie snarled.

"Just asking that's all. He's a darling; I wouldn't mind a piece of him." Susie tried to ignore her comments but the woman was drilling into her and making her blood boil. "Is he calling here later then?"

Susie snapped and her face turned red. "Yeah he is. Not that's it's any of your fucking business. Ashley has a girlfriend you know, so back off."

Pippa stood up and rested her chin in her hands as she spoke again. She was winding her up. "Well he's not told me about any so called girlfriend. In fact he's told me we can go out together."

"Get a grip ya hussy," Susie snarled. "I know Ashley's girlfriend and I know he wouldn't look at a tramp like you."

Pippa stood her ground. She tapped a long red fingernail on the wooden desk. "Don't make me laugh Susie. Take your head from your arse and smell the coffee. The man's a player." She swung her hair away from her face.

Susie looked gobsmacked. "Ashley is taken, so fuck off will you!"

Pippa stood for a minute thinking. She knew exactly what she was doing and added more fuel to the fire. "Well I'm going to make him my man anyway. I don't care about any girlfriend. The guy's gonna be mine."

Susie knew she couldn't tell her the truth and ignored her. She heard her heels clicking away in the distance. The till was over eighty pounds down. Susie had checked the figures over and over again and no matter how many times she looked at it, money was missing. Joan was in her office and with a sprint in her step Susie went down the corridor to confront her.

The office was quiet and stank of stale cigarettes. A small lamp in the corner barely gave off any light. Susie crept inside and held her breath. She could hear movement in the toilet at the back of the room. Creeping over she made her way to the noise she'd heard. The door was opened a little and she could just about see inside. Susie stretched her neck around the door. Joan was sat on the toilet and she could see her smoking crack. Susie booted the door open with force. Joan fell to the ground and guarded her drugs with her life. Susie ragged at her hair and dragged her up from the floor. "You dirty fucking crack head. I knew you were bang at it, you lying slag!"

Joan looked spaced out. Her eyes were all over the place. Susie gripped her from the toilet. Joan was fighting back now and she wasn't giving up that easy. "Take you're fucking hands off me you silly bitch," she shouted. Susie kicked her high heels from her feet and was ready for war. Joan reached to the small oak table at the side of her and fumbled as she gripped a glass bottle. Her hands come up as she smashed it against the wall. The jagged edge now faced Susie. Joan was wafting it about in front of her face. "Come on then if ya want a piece of me!" Joan screamed at the top of her voice.

Susie looked at the weapon and knew Joan wouldn't think twice about using it. Scanning the area the only thing she could find was an umbrella. Reaching for it she held it tightly in front of her trying to protect herself. Susie's chest was rising frantically and her lips looked dry. "Come on then shag-bag. Don't think you scare me one little bit."

Joan came forward now with the bottle held out towards her. Her face was sweating and her eyes looked menacing. She seemed on another planet. "Who do you think you are? Everything was running fine here, until you stuck ya nosey beak in."

Susie was holding her own and protecting herself. "You're a thieving cunt. Did you think nobody would ever find out? Tim's been onto you for a long time ya crack- head." She was moving towards the door. Joan bent down and quickly picked her bag up. Her eyes never left Susie. A few of the girls had heard the commotion and were gathered in the corridor outside the room.

Pippa flew at Joan with rage. She grabbed the bottle from her hand and twisted her arm up her back. "For fucks sake Joan, what are you playing at? We don't deal with things like this."

Joan was yelling out in pain as Pippa overpowered her. Susie looked white and stood frozen for a minute. Once, she saw the broken bottle in Pippa's hand, she pounced on Joan. "Ya dirty scrubber. Let's see what you can do without your weapon." Susie pummelled her fist into Joan's face. The girls looked on in disbelief. Susie could really fight.

Joan was finally dragged to the exit. She had blood dripping from her mouth and one of her eyes was starting to swell up. Her voice was loud as she struggled to stand to her feet. "You shower of shit. The fucking lot of you. You were all slagging Susie off the other day, and look at you now. You're like flies round a pile of shit."

Pippa stood watching and nodded her head slowly as she spoke. "Listen Joan, if you've been caught with ya hands in the till, you have nobody to blame, but ya-self."

Joan yanked the door open. Her hands were trembling. Turning to face them for the last time she held an evil look in her eyes. Lifting her hand up, she pointed her finger at each of the girls, then focused on Susie. "Watch you're fucking back, because nobody talks to me like that and gets away with it."

Susie ran for her again but Pippa held her back. "Just leave it love. She's off her head. She'll be back tomorrow, begging for her job back."

Susie huffed. "Not a fucking chance. The slut is out on her arse for good. She's a thief and a dirty crack- head." Her voice was loud as she yelled after her. One by one the brasses left the doorway. All that was left now was Pippa and Susie.

Susie wiped the trickle of blood from her face. Joan had scratched her, and the gash was still bleeding. Pippa took her by the arm and led her back upstairs. "Come on let's get you cleaned up."

Susie started to walk up the stairs and shook her head. "I can't believe what has just happened. She tried to bottle me, the bitch!"

"That's the drugs that love," Pippa sighed, "I knew she was on summat, but I just kept my nose out of it. I mean it's got fuck all to do with me, has it?"

Susie squealed as Pippa dabbed antiseptic on her face. Taking a minute to speak she plonked herself on the sofa with a white tissue held closely to her eyes. "It's just one thing after another in this gaff. I don't know how Tim has coped with that loony bitch. I think he just did anything for an easy life. That's why she took the piss."

Pippa stared at her for a moment; she looked as if she was thinking. "Joan's alright yanno. It's just the drugs. She told me a while back that she used to have a bad habit, but she said that was ages ago. I didn't think for one minute, she was still dabbling". Susie's phone went off. Standing to her feet she walked to the other side of the room. Tim's name flashed on the screen.

Hearing Tim's voice brought tears to Susie's eyes. She struggled to talk as she started to tell him about the saga. After a few minutes her face changed and she looked angry. "Yeah I know I haven't been to see you. Fucking hell Tim don't you think I've got enough on my plate at the moment?" Her ear was glued to the phone as she held her head back and shook her head. "Right I'll sort it out. Vicky said she wouldn't do it again, so I think you're pissing in the wind. Right, right, I'll ask her to visit you and do a drop." The phone was still held in her hand and she held it out from her ear looking up to the ceiling. After a few minutes she spoke again. "Right Tim, I love you too. Yeah stop stressing I'll sort it." The phone call ended.

Ashley had arrived while Susie was on the phone and quickly took a seat next to Pippa on the sofa. He didn't know Susie was watching him. She could see his hand resting on the whore's leg as he looked into her eyes. Susie screwed her face up as she marched towards them like a raging bull. "How long have you been here?"

Ashley's face looked vacant. "Just this second. Why?"

"Because it's been like World War Three in here, that's

fucking why."

Holding her face she showed him her war wounds. Jumping to his feet he was by her side. His knees bent as he came closer to her and he slowly ran his fingers over the deep scratch. Susie was filling him in on the full story.

Pippa sat back watching the pair of them together and the penny dropped. Ashley was in love. Slowly Pippa stood up. She looked at Susie and smiled. "Right I better get back to work, and leave you two love-birds to it." None of them answered her and she knew she'd hit the nail on the head. Everything made sense now. Susie was definitely screwing Ashley.

Checking her watch Susie reached into her bag for her phone. She needed to set a visit up for Tim. He'd asked for Vicky to come and take the drugs straight to him. Susie wasn't arsed one little bit. As long as he was off her case, she didn't have a care in the world.

"Hiya Vicky love, sorry it's late. Are you alright to talk?"

Ashley left her and made his way to the toilet. Just as he pushed the door open he could feel someone behind him. Turning his head back, he could see Pippa stood there smiling at him. She knew she needed to be quick. Her head was watching the door constantly. "So big boy, are me and you gonna get it on or what."

He chuckled nervously. Checking no one was about he stretched his arms out and dragged her into the toilets with him. Sinking his lips onto hers he kissed her passionately. His hand slid between her legs and you could see him rubbing at her crotch. "You're a horny bitch you are," he whispered into her ear. It was obvious she wanted more.

"Is that it? Is that all you've got," she giggled.

Ashley chewed on his lips. Rubbing at his throbbing member he pressed her up against the wall with his arm hanging over her head. "You'll see exactly what I've got later. Let me get rid of Susie, and I'll be back for you." Susie's voice could be heard shouting his name from outside. He panicked as he placed a finger up to her lips. Straightening his clothes he told Pippa to stay inside the toilet until it was safe for her to come out. With one last kiss he left her gagging for more. "I'm here Susie, what's up."

Susie was at the other end of the corridor and quickly trudged back towards him. "That was Tim on the phone. He wants me to sort a visit out for another drop," Ashley snarled.

"Well as long as you're not going anywhere near him, you can do what the fuck you want." Susie looked at his face and knew to keep schtum. Walking back to the reception Ashley draped his arm over her shoulder. "You look done in love. Do you wanna go home, and I'll finish off in here for you?"

Susie sank her head into his arm. It had been a stressful day. "Yeah I'll go home Ash. I don't think I could stand another minute in this place." Pushing the door in front of them Ashley turned his head back down the corridor. A cunning smile came across his face as he watched Pippa leaving the toilets. Patting Susie's arse with the flat palm he giggled to himself.

Vicky sat at her laptop. She looked excited as she typed at speed. Tim was talking to her on facebook. He just told her that he'd asked Susie to get in touch with her to sort a visit out. Tim was clever and Vicky loved that she could go and sit with Tim without any fears of anyone seeing her. Her own boyfriend Blake had been shipped out of Strangeways and he was allocated to another jail called Lancaster Farms HMP in Lancaster. He was well out of the picture now and this left her free to try and have a bit of well deserved fun.

The chat between them was getting hot. Tim was talking about sex and you could see Vicky blushing. She knew she should have ended the chat there but she just couldn't help it. He was like a drug and she was slowly becoming addicted to him. Licking her bottom lip she began to type back on the keyboard. Once she'd finished writing she sat back and searched for her cigs. The notice flashed at the bottom of the chat box that he was writing a message back. Her hands were shaking as she popped a cig in her mouth. Vicky sat up straight as the text appeared. "Fucking hell," she giggled. She'd asked Tim if he fancied her, and as she read his reply he was more than happy to get her knickers off. Tim stayed online for a few minutes more. He told Vicky he would see her tomorrow. His last comment made her laugh out loud, the cheeky fucker had asked her to wear no knickers on the visit. Vicky told him she couldn't wait to see him and get to know him better. Four kisses now came back on his last reply. Logging off the computer Vicky's head was all over the place. Her love for her own boyfriend had completely disappeared. Tim was the one holding all the cards now, he could change her life. With a grin on her face she switched the lights off downstairs and headed upstairs to bed.

The bedroom was cold as Vicky entered it. She was rubbing at her arms trying to get warm. The lonely double bed at the back of the room stared back at her.

The bedding was old and the quilt inside it looked as flat as a pancake. Walking over to the window she pulled back the net curtain and looked outside. She could see some lads sat on a wall close by. She chuckled as she saw them fucking about. Dropping the curtain she peeled her clothes from her perishing body. Grabbing an old t-shirt from the floor she quickly yanked it over her head. Diving in the bed she tossed and turned trying to get warm. You could just see her head sticking out from the top of the quilt cover. Crying could now be heard. "Fucking hell," she moaned as she sat up. Declan was stood at the bedroom door bawling his eyes out. "Come and get in my bed then mard arse," she moaned. Holding her hands out towards her son he quickly ran to her bedside. They snuggled up together. Vicky was secretly glad he was in her bed; otherwise she would have used the other pillows at the side of her for comfort. Looking at her son's eyes in the moonlight she pulled him closer and kissed his head. "I'm gonna get us out of this mess Declan. Don't worry son, we won't always be like this."

Declan looked up at his mother's face. His eyes were slowly closing as he mumbled under his breath, "I want my daddy back." Vicky sighed. He was always shouting for his dad when he was upset. It did her head in. Closing her eyes she drifted off to sleep. Tomorrow was the start of her new life. Snuggling up in bed she looked content as she lay beside her son.

Susie lay in her bed. Ashley stayed with her for a while but he was getting ready to leave. Dipping his head he kissed her cheek. "Right babes, I won't be long. You get some sleep."

Susie smiled at him and pulled the blanket over her shoulders. "Thanks Ash, you're a star. I don't know what I would do without you." With one last glance at her he was gone.

Susie's stared out of the window. The moonlight was shining in through the blinds. It looked so peaceful and made her feel calm inside. The stars danced in the midnight sky as if they were celebrating something. Her eyes flickered rapidly and she was slowly drifting off to a place where she was much happier. After a few minutes she was fast asleep.

CHAPTER ELEVEN

Vicky's hand trembled as she opened the sticky mascara bottle. She hadn't applied make-up in ages. The last time she'd even thought about dressing up was when her boyfriend was out of prison. She didn't see the need anymore. Holding her head to the side she opened her mouth and brought her face closer to the mirror. You could see her concentrating. With long even strokes, she fanned out her lashes and made them look a lot longer than they really were. Standing back from the mirror she giggled to herself. "Not bad," she mumbled.

Vicky looked at herself fully in the long mirror in the hallway. Her face looked troubled. Gripping her skirt at the edges she yanked it down. Vicky had no knickers on and you could see the image of her lady garden in the reflection in the mirror, she blushed.

Susie had sorted a babysitter out for Declan and she'd picked him up about an hour before. Vicky was looking forward to a stress free few hours without her whinging son by her side. Patting her bra Vicky made sure the drugs inside couldn't be seen. Pressing her fingers deeper inside it she pushed the bags of powder further. The fear of taking drugs into the prison had left her. All that was on her mind was pleasing Tim, and looking her best. She had big plans for the visit today and she just hoped all her hard work was going to pay off. With one last look in the mirror she left the house.

Sitting in the visitors centre Vicky felt special. She was wearing the shoes that Susie had given her. The high heels seemed to be magical and gave her so much confidence. For the first time in ages she was standing tall and held a look of happiness in her eyes.

As usual, names were shouted out for the visits. At first she forgot she was visiting Tim and was waiting for Blake's name to be called out. Hearing the name of the inmate she was going to see, she stood up. Her legs looked long and slender today and she'd even put some false tan on them hoping to give them a sun-kissed look. Tossing her hair over her shoulders she began the walk over to the prison.

All the visitors seemed to be on a mission. They walked at speed and all held that hard-knock look on their faces. Kids were moaning as the rain started to fall. One by one they entered the walls of HMP Strangeways. Today everything looked different. Screws were stood with stern faces and they seemed to be double- checking every movement they made. Vicky felt anxious. Holding her neck with one hand she began to take her shoes off from her feet to begin the search. The female officer was taking her time today. Usually she would have just given her body a quick frisk, but today she was searching every nook and cranny on her body. Vicky looked white in the face. Her heart was beating ten to the dozen. Lifting her feet in the air the screw scanned every inch of her foot. "Open your mouth," she asked. Vicky stretched it as wide as she could and stuck her tongue out, her search was over.

Walking up the flight of stairs seemed to take Vicky, ages. Her feet seemed heavy as she dragged them up each stair. The sound of people talking seemed to help calm her down. Scanning the area she realised that no sniffer dog was on duty today. "Thank fuck," she whispered. Going through the last part of the search she stood at the glass door waiting to enter to see Tim. The other visitors were behind her, eager to get inside, they were pushing and shoving. An officer stared at her through the glass window. Vicky was crapping herself. Turning her head unsure of where his eyes were focused she checked behind her. He was definitely looking at her without a shadow of doubt. Vicky noticed it was the same screw who had stared at Susie weeks before, it was Jenkins. She had no idea that he was the one making sure all the drugs got inside the prison for Tim. His eyes looked evil and she was debating running down the stairs away from the visit. Watching his hands slowly open the door she dipped her head and refrained from any eye contact with him. As Vicky passed him, she could feel his warm breath on the back of her neck. He looked as if he wanted to say something to her, but he was hesitating. Tim was now waving his hand at her. Bringing a smile to her face she made her way towards him looking embarrassed.

"Hello sexy," Tim said as she sat down at the table. She was fidgeting about and pulled a crumpled ten-pound note out from her pocket that Susie had given her for the visit.

"Do you want any drinks or owt?" she asked

nervously.

Tim leaned nearer towards her. "Nar I'll just have a kiss for now. The food can wait,"

Vicky panicked. This was the real thing. She was no longer hiding behind her lap-top flirting. She was sat facing Tim. Licking her lips she bent her head over to him and puckered up. The kiss was quick and nothing to write home about. "Did you bring the parcel?"

Tim asked, with a cunning look spread across his face. His eyes were all over the show watching everyone around him. Vicky nodded. In a low voice she spoke. "It's in my bra."

He looked at her and smirked. "Good girl, you've done well." Jenkins was walking up and down the aisles scanning the prisoners. He seemed to linger near Tim for a lot longer than necessary; he nodded his head at Tim slowly. Vicky looked terrified. This warden was throwing her looks and she was sure he was onto her. "That nob-head Jenkins is at it again. I swear to you he's out to get me, the daft cunt." Tim shot him a look and growled. The officer was definitely up to something and small droplets of sweat were visible on Tim's brow as he watched him walk away.

"Go on then Vicky. Go and get us a brew then. I'll have some chocolate as well."

"Which one do you want," she asked in a timid voice.

"Erm, I'm not arsed love. As long as it's as sweet as you, I don't care." Vicky stood up from her seat and smiled softly. She could feel his eyes burning into the back of her as she joined the queue for the food.

Lots of people were stood in a line as Vicky queued up behind them. Loud shouting could be heard. Vicky turned her head quickly and watched five or six officers running towards a table in the distance where an inmate was sat on his visit. Vicky moved away from the crowd and got a better look at the goings on.

A prisoner could be seen getting twisted up at the table. A screw had his hand held tightly around the convict's throat. He was trying to stop him from swallowing something. "Get it out!" the warden screamed. The room was in complete silence and all you could hear were the inmate's groans. The prisoner was thrown to the floor with force. He looked purple in the face. Visitors were up in arms and Vicky could see the inmates own visitors trying to walk away. They were stopped and restrained straight away.

"You're gonna fucking kill him. Let him breathe ya wanker," a nearby prisoner shouted. He was stood up from his chair ranting loudly with his hands held out in front of him. He was soon quietened down though as Jenkins walked to his side and whispered something into his ear. Four officers now carried the prisoner away from the table. He was shouting and kicking and it was obvious he'd swallowed whatever it was in his mouth. Vicky listened to the other people as she joined the queue again. The man in front of her was speaking loudly. "At least he got it in, the bastards never got to him fast enough." He was giggling and high-fived his mate at the side of him. Vicky's heart was beating faster than usual and she sighed rubbing her arms vigorously.

Tim helped Vicky place the tray on the table; he could see she was nervous. Once she was sat down, he jerked his head back and stretched his arms above his head yawning. Vicky chirped in. "Fucking hell did you see those cranks with that prisoner? They nearly choked the poor fucker to death."

Tim chuckled. "He's fucked either way now, because he'll just be shoved down the block. They'll just wait until he takes a dump to see what he was concealing. I think it was smack, because the lad's a bad bag-head."

"What will happen to his visitors now?" she asked with an anxious face.

"Fuck knows. They'll probably get nicked when they take them downstairs." Vicky gulped hard and Tim could see her face dropping. He reached for her hand and tried to comfort her. "You'll be sweet babes. Don't you worry about a thing?" His head tilted to the side now and he smiled from cheek to cheek revealing his pearly white teeth. "So have you got any knickers on or what?"

Her face went bright red. Moving about in her seat she tried to look confident. The corners of her mouth curled. "You'll have to wait and see won't you."

Tim was aroused. Susie was a right boring cow and this girl seemed to be up for a good time. "Put your hand under the table and give my trouser snake a bit of a stroke then." Vicky moved forward in her seat. Pulling his head towards her she sank her lips onto him. Her hand disappeared under the table and Tim's face changed. He looked excited. With slow movements Vicky strummed his penis. It was much bigger than Blake's, and she felt cheated that these things came in different shapes and sizes. "Take it easy," Tim moaned. Looking around the area Vicky could see lots of other women doing the same thing as her. Their arms were under the table too.

Tim and Vicky looked like a normal couple. You would have never had known they'd just met. Once Tim had shot his load he dropped his head on the table and Vicky pulled her arm away. "I've got wanker's cramp," she giggled as she flexed her fingers out in front of her. Tim didn't speak straight away. He was trying to regain his composure.

"That was mint ,Vicky," he gasped. Holding her head back she chuckled. This was so out of character for her and she was acting strange. Tim looked about the room and pulled her back towards him. Dipping his hand in her bra he pulled the drugs from it quickly. His fist was clenched as he sat back at the table. One of his hands disappeared down his tracksuit bottoms and he quickly rammed the parcel up his ring-piece. Tim looked hot; he was wriggling about on the chair.

"What's up,"Vicky whispered.

"My arse is on fire, fucking hell I feel sick." Tim dropped his head on the table and blew through his mouth. His face looked white."Just give me a minute and I'll be fine," he said in an anxious voice.Vicky rubbed his head and played the part of a concerned girlfriend.

"It must be because my arse is a virgin," he pulled his head up and smiled.Vicky could see the colour returning to his face and started to relax again.

"How the fuck do you get it up there anyway," she whispered.

"I greased my arse-hole before I came out on the visit. It should have just slid up there no problem."

Vicky was holding her belly laughing. "What do ya mean greased your arse-hole up?"

Tim chuckled. "I put some Vaseline on the rim of it, that's all. All the lads do it. They said it should go up with no problems." He looked concerned now as he continued."Perhaps I should have practiced it a few times in my cell first, shouldn't I?"Vicky was chewing on her lips trying not to laugh anymore. Everyone was looking at them. "Well I'll tell you summat love, I won't be doing it again. I feel violated," he whispered, Vicky's face dropped. If he didn't want any more drops, where did she fit into his life? She wanted him more than ever now, and spoke in a clear voice.

"What? Don't you wanna see me anymore then?" His face screwed up and he grabbed her hands over the table. "Yeah, ya muppet. I'm just saying you won't be bringing me any more parcels in, that's all." She looked happy but then she shook her head. "But I need the money," she moaned. "I get one hundred pounds for each drop. That makes a big difference to me, yanno?"

He sat upright and jerked forward. He was gritting his teeth. "What do you mean you get a ton? It should be two hundred quid for each fucking drop."

Vicky shook her head. "Susie just gives me a oner that's it."

"The snidey cunt," he snarled. "Why did I ever think I could trust her? She's one conniving bint."

Vicky was onto it now and her face was angry. "So are you telling me, she's been having me over?"

Tim sighed as he rubbed his fingers through his hair. "Yeah love, but don't worry I'm gonna phone her and tell her to sort you out."

Vicky was fuming "She's a cheeky cow. What the fuck is she playing at? She knows how much of a risk I'm taking, bringing shit in here." She blew a hard breath. "And she thinks she can pull the wool over my eyes. We'll see about that." Tim agreed as Vicky cursed Susie.

Tim sat talking with Vicky for the rest of the visit and he found out all about her life. He looked at her endearingly. The girl had so much to offer him and he was smitten already. With a cunning grin on his face he spoke to her in confidence. "Me and you could have something special, yanno? Susie can't be trusted and I want you to be my eyes and ears on the out." Vicky was hanging on his every word. As he continued she was debating telling him some home truths about Susie. After all, the woman was a sly fucker and she couldn't be trusted. Licking her lips Vicky decided to grass her up. Watching his face she started to confide in him.

"You know she's shagging your mate Ashley. She has been for the last few years."

Tim's face dropped. "Nar has she fuck. Where have you heard that bullshit from?"

Vicky moved in closer. "Truthfully Tim, she told me herself."

Tim was gobsmacked. He was cracking his knuckles and his nostrils were flaring. "Are you kidding me or what? Don't wind me up love. This is serious."

"Listen Tim, the woman's a dirt-bag," she snapped, "she was sat in my house and poured her heart out to me. She doesn't deserve you. Trust me; she's having an affair with Ashley." Tim was bubbling with temper and at one point he nearly stood up and left the visiting room. Sitting clenching his fist at the table he nodded his head slowly. Vicky was looking around the room now and felt uncomfortable. "Right Vicky, don't you say a fucking word to anyone about this. This is our secret. Oh.... those two cheating bastards are going to get what's coming to them. Just you wait and see!"

"I won't say fuck all," she smiled, "I'll do whatever I can to help you," she simpered.

Tim kissed Vicky at the end of the visit. He told her he would phone her later that evening. Walking away, she could see him sat with his head on the table with his face covered. She moved fast now as she watched the screw stood near the doorway. As she crept past him she could see him tapping his finger on the wooden ledge at the side of him, she quivered.

Vicky left the prison and made her way back to the visitors' centre. Her heart was in her mouth. Her arse was twitching. Running to the toilets she looked like she was squeezing a penny between the cheeks of her arse. Opening the toilet doors she ran inside the cubicle. Sweat was trickling down her face.

Heading out into the daylight, Vicky pulled her coat tighter around her body. She felt sick. Her temper was boiling and she couldn't wait to go and see Susie and tell her that she knew she was short- changing her. Walking up towards Cheetham Hill, she looked at the shopping Fort in the distance and wished she could go on a spree right there and then. She looked serious as she crossed the busy road.

Vicky walked towards Susie's house. It looked posh and well maintained. Walking down the garden path she could smell the scent from the red roses at the side of her. Her fingers lifted the letterbox as she tapped at it gently. She could hear Declan shouting from inside. Susie opened the door and spoke in an animated voice. "Told you, she wouldn't be long didn't I?"

Declan snivelled. "Orr has he been upset," Vicky asked as she bent down to kiss her son.

"No, just these last ten minutes. Kerry brought him back about half an hour ago. She said he's been as good as gold."

Vicky lifted him into her arms. Swinging him up to her chest she cuddled him. "Orr have you been a good boy?"

Declan was smiling now and wriggled to get back down to the floor. "Mummy come and look in here, they've got a Play Station. Can I have one?" Vicky followed him to the living room as he grabbed her hand pulling her with him. "Look mummy look," he shouted. Declan sat down on the floor and continued playing on a 'Playstation' game.

Susie smiled at Vicky. "Sit down love. Do you want a brew?" Vicky nodded. Her mouth felt like sandpaper and she needed a drink to help her find her words again. Susie went into the kitchen and Vicky sat down. The house was mint and a million miles away from her depressing abode. Everything was polished and in tip-top condition. "Posh cow," Vicky mumbled.

As Susie made the brews, Vicky prepared herself for some action. There was no way the slag was ripping her off; she was getting herself ready for war. Dragging her coat from her shoulders she placed it on the arm of the chair. Susie appeared at the door and was carrying two cups that looked hot. Bending her knees towards the table she looked at Vicky and gave her the eye. "Just grab two of them mats there love." Vicky reached over and took two glass coasters from the centre of the table. "It cost a fortune this table, that's why I don't want any marks on it." Vicky huffed and sat back in her chair. Susie went back into the kitchen and come back with a plate of biscuits. "Get some of them love," she urged. "So how was it? Did you get the parcel in or what?"

Vicky's face creased as she sat forward. Wriggling about in her seat she replied. "Yeah it was sound. That fucking screw, remember that one who fancied you?" Susie eyes opened wide as she nodded her head. "Well he was acting really weird. He kept staring at me. And when we were on the visit Tim said he had it in for him too. He spooked me out yanno?" Susie looked nervous as she pulled a cig from her packet. Lifting her eyes up, she offered Vicky one, with her own cig hanging from her mouth. Lighting the fags they both inhaled deeply.

"So did he get the drugs?" Susie continued.

Vicky nodded. "Yeah he did, but he said you should be paying me two hundred pounds not one." Susie went red in the face, and couldn't look at her. Vicky made a point of saying it again. "So is that right then, you should be paying me two ton a visit not one?"

Susie sat back in her chair; she looked agitated as she stroked her neck with her hand. "Nar it's up to me what I pay for a drop, not Tim".

Vicky was up in arms now and held nothing back. Her face was red and her arms were waving about in front of her. "Listen Susie, I'm taking a big risk taking drugs into the nick. Tim told me he's gonna phone you later and tell you to pay me what I'm owed." Susie bolted up from her chair as if boiling water was being poured over her and stood up. She was pacing about the living room shouting. Declan looked scared and moved to his mother's side. "I want to go home now," he whispered.

"Who the fuck does Tim think he is. I'm the one calling the shots round here, not him. I pay one hundred pound per drop, love. If ya don't wanna do it anymore, then fair enough. There's loads of people out there who would bite my hand off for that much cash for a drop."

Vicky stood up and started to put her coat on. Her eyes burned into Susie. "Just give me what you owe me then. I'm calling it a day. It's not worth it to me anymore."

Susie snarled. "What, are you saying that you're not doing anymore drops?"

"Correct," Vicky hissed. "If you think you're having me over, think again. Tim has told me what he told you to pay me, and you're just taking the piss out of me. You must think I'm some kind of nob-head." Vicky was in Susie's face. "If you think you can rip me off, you've got another thing coming." Her hand sat on her hip as her nose touched Susie's. "You can think again sweetheart, I'm no dick."

Declan was huddling next to his mother now getting ready to cry. Vicky was stroking his head at the side of her but her eyes were fixed on Susie.

Susie looked uncomfortable and searched for her handbag. Once she'd found it she grabbed her purse from it and pulled out a wad of cash. Counting out five twenty-pound notes she handed it to Vicky. "So you're not paying me the rest?" Vicky growled.

"Am I fuck, Vicky. It's up to you. Take it or leave it?" Vicky shoved the money into her coat pocket and scanned the area for Declan's coat. Once she'd located it, she sat on the chair and helped him put it on. Susie was stood watching them both like a hawk.

Vicky made her way to the door holding her son's hand. Susie was walking behind them and looked frustrated. The sound of Vicky's heels clicking down the garden path could be heard. Susie looked like she wanted to say something. She stepped out from the front door but quickly jumped back inside. "For fuck sake," she huffed as she slammed the door shut behind her.

Susie walked back to the living room. There was an eerie silence. Her mobile phone hadn't rung for ages and she kept checking it to see if it was working properly. Lighting a cig she sat puffing away while she tried to gather her thoughts together. She looked stressed.

Vicky walked with haste and dragged Declan alongside her. She was fuming. Reaching into her pocket she pulled out her mobile and tried to ring Tim. It was going to voice-mail all the time and she knew she'd have to wait until later that night when she could speak to him.

Feeling the cash in her coat pocket she smiled at her son. "Do you want a have a Happy Meal from McDonald's?"

Declan was jumping about and he looked excited. "Yeah! I want one, I want one." Vicky smiled at him with endearing eyes. Even though he was a handful she still loved him with all her heart. They both set off to get something to eat.

CHAPTER TWELVE

Tim sat in his cell and stared at the four walls. He was cracking his knuckles and wriggling his feet on the floor. His pad mate was on a visit and he was sat alone with his thoughts. Susie and Ashley were lying heavily on his mind and had been for many weeks. Every minute of every day he was plotting to ruin the pair of them. "Bastards," he muttered under his breath as he dragged his fingers through his hair.

Looping his arms behind his head, he closed his eyes as his head sank into his pillow. Tim was in pain and you could see his hands gripping the grey bedding, tightly. "Bitch, bitch," he whispered to himself. Slowly he opened his eyes and looked at the wall at the side of him. He could see Susie's photograph looking straight at him. His face screwed up as he stared at it with piercing eyes. Bolting up from the bed he dragged the snapshot from the

wall as if it was on fire. Tim's fist was turning white as

he squeezed the photograph hard in his hand.

Tim looked anxious; he kept lying on his bed and then jumping back up as if he was practising a movement. At association he sprung to his feet and walked from his cell towards the phone. Heading down the landing, he swung his arms about at the side of him like a soldier going to war.

The prison was busy. Shouting could be heard all over the landing and the daily life of the prison system was in full swing. Tim stood behind an inmate and waited patiently to use the phone. He looked nervous as he stood with his back against the wall fidgeting. Finally after about five minutes it was his turn to make a call.

"Alright Helen, it's me Tim." His mouth pressed up close to the receiver as he whispered. "I need your help, sis. I need you to do a few things for me urgently. I need you to get my spare bank card from my Mam's and draw my money out. I want every fucking last penny out of my account as soon as possible." Tim stood relaying his instructions to his sister and by the end of the phone call a small smile appeared on his face. Once he'd said goodbye to Helen he went to join the rest of the convicts in the prison for association.

The prisoners were playing cards when he reached them and he looked eager to join in. Within minutes Tim's mood seemed to have lifted. He was laughing and joking with the other cons and he seemed like he was the life and soul of the party.

Helen marched to her mother's house like a woman on a mission. The wind was howling and it had just started raining heavily. Pulling her hood up over her head she waddled onto the estate.

"What are you doing out in this weather? It's freezing out there,"Tim's mother exclaimed as she let her in. Helen sighed as she peeled her wet coat off. Throwing it on the small hall table she went straight inside the front room. Mary was still moaning. "You must be a butty short of a picnic coming out in this weather."

"I know," Helen nodded, "but I've got shit to do and it couldn't wait." Tim's mother watched as her lard arse daughter plonked her damp body on the sofa. She was drenched from head to toe.

Mary could tell by Helen's face something was on her mind. Even from being a small child she was always able to tell when she was up to something and today was no different. Helen was rubbing her purple hands together as she spoke to her mother. Her voice was loud and she sounded distressed. "Mam, our Tim wants me to get all of his money from his bank account, as soon as. He said you have the spare bank card for it."

Tim's mother shook her head and sat back in her chair. Screwing her face up, she held her head back and raised her eyes to the ceiling. "Over my dead body, am I giving you our Tim's bank card. When I hear it from him then I will. You must think I was born yesterday."

Helen sprang from the sofa waving her hands in the air. "Mam, Tim has rang me and told me to do it. Fucking hell, do you think I would lie about summat like that?"

Mary snarled and gave a sarcastic laugh. "Are you forgetting the last time you asked me for Tim's money love? What was the money for again?" she chuckled and sat forward in her chair before she continued. "Oh yeah... You said the cash I was holding for Tim was to be given to you. 'His orders' you told me." Her index finger was held up to her lip as if she was thinking. "Yep you told me, he said you could have eighty-quid from it didn't you?" she sniggered. Staring right at Helen she continued. "But when I saw Tim, he said he'd said no such fucking thing. You were lying. And who did he go mad at?" she paused and pointed to herself. "Me, that's fucking who, so there's no chance I'm giving you a penny of his money without his say so."

Helen dropped down on the sofa. Her mother was right. She had lied in the past to get some money but she was on her arse at the time, and needed some money to feed her kids. Helen was angry. "Mam I admit, I've told porkies in the past, but come on, our Tim is loaded and I didn't have a pot to piss in," she shrugged her shoulders as she continued. "I paid him back though didn't I?"

Mary huffed and shook her head. "Yeah you did, but in fucking dribs and drabs. And I bet you didn't pay him the full amount back did you? I know what you're like. You're forgetting I know you of old." Helen marched about the living room, dragging at her greasy locks. Pulling the white crisp net curtain back from the window she stared from it looking like a wounded dog. As she leant on the windowsill she smiled as she watched one of the neighbours struggling to hold an umbrella up in the rain.

Tim's mother lit a cig and sat back in the chair. She could tell her daughter was ready to have another go at her and prepared herself for round two. Helen disappeared into the kitchen to brew up as Mary started to read the newspaper at the side of her. Finding her horoscopes for the day she shouted into the kitchen to Helen. "Ay, my stars say I should be careful today, and not be foolish where money is concerned."

Helen came back into the room and lifted her eyes to the ceiling. "Stop fucking lying mother. Sometimes you just go right over the top, yanno. You just wait for Tim to phone, and then you'll know the truth." A grin now filled her face as she placed her mother's cup of tea on the table. Helen looked cocky as she continued. "Then, when Tim knows you didn't give me the bank card you'll be the one up shit creek not me."

Mary reached for her brew as she replied. "Well that's a chance I'm willing to take."

Helen sat down and ripped open the packet of biscuits with a firm grip. Her mother watched her and sighed. "I thought you were on a diet?"

Helen shot her a look, "I'm having a couple of fucking biscuits with my brew that's all. I've hardly eaten anything all day."

"Little pickers wear big knickers you know?"

Helen blushed and threw the rest of the biscuits to the floor in temper. "Fucking hell, Mam. I'm stressed out and need a bit of comfort. Is that such a big sin?"

"I'm just saying, that's all. You're always moaning about your weight, so I'm trying to help you." Mary held the newspaper up to cover her face. "A moment on the lips is a lifetime on the hips," she giggled; Helen could see her mum's shoulders jerking about behind the newspaper.

"No need, mother," Helen huffed as she shoved the rest of the biscuit in her mouth.

Helen had waited long enough now and she couldn't wait to tell her mother about Tim's phone call. Coughing loudly she let her know she had something to say. Mary dropped the newspaper onto her lap and looked at Helen. "What's wrong?"

Helen licked her bottom lip. She knew she had her

mother's full attention. "Oh shag-bag has been at it again. I knew she couldn't be trusted."

Mary looked at her in surprise. "Who are you going on about now? Who's a shag-bag?"

"Fucking Susie, that's who. She's only been sleeping with Ashley. Apparently it's been going on for years!"

"Will you stop listening to gossip? Every fucking time I see you, you're always the same, slagging someone off."

Helen sat forward in her chair and cupped her hands together. "Not this time mother, Tim told me himself. This is straight from the horse's mouth. I don't know how he knows but he does."

"I bet it's someone telling lies. You know what it's like round here. Susie loves our Tim to death."

"Come off it mother, she loves the money he has, nothing else. She's a grabbing cunt."

"You're just jealous of her, Helen. You always have been. You've never had a good word to say about her since our Tim met her."

"Susie has always been the same," Helen retorted, "and I know it's her who grassed me up to the benefit agency." Mary reached for her cigs. As per usual Helen didn't have any and she bummed one from her.

Tim's mother sat in silence for a minute. Licking her teeth she crossed her legs and sat looking at Helen. "You don't know for sure Susie was the one who grassed you up. That's just you presuming. Come on," she puffed on her cig, "I mean you sit with all your mates all day calling every fucker under the sun. So it could be someone in your own circle of friends who bubbled you, not Susie."

Helen nearly choked on her cig. "Why do you always stick up for her? You're such a brown-noser. I just can't wait until Tim phones and tells you the truth about her.

She's scum, end of." Mary picked her paper back up from her lap and continued reading it. Helen could be heard puffing and blowing in the background. Sitting back in the chair Helen found the remote for the TV and found something to watch.

A few minutes later the house phone started ringing. Mary jumped up from her seat. Helen was going to answer it but her mother pushed her back in the chair with her hand and told her she would deal with it. The phone sat in the hallway and Helen was already leant forward in her chair trying to earwig.

"Hello son how are you?" Helen bolted from the chair and made her way to her mother's side. She held one hand on the door frame as she listened to the conversation. Her face was smiling as she yanked her tracksuit bottoms up over her arse cheeks. "How do you know that Tim?" Mary asked in a distressed voice.

You could now see her shaking her head and running her fingers through her grey hair. "Oh well son. If that's what you want me to do, then fine. Do you want me to get the money out for Helen?" Mary was concerned as she continued. "I'll get it out, but you will have to write me a cheque out because the cash machine only allows three hundred pounds a day."

Helen held a concerned look on her face. "Tell him I will sign the check for him, I'm mint at forging his signature." As soon as her mother placed the receiver down her daughter was on her like a rash. "Well then, what did he say? Did he tell you Susie was fucking about with Ashley?" Mary ignored her and barged past her back to the front room. Plonking herself on the chair she tried not to look at Helen. "So was I lying or what?" Helen piped up.

Mary looked flustered. "No, you weren't, for a change. He wants me to draw the money out of the bank, but you can go and get it for me. I'm not going out in this weather."

Helen chuckled and held her head back. "See, I told you that yo-yo knickers was at it. What are you saying now, who's chatting shit?" Helen gave a victory punch into the air. You could tell by her face she loved every minute of Susie's downfall and she wasn't holding anything back. Mary looked worried. "He's told me to write a cheque out in my name from his bank account for fifty five thousand pounds."

Helen's eyes nearly popped out of her sockets. "Fifty five grand! Our Tim's fucking wadded."

Mary blew hard as Helen watched her with eager eyes. "Right where's his cheque book. No point in wasting any time is there?" Helen was bouncing about the front room looking anxious as Tim's mother planned her next move. "Go upstairs in my bedroom and there is a red box under my bed. I think the cheque book in there."

Helen bounded upstairs. She sounded like a herd of elephants. Struggling to bend down under the bed, she rolled onto the floor. Her arm was stretched out flat as she searched for the red box. Helen's head was held to the side as she pushed her face deeper under the bed trying to locate it. She was struggling and moans could be heard. Dragging the red box out she shouted downstairs to her mother. "Mam... Do you want the box bringing down, or should I just get the cheque book out of it?"

Holding her ear to the door she could hear her mother's reply. "Just get the cheque book." Helen sat on her mother's bed and her eyes looked eagerly inside the shoe box. Her fingers looked like bunches of bananas as

she lifted the lid. Helen was like a kid in a sweet shop. Lots
of Tim's personal things were inside the box. Her eyes
flickered as she clocked a sparkling diamond ring in the
corner of the box. Checking no one was about she slid
the gold ring over her fingers. She was struggling to get it
past her fat knuckle. Her face looked stressed; you could
see her finger turning white. Sliding her teeth down her
finger she dragged the ring onto it. Sitting back on the
bed Helen held her hand from her face. The ring was
way too small for her but somehow she squeezed it onto
her fat finger. Her mother's voice could now be heard
shouting from downstairs. "Helen what the fuck are you
doing up there? I hope you're not rooting about."

Helen grabbed the cheque book quickly and came
to the top of the stairs. "I'm here now. It was right at
the bottom of the box." Mary gave her a look from the
bottom of the stairs.

"Right bring it down then, if you've found it." Helen
bounced down the stairs. Mary listened to the noise she
was making and shook her head. The house was trembling
with her body weight coming down the stairs.

Helen was at the living room door looking hot and
flustered. "There you go, do you need a pen?"

Mary sighed. "You're loving every minute of this
aren't you?"

Helen smirked. "Yep, fucking dead right I am. I want
to see the slut come down to earth with a bang." Helen
burst out laughing as she reached onto the windowsill to
pick up a pen. "Every dog has its day, mother. And this is
my day." She smirked and passed the black pen over to
Mary.

Once the cheque was written, Helen forged Tim's
signature. She went into the hallway and grabbed her

damp coat. Re-entering the room she started to put her coat on. "Right mam, give us that cheque and I'll pay it into the bank for you. In five days it will be cleared and then the bitch won't have a pot to piss in. Welcome to my world, Susie!" She cackled like a witch. "Let's see how long you're smiling when you're skint."

Tim's mother passed her the cheque with trembling hands. You could see she was hesitating. Helen snatched it. "Come on woman, I've not got all fucking day."

Helen marched to the shopping precinct with haste. The rain had stopped now but the wind was still cold. Looking down at her finger she looked at the diamond ring shining like a star. It looked expensive, for once Helen looked happy.

Once she'd paid the money into the bank she looked relieved. Her face was red and small droplets of sweat were visible on her forehead. That was one job from Tim's list done now. Her next destination was to go and see Joan. Tim knew all about her ripping him off but that didn't matter to him anymore; he needed her to come back and manage 'Delia's' until he got home.

Tim's sister jumped on the bus and headed down Rochdale Road. Her eyes never lifted from the ring sitting on her finger. Standing to her feet she got ready to get off the public transport. With her head dipped through the window she could see Mays Pawnbrokers just in front of her. Helen jumped from the bus with a spring in her step. Checking the area first she headed inside with her head down.

Helen's teeth sank round the ring on her finger as she tried to pull it off. Her face looked strained, and every now and then she shook her hand out in front of her in pain. Her finger was turning purple, it had swelled. Joining the queue of desperate people she finally managed to pull the ring off. Wiping her spit from it, she twirled it on her finger. Waiting patiently she looked around the shop.

Helen got twelve hundred pounds for the ring. Folding the pawn ticket in her hand she shoved it deep inside her coat pocket. Her face looked white as she stepped out from the shop." "Fuck me," she whispered. This was more money than she ever imagined. A cunning smile filled her face. She was a conniving bitch.

Flagging a taxi down from the main road, Helen headed to Joan's house. The money in her pocket was carefully hidden away and she kept patting her pocket every now and then to make sure it was still there. After paying the taxi she made her way to Joan's house. Rapping on the letterbox she stepped back from the house looking up at all the windows for any sign of life. She saw the net curtain moving about and knew someone was inside the house. Bending down, Helen shouted through the letterbox. "Joan it's me Helen. She stood twisting her body about waiting for someone to open the door. When the door opened, Joan looked like she'd just got out of bed. Her hair was stuck up all over the place and she looked different. "Alright sweetheart, can I have a quick word with you?"

"What the fuck do you want?" Joan scowled.

"Ay Mrs Attitude, don't be stressing with me, I'm here to help." After a pause Helen tried again, "Fuck me Joan; are you letting me in or what?" Joan didn't speak and just held the door open for her to come inside.

Joan's living room was a shit-tip. Clothes all over the place and old magazines were scattered about the furniture. The place stank of sweaty feet and stale cigs. Helen screwed her face up. Her own house was a disgrace but Joan's took the biscuit. Lifting some old newspaper up from the couch, Helen parked her arse. "You look rough Joan. Are you feeling okay?" Joan sat down and searched the ashtray for cig dimps. Helen watched her carefully as she unfolded a cig butt out with caution. Joan's face was screwed up as she tried to light it from the flame. Watching Joan drain every bit of nicotine from it, Helen shot her a look of disgust.

"Right what the fuck do you want, I'm busy," Joan moaned.

Helen shook her head and smirked. "Stop being so fucking nasty, will you. I've done nowt wrong to you, so remember that."

Joan wrapped her arms around herself and pulled her skanky housecoat tighter. "I know love, but I'm just pissed off and all that. No work, no money what do you expect, a laughing clown?"

Helen held her head to the side. She loved the control she was feeling and it was written all across her face. "Our Tim wants you back running 'Delia's'."

Joan coughed loudly and at one point she looked as if she might be choking to death. Once she'd caught her breath she replied. "Are you having a laugh or what?" she replied sarcastically.

"Nope, seriously love. It's all going pear-shaped in there and Tim wants Susie out of the joint as soon as possible."

Joan smiled as she scanned the ashtray for more cig ends. "I knew that slut wouldn't be able to hack it."

Helen jumped in and stopped her dead in her tracks. "Oh she could hack it, Joan. That's not the reason why he wants her out." Helen spoke in a low voice now, and made Joan swear she wouldn't tell anyone of what she was about to tell her. Once she had Joan's word, she continued with an excited tone. "Susie's only been shagging Ashley."

Joan's face dropped and her mouth was wide open in shock. "No way," she huffed.

Helen was on fire now and couldn't wait to spill the beans on Susie. "Our Tim said she's been at it for years, the dirty slapper."

Joan was on one now, her face was alive again. "I fucking hate that woman with a passion, I'm so glad she's been knocked off her high horse. When you think about it..." she held her head to the side and held one finger inside her mouth, "they were always together and he was always defending her when I slagged her off."

"Well she's up the creek without a paddle now," Helen butted in, "He's asked my mam to draw all his money out of the bank, so the shit will hit the fan when she finds out." Helen sat upright in her seat. "Swear to me Joan. You won't breathe a word of this to anyone, because if our Tim knows I've been chatting his business he'll go sick at me."

Joan looked happy. A smirk appeared on her face. "Does she know I'm coming back to 'Delia's'?"

Helen shook her head. "Does she fuck, Tim's gonna tell her some story and say some bad arses are giving him shit and that they have threatened to go in the brothel and cause shit for you all."

Joan nodded her head. "Right. Am I starting back there tonight or what, because I have to sort my shit out."

Helen twisted her greasy locks in her fingers. She looked like a sergeant major getting her troops ready for war. "Yeah be there for about nine. Tim should have phoned her by then and told her the script." Helen held her belly as she laughed out loud. "Oh, I wish I could be a fly on the wall when she knows her empire is crumbling around her." Both women sat looking happy at Susie's downfall. Helen patted the money in her pocket and stood from her seat. "Right I've got to go to ASDA and get some shopping. My fridge is bare as fuck. I feel like old mother Hubbard."

Joan followed her to the door. "Thanks love," she whispered as Helen stood outside her door. "I'm gonna sort my shit out now. I've been all over the place lately and this is just what I need to make me pull my finger out."

"Right love, I'm here for a good time, not a long time. See you later about nine at Delia's." Walking away Helen held her arm up behind her head and waved goodbye. Joan stood for a minute and checked the area. Everything seemed quiet for now. Closing the front door she rubbed her hands together, feeling excited.

CHAPTER THIRTEEN

Susie was dressed and just about ready to go to the brass gaff. She could hear someone knocking at the front door. Checking her watch she went to open it. "Who the fuck is that? at this time," she whispered as she marched to the door. Helen was stood looking at her with a cocky face. Susie was livid. "What the fuck are you doing here?" Helen placed her hand on her hip.

Tim had already made Helen's day by telling her earlier that she could tell Susie she was no longer running the brothel. He was going to tell her himself, but he said Helen could tell her and make it all seem real. Helen began with concern in her voice. "Listen, Tim's in big trouble.

He's asked me to come round here to fill you in. Don't think for one minute I would be here otherwise." Susie snarled at her and gritted her teeth. You could see her fists clenching together as she told her to come inside.

Once they were both in the house Helen began. She looked so convincing and at one point she shed a tear for her brother's safety. "It's all going off Susie. Remember them guys who Tim had trouble with ages ago?"

Helen was holding her hands out in front of her. Susie was shaking her head as she paced the front room. "No who?"

"The Jones crew from Blackley. The lads who sell the brown and sniff up there."

Susie sat down and Helen joined her sitting by her side. "Yeah I know who they are. What the fuck have they got to do with Tim?"

Helen spoke slowly. She looked as if she was remembering her script. "Well Dominic, you know the fat guy?"

Susie was hanging onto her every word. "Yeah yeah," she huffed.

"He's in Strangeways with our Tim and they've been at war. Tim said they've been fighting." Susie rubbed her arms. You could see goose pimples appearing on her skin. Helen carried on. "Apparently he's sending some guys to the brothel tonight to smash the place up. Tim said he doesn't want you near the place, because this man is a mad-head and he knows he wouldn't think twice about getting his foot soldiers to slice you up."

Susie looked scared "Why are they fighting?"

Helen sighed. Susie knew Dominic Jones personally and he was a main head in the area. She'd heard some bad stories about him in the past and knew he was someone not to be messed with. Helen dug deep in her pockets and pulled out a packet of twenty cigs. Slowly opening them she pulled two cigs out and offered Susie one. Once they were both smoking Helen told the full story.

"Dom knows our Tim has cash and he wants to knock him down a peg or two. I mean our Tim is on even par with him and his men, isn't he?" Susie just listened and never replied. Blowing smoke from her mouth Helen looked at Susie with evil eyes. "It's war love. Tim wants you out of the place and nowhere near it. Joan's going back there tonight."

Susie screamed out now at the top of her voice. "What do you mean Joan's going back to 'Delia's'? Over my fucking dead body she is. The woman's a raving crack-head."

Helen knew she had to up her game and stood up from her seat. "You can't go anywhere near the gaff love. Joan will be able to sort them out if they come. She's dealt with this kind of shit before. Think about it. If Dom's men see you there, they'll just waste you to spite Tim."

Susie was stood frozen for a minute. No words were coming from her mouth. Sitting back down she looked up to Helen who was standing over her. "Why hasn't Tim told me all this? Why has he sent you to tell me?"

Helen maintained eye contact with Susie. "Fucking hell, Tim's probably protecting you. He probably doesn't want to speak in front of anyone in there. You never know whose listening, do you?"

Susie was tapping her fingers on her front teeth. "What about Ashley, why isn't he sorting it all out?"

"Dunno love, our Tim said he wants to see Ashley on a visit as soon as possible. He wants you to sort the visit out."

Susie reached for her mobile phone. Her hands were trembling. Finding Ashley's name she began to ring his number. Helen sat back down in her chair and watched her slowly falling to pieces right in front of her very eyes. She loved every minute of it. Susie held the phone to her ear. After a few minutes she flung her mobile phone down beside her. "The prick isn't answering."

Ashley looked at his mobile phone as he lay on his bed. An arm was draped over his body and he looked back at Pippa with a smile on his face. "Who was it?" she asked in a cocky voice.

"Susie," he replied. Pippa snuggled up beside him and kissed his body slowly.

"Phone her back and tell her ya banging me."

Ashley laughed out loud. "Pippa you are so blunt. I can't just say that to her."

"Why not? When I see her I'm gonna tell her anyway."

Ashley rolled on top of her and pinned her arms down over her head. She was giggling as he bit her breast softly. "I'm gonna tea-bag you, you filthy animal." Ashley chuckled as he moved his arse up over her face. Dipping his ball bag into her mouth she could be seen squeezing her mouth tightly shut. "Open wide," he shouted as he moved further up the bed. Pippa was wriggling about underneath him, as his bollocks whacked against her mouth. They were both laughing their heads off.

Susie sat watching the clock on the wall. Helen was still sat there watching her every move. "I'm going to Delia's.

Fuck, sitting here all night. If they come I'll just have to deal with them won't I?"

Helen went red in the face. "Are you right in the fucking head? Tim has told you, he doesn't want you anywhere near the place. Just do as you're told for once in your fucking life."

Susie shook her head. She sat fidgeting, twisting her fingers. Chewing her bottom lip she replied. "I can deal with them. You can come with me if you want?"

"Don't be daft" Helen ranted, "Do you think I'm going anywhere near the place after Tim has told me what's going to happen? It might not happen tonight, correct, but mark my words the lads will come, and I for one don't want to be any part of it."

Susie knew she was right and stood up. "Do you wanna drink? I've got a bottle of wine in the fridge?"

Helen looked relieved. "Yeah I will do. Haven't you got any Cider instead?"

Susie shook her head. "No I don't drink it. It's fucking loony juice." Susie left the front room and Helen looked pleased with her performance. Susie stood in the kitchen and typed out a text message to Ashley. "Where the fuck are you? Phone me as soon as you get this message. It's important." Once the message was sent she placed the phone in her pocket and dipped her head inside the fridge. Grabbing a bottle of red wine she searched for two glasses in the cupboard.

Helen was smoking as Susie came back into the room. This was the first time she'd ever seen Tim's sister with a twenty packet of cigs. Laughing she placed the two glasses on the table. "Fucking hell have you won the lottery or something? Since when do you buy twenty cigs?"

Helen chuckled. "I know, I just thought I would treat

myself with the budgeting loan I got from the Benefit Agency." Helen was watching Susie like a hawk and began to tell her about her misfortune. "Did I tell you someone grassed me up to the fucking social?" Susie shook her head as she sipped from her drink. Helen reached for her glass of wine and began to tell her more details. "Yeah some slimy bastard phoned the benefits on me and Mike. They told them I was living with someone and that I was claiming as a single parent."

Susie looked uneasy. "No way did they? Did they tell you who it was?"

"Nar did they fuck. They just said they had a phone call from someone who wouldn't give their name." Susie lit a cig and tried to change the subject, but Helen was still on it and carried on with a sarcastic tone. "Whoever it was, will get what's coming to them. Trust me. What goes around comes around. An eye for an eye and all that." Susie agreed.

Susie had a text alert; she pulled her mobile from her pocket and read the message. It was from Ashley telling her he wouldn't be long. Shoving her phone out of the way she knew she'd have to get rid of Helen as soon as possible. With a concerned look on her face she spoke to her. "I'm so tired, every day since Tim's been in nick, I just can't find the strength to do anything. I mean he's been inside now for over six months hasn't he?"

Helen blew a hard breath from her mouth. "Wow is that how long he's been gone. Time's flying isn't it?"

Susie agreed. If she was truthful to herself, she was missing Tim and she was starting to realise just how much she loved him. Helen quickly looked up at the clock on the wall. "Right I better be off. Mike will be climbing the walls. I've been out ages all ready." Susie stood to her feet.

The sooner Helen was out of there the better.

"Thanks for telling me about Tim. I hope he sorts it all out. I'm going to be worrying all night now. I'll try ringing his mobile phone when I get in bed, hopefully it will be switched on." Helen didn't say much more. Walking down the garden path she said goodnight.

Susie lay in her bed. The quilt was stuck under her chin and she was cold. Checking her mobile again she sat worrying where Ashley was. He'd changed so much lately. He hardly ever rang her anymore and she was sure he was losing interest in her. Part of her was glad but the other part craved his attention. Switching the TV on Susie sat staring at the screen trying to watch a programme about giving birth. Her face went white as her hand felt the lower part of her stomach. Jumping from the bed she searched for a calendar. Flicking the white sheet over to the month before, she could see the date she had her last period. She'd drawn a ring around it. Her fingers touched every date as she counted the days. She was over two weeks late for her period. Sinking to the floor with the calendar in her hands she counted the days over and over again to make sure it was right. Susie was definitely late with her period.

The sound of something being thrown at the window could be heard. Someone was throwing stones at it. Diving up from the floor she could see Ashley stood in the back garden. He was waving his hands at her frantically. Grabbing a jumper from the side of the bed she threw it on and went downstairs to let him in.

"Where the fuck have you been? I've been ringing you for ages. You're not gonna believe what's happened."

Ashley barged past her and came inside the house. "I've been busy. I've not had chance to fart. Why what's up?"

"Come on let's get in bed and I'll tell you all about it. It's fucking freezing down here."

Ashley told her to go upstairs without him. He was moaning telling her he was starving and needed something to eat. Opening the fridge door he started moaning. "Fucking hell Susie, it's bare in here. When was the last time you went shopping?"

Susie was shouting as she went up the stairs to bed. "Come on stop moaning. We'll phone a Pizza from the takeaway if you're hungry."

Ashley slammed the fridge door shut and followed her up. Susie told Ashley about what Helen had told her. He looked shocked. "So are you saying Tim's having problems with Dom Jones in jail?"

"That's what Helen told me."

"Why the fuck is he involving me. When is the visit booked for?"

"I haven't booked a visit yet, but I'll do it for you tomorrow if you want?"

Ashley stripped off and jumped into the bed next to her. "Yeah book it for tomorrow. I'm gonna tell the prick once and for all. I'm sick of fighting his battles for him. I've got my own shit to deal with."

Susie could see his nostrils flaring at the side of her. Caressing his chest with her fingers she spoke in a low voice. "Ashley, I think I'm pregnant. I'm two weeks late for my period."

He bolted up from the bed. His eyes were staring at her and she looked scared. "Oh that's all I fucking need. If you are you'd better be getting rid of it. I don't want any bin-lids. I'm too young to be a dad."

Susie looked at him. Tears were forming in her eyes.

She was definitely hormonal. Never in a million years would she have been feeling like this unless she was pregnant. She looked weak as she spoke. "Why are you being so nasty to me?"

His head touched hers and he opened fire on her. "Nasty? Fucking hell, I only said, get rid of it. Don't tell me you wanna keep it?"

Susie knew she had to pull herself together and retaliated. "No I don't want it either, but it would have been nice for you to show some fucking support. Don't you give a fuck about me anymore?"

Ashley turned away from her and pulled the blankets over his head. "Stop fucking pecking my head will you? I'm tired, I'm going to sleep." Susie lay staring about the room. Her life was falling apart right in front of her eyes and there was nothing she could do to stop it.

CHAPTER FOURTEEN

Vicky sat on the chair re-reading Blake's prison letter. She'd written to him weeks before telling him it was over, but he was having none of it. He'd been phoning her constantly threatening to kill her if she didn't have him back. Blake meant every word he said. She looked pale and she feared for her life. Vicky's hands were shaking as she turned the white pages of his long letter. She was chewing on her fingernails. Blake told her his appeal was coming up soon and if he won it, he'd be back on the out. His solicitor was confident he would win his case and in each line of the letter he was telling her she was making the biggest mistake of her life. He was a crank.

Vicky held her body and rubbed her arms. Small goose pimples were appearing on them. This man was dangerous and she knew if he ever found out she'd been unfaithful he would slice her up. He'd told her so many times in the past, and she knew without any shadow of doubt that he would stick to his word. Blake was not to be messed with. If he couldn't get to her, she knew he'd get somebody to sort her out on his behalf. In the past Blake's mates had shaved the hair from some girl's head because she was fucking about with her boyfriend's head whilst he was in jail. Vicky knew they wouldn't think twice about doing the same thing to her. She gripped her hair and sighed.

Vicky was doing well now and she was the one organising all the drops inside the jail. The people she'd got involved with didn't seem to mind taking drugs into the nick. They were desperate people just like she was and they'd do anything just to earn an extra few quid. Vicky always made sure she paid them the going rate and never took them for granted. She was supplying most of Strangeways with drugs now and her life seemed to be on the up.

Vicky's appearance had changed completely. She looked amazing. Her hair was always neat and tidy and she even applied make-up to her face. Tim was in love with her. He'd told her so, the last time she'd visited him. If she was true to herself she loved him too. He made her heart race every time she looked at him. Vicky hadn't seen Susie for weeks. She was dreading bumping into her and knew the day would come pretty soon when she'd have to face her demons. Vicky was involved with Pippa and Joan. She'd been to the brass gaff lots of times and she got on well with both the women. Tim had phoned Joan and told her the script regarding Vicky. She loved it and enjoyed every moment of Susie's pain. Joan was no longer the underdog that Susie could walk all over. They all loved that she was getting a taste of her own medicine.

Vicky sat in the brothel. She was watching everything that was going on around her. Pippa was in the corner of the room and she could see her sat with her legs crossed talking on her mobile. Tapping her finger on the side of the table she could tell this woman was up to something. Sneaking over to where she sat, she hid away behind some boxes and listened to her conversation. With one ear held towards her, Vicky looked shocked and covered her mouth with both her hands. She could hear the conversation coming to an end and tiptoed back to her original seat. Pippa strolled back towards her. She could be seen smiling from cheek to cheek. "What are you so happy about?" Vicky giggled.

Pippa threw her hair back from her face and smirked. "I think I'm in love yanno."

Vicky screwed her face up. "Who with?" she sniggered. "You don't even have a fella?"

Pippa tapped the side of her nose with her long fingernail and chuckled. "Well that's where you're wrong sweetheart, Just because you don't see me with anyone in here, it doesn't mean I'm a loner."

"Yeah I know that but," Vicky mumbled.

"But nothing love, I do have a life outside these four walls you know." Pippa nodded her head at Vicky and continued. "I've been going strong with my man now for over a month."

Vicky knew her secret and was waiting for the right moment to tell her she was onto her. She sat upright and got herself ready to knock the smile right from Pippa's face. Vicky coughed and cleared her throat. "It's Ashley innit?"

Pippa nearly dropped down dead on the spot. Her face was white and she looked flustered. She gave a nervous laugh. "Ashley, you mean Tim's mate?"

Vicky nodded her head. "Yeah, you know exactly who I mean."

Vicky sat up and grabbed at Pippa's hand. She made sure no one was listening. "Listen love. I'm not arsed who you're sleeping with. Who am I to talk," she held her hands out in front of her. "I'm with Tim aren't I?"

Pippa was desperate to tell someone her secret and sat closer to Vicky. "You're right. I am with Ashley, but nobody's knows yet, so I need you to keep quiet until he tells his girlfriend."

Vicky chuckled and played with her hair. "Who do you mean, Susie?"

Pippa's eyes nearly popped out her head. She was gobsmacked. "How do you fucking know about her? Ashley said nobody knows."

Vicky moved closer to her. She was a conniving bitch. "Susie told me," she whispered.

Pippa looked blank. "How? When?" she gasped. Vicky told her all about how she met Susie and how she'd ripped her off. Pippa was hanging onto her every word. She knew Vicky was seeing Tim but she'd never asked any questions about how they first met. Tim had always had women when he was on the out and she just thought Vicky was one of his knock-offs. Pippa sat back in her chair and blew her breath. "Right I'm with you now, you've only just started seeing Tim. I thought you were seeing him before he got nicked."

Vicky shook her head. She leant closer towards her and whispered into her ear. "I grassed Susie up to Tim."

Pippa tilted her head to the side and twisted her fingers

in front of her. Vicky continued. "Susie's an evil cow. She thought I was a nob-head and that she could have me over. She doesn't deserve Tim anyway and I'm glad I told him she was shagging his best mate." Pippa looked at this young girl in more detail. She couldn't be trusted and she knew she would have to hold her cards close to her chest with her. This girl was out for what she could get and she didn't care who she hurt in the process.

Banging noises could be heard at the front door and both girls looked towards the camera. After studying it for a few minutes they realised it was Susie. Vicky swallowed hard and jumped to her feet. She looked frightened. "Where's Joan," she yelled. "Find fucking Joan."

Pippa sprang to her feet and ran out of the reception. "Joan, Joan," she was shouting at the top of her voice as she ran down the corridor. Vicky ran to the CCTV and just stared at it. "Fuck, fuck, fuck," she mumbled under her breath. Pippa bolted into Joan's office. It was dark and she was struggling to see. "Joan where the fuck are you?" she was screaming at the top of her voice. Pippa kicked hard at the toilet door. She could see Joan leant over the toilet smoking crack. Dragging at her hair she yanked her up from the floor. "Are you fucking right in the head? I thought you were off that shit?" Joan was off her head. She looked on another planet. Pippa dragged her to her feet. She was struggling to hold her up. "Susie's banging at the front door Joan. What the fuck are we going to do?" Joan was slurring her words and nothing she was saying was making any sense. Pippa dropped to the floor. She stood watching Joan trying to get back on her feet. "You're a waste of space you are Joan," she ranted as she ran back to the reception.

Susie swung the reception door open. Vicky had

pressed the button to let her in and she was sat down waiting for all hell to break loose. Susie's hair was all over the place as she walked in; she looked pissed out of her head. Pippa came back into reception and their eyes locked. You could see Pippa's chest rising frantically. Susie shot her a look and snarled. Vicky was sat on the sofa at the side of her and she was jerking her knees up and down. Once Susie saw her all hell broke loose. "What the fuck are you doing here? You little skank?" Vicky swallowed hard and you could see her face going red. Susie shouted into her face, and stood over her watching her like a hawk. "I said what are you doing here? Are you fucking deaf or summat?"

Pippa sprinted over to where Susie stood and nodded her head. Her nostrils were flaring and you could see her clenched fist at the side of her. "She's come to see me Susie. Have you got a problem with that?"

Susie spun her head around to face her. "How do you know Vicky? And what's she seeing you for?"

Vicky felt intimidated and sprung to her feet. She didn't need anyone to fight her battles. Her arms were held out swinging about in front of her face. "Ay gob-shite. Don't ask Pippa about me. I'm sat fucking right here."

Vicky's face was boiling with temper. Susie went nose to nose with her and they were close to fighting. "Who you calling a gob-shite? You fucking trollop."

Vicky pounced on Susie. She dug her nails deep into her face. The two women were going for it, but Vicky was fighting a losing battle. Pippa had to jump in to stop her getting hurt. She gripped Susie's hair and tossed her across the floor. Vicky was bleeding and blood was trickling from her nose. Susie looked shocked and struggled to get back to her feet. When she regained her balance she ran at Pippa with an evil look in her eyes. "Fucking slapper, come on then if you want a piece of me. Bring it on."

Pippa stood her ground as Susie ranted into her face. Pippa looked calm. "Listen Susie, if you want to fight me then let's have it. You don't scare me one little bit. Vicky's a fucking kid and you're taking liberties with her, there's no need for it. You need to get a grip." Susie was bouncing about the room. The other working girls were stood at the door watching the goings-on.

Susie snapped at them. "Right you lot. Get ya fucking stuff sorted out, and get the fuck out of here. As from now on Delia's is closed. Do you hear me, fucking closed."

Pippa growled. Her head was spinning round looking in all directions. The girls huffed and one of them stood with one hand on her hip as she spoke directly to Susie. "You can't close this place. It's our livelihood. You're fuck all to do with it anymore. Joan's running things now. So when she tells us it's over, that's when we'll go."

Susie screamed at the top of her voice. Spit hung from the corner of her mouth as she ran at the girls. She dragged the one who was talking and marched her back into the corridor. Susie could be seen pummelling her fist into her face. Vicky looked at Pippa. Her lips were trembling. "Where's Joan?"

Pippa held her hands out in front of her and hunched her shoulders. "She's fucked love; I've just left her in the office. She's been smoking crack again." Screams could be heard from the corridor and they both ran to see what was going on. Dragging the door open they both looked shocked. Joan had hold off Susie's hair from behind and she was dragging her all over the place. "You dirty crack-head. Get your fucking hands off me," Susie screamed. Joan looked demented. She looked like a woman possessed as she ragged Susie's body all over the place.

Susie was launched out of Delia's. It took five of them to get her down the stairs. She was kicking and screaming all the way to the exit. Joan stood tall as they watched Susie get up from the floor. She was livid as she spoke. "You think you're smart you lot. Just wait until Tim knows what's happened here. The lot of you will be out on your sorry arses."

Joan spat at her and pulled a small silver knife from her side pocket. The blade shone in the night and one girl covered her face as she saw it shining in her hand. Joan walked up to Susie and wafted the blade near her face. Susie backed away slowly as Joan gave her a piece of her mind. "Listen to me Susie. Tim's asked me to run things now. He doesn't want you anywhere near here. So deal with it. I swear, if I see you within an inch of this place, I'll slice you up good and proper. Do you hear me?"

Susie looked scared and nearly fell as she backed off. Her hair was all over the show and her blouse was ripped to shreds. Walking off into the night she shouted back at them one last time. "This is far from over Joan, mark my words, you'll get what's coming to you. You fucking whore."

Joan ran for her again, but Pippa held her back. "She's not worth it love. Just leave her." Joan was angry and stood shouting behind her. Susie didn't look back and kept walking.

The girls went back inside the brothel. Vicky looked white, she was trembling. She still had tissue hanging from her nose and blood was still pumping from it. Pippa held her arm as they went back upstairs. She looked like she was going to faint. "Are you okay love?"

Vicky sniffed hard and tears were forming in the corner of her eyes. "Yeah just a bit shocked that's all. Susie's off her fucking head. She was like a wild woman."

Pippa agreed with her. "Yeah she's got some serious issues. Good job Joan sorted her out wasn't it?" Vicky tried to smile but she was in severe pain. Heading into the reception Pippa led her into the bathroom. "Come on let's get you cleaned up."

Joan was pacing reception. She tried Tim on his phone but it was switched off. She was shivering and her lips were blue. Sitting down on a nearby chair she sat cracking her knuckles. "Fucking tart," she mumbled under her breath. Pippa came into view with Vicky walking slowly behind her. Joan sighed and shook her head. "We'll have to watch our backs now yanno. I don't trust Susie one little bit she's a snidey bitch."

Pippa pulled her cigarettes from her pocket and handed them out. As Vicky took one her hand was still shaking. Joan reached for her hand and rubbed at her bony fingers. "Vicky are you okay? I'm sorry I wasn't there straightaway."

Pippa scowled at Joan and coughed loudly. "You need to sort your shit out, you do," she raised her eyebrows at her as she took a deep drag of her cig. Pippa continued. "If you're smoking that shit again, I'm off out of here. Do you hear me? I'm gone. Seriously," she stared at her.

Joan was fidgeting, she looked edgy. Small droplets of sweat were visible on her forehead. She dropped her head and looked ashamed. "I'm sorry love. I'm trying my best. It's just when I get stressed out, I can't help myself."

"Like I said, sort it out Joan," Pippa huffed. She stubbed her cig out in the ashtray and left them both alone.

When she got into the toilet, Pippa pulled her mobile

from her pocket and dialled Ashley's number. When he didn't answer she texted him to tell him what had happened and told him to come and pick her up as soon as he was free.

Meanwhile Susie sat watching Delia's from afar. She was fuming and wanted revenge on the girls inside, especially Vicky and Joan. Who the fuck did they think they were talking to her like that? Hiding away in a bus shelter she could see the entrance to the brothel. The night was cold and she was jerking her legs up and down trying to keep warm. Her warm breath could be seen blowing out in front of her. Susie's eye looked swelled and you could see her hands holding one side of her face. She was in pain.

Looking at her mobile phone she decided to phone Ashley. He was the only person who could help her. She felt so alone. Listening to the ring tone for a few minutes she gave up trying. It was obvious he didn't want to speak to her. Usually he would pick his phone up straightaway. Susie now held herself back in the shadows of the bus shelter. She could see the front door of Delia's opening slightly. Vicky could be seen leaving. She talked to Pippa for a few minutes before she left after they gave each other a quick hug. Pippa was still stood at the door scanning the area. Susie stood to her feet and pulled her black coat tightly around her body. Dipping her head she was about to follow Vicky. Susie paused. She looked frozen. She could now see Ashley's car pulling up not far from where she was stood. She watched him sitting in the car park and she could see he was on his mobile. Stepping out onto the road she was just about to run over to the car when she saw Pippa coming out of the brothel. Sliding back into the shadows she watched on.

The brass jumped into the car with Ashley. She watched him pull her towards him and kiss her passionately. Susie melted to the floor as she covered her mouth with her hands. Her breathing was rapid and she was struggling for breath. Watching them pull out of the car park she hid away from their view. Her hands now cradled her stomach and tears ran down her face. Ashley's baby was growing inside her and she felt suffocated as she fell onto the cold floor. "Bastards," she sobbed as she punched her clenched fist onto the plastic bus shelter.

Susie knew she was in no condition to confront them both. She needed to go away and think it through. Ashley thought he was having one over on her and she wanted to make sure she wiped that smile right off his face. Pulling herself up from the ground she wiped her nose with her sleeve. Heading from the bus-stop she started to make her way to her car parked in a nearby side street. Tomorrow was another day and once she'd slept on it she was sure her mind would be full of plans to pay the lot of them back, especially Ashley.

CHAPTER FIFTEEN

Susie lay wide awake in her bed as the morning light broke through her bedroom window. Her face felt swelled and sore. She looked sad lying there just staring into space. Rolling slowly about the bed she reached for her mobile phone. Scrolling down the contact numbers she stopped as she came to Tim's name. Lifting her head up, she focused at the clock on the wall. Tim would have his phone on at this time surely. Susie was desperate to speak to him. Taking a deep breath she pressed the green button to start the call.

Susie looked in pain as she sat up in the bed. "Hi baby it's me Susie." Her feet were curling up at the end of the bed as she fidgeted about trying to get comfortable. Her tone was low as she spoke to her boyfriend. "Yeah I know Tim. I'm coming to see you soon. I've just had loads to do. You know how it is, don't you?" Susie was listening to Tim and she kept rolling her eyes. "Yeah I know. Listen I'll book a visit for two o'clock today. We can sort it out then." The phone call lasted a few more minutes and she finally said goodbye. "Arse-hole," she mumbled under her breath. Sighing, she fell back onto the bed. Reaching for the remote for the TV she flicked through the channels looking for something to watch. The sound of her phone ringing could be heard. Pulling the covers from the bed Susie searched all over for it. "Where the fuck is it?" she moaned. She was throwing the duvet all over the place. Finally she found it. Ashley's name was on the screen flashing. She scowled as she answered it. "What do you want?" she answered angrily. Susie stood up from the bed and her face was going red as she raised her voice. "Nar, you should have been here last night. You can't just come here when you feel like a leg-over." Susie shook her head as she listened to him talking his way out of it. Her eyes were raised to the ceiling. "Yeah alright, I'll see you in five minutes. Just come in the back way. The door's already open."

Susie looked white in the face and gripped her throat with one hand. Covering her mouth she sprinted to the bathroom. Her cheeks suddenly filled out. The sound of retching could be heard. Susie's head was hung over the toilet bowl and yellow liquid was pumping out of her mouth. Lifting her head up every now and then she looked like she was struggling to breathe.

"Susie where are you?" Ashley shouted as he climbed the stairs.

Standing behind the bathroom door she yelled back to him. "I won't be a minute I'm just getting a wash. Go in the bedroom." His footsteps could be heard going past the door. Susie wafted her hands in front of her face. She was hot and flustered. Walking to the mirror she could see her skin had changed to a light grey colour. Bringing her hands up to her cheeks she slowly slapped at them trying to bring some normality back to her face. She didn't look well. Dragging her hair from her face she grabbed a hairgrip from the side of the sink and tied her hair back. Susie ran some cold water into the sink and started to splash it all over her face.

With her head still stuck in it she could hear Ashley shouting her from outside the door. "What are you doing in there? Fucking hurry up, I need a piss."

Susie lifted her head up and reached for a towel. Patting it on her wet skin she replied. "Hold you're fucking horses, I'm coming now."

Opening the bathroom door with the towel still covering her face Ashley walked inside. Unzipping his jeans quickly he stood pissing at the side of her. "Phew, I needed that," he sighed. Susie's eyes darted into him. She could see his manhood from where she stood and knew without any doubt in her mind that it had been stuck up Pippa all night long. Susie coughed and stared at him. Sitting on the edge of the bath she casually swung her legs out in front of her. Her face was cocky as she licked her lips.

"So come on then, where were you last night." Ashley shook his penis and zipped his jeans up. He looked agitated. Following him into the bedroom she was still interrogating him. "Are you ignoring me or what?"

Ashley turned his head back to her and shot her a look and sniffed hard, she knew he was ready for snapping. His teeth were gritted together and she could see the vein in the side of his neck pumping. He was close to breaking point. "I was out with my mates," he groaned.

"Fucking hell, am I not allowed a life now?" Susie retaliated. "Oh you've changed your fucking tune, it was only last week when you was up my arse telling me you wanted to be with me twenty- four- seven." She was pacing around the bedroom kicking things on the floor.

Ashley came up behind her and dragged her by the hair. He was in her face. "Don't get lippy bitch, perhaps I've got sick of your shite and moved on. How about that?" He spat into her eyes. Susie was trying to break free; she was kicking her legs out in front of her. Her body looked weak and she was fighting a losing battle. Ashley threw her onto the bed like a rag doll and stood in front of her. Jumping back up from the bed she spat into his face.

"Well fuck off back to where you were last night then. Don't be coming round here chatting shit to me."

Ashley chuckled menacingly. Gripping her face in his hands his knuckles were turning white, he squeezed her cheeks together. "Orr did you miss me. Come here and give me a kiss then." Ashley's moods switched like the weather and she knew she would have to back down otherwise he would have kicked the living daylights out of her. The sound of lips smacking together could be heard. Susie cringed as he stuck his tongue into her mouth. Her nostrils were flaring as she inhaled deeply, she could smell perfume all over his body. Pushing him away with a firm hand she sat on the bed.

"I'm going to see Tim later." She watched his face and not one bit of emotion was visible. She nudged him in the waist. "Are you listening to me? I said I'm going to see Tim later."

Ashley turned to face her. Cupping his hands under his chin he looked at her. "Does this face look like it gives a fuck? Do what you want, I'm not arsed anymore. I'm sick of waiting about for you."

Susie's eyes welled up. She wasn't usually this emotional but she couldn't control it. Tears trickled down her face. Ashley looked at her and shook his head. "Fucking hell, what have I said now?" Susie dropped her head into her hands and sobbed. Her shoulders were shaking up and down and finally he comforted her. "Why you crying love?" lifting her head up she stared deep into his eyes.

Taking a minute to find her words she spoke. "I'm hormonal I think."

Ashley bolted up from the bed. Dragging his fingers through his hair he stood at the window. "Right you better get it sorted. I've told you before I don't want no bin lids running about. You need to get rid as soon as possible. How much is an abortion?"

Susie bit hard on her knuckles. She stood up and walked to his side slowly. "Is that what you want, for me to get an abortion? I thought you loved me?"

Ashley held his head back and laughed. "I love everyone me darling. I've told you I don't want a baby." He leant on the windowsill and sniggered. "Me, having kids! Are you having a laugh or what? You can get that fucking daft idea right out of your head."

Digging in his pockets he pulled out a wad of cash. Quickly counting it in his hands he threw it onto the bed with a flick of his wrist. "There's about five ton there, get it sorted." Silence filled the bedroom and Susie plonked herself back on the bed. Touching the money with her fingertips she gathered it together and placed it on the side.

Ashley was stood next to her, he looked edgy. Cracking his knuckles he blew a deep breath. "Right I'm getting off. I've got some graft to do today with Duggy, and Jethro."

Susie looked deflated as she replied. "Why, what's going down? You haven't worked with them two for ages."

Ashley tilted his head to the side and nodded. He could see himself in the mirror not far from him and stroked his chin slowly as he answered her. "They're meeting some big- head from Cheetham Hill. He's got some brown for sale and if it all goes to plan we should be in for a right few quid."

Susie was up in arms. "Fucking hell Ashley, why are you getting mixed up with heroin? Just do your normal grafts. You don't wanna get caught up in all that do you?"

His eye lids flickered rapidly. With his hands waving in front of him he shouted at her. "Why are you so concerned all of a sudden? You usually don't give a flying fuck."

Susie huffed as Ashley eyes pierced into her. "I'm just saying, that's all. Do what you fucking want then, I'm not arsed." Flicking her hair back from her shoulders she listened to the details of the job. Her face changed. Gripping the money from the side of the bed she stroked every note with her long talons. "Well I better get myself sorted then, hadn't I?"

Ashley nodded, and sprung up from the bed.

Checking his watch he looked at her and squeezed his crotch. "Right I'm off. Do you fancy a quick shag before I have to go or what?" He was pulling her legs apart and pouncing on top of her. Before she knew it he was inside her. She looked in pain. As he mounted her she started to tell him about the troubles at Delia's. He looked angry as he placed his flat palm over her mouth. "Will you shut the fuck up? Here's me trying to bone you and you're chatting away as if we're just sat talking. Fucking concentrate will you?" Susie's eyes closed and she made a few noises but she was faking it. Ashley's arse could be seen moving up and down now like a fiddler's elbow, and by the look on his face he was ready to shoot his load. Ashley's face looked like a pig in a fit as he found heaven. Susie just lay underneath him and watched his face screw up. His eyes were closed and his nostrils were flaring. Once he'd finished he rolled from her body and sighed.

"Just what the doctor ordered that was." Susie had to bite her tongue. She was ready to tell him that she knew about Pippa. Her fingers gripped the white sheets on the mattress and her eyes were closed tightly together. Her mouth was moving, but no sound was coming out. Lighting two cigs he passed her one. The sound of him inhaling the nicotine could be heard. Both his cheeks were sucked in at the side. Susie watched him with wide eyes. The bastard thought he was God's gift! He patted his stomach. "I better get back to the gym later. I'm piling the weight on, aren't I?"

Susie looked at his lean body. She knew exactly what she was doing as she replied to him. "Yeah I thought you'd put weight on but I didn't like saying."

He bolted upright. "You cheeky cunt. What do you mean?"

Susie knew she'd struck gold and watched his face drop. She could see him breathing in and out now and patting his chest. She smiled at him. "You were the one who said you'd put weight on, not me. I was just agreeing with you." He was in a strop now and slid out of bed. Pulling his jeans back on he stood up in the full- length mirror. He was turning from side to side and you could see his cheeks sucking in and out as he checked out his physique. Turning his head back to her he sniggered.

"Fat, my arse. I'm all muscle me."

Susie sighed as she watched him flexing his arms in the mirror. "Posing fucker," she whispered under her breath.

Ashley left once he'd had a wash. He was in a hurry. Standing at the window she watched him get into his car. The music could be heard pumping as soon as he got inside it. Susie froze for a moment. Pulling the curtain back slightly she could see him driving away. Cradling her hand on her stomach she looked in deep thought. Quickly she ran back to the bed and grabbed her phone. Holding it to her ear she looked scared. Her lips were trembling. "Hello police please. I would like to report a big drugs deal that's happening today." Susie was on the phone for at least five minutes. She told the police every bit of information she knew about Ashley's dodgy deal. As she finished the call she nodded her head. Her voice was low as she whispered to herself. "Let's see who the smart arse is now, prick." Her face held a cunning look as she started to get ready.

Susie sat waiting in the visitors' centre at Strangeways prison. It had been ages since she'd been to see Tim. She looked tired and her usual fashion sense had gone right out of the window. She looked as rough as a bear's arse. Her lips were still swollen and she hoped as soon as Tim saw the state of her face he would close Delia's down and make sure Joan was dealt with good and proper.

Looking about the room nothing had changed much. The walls were still depressing and a few pictures hung on them that inmates had painted. Kids still ran about the centre and nobody seemed to care about life any more. The names were soon called for the visits. All the visitors made their way to the main prison for the normal searches.

Waiting patiently at the top of the stairs Susie could see the visiting room. The inmates were sat there waiting eagerly. A screw now came to let them inside. Susie's face changed as she saw it was Jenkins who was opening the door. Pulling at her clothes she stood tall. She was coughing.

Visitors pushed past each other to get to the convicts. Every minute was precious to them. Susie stood in front of Jenkins. Their eyes locked. Making sure no one was listening he whispered to her as he slid past her. "I want to see you tonight. I want this shit over and done with okay?"

"No worries I'll phone you later," Susie nodded. As she walked to Tim's table she turned her head back over her shoulder and she could see the screw looking flustered. "Dirty twat," she mumbled under her breath as she walked further into the prison.

Tim was fidgeting nervously as she walked over, he looked agitated. "So, to what do I owe the honour?" he asked sarcastically. Susie pulled her coat from her body and hung it on the back of her chair. Turning back to face him, she smiled. Tim noticed her bruised lips and shook his head. "Is that what Joan did?" he asked.

Susie gasped, "Has she already been in touch with you telling her side of the story?" He nodded. Susie's eyes welled up. Reaching over she tried to touch his hands but he pulled away. He couldn't look at her. Dipping her head she knew she'd lost Tim for good. It was all her own doing and she knew that more than anyone. Licking her dry lips slowly she spoke. "Do you want a brew?" Tim nodded.

"Yeah get me a coffee and some choccy biscuits." Standing to her feet she went to join the queue for food. Tim looked at her in amazement. This was so out of character for her. She was being too nice.

Jenkins could be seen walking towards Tim. Their eyes locked and they grinned at each other. Tim dropped his head into his hands as he walked past.

Susie sighed as she sat back down in her chair. Placing the cups on the table she slid one towards Tim. She looked exhausted and her hands were shaking. Tim slouched back in his chair and scanned her face. He could see she wasn't herself. "You look rough." Susie stared at him and tears fell onto her cheek. Tim struggled to hold back his emotions and just did what came naturally to him. Grabbing her hands he tried to comfort her. "Ay what's all this about. This isn't like you."

She snivelled and wiped her tears away with her hands. "Tim I'm sorry. I've been a right bitch since you've been in here. It's just all got too much for me."

He shook his head. "I know, I know," he whispered. Susie picked at her fingernails as she looked at Tim. He was unsure of her and was waiting for the usual nasty Susie to return. Leaning over the table she spoke in a low voice. "Tim, can we start again?"

She looked sincere. Tim was huffing and puffing. He was finding it hard to keep still. "Susie you haven't been to see me in moons. What do you expect? It just seems to me that since the money has stopped you want to play the devoted girlfriend." He rocked back in his chair and rubbed at his crotch. "I needed you Susie and you left me to rot in here. You didn't give a flying fuck about me."

She snapped as she tried to reach his hands. Tim pushed her away as she pleaded with him. "I didn't leave you to rot. I was sorting out all the shit for you on the out." Her hands were all over the place now and she was dragging at her hair in desperation. "You left me to cope on my own Tim. It's hard, yanno." He yawned and stretched his arms over his head. She looked stressed as she stretched over the table towards him. "I want my old life back, and I want you back too."

Tim was gobsmacked. Blowing his breath he gritted his teeth together. Making sure no one could hear him he snarled at her. "What's up? Has Ashley fucked you off now?"

The colour drained from her face, she was stuttering. "What do you mean has Ashley fucked me off?" Tim realised what he'd said and backpedalled. There was no way he wanted her to know he knew about her sordid affair with his best mate.

He calmed down and sipped at his brew. His fingers were tapping on the table. "I mean Ashley was helping you out wasn't he, has he fucked you off now?" Susie looked relieved. She was off the hook. She didn't have a clue he was onto her.

"Yeah he's a full time prick, a complete waste of space." Tim's eyes were all over the prison he wasn't listening to a word she said. He was constantly scanning the area. A few lads were getting drops in today and he hoped the drugs got in without any problems. Seeing one inmate on a table not far from him he started to relax. The convict winked at Tim and nodded his head slowly, the drugs were in. At least now he could make a few quid when the parcel got back to the landing.

Tim was one of the top suppliers in the jail now thanks to Jenkins, and everyone was up his arse. He was the main man on his wing. Sipping his coffee from a white plastic cup he looked at Susie in more detail. At that moment he knew he didn't love her anymore. She was an evil self- centred bitch and he planned to hurt her, just like she'd hurt him.

Susie pleaded with Tim throughout the visit but although he knew in his heart she was sorry, he was done with her. Vicky was his girl now and Susie was his past. Pulling Susie closer he whispered into her ear. "Right I need you bringing some parcels in here for me."

Her eyes opened wide and her mouth dropped. "What, me bring drugs in jail, are you being serious, I've already sorted it so Jenkins lets the drugs in here, so why do you need me involved?"

Tim nodded. "I can't afford to pay anyone anymore so it's up to you to do it. I'm on my arse in here and need to make a crust." He was lying through his teeth. Tim was raking the cash in and he was never short of anything. Everyone was his mate in the jail and he could get anything he wanted for a few bags of smack. Susie looked deflated, dropping her head onto her folded arms she rested there for a few seconds. Raising her head up, she shot a look at Tim.

"Right I'll do it."

Tim rubbed his palms together. He was right after all, Susie would do anything to earn a bit of money. She was playing right into his hands and he smiled back at her. Licking his teeth slowly he looked happy. "Good girl. We both can earn a bit of cash now can't we?"

Susie raised a struggled smile back at him. "Hopefully," she said.

The screw Jenkins was at the table. "Finish your visits now please," he shouted in a loud firm voice. Patting Tim on his shoulder he walked to the next table.

"No worries boss," Tim replied as he walked by. Susie kept her eyes low and tried not to look at the officer. She was an evil bitch and she deserved everything that was coming to her.

CHAPTER SIXTEEN

Susie stood on the corner of Rochdale Road. Once a passing car honked its horn at her she ran back to her car. Jumping in her vehicle she quickly pulled out of the car park. The male driver of the other car was pulling over with his hazard lights flashing at the side of the road. Driving next to it Susie made the driver aware she was ready for him to follow her. Both cars drove up Rochdale Road.

Susie turned her music down and stared in her rear-view mirror. She could see Jenkins driving up her arse. He looked serious. Turning her music down, she headed up Charlestown Road and made her way to the park up there. Boggart Hole Clough would be deserted at this time of the night. It was an ideal place to carry out her business. Turning the heating on full she struggled to keep warm.

As predicted the park was empty. The lighting was poor and nothing but one dimly lit street light, lit up the area. Susie pulled up and turned her engine off. Her chest was rising at speed and she looked nervous. The sound of a car door slamming could be heard. Twisting her head over the passenger seat she could see Jenkins approaching.

Paul Jenkins was thirty- two years of age. He's been a screw for over five years at Strangeways prison. He loved his job and his wife. The woman he was meeting was ruining his life and he wanted it to stop as soon as possible. His home life had been struggled during the last few months. He and his wife Julie had lost their son to cot death. She was suffering from depression at the moment and any sex with him was a million miles away from her mind. Visiting Delia's was just a one- off for him. He was a man with needs and paying a brass for sex was so out of character for him. His mate James was the one to blame for his downfall and he regretted ever telling him he was going short of sex at home. Paul was just caught up in the moment and only agreed to sleep with a prostitute to look the big man in front of his mate.

Jenkins looked angry as he dragged the car door open. Darting his eyes at Susie he looked like he was going to do her in there and then. Pulling the car door shut he turned to face Susie. You could tell he'd prepared a speech before he joined her. Paul was a good- looking man and if Susie wasn't up shit- Street she would have seriously thought about shagging his brains out. Tapping her fingers on the steering wheel she waited for him to begin. Paul sniffed hard and banged his hand on the dashboard. "Right just tell me what you want from me, I can't do this anymore. You've already had over two thousand pounds from me."

He looked stressed and he was close to tears. Susie smirked. Looking into her rear-view mirror she straightened her hair. "I don't want any more money love…"

"Thank fuck for that, because I haven't got any."

Susie chuckled. Taking a deep breath she turned to face him. "I need to get some more parcels into the jail."

Paul shook his head. This was putting his job on the line and if he was caught he could end up in jail too. "Are you joking?"

"Nope, I'm being deadly serious."

Paul dropped his head into his hands. "This is my life you're messing about with, you stupid bitch." He stretched his body over to her and yanked at her clothes. Pulling her closer he screamed into her face. "You're a grabbing bitch. You're ruining my life. I have a wife you know."

Susie yanked herself from his grip and pushed him away. "You should have thought about that before you started paying for sex."

Tears filled Paul's eyes as he punched his fist onto the dashboard. Gritting his teeth he turned his head to her. Quickly checking the area he grabbed her by the throat and started to squeeze it hard. Susie was struggling to breathe and her legs were kicking hard under the steering wheel. His warm breath was on her face. "See that's how easy it is to do you in. Nobody would miss you. I could take you over to the bushes and leave your sorry arse to rot." He scanned the area for signs of life. He was definitely thinking of killing her. Suddenly his face changed and he fell back onto his seat. His hands were shaking. Lifting them up to his eyes he screamed out. "Look what you have made me. I'm not a violent man, but you're making me do this."

Susie gasped for breath. Opening the door she fell forward and started vomiting. Paul jumped out of the car and ran to her side. As she spewed up he rubbed her back. "I'm sorry, I'm sorry," he moaned.

Susie was taking in deep breaths and panting like a dog. Once she'd recovered she jumped back in the car. Holding her neck she looked at Jenkins at the side of her. "Get back in the car, prick."

Paul trudged back to the other side of the car. Jumping back in, he stared at her. "Right I'll sort it. But I want the photos you took, this ends here, do you hear me, this is the last time."

Susie was still trying to find her breath. Coughing loudly she nodded. "Once I get a few parcels inside the nick, then you can have the photographs."

"Listen, you conniving bitch. You can do the drops but I want the pictures before I sort anything out. I mean, how do I know I can trust you."

Susie giggled as she pressed the button to open the window. "You can trust me mate. Do I look like someone who would have you over?"

Paul reached in his jacket pocket. Grabbing a cigarette he searched for his lighter. Flicking it, he stuck his head down towards the flame and sucked his cheeks in. His mouth blew the smoke into Susie's eyes. Wafting her hands she choked. Everything was making her feel sick these days and if this was what it was like to be pregnant she wanted the baby out of her as soon as possible.

"Right I'm gonna be in the jail over the next few months," Susie continued, "I just need to do a few drops then all of this nightmare will be over for you. I need you to watch my back and tell me the best days to come and where to sit."

Paul huffed and blew a struggled breath. After a few minutes he agreed. Gripping the handle to open the car door he turned his head to her before he left. "I want those photos. If you think for one minute you can blackmail me forever, think again. Because if this doesn't stop soon. I'll do you in. Do you hear me? I'll kill you."

Susie smiled at him. Inside she was shitting her knickers but she had to keep a straight face. "I've told you Paul, you scratch my back and I'll scratch yours." He was gone. Susie was panting. Rubbing her neck she clicked the central locking. Jenkins was a mad man and she knew she'd pushed him too far this time. Watching him pull away from the car park she turned her engine on. Susie's face was on fire and she had to open the car window. Driving along the cold night air blew onto her face.

Susie drove down Moston Lane and the aroma of the takeaways filtered into the car. She'd not eaten a scrap all day. Pulling over at Pizza Lane she grabbed her handbag from the back seat. Heading inside she scanned the menu and licked her lips. There were a few people in the shop and she didn't notice Tim's sister Helen sat on the chair in the corner of the shop. Susie walked to the counter and waited for the Asian man to come and take her order. Leaning on the counter she tapped her nails on the surface. Once the bearded Asian stood in front of her, she reeled off her hearts desires. "Can I have a Doner kebab in a Nan bread with chilli sauce on it, and one lot of chips please."

The man was writing her request on a small piece of white paper in front of him. "Is that it," he asked.

Susie cast her eyes on the large menu board. "Nope, can I have a portion of onion bhajis and a can of Coke as well please?" The assistant left her side and shouted in a foreign language to his co-worker. Susie backed away from the counter and stood at the back wall of the shop.

"You'll end up like me if you carry on eating like that!"

Susie twisted her head to look for the familiar voice. Once she saw Helen she smirked. Helen wasn't that bad she thought and after all she needed cheering up. She plodded over to her. "See, you're still on the eat all you can diet."

Helen held her belly as she chuckled. "Yep you know me. I can't be arsed with all that dieting anyway. I'm fat and that's the end of it. Why should I be hungry and sad all the fucking time?"

The two men at the side of them giggled. One of them agreed with Helen and patted the middle of her arm. "That's right, cock. You eat what ya want. Fuck all them skinny cows, us men love a woman who has a bit of meat on them, don't we Eddie?"

His mate was laughing out loud as he answered him. "Correct mate. You don't look at the mantelpiece when ya poking the fire." The two men were pissed out of their heads and they were both swaying about as they waited for their food. Helen had a bit of banter with them and they finally left the shop carrying their food.

Helen leant forward and rested her elbows on her knees. With a gasping breath she spoke. "So what's new with you?"

Susie now dropped her handbag on the floor. "Nowt really, just a bit pissed off lately that's all."

Helen looked shocked. "What do you have to be pissed off about Lady Muck, you have everything. It's me who should be fed up. I mean, no job, crying kids. Do I need to go on?" Lifting her eyes to the ceiling she sat back in her chair. "Come on then tell me what's up?" Susie was cagey at first but after a few minutes she filled her in about the trouble at Delia's. "Fucking hell," Helen gasped. She knew exactly what had gone on but acted like she didn't have a clue. "So Tim has had you flung out of there for good?"

Helen tried to hide a smirk as she asked more questions. "Yep Tim has carted me. I went to see him today though, so hopefully I'll be back in his circle of trust pretty soon."

Helen cupped her hands together and rested them under her chin. "So how are you doing for money then? I mean you won't have any cash coming in now will you?"

Susie tapped the side of her nose and giggled. "I've got a few tricks up my sleeve, so hopefully I'll be back on track pretty soon." Helen screwed her face up; you could tell she hated the thought of Susie getting back on her feet. Susie's order was ready.

The assistant placed a brown paper bag on the counter and read out the order. Standing to her feet Susie went and paid for her food. Helen's order was ready now too and she stood at the side of Susie patting her stomach. "Oh I'm gonna enjoy this scran, I'm starving," she chuckled. Once they'd both paid they walked outside together into the night air. There was silence for a minute and they both looked uncomfortable. "Any chance of a lift home, or what?" Helen said finally.

"Fucking hell, some things never change do they? Come on then, jump in." Susie sighed. Helen held onto her food for dear life as she opened the passenger door. Susie placed her food neatly on the back seat and joined her in the front. Helen had made a hole in her wrapper and was pulling out long pieces of meat through the gap she'd made in the paper.

"Just wait until you get in, you starver." Helen ignored her and carried on stuffing her face.

The roads were quiet; the only sound you could hear was Helen munching on her food. Susie headed to drop Helen off. Sat waiting at the traffic lights she spoke to her. "Why don't you come on a visit to see Tim? I bet he would love to see you."

Helen nearly choked. Spluttering, she stuttered her words. "Yeah I would love to see our kid. Just give me a shout when you're going and I'll sort the kids out with a babysitter." Helen was buzzing, she sat nodding her head. "I've not been to see anyone in nick for years," her eyes shot over to Susie who was driving. "Ay, I could have got slammed when the benefits were on my case. Good job I got off with it innit, otherwise you might have been visiting me too," she cackled but she was still watching Susie's face to see if she showed any sign of being the snitch. Susie completely ignored her; she looked like she was thinking.

Pulling up outside Helen's house she could see every light on inside it. Helen blew her breath as she grabbed her food from the floor. "Fucking hell, it's like Blackpool illuminations in there. Why do they need every fucking light on in the house?"

Susie giggled. "I bet your electric bills are sky-high?"

Helen nodded and leant closer to her. "We have it on the fiddle, even the gas too. Fuck that, I couldn't afford to pay them big bills."

Susie shook her head in disbelief. This woman didn't have an ounce of shame. "If you want, I can rig yours up too. It won't take me long," Helen offered.

"No you're alright," Susie replied.

"Well if you ever change your mind, just give me a shout. I've done loads of people's on the estate. I only charge fifty quid."

Susie knew Helen would sell her own mother to earn a few quid. "Right I'm gonna get off. I'll be in touch about the visit as soon as you've booked it. Is that okay?" she said as she lumbered out of the car clutching her food.

"Yep, no worries." Susie giggled to herself as she saw Helen yanking her trackie bottoms up as she walked away. You could almost see the cheeks of her arse. "Fucking skank," Susie said.

CHAPTER SEVENTEEN

Days passed and Vicky was doing everything she could to get by. As she in lay in bed with her son, her face looked tired. Her eyes seemed heavy and the amount of cigs she was now smoking was visible on her face.

Declan was lying beside his mother in bed. He was kicking his legs up and down and pulling the blankets from her body as the morning light streamed in through the window. "Stop it ya little nob-head," Vicky growled at him. Turning over to face the wall he was still jumping all over her body. "For fuck sake, if you jump on me one more time, you can get in your own bed." The child was still bouncing about and her face went red with anger, she was losing her patience. Jumping up from the mattress she dragged him by the scruff of the neck. He was moaning and trying to fight her off. "Don't you ever listen to a word I say?" she screamed.

Vicky was carrying him back into his bedroom now. "Bitch, bastard," he yelled at the top of his voice. Throwing him onto his bed by one and arm and leg she turned and walked out of the room. One of his toys just missed her head as she slammed the door shut behind her.

Vicky was at her wits end. She hadn't been getting much sleep lately. Tim was always on the phone until late and last night was no different, she didn't get asleep until three in the morning. Tim had told her about his visit with Susie and she was unsure of how to feel anymore about their relationship. He'd told her point-blank that he and Susie were more than over but she had a gut feeling he was lying to her. All he seemed to do these days was to ask her to talk dirty down the phone to him. She didn't mind it at first but it was boring her now. Vicky was all about earning some decent cash and tried to put her feelings for Tim to the back of her mind.

Diving back in the bed Vicky tried to warm herself. Her skin was cold and small goose pimples were visible on her pale arms. Her legs could be seen rummaging about under the covers. The sound of her son's high pitched screams caused her to hide her head under the blankets further. "Shut up, shut up," she gasped under her breath. Vicky knew he would be back in her room pretty soon and made sure she wasn't in view. All of her body was covered with the blankets. The sound of him kicking his bedroom door could be heard throughout the house and the usual abuse he gave her was filtering through the walls. Vicky lifted her head up from the covers after a few minutes. It was quiet. Holding her ear to the door she listened carefully with a look of concern on her face. Her body fell back onto the bed. Her mind was doing overtime and she remembered the last time she'd left him after a tantrum that he'd smeared her nail polish all over the walls.

Jumping to her feet she yelled his name. "Declan, what are you up to? If you're fucking about, again, I'm gonna smack your arse until its red raw." There was still no reply. Pushing the bedroom door open slowly she could see him sat on his bed with a smile on his face. Her eyes shot about the bedroom. The window was opened fully and the curtain was blowing wildly from it. She screwed her face up at him. Vicky clenched her fist and was getting ready to pummel him. He'd pushed her too far this time.

As she headed towards him he shouted out in a giddy voice. "Daddy's here!"

Vicky shook her head and walked to his bedside. "I'm sick to death of you, you're gonna get it now." The sound of the bedroom door shutting behind her made her turn her head. Her face was white and she lost her balance and fell onto the bed.

"Blake," she gasped. Her breathing was rapid and her chest was moving up and down frantically. "How did you get in here?" she stuttered. Blake just looked at her and nodded his head, he looked disturbed.

Vicky bolted up from the bed and stood tall; she had to show him she wasn't scared. She gripped her son in her arms and pierced her eyes into his face. Blake looked demented, his look was frightening her. Her breathing was struggled and Declan was trying to break free to get to his dad. Blake bent his legs down and held his hands out to his son. "Come on then lad, let's have a cuddle." Declan wriggled free from his mother's arms and ran towards his father. Vicky was left feeling vulnerable; she was an easy target now. Pulling her t-shirt over her legs you could see she was cold, her legs were purple. Her lips were trembling as she spoke.

"What are you doing here, Blake?"

He picked his son up from the floor. Swinging him round by his body he darted his eyes into her. He was gritting his teeth. "I'm here to get my family back. I told you I would come for you didn't I?" he snapped

Vicky sighed. "Blake you've broken into my house. I'm going to phone the police if you don't leave. I've told you before, it's over between us." She sat cracking her knuckles, her lips looked dry as she slowly slid her tongue over them. Blake coughed and put his son back to the floor.

Opening the door he told him to go downstairs to get some biscuits. Declan was toddling past him without a care in the world. "Do you want a biscuit daddy?" Blake smirked at him and nodded. Declan could be seen walking down the stairs. Vicky knew she was in deep shit.

"So, let's get this sorted then." Blake moved towards her and sat on the edge of the bed by her side. Her legs were jerking up and down and she knew by his face she was in serious danger. Standing to her feet she tried to walk past him. His face screwed up as one of his hands grabbed at her. You could see white patches appearing on her skin as his grip tightened. "Sit fucking down there, you stupid cow." He grinded his teeth together and dragged her back onto the bed. Her head swung to the side as his fist pummelled into the side of her face. Blood spurted from her nose as his fist connected. Vicky tried to scream but it was no good. His large hands reached over her mouth as his teeth bit into her cheeks. "Did you think you could just treat me like a prick, and think you would get away with it? I told you I'd be back, you daft slag." His fist was pounding into her body.

The sound of Declan bouncing back up the stairs could be heard. Blake spat into her face and jumped up from her body. The door opened and Declan was stood with a handful of biscuits. The side of his mouth was covered in chocolate and he was speaking with a mouthful of food. "Why's my mummy crying?" he walked nearer to Vicky. "What's all that red over your face, mummy?" Blake quickly dragged the white sheet from the bed and covered Vicky's face.

"Get cleaned up," he whispered. Vicky was trembling and her hands were shaking as the white cotton sheet filled with the pumping blood from her nose. The sound of her mobile ringing from the other room could be heard. "I'll get it mummy," Declan shouted. Vicky's face dropped. Her mouth was open but no words were coming out. It was too late he was gone.

Declan walked back into the bedroom. The phone had stopped ringing. Walking towards her he held the phone out, Blake gripped it. "Thanks Son." Looking at Vicky he held a menacing look in his eyes. His fingers pressed the button on the phone. As he flicked down the messages he raised his eyes towards her. Sliding down onto the floor, you could see him going through all her text messages. Blake was biting down on his lip and you could see his fist clenching. His head lifted up and he stared at her nodding his head.

"Declan you go and put a film on downstairs. Daddy wants to talk to mummy for a while."

Vicky jumped up from the bed. She knew if she let her child go she would be in big trouble. "No," she screamed.

"He can't turn the telly on himself. I'll have to do it for him." Picking Declan up in her arms she held him close to her body. Blake bolted up from the floor and was right beside her. His eyes were all over the place and he was making sure there was no escape for his cheating girlfriend. The mobile phone was still held tightly in his grip.

Walking into the front room, Vicky opened the curtains. Casting her eyes out of the window she hoped she would see someone she knew and beg them for help. No one was about. The blood was still pouring from her nose, holding the blanket tightly next to it she bent down to turn the TV on. The phone started ringing again. Vicky gasped and looked about the front room. Blake held it up to her. His face was angry.

"It's Tim." Vicky swallowed hard. "Who the fuck is Tim?" he growled. Walking out of the room she went into the kitchen. He was behind her and she could feel his warm breath on the back of her neck. Shoving the phone into her face he ranted at her. "Go on fucking answer it." Dragging her hair he rammed the phone to her ear. You could hear Tim's voice at the end of the line shouting her name but she remained silent. Blake was on top of her now and the phone was flung against the wall. He was kicking ten tons of shit out of her. "Is this your new guy, fucking Tim?" his hands were dragging her all over the place. "I swear to you Vicky, I'll kill you both." Vicky cowered in the corner of the room holding her two hands over her head. He was beating her bad.

The kitchen was quiet and Vicky lay on the floor barely breathing. Blake sat behind the door and you could hear Declan crying to come inside. "Hold on a minute son, go back in the living room and play with your toys, I'll be with you in a minute." Walking over to Vicky he kicked at her body softly. "It's what you deserve you lying slut. You should thank your lucky stars I haven't finished you off, because I could have, yanno." His deep breathing could be heard and he kept sniffing loudly. Dropping to the floor he stroked her hair as he watched her sobbing at the side of him. "Turn over so I can see you face, Vicky." She didn't move at first but after he raised his voice again, she struggled to obey him. Groaning could be heard as she rolled over. Her face was a mess and her eyes were barely opened. Vicky's face looked like it had swelled twice its normal size. Blake shook his head as he looked at her. "See what you've made me do." His hands dragged through his hair and he was sweating. "I've sat in my cell for months going over in my head, all the things I was going to do to you. This is what you deserve," he sighed. "You've got off lightly, I can tell you." He leant in towards her face and whispered into her ear. "I planned to kill you, yanno."

He pulled his head back up and rested it on the cream painted walls. Slowly he banged his head against it. "Fucking why, why?" he mumbled. Tears fell from his eyes and he cupped his face into his hands. "I thought you loved me Vicky, how can you give up on us just at the drop of a hat. We have a kid together."

Declan was booting the door with force and screaming. "Let me in you bastards." The child's temper was broken and he wasn't giving up for love nor money.

Blake screwed his face up and jumped to his feet. Dragging the door open he snapped at his son. "Who are you calling bastards?" Declan dropped his head and was trying to get past his father but he was having none of it.

Blake dragged his hand and swung him up onto his body. Snarling into his face he scared the life out of the young boy. "Don't let me ever hear you saying that word again."

Declan was wriggling free. He was bawling his eyes

out now. "Mummy mummy," he shrieked.

Vicky sat in the front room on a chair. Declan was sat next to her and the both of them looked scared to death. Blake made her put a bag of frozen chips on her face to stop the swelling, she struggled to hold it. The TV was switched on and even though the three of them were watching it none of them looked interested in it.

Blake's eyes were all over Vicky. Declan looked tired. He'd cried for hours now and it was finally taking its toll on him. Vicky forced herself up and placed him on the sofa nearby. He gave out a little moan but he finally settled back to sleep. Blake stood from his chair and sat on the floor facing her. His head was dropped between his legs and he held his chin in his hands. Blake was all skin and bone. His skin looked grey and you could see in his eyes that the time he'd spent in prison hadn't been easy. "I got out yesterday," he spoke in a low voice. "I won my appeal." Twisting his fingers nervously he reached over and stroked her hand softly. "If you tell him it's over, we can start again." Her eyes welled up as she looked at him. She shook her head as tears trickled down her cheeks. As he watched her reject him his face changed. She tried to backpedal knowing he was on the edge.

"Blake we want different things now. I can't live my life waiting for you in prison all the time. I loved you with all my heart, and you let me down big time." Her tears streamed down her face. "It's been so hard on my own. I've been to hell and back. You're okay in prison; three meals a day, no bills, no worry where you're gonna get money from, for electric and that."

"I worried about you and Declan every day," Blake protested, "don't think for one minute it was easy for me," he sighed with his hands held out in front of him.

She carried on speaking. "I can't do us anymore Blake. I need more."

"I'll change," he sobbed as he sat on the arm of the chair.

Vicky looked like a woman twice her age as she tried to pull her aching body up. Taking a moment to gather her breath she placed one hand on her hip. "I've got a chance at life Blake. Me and Declan can be happy. Why don't you just move on?"

Blake fell to the floor like butter melting from hot toast. His shoulders were shaking as he broke his heart crying. "I did it all for us Vicky, everything I did was to give us a better life."

"No," she yelled. "You did what you did, for you. You made sure you were okay and then if anything was left that's when you thought about us." He lifted his head up as she continued, he was a broken man. "Even when I was pregnant I had to find the money myself, you didn't give a fucking shit." Vicky's face changed as a sharp pain surged through her body. Holding one hand on the wall she keeled over in pain.

Blake looked at her and jumped to his feet. "Orr baby, are you okay."

"Take your fucking hands off me. It's because of you that I'm like this." She was panting.

"Vicky please give me one last chance, let me prove I can change."

"Never in a month of Sundays. I'm thinking about me and my son now, no one else. If you're gonna kill me then get it over with, because there is no way I'm going back with you."

"Oh what's lover boy promised you. He's just using you for a shag you daft bastard. Are you right in the head," his finger was ramming into the side of her head. "Men say anything to get into your knickers Vicky, you need to get a grip and take off your rose-tinted glasses. He's using you for a leg- over."

"You don't know shit about him. I've not even slept with him yet, he's in prison."

Blake's face dropped. His jaw was swinging as he tried to run her words through his mind. He was stuttering. "What, who's in prison, you mean you've met a fucking prisoner?" Vicky nodded. Her arms gripped tightly around her body.

Blake was pacing the floor again when her mobile phone started ringing. His eyes and ears were all over the show and he ran back into the kitchen to find it. The back of the phone was in bits on the floor but it was still working. His hand stretched under the kitchen table to get at it. Casting his eyes at the screen he could see Tim's name again. Dragging it out from under the table he pressed the green answer button and held the phone to his ear. "Vicky is that you. What's going on love, I'm worried about you." Blake held his hand over his heart and his nostrils were flaring. He listened further as the voice continued. "Vicky I love you yanno, and if all this is because Susie's been on the scene, I can tell you one hundred and ten percent that she means fuck all to me. Vicky please speak to me baby. I love you." Blake dropped the phone to the ground and stamped all over it. He was jumping high in the air and making sure the phone would never work again. Sinking to his knees he cried like a baby. His fists were punching into the vinyl tiles and his legs were all over the place.

Vicky was in the front room, Declan had just woken up and she held him in her arms as she struggled to get the key in the backdoor. Her heart was pounding and she couldn't get the key inside the lock quick enough. The gold keys were rattling in her hands and her son was moaning because he'd just woken up. "Are we going out," he shouted in a loud voice. Before she could answer him she felt Blake's hand on her wrist. Her escape was over. The look in his eyes told her to do what he said. Jerking his head back she knew she'd have to go back into the front room. There was no escape.

The room was filled with cigarette smoke. The pair of them were chain-smoking. Declan was watching a DVD and sat quietly for a change. Vicky was in pain and every movement she made was hard. Blake just sat staring into space, he seemed in deep thought. Stubbing his cig out into the ashtray he gazed at her. "Vicky we can make it work, whatever he's promising you is a load of shit. I'm here now, I can look after you. Give me a chance, for crying out loud."

Vicky seemed quiet. Searching in her bag at the side of the chair she pulled out a wad of cash. Waving it about in the air she threw it over to him. "I can earn cash like this every day. I don't need any man."

His face screwed up as he focused on the notes lying on the floor. "Yeah but what are you doing to earn the money, are you selling your fanny?" He was hanging onto her every word.

"Am I fuck selling my fanny ya nobhead. What kind of girl do ya think I am?"

Blake huffed as he blew his breath into his fist. "Vicky I don't know you anymore, you could be into anything these days." Biting down onto her bottom lip she shrugged her shoulders. Who the fuck did he think he was? She was going to wipe the smile right from his face.

Clearing her throat she began to speak. "I get drugs

into the prisons. I organise the drops for the lads." He darted from his seat.

The penny had dropped at last. "It's that fucking Tim who I gave the drugs to last time innit? You're shagging him aren't ya?"

Vicky held a cocky look on her face. "He's in prison, prick, so how do you work that out."

Blake was bouncing about the room waving his hands in front of his face. "How have you got in with him? You don't even know the piss taking cunt."

Vicky knew she should have kept her mouth shut but she couldn't help but tell him the truth. Once he knew how they'd met he sat on the chair facing her, he was stuttering. "Vicky, we can run this thing together. Me and you, no one else. This guy Tim is taking the piss out of you, please see that." Vicky was listening to him as he carried on. "Let's have him over; we can start again somewhere new, let's move away." She liked what he was saying, it was all making sense now, he was right, Tim was just another man sat in the nick chatting shit to her. If he loved her, why was Susie still going to see him? Grabbing another cig from her packet she encouraged Blake to continue. Dragging his grey tracksuit jacket from his body he sat on the chair next to her. "Baby let's start over. Tell me how you get the drugs for him and all that."

Vicky took a long drag of her cig, she was telling him everything. "He just gets it dropped off here for me. It's already bagged up; all I do is hand it to whoever's taking the drugs into the jail. He gives me the money to pay them too, there's a bent screw who sorts it out so they don't get caught."

Blake placed his hand on her lap. Softly stroking it, he looked at the state of her face. "Vicky I swear to you now, I'll never lay a finger on you again. I'll be everything you want me to be," his eyes looked over to his son. "Just think Declan will have a good life away from this shit-hole." He was working his magic on her now and she believed every word he was saying. "If we plan this right we can make a good butty and have enough to get off from round here. Trust me baby, please, we can make it work." Vicky nodded her head. He was making sense.

Vicky sat pondering her thoughts, Blake was on the out now and he was the father of her child. Tim was just using her to line his own pockets; she knew that deep down inside her. The both of them now sat together talking about how they could rip Tim off. They needed to make sure that when they had him over, they'd have enough money to leave the area. Blake and Vicky kissed each other as Declan ran and jumped on them both. "I love my mummy and my daddy," he yelled at the top of his voice.

CHAPTER EIGHTEEN

Helen stood at Susie's door. Her face was squashed up against the glass as she shouted out her name. You could see her banana-like fingers rapping on the door panel. "Susie it's me Helen, open up."

Susie wasn't feeling good and she was sat in the front room watching TV. She'd not long since spewed up and her face looked yellow. Hearing the continuous banging on the door, she bolted up from the chair and sighed. "For fuck sake." Her pink fluffy housecoat was pulled tightly around her body as she walked into the hallway. She couldn't chance anyone seeing her belly. Dipping her eyes down to her stomach she made sure it was fully covered.

Susie had decided to get rid of the baby but it was just finding the time. She was always too busy and tried to put it to the back of her mind until she was ready to deal with it. Ashley was in jail now too. She'd done her job well in informing the police of his criminal activities. The word on the street was that he was looking at least seven years. The local paper said he'd been caught with over eighty thousand pounds worth of drugs and firearms. Susie regretted grassing on him at first but now he was locked up behind bars she felt happy knowing he wasn't causing her any more grief.

Pippa was still lying heavy on Susie's mind. Every night before she closed her eyes to sleep she was plotting to wipe the smile from her face. Ashley was banged up in Strangeways prison along with his co-accused. Susie knew Pippa had been visiting him because Tim had told her. She hated the bitch with a passion, and she couldn't wait until the day came when they were both on a visit at the same time so she could see Ashley's face drop.

Susie wanted Tim back; she was doing everything she could to keep him onside. The drops in the jail were going well and Tim was more than happy with her performance. Susie had got at least eight parcels inside the nick already and the screw Jenkins made sure everything ran smoothly. Susie was taking small parcels into the jail at first, but nowadays she was packed up to the eyeballs with drugs. She'd brought heroin, cocaine, steroids, ecstasy tablets and anything else the inmates requested into the prison. Tim was getting greedy too, and she'd told him on one or more occasion that he would have to curb his demands. If Susie was ever caught with any of the shit she was taking in the prison she would have been slammed for years.

Tim watched Ashley walking along the prison landing as if he owned it. He snarled as he watched the cocky fucker bouncing towards him. Ashley thought that things were sweet between them both and didn't have a clue that Tim was out to make him pay for his betrayal. Tim was playing the role well and kept Ashley by his side as much as he could. He needed him to trust him and to think he was his wing- man again.

Jenkins and Tim always had their heads together. They were always whispering and passing each other bits of paper. Jenkins looked as if he'd lost some weight and his black pants hung from his waist as he walked about the landing.

Paul Jenkins was on edge all the time; he looked scared of his own shadow. He couldn't wait for this whole mess to be over with, so he could get back to feeling normal again. Tim told him that after these last few parcels had been dropped, he would be off the hook forever. He reassured Paul that his secret would never be revealed. Tim liked Jenkins and even though he was a screw, they had a laugh together. They both knew Susie was a bitch and both of them couldn't wait till she got her comeuppance.

Tim lay on his bed, with his arms looped behind his head. His pillow looked flat and scruffy. Vicky had been a bit off with him lately and he was sure she was going off him. Dialling her number he listened to the ringing tone. She answered. "Hiya chicken," he whispered as he raised his head from his bed checking no one was listening. It was late and the screws were patrolling the landing, he had to keep his voice low. "Where are you, are you in bed, babes?" Vicky replied to him and you could see him rubbing his hand at his crotch. He loved this time of the night when he got a bit of female attention. "Come on then Vicky, let's get down to business, these cunts are all over the landing tonight, so I haven't got long. Talk dirty to me, my balls are gonna explode if I don't shoot my load soon." His eyes were closing slowly and he held his head to the side so he could grip the phone in the crease of his neck. His hands were twisting his throbbing manhood. "Say it Vicky, come on love, do that sexy voice you always do." His palms were firmly fixed around his penis; he looked like he was strangling a pigeon's neck. Tim was yanking his cock up and down.

Groaning noises could be heard and it was obvious he'd emptied his sack. Yawning he wiped his penis on the blanket and he carried on speaking to her after he'd tossed the cover from his body. "That was bang on, that was. You're a right dirty fucker, where did you learn all that perverted talk from?" his head tilted back as he giggled. Talking in a low voice he lifted his head from the bed to make sure no one could hear him. "Have you sorted out all those drops now?" He was nodding his head as he listened to her. "Yeah fucking hell, Vicky it's cost me nearly six grand to sort this lot out. It better not go pear-shaped otherwise I'm going to be fucked." Pulling the blanket up to his neck he snuggled down underneath it trying to get comfy. His whispering voice could be heard and he looked tired. Once the call was over he turned on his side and started to drift off to sleep. Tim had plans for the next day and he had to be fresh. Ashley was going to get what he deserved.

Morning light broke through the bars of HMP Strangeways. Stretching his hands over his head, Tim dropped his legs from his bed. Hearing the sound of pigeons cooing outside his cell he walked to the window. The bird looked at him as he poked his face through the bars. Laughing to himself he spoke to his feathered friend. "You've got it easy you, you have mate, free to fly wherever you want and no women to worry about." The pigeon was turning its head looking at him. "Go on fuck off now then, waking me up at this time of the morning, ya, little bastard." Tim pushed his hand through the bars and watted it towards the bird "Shoo, shoo," he shouted.

The sounds outside his door let him know that prison life had begun for another day. Every morning was the same, people shouting and laughing outside their doors. Dipping his face in the sink he splashed cold water over his skin. Dragging his cheek bones in his hands he realised how much weight he'd lost since he'd been in prison. Tim was hammering the steroids every day but he was nowhere near the size he used to be. Ashley was still big and he was forever ramming his muscles into everyone's face, the posing fucker. Tim was jealous of Ashley's body shape.

All the inmates were walking down the stairs to get their breakfast. Tim saw Jenkins and gave him the nod as Ashley came to join him. Jenkins could be seen heading back to the pads with a concerned look on his face. Tim rubbed Ashley's hair as he stood at the side of him. There was a cunning grin spread across his face. The convicts all stood in the queue waiting to get their breakfast. The noise was deafening.

The prison canteen was busy. The men in the queue held that hard knock look in their eyes. Their skin looked grey and you could tell for a lot of them that this was their worst nightmare. The sound of cutlery being banged about could be heard. The server looked at Tim. "What ya having mate?" Tim's eyes scanned the food and his face screwed up. The eggs looked like they'd been stood there for days and the toast looked hard as nails. "Erm... I'll have some beans on toast." The man stood behind the counter, he dug his large silver spoon in the beans and scooped them onto the piece of burnt bread. Before Tim could say anything the server was already asking Ashley the same question. Each inmate looked at the food with disgust. Prison life was shit.

The sound of cutlery clattering on plates could be heard. Ashley sat next to Tim and chuckled. "Fuck me mate, how have we ended up in this place?"

Tim lifted his head from his plate. "Fucking hell, tell me about it, you just need to get ya head down and take every day as it comes, that's what I do."

Ashley gasped as he folded his toast in his fingers. "You're alright mate; you know when you're getting out. I've still got to be sentenced yet."

Tim patted the middle of his arm. "Nar, you won't get long, there are loads in here what've been caught with drugs and they only got four or five years."

Ashley's face dropped. "I can't do fucking five weeks mate, never mind five big 'uns rammed up my shitter. I just hope my barrister is good and he gets me off with it."

Tim nearly choked on his food. "Get you off with it, you was caught bang to rights ya dick-head. You need to start telling yourself that you're gonna be doing jail mate, because if you don't, you're in for a big surprise when you get slammed."

Ashley pushed his white plate out in front of him. Slurping on his brew he looked deflated. Tim could see he was struggling and tried to make him laugh. "So you're all loved up with Pippa then, she's an alright woman you know."

Ashley shot him a look and Tim laughed out loud. He punched Tim playfully in his arm. "Don't tell me you have banged her first?" Ashley asked.

Tim held his belly as he stuttered his words. "Fucking dead right I've shagged her. I met her in a club ages ago and that's how she ended up working in Delia's. I mean, if she's selling her fanny I have to make sure it's worth it don't I?"

Ashley's head sunk. Tim had always got more women than he did. He never thought in a million years he'd slept with Pippa, he'd hid it well. Tim was out to break Ashley in two, and carried on with the banter. "Yeah, she was a top ride. Next time you're licking her motty, just think my tackle has been inside her." Tim roared laughing.

Ashley bolted up from his chair. "You sick bastard, don't be saying shit like that, you'll put me off her."

Tim pulled at his arm and dragged him nearer. "Stop being a mard arse, I'm only joking with you."

Ashley plonked back down in his chair and carried on drinking his brew. Tim reached over and grabbed his hand and stroked it slowly. "Ay I've never thanked you for looking after my Susie when you were on the out."

Ashley swallowed hard and his lips were dry. He kept his eyes on the table as he replied. "No worries mate, that's what friends do for each other." Tim scowled and had to turn his face away from him. His nostrils were flaring and you could see his clenched fist lying on his lap under the table. Jenkins was stood at the doorway and shot Tim a look.

Breakfast was over and the inmates headed back to

their cells. Tim always used this time to write a letter to his mother, he loved writing. It was bang up now for a few hours and you could see by the convicts faces that they hated this time of the day. "Are you busting the gym later, Tim?" Ashley shouted as they parted ways.

"Yeah I'll see you down there later."

Ashley flexed his muscles at Tim and kissed his bulging bicep. "You better had because you need it. You're all skin and bone these days," he sniggered. Both men disappeared into their pads now. The sound of door slamming could be heard.

Tim walked to his window and gripped the bars, his knuckles were white. "Let's see whose laughing now, smart arse," he whispered under his breath.

Ashley lay on his bed. He was preparing himself for an early morning wank when the door flew open. Bolting up from his bed he yanked his shorts up. "What the fuck," he yelled. Five screws were in his pad. He was being spun over. This was normal in the jail, and every week at least five or six cells were turned over. The screws were wearing plastic gloves and their eyes were all over the show trying to look for hiding places. Jenkins led Ashley outside. He was made to stand with his back against the wall. Lots of noise was coming from the cell and Ashley was going ballistic as he popped his head back around the door trying to see inside. "Fucking no need for all this. I hope you're gonna clean it all up when you've fucking finished." A hand met his body and pushed him back up against the wall.

Minutes passed and laughter could be heard coming from his pad. Jenkins stood at Ashley's side and stretched his neck over to see what was going on. He could see an officer holding a large bag of drugs in his hand. The powder was white and it looked like cocaine. Tim knew Ashley's downfall came at a price and he'd made sure there were enough drugs found in his cell to get years added to his sentence.

"Result," one of the officers shouted.

Ashley looked agitated. "What the fuck are they waffling on about in there?" he protested to Jenkins.

Jenkins cleared his throat and came to Ashley's side. "They've found drugs." His face dropped and Jenkins had to call for help to restrain him. He was up- in- arms shouting at the top of his voice. "Fucking no way in the world is there any drugs in my cell. If there is, you've stitched me up, you shower of bastards." Ashley was sprawled across the floor; his face was forced into the cold concrete. He was trying to fight back but within minutes he was handcuffed and lay on the ground with a screw on top of him with his arms held behind his back. "Fucking cunts, you've set me up," he ranted.

The screws came out from his pad and they looked happy at what they'd found. All in all six bags of drugs were seized. The other inmates on the landing were all kicking off from behind their doors. They were banging and going wild and shouting abuse at the screws. Ashley was dragged to his feet. He was still trying to fight back and tried head-butting a nearby officer. The wardens worked together and marched the prisoner down to the block. Solitary confinement was somewhere every prisoner dreaded going. All they had was a bed in a room with no television, no radio. It was the worst place in the prison to be.

Ashley was flung into his cell. Once he pulled himself up from the floor he ran back at the officers but it was too late, the door was closed. He pummelled the iron door with his fists at speed. Ashley looked demented; he was like a madman. "Bastards!" he yelled at the top of his voice. After a few minutes he realised it was pointless. Sliding down the wall he sat with his head held between his knees. Tears ran down his face and he sobbed as he realised that no matter what, he would be spending a long time locked away behind prison doors.

Tim was quick to hear the news about Ashley. Everyone on the landing was talking about it. One inmate at the side of him started to claim he'd seen all the commotion through the peephole in his cell door. He was bouncing about at the side of the convicts as he told his story. "I swear lads; Ashley took at least three of the bastards down. He had one in a head- lock and he round-housed another two. He was going sick at them." The story teller was talking fast. "It took eight of them to hold him down."

Another convict jumped in, they knew the prisoner was chatting shit and told him straight. "How the fuck did you see all that, when we were banged up. Stop telling fairy-tales ya muppet."

The witness looked shocked, his mouth was opened wide. "Nar, I swear on my mother's life, I saw it all." His two palms were now held out in front of him.

"Fuck off Billy bull-shitter!" the other criminals laughed.

Tim sucked on his lips as the convicts went down the stairs. It was association time and the men looked relieved to be out of their cells again. Parking his arse on a chair at the side of the pool table Tim saw Jenkins head towards him. He looked happy, as he casually stood behind Tim. Bending down, he spoke to him. "The job's a good 'un, he's going off his head down there in the block."

Tim rocked back on his chair and tilted his head back at Jenkins. "Good stuff," Tim whispered under his breath.

Jenkins moved forward and covered his mouth with his hand as he mumbled. "He should be shipped out soon. He's fucked now."

"Right just one last thing Paul and you're a free man too" Tim nodded, "If you pull this next job off, I promise you, you'll never hear from me again."

Jenkins was sweating and a small droplet of sweat was visible on his forehead. "I'd better not," he moaned as he walked away from the prisoner.

The inmates enjoyed the time out of their cells. They seemed to be human for at least the time they were among each other. Being locked away in a small room for most of the day and night was enough to break even the toughest men. Ex drug-addicts sat about the room, hugging their bodies, they were still craving drugs. You could see life without a fix was having an effect on them, they were roasting. Strangeways was a prison every drug addict hated. Many a late hour you could hear smack-heads screaming in pain as their bodies called out for a hit. Each one of them had to rattle and they knew that no matter what, they would have to roast their nuts off, because no one cared if they lived or died behind these prison walls.

Tim lay on his bed; he looked like the cat that had got the cream. Tapping his fingers on his cheek, he checked the time on his watch, it was wank time. Searching for his mobile phone he cautiously pulled it out from its hiding place. He'd been trying Vicky all day but she wasn't answering. He looked concerned as he listened to the ring tone. Still no answer. His fingers quickly typed a text message and once he'd sent it he hid the phone away back in its secret location. Reaching under his bed he grabbed a fanny mag. One of the inmates had given it to him and it was the unwritten law of the jail, that you shared your porn with all the other inmates. Tim tried to open the first page of the glossy magazine but it was stuck solid. Tim giggled; some dirty bastard had shot his load all over the page, it looked like cardboard. Gripping the next page his eyes looked contented. A big hairy fanny stood out from the page. Rolling his boxer shorts down, he spit onto his palms. Moans and groans could be heard and it wasn't long until Tim had emptied his sack. This was all that inmates seemed to do in the jail; eat, sleep and masturbate.

Tim looked through his collection of photographs. Holding one of Susie to his face he gritted his teeth together. "Now it's your turn bitch." Laughter filled the room and he looked menacing. His fingers scraped at the snapshot and he flicked at Susie's face with the end of his finger. Tossing it on the floor he turned the radio on and tuned in for the late night love hour. Tim snuggled down under his sheets and his eyes lay staring into space as he listened to the love songs being played on the radio station. Nodding his head slowly you could see his feet tapping to the beat of the song. His eyes were closing.

CHAPTER NINETEEN

Vicky zipped her coat up as she pulled the curtain back to look out of the window. The wind looked fierce and she was dreading going out into the cold weather. "It looks fucking freezing out there," she moaned.

Blake was by her side drooling all over her. He draped his hand over her shoulder as he pulled her in towards his chest. "You and me baby. Once we get that cash, we're off from this shit-hole and starting our new life."

Declan ran to his side and he yanked him up by one arm pulling him up, Vicky smiled. This was all she ever wanted. Looking at her son's smiling face she knew she'd made the right decision, she pulled away from Blake. "Right I'm going. Joan said she'll be at the brass gaff to meet me at two o'clock, so I'd better move my arse."

Blake watched her with cunning eyes. His lips met hers one more time and he looked so in love with her. "Yeah, hurry up, don't leave us on our jacks for hours, I'll miss you too much," he chuckled at her with endearing eyes.

Vicky hugged him quickly and made her way to the front door. "See you later," she shouted as she pulled her hood up over her head

The wind gripped her body and she was struggling to walk out from the street at first. Her head was dipped low and you could only see her eyes peering out from her hood. Vicky walked at speed and finally reached the bus-stop. Placing her hand inside her pocket she found her money for the fare. The bus was approaching. Vicky had a smile on her face.

Sitting on the crowded bus she gawped about at all the different characters sat near her. Pulling her hood down her face looked hot. With one hand she straightened her hair and tried to look half decent. Her nostrils flared as she inhaled deeply. The man in front of her stank of stale cheese. Shaking her head she looked out of the window. "Fucking scruff," she mumbled under her breath.

Joan was sat smoking in the reception when Vicky walked in, she looked flustered. "Hiya love, I won't be a minute," she moaned. Joan looked off her head again. Her eyes were dancing about and her words were slurred. Joan stood to her feet and left Vicky alone for a minute. Tim had arranged for some cash to be dropped off there for her. She was expecting over six grand in total. Rubbing her arms she felt cold. Plonking herself down on the sofa she could hear Joan having a coughing fit in the distance. She sounded as if she was on her last legs. Standing to her feet she trudged towards the door. With a hard tug she pulled it open. Joan's face was white and she was struggling for breath. Vicky quickened her step and stood at the side of her.

"Fuck me Joan, you need to go to the doctor's with that cough, you sound as if you're dying," Vicky said, patting her back with a flat palm. Loud coughing could be heard and Vicky led her to the chair at the side of them so she could rest. Vicky looked concerned. "Park ya arse there love, I'll go and get you a drink of water."

Joan reached for her hand and looked at her with desperate eyes, regaining her breath she spoke. "Orr love, go down to my office and get my vodka that will sort me out, it always does."

Vicky sighed and blew a laboured breath. "What are you like you, Joan? You're gonna end up dead, if ya carry on." Joan was having another coughing fit and she just waved her hand out at Vicky for her to leave her.

The office was a mess. It stank of cat piss. Vicky cast her eyes to the table and could see the half a bottle of vodka. Reaching down to the table for it, her eyes caught sight of a wad of cash nearby. Vicky froze for a minute. Slowly walking towards it she checked nobody was about. Her fingers stroked the money slowly. There was a piece of paper stuck on top of it with numbers written on it. The money was the monthly takings from Delia's, she was sure of it. Four thousand pound it said on the yellow piece of paper stuck on the top of it. Without thinking any further she rammed the money into her coat pocket. She looked white as she fidgeted about trying to conceal the cash. Gripping the neck of the vodka she quickly turned around and went back to Joan.

Joan was sat on the chair with her head dipped between her legs. Vicky came into view on the corridor. Joan heard her footsteps and lifted her head up. "Oh thank fuck for that love, give it here while I have a quick mouthful." Vicky passed her the alcohol. Her hand was shaking as she tried to get the top off it. Licking her lips frantically she finally unscrewed the bottle. Joan gulped at it as if her life depended on it. She'd drunk at least half of it before she came up for breath. Taking a few minutes to steady herself she looked at Vicky. "I needed that, yanno. Whenever I start coughing like this," she held her throat with one hand. "This shit sorts me right out."

Holding the bottle towards Vicky, she offered her a swig. Vicky shook her head. "Nar I have to hurry up," she lied. Joan's breathing returned to normal, she was right; the vodka did sort her out. Standing to her feet Vicky walked with her back to the reception. "Have you got that money from Tim," Vicky asked in a low voice. You could see her hand in her pocket and she was constantly feeling the stolen money. "Yeah, just bare with me a minute and I'll sort it out for you," Joan mumbled.

Joan went behind the reception desk and dipped down, she was out of sight. Pulling out an old box, she dug deep inside it. With a smile across her face she sighed as she lifted her head back up. "I've put it in here as a hideaway. You never know, anyone could run in this place and try to have us over, that's why I always stash the money away from prying eyes." Joan pulled out a brown envelope. It looked full. Vicky held her hand out for the package, but Joan was still waffling on about when she had to fight off two men who came into the gaff demanding money.

Vicky coughed and swung her body about nervously. "Joan I have to get going." Joan huffed and passed the money over to her. With a quick goodbye Vicky was halfway down the stairs before she could get another word in. She shoved the envelope inside the front of her jeans and was holding onto it for dear life.

Blake sat watching the clock; Declan was doing his head in at the side of him. His face looked stressed as he tapped his fingers on the kitchen table. "Come on Vicky, where the fuck are ya? How long does it take you to pick up a bit of fucking money?" he mumbled. Declan was pulling at his sleeve trying to drag him from his chair. He snapped at him, "Will you fuck off, you little cunt," he snarled. Declan knew he meant business and slowly melted into the background. Blake picked up the blue pen from the table and carried on writing his letter. He was guarding the words he was writing with his life. Once he'd finished writing it, he shoved the piece of paper into a white envelope and tucked it inside his pocket. He smirked as he patted the paper down.

Vicky neared home. Her cheeks were red and she was sweating. Once she saw her house in the distance she picked up speed and started to jog. She could see a face at the kitchen window; she waved her hands in the air. Blake was stood at the front door with his hands tucked down the front of his tracksuit- bottoms looking anxious. He shouted to her as she walked towards him. "Hurry up slug, fucking hell; I've been worried out of my mind. Did you get it?" Blake's eyes were all over her like a rash as he licked his lips. Vicky nodded her head; he dragged her inside the house by her arm.

Stood in the hall way Blake bounced about. "Let me see it, let me see it," he said in a stressed voice. Vicky peeled her coat from her shoulders and threw it over the banister. "Hold your fucking horses," she chuckled. Marching into the front room Blake and Declan followed her inside like two ducklings. Her hands dipped inside her jeans. Pulling out an envelope she held it out in front of her with a great big smile spread right across her face. "There you go, that's our future Blake," his eyes shot straight to the money. Reaching over he hugged her and made sure he got his hands on the cash. The two of them stood kissing passionately in the front room. Holding her face in his hands he squeezed her cheeks together. "Well done Vicky, it's just what we needed."

She pulled her head back from him as she broke free. "Hold on, that's not it," his face looked surprised.

"What do ya mean, it's not it?" her hands slid back into her jeans.

"There's another four grand in there, I had the takings away as well."

Blake's eyes danced about with excitement as he rubbed his hands together. "Fuck off, no way, did ya?"

Vicky looked proud. "I sure did, it was just there staring at me, so I thought fuck it."

Blake was pacing the front room, nodding his head; he made his way to the sofa. "Give me a cig Vicky, my nerves are shattered."

"Yours are, I'm fucking shitting myself," she giggled as she came and sat by his side. Her face looked concerned as she spoke.

"Once Joan clocks the money missing, she'll be on

the war path for me, she'll know it's me straightaway, I can just feel it."

They both lit a cig each, inhaling deeply Blake spoke. "Right, let's get things moving. Give me the cash and I'll go and get us a runner. We don't need out flash do we? Just something for about six ton, we need a car don't we?"

Vicky nodded her head. "Yeah, you go and buy a car and I'll start packing our stuff up." Gathering all the money together she passed it to him. "Blake we're gonna be alright aren't we?" she whispered as her eyes watched Declan playing with his car at the side of her. Blake coughed loudly as he stood to his feet. "Yeah, yeah course we are, I'm gonna get off now, and sort us some wheels out."

Vicky smiled. "Right get going then, the sooner you're gone, the sooner you'll be back, and then we can get out of this depressing place." Blake grabbed his coat from the side. He paused for a minute and stood frozen. Turning back towards them both, he leant down and kissed Declan. "I love you son," he whispered. He was gone.

Vicky sat tapping her fingers on her teeth. After another cig, she jumped up from her seat and headed into the kitchen. Bending down she searched under the sink. Grabbing some black bags she shouted out to Declan. "Come on son, I'm going upstairs, we need to start packing our stuff up." He followed her, and they both went up the stairs together.

Vicky was like a mad woman, as she opened the wardrobe doors and started scooping piles of clothing into bin-liners. She did the same with all the drawers. The sound of her mobile phone ringing could be heard.

Digging her hands deep inside her jeans pocket she struggled to pull it out. Her face looked distraught, it was Tim again. He'd not stopped ringing her all day. Holding the phone tightly in her grip she sighed. It stopped ringing now and she threw it onto the bed. "Right Declan, I need you to help mummy. Go in your bedroom and get all the toys you want to take to our new house." She passed him a black bag.

Declan started stamping his feet, he was having a strop. "I don't want to go to a new house, I want to stay here."

Walking to his side she bent her legs down and was at eye level with him. She spoke in an animated voice. "Declan we're going to a better place and you'll love it."

The child fell to the floor and started rolling about. "No I'm staying here," he bawled.

Blake walked up Rochdale Road. His arms were swinging at the side of him. Seeing a post box not far from him, he sat on a nearby wall. Grabbing a pen from his coat he pulled out the white envelope from his back pocket. Once he'd scrawled the address on the letter he jogged to the red postbox. His hands held the letter for the last time; he held a cunning look in his eyes. The envelope disappeared inside the box and he carried on walking to his destination. Pulling his mobile phone from his jacket he dialled a number. Holding the phone to his ear he was waiting for someone to answer. "Yo Conrad, its Blake, what's happening bro?" he was laughing out loud. "Yeah mate wait there, I'm on my way. I've had a good earner so get ya partying clothes on."

Vicky sat with piles of black bags next to her, they were scattered all about the living room. She kept looking at the clock on the wall and looking out of the kitchen window. There was no sign of her boyfriend, he'd been gone ages. She tried ringing his phone, but it just kept going to voicemail. Lighting a cig up, she stared at the TV. Smoke filled the room and she waved her hand in front of her face to try and see clearly. Declan was munching some crisps at the side of her and he was restless, his body was moving about all the time. He was bugging her, "Keep fucking still," she snapped.

"I wanna go out," he yelled.

Pulling his body from hers she answered him. "We will soon, we're just waiting for your dad to come back, and then we can go to McDonald's for something to eat."

Declan was cheering, jumping about on a chair. "I wanna go now, I wanna go now," he screamed out. Vicky gasped her breath and tried to console him, he was doing her head in and she was losing patience.

Night time fell and there was still no sign of Blake. Declan had fallen asleep ages ago and Vicky decided to put him in bed. Smoking another cig, she stood at the front door and pulled it open. The night air was cold and she was shivering. Her eyes scanned the area looking for her boyfriend. Vicky stood on her tiptoes to see if she could see him in the distance, he was nowhere in sight. "Where the fuck are you?" she moaned under her breath. Turning around, she trudged back inside the house. Lying on the sofa she dragged her coat over her body, she looked perished. Her eyes looked tired and she was struggling to stay awake. After hours of staring into space, Vicky finally fell asleep.

Vicky opened her eyes, it was morning time. The telly was still on and she realised she'd been asleep. The sound of the letterbox being flicked up and down made her jump up from the sofa. She thought it was Blake returning.

Running into the hallway she could see two letters on the floor. Opening the door, she glanced outside and could see the postman walking away with his bag held over his shoulder. Bending down she picked up the two letters. Heading back to the front room she reached for her phone and tried Blake's number again. She looked worried; the call was going to voice mail again.

Declan could be heard shouting from upstairs. "Mummy can I have some Coco pops for my breakfast."

"Yeah, come down here then." She could hear his footsteps coming down the stairs, he was singing.

Declan sat on the floor with his bowl of cereal. They were dropping all over the floor and Vicky was shouting at him. "Scruffy twat," she moaned as she picked up the mess from the carpet. Once he was sorted out she plonked her body back on the sofa, she looked deflated. Seeing the two letters nearby, her hands reached over and grabbed at them. The first one looked like a bill; she flung it to one side. A white envelope now stared back at her, her face frowned as she recognised the handwriting on the front of it. The writing was Blake's, she was sure of it. Her fingers quickly ripped the letter open she looked distraught as she sat reading. Every word she read was like a knife being twisted deep inside her heart.

Yo Vicky,

Hope you slept well? Did you really think I was gonna have you back after you cheated on me? Get a grip ya daft slag. I wouldn't touch you with a bargepole now. The money is … let's call it disturbance money for all the sleepless nights you caused me when I was lying in my prison cell. I hope you get everything you deserve and people see you for the cheap little slut you really are. Goodbye Sucker, I wish you nothing but bad luck, you're a life wrecking bitch,

    Blake

Vicky dropped the letter from her hands and her mouth was wide open. "No," she screamed. She bolted up from her chair and was punching her fists into the wall. With the last blow she fell to her knees and curled up like an injured animal. Declan was at his mother's side, he looked scared. Sitting next to her he just scraped his fingers into the carpet and looked about the room.

Vicky remained lay in the same spot for over an hour. Turning her body over you could see the tears she'd cried. Her face looked swelled and pieces of hair were stuck across her forehead. Sitting up, she brought her knees up to her chest and rocked about in the same position. Shaking her head from side to side, she sobbed.

A loud banging noise could be heard. Jumping to her feet she ran to grab Declan in her grip. The living room door swung open and she could see Joan stood there with two stocky looking men. Joan growled at her. "You know why I'm here don't you, you cheeky bitch."

Vicky cowered in the corner and held her son close to her body. "Joan please, my son's here, he's scared, please."

Joan walked to where she stood and yanked the screaming child from her grip. Declan was punching and kicking her but it made no odds. Joan passed him to one of the men at the side of her. "Sort that crying cunt out will you, while I deal with this thieving fucker." The man obeyed her orders and dragged Declan out from the room. Joan pounced on Vicky like a preying lioness.

A piercing scream could be heard, Vicky was curled up in a ball on the floor, pleading for her life. Joan's face was on fire. Her hand went into her pocket and a small silver blade could be seen. Gripping it tightly in her hand she swiped it across Vicky's face with one quick movement. "You won't rob from me again in a hurry, you low life slut." Blood surged from Vicky's face and she was yelling at the top of her voice for help, no one came.

Joan ragged Vicky by her hair. "Where's my fucking money," she growled into her face with her teeth gritted, Vicky remained silent. "Don't make me ask you again." Vicky knew she was in danger, and pleaded with her. "Joan please, it was Blake who made me do it. I don't have the money, he's got off with it and the money Tim gave me too. Read the letter over there, if you don't believe me."

Vicky pointed to the arm of the chair where the letter lay. Joan nodded to the man at the side of her, "Pass me that!" Joan hissed. Joan sat down and her eyes squinted together as she held the letter up to her eyes. Her face looked serious. All of a sudden she laughed out loud. "She's been ripped off, by her boyfriend, the fucking daft bastard." Vicky was trembling in the corner; her lips were quivering as she came to her side again. Joan bent down and rammed her finger into the side of her head. "Never trust a man," she chuckled, "Because now," she paused, "You have to pay for his sins." Joan held Vicky's head back and you could see her fist clenching together at the side of her. Her head swung about as Joan's fist pummelled into her face. The man in the room stood behind the living room door and dipped his head as each blow connected with the young girl's face. Joan was beating her within an inch of her life; he closed his eyes and looked away.

Joan plonked onto a chair. She looked over at Vicky's lifeless body on the floor. She knew she hadn't killed her because she could see her chest still rising. "Get her cleaned up Rob."

The man, who looked around thirty years of age,

walked to Vicky's side, he yanked her from the floor and struggled to hold her up. Rob looked horrified when he saw her face for the first time and shot Joan a look. "Fucking hell, she's a mess," he moaned.

Joan heard his words and screamed out in a loud voice. "What do ya expect, ya fucking fairy. I'm here because she owes us four grand," she gasped, "I'm not here to sit and chit-chat with her." Rob raised his eyes and led Vicky to a chair before he left the room. Declan could be heard still crying upstairs. Bob shouted upstairs to the other man. "Brad, keep the kid up there, until we've cleaned her up, she's in a right mess."

Brad came to the top of the stairs and bent his head over the banister so he could see Rob. Declan was trying to get past him, but he held his hand round the kid's clothes so he couldn't move any further. "Get back in there," he shouted at the kid.

Declan was heartbroken. "I want my mummy," he wailed. He was dragged back inside the bedroom.

Rob started to clean Vicky up. Her cheek was still pumping out blood and he commented that she would need stitches in the deep gash across her face. Joan sighed. "Once we've sorted out the little matter of the cash she owes us, then she can go and get it sorted out, but for now, she's going nowhere. I don't give a fuck if she bleeds to death or not. I want that fucking money back." Vicky held her hands around her body and looked in pain. Rob pressed the white dishcloth firmly on her face, she was squealing.

Once he'd backed off Vicky sat with a distressed look on her face. "Joan tell me what I can do, I'm fucked. I don't have a pot to piss in; you know that, so how can I pay you back."

Joan inhaled deeply on her cig. She looked deep in thought as she flicked her ash on the floor. A cunning look appeared on her face. "You'll have to work it off then, won't you?" Vicky shrugged her shoulders.

"What do mean, work it off?"

Joan stubbed her cig out on the wall and flicked her cig end onto the floor. "In 'Delia's', you'll have to work for me there until you've cleared you're debt."

Vicky shook her head slowly as Joan's words registered. "I can't do that; please Joan, anything but selling my body."

Joan cracked her knuckles and nodded her head at Vicky. "It's the only way love. You owe Tim over ten grand, and there is no way in this world he's gonna let you off with that much money."

Vicky chewed rapidly on her fingernails. Tears trickled down the side of her cheeks. Joan was staring at her, waiting for an answer. "Well," she prompted. Vicky gasped for breath and held one hand around her neck. Joan was right; there was no other way she could pay the money back. Slowly she whispered. "Yes."

Joan darted up and walked to where Vicky was sat. "You know it make sense girl." She held Vicky's face in her hand and examined her wounds. "Right, get to the hospital and get that looked at, a few stitches will sort it out. I'll be back later to see you."

Vicky remained silent; she was watching her every move. As she watched her make her way to the door she could feel her heart beating rapidly inside her chest. Joan placed her hand on the door handle and slowly turned back to her. Rob was already out of the room. "Vicky don't even think of doing anything daft, because I'll find you, and you know what will happen then don't you."

You could see the terror on Vicky's face as she replied. "No Joan, I promise, I'll keep my word. I will, honest." That was all Joan needed to hear, she left the room and you could hear Rob shouting his mate from upstairs. Vicky was on her feet and made her way to the living room door.

In seconds Declan was stood at the door screaming, "Mummy, mummy what's happened to your face? I don't like it." Vicky gripped him in her arms and the blood from her cheek was trickling down her son's face as she pressed him up against her. Running to the front door she could see the lock was hanging from it. Pushing it shut, she fell to her knees with her back pressed against the door. There was no way out of the mess she was in, and Vicky knew no matter what, her life would never be the same again; she'd have to become a prostitute to pay her debt off. Cradling her son in her arms she whispered into his ears. "I'm sorry son, I did it all for you, yanno. It's all such a mess, I'm sorry, I'm sorry."

Vicky went to North Manchester General Hospital and had eight stitches in her face. The doctors wanted to know how she'd done it, but she talked her way out of it so the police weren't involved, she couldn't stand anymore stress. Blake's phone was still off and she knew now that the bastard was only really ever interested in the money she was getting. She was a fool and knew that more than anyone now. Blake had pulled the wool over her eyes and had her right over. Vicky cursed Blake every minute she sat in the hospital waiting room. She promised herself that one day she would pay him back for ruining her life. Vicky looked in a bad way as she left the hospital.

CHAPTER TWENTY

Susie sat in her front room. She felt tired as she bagged the last lot of drugs she was taking into the nick. The cling-film was tightly wrapped round each bulky package. This was the biggest drop she'd ever done. She sat smiling at the parcels as she puffed hard on her cigarette. The money she'd pull in from this drop was more than enough to pay for her abortion. She'd already spent the money Ashley had given her and this was her only way of ever getting it done privately.

The telly blared out in the front room, she didn't look as if she was watching it, Susie was anxious. Helen was due at any minute now and she knew she had to make a move to start getting ready. Dragging her body up from the sofa she sighed. The usual glow that rested on her face had disappeared. Heading upstairs she went inside the bathroom. Susie tweaked her fingers at her skin. She looked pale and her skin looked grey in colour, she didn't look healthy. Reaching for her make-up bag from the side she started to try and look half decent. As she bent over towards the mirror, a knock at the front door could be heard. Throwing her mascara back on the window ledge she headed downstairs. Susie forgot she was only wearing a vest top and some pyjama bottoms and opened the door.

Helen was stood there munching on some crisps. "Aren't you ready yet?" she moaned.

Susie just held the door open, and Helen followed her inside. "I'm getting ready now, my clothes are ironed.

I just need to have a wash and that".

Helen's eyes shot to Susie's stomach area, and her jaw dropped. "Fucking hell, Miss Piggy, what have you been eating?" she walked towards Susie and patted at the pink flesh she could see. "You better start dieting like me; otherwise you'll be fat as fuck, if ya carry on. It just creeps up on ya, yanno."

Susie yanked at her vest top that had ridden up. Pulling it down with her hand she snarled at Helen. "I'm due on my period; I always look frumpy when I'm due on."

Helen chuckled and carried on eating the last crumbs of the crisps from the packet. "I'm just saying, that's all, you wouldn't want me to lie to you, would you?"

Susie marched back up the stairs in a mood. "I won't be long, go into the front room." Susie bounced up the stairs back to the bathroom; she'd definitely spat her dummy out.

Helen parked her arse on the sofa. Clocking all the drugs on the table she had a cunning look on her face. She knew exactly how much this kind of stuff sold for on the streets, and wanted a little earner for herself. Quickly tiptoeing back to the living room door she shouted up to Susie. "Do you want a brew?" Helen held her ear to the door, there was no reply. Bouncing back to the table, she quickly pulled one of the parcels open. Her fingers were trembling as she yanked a few bags of heroin out of them. She continued to do so to all the other packets, and made sure she had enough drugs to earn herself some decent cash. All the parcels were sealed back up, and you couldn't tell she'd interfered with them. Quickly catching her breath she sank the drugs into the lining of her coat. She could hear footsteps coming down the stairs; Helen looked flushed as she reached for the TV remote and pretended to be flicking through the channels.

Susie was ready; her make-up hid a multitude of sins on her face. Checking the clock on the wall she spoke to Helen. "We'd better get a move on, the visits in an hour." Helen watched Susie clearing the table of the drugs. She knew she was taking them into the jail, but she didn't have a clue that the screw Jenkins was making sure she never got caught. Susie reached for her handbag, and hunged the parcels inside.

Helen was watching her from the corner of her eye, she didn't have a clue she'd been inside them. With a cunning look on her face she stood up and stretched her hands over her head. "Don't you ever shit yourself taking all that gear into the jail, I mean fucking hell, you'd get years, if you ever got caught."

Susie chuckled and started to put her coat on. "I'm too good to get caught love, I mean," she placed her hand on her hip and pointed to herself. "Do I look like a drug smuggler," she giggled. "They don't search people like me. It's people like you who look dodgy who get searched."

Susie watched Helen's face drop and grinned. "Ay, ya cheeky bitch, I don't look dodgy. I look like a normal everyday person."

"Yeah right" Susie sniggered.

Helen looked upset; Susie could always make her feel like shit at the drop of a hat. Helen hated that she could never win an argument with her. Growling at her she tried to retaliate. "Let's hope you're right, because I'd hate to see you land up in the clink. You wouldn't last one night."

Susie ignored her and grabbed the car keys from the side. "Come on then, dodgy dealer," she chuckled.

"Fuck off," Helen snapped as they headed outside.

The weather was cold and the grey clouds in the sky told you it wouldn't be long before the heavens opened. The smell of smoke filled the air, in the distance you could see a car that had been burnt out. Small kids were congregating round it and you could see the mischievous looks written across their faces.

Susie pulled out from her street. Her tunes were on low and Helen sat nodded her head to the beat as they waited in traffic. Helen started to sniff, her nostrils were flaring. Yanking at her sleeve she grabbed the armpit of her jumper. Her face screwed up as she smelt the stale aroma. "Fucking hell, I stink like a pig's arse-hole, have you got any spray or owt?"

Susie huffed as she dropped her eyes to her handbag. "There's some 'Impulse' spray in there, get some of that."

Helen dipped her head and rummaged about in the handbag. Holding the aerosol out in front of her she giggled. "Fuck me, I'm gonna smell like a prostitute's handbag." Her eyes scanned the white bottle in front of her. "Vanilla Musk, what the fucks that?"

"Just spray it will you," Susie moaned. Helen was really doing her head in now and she just seemed to know how to wind her up.

Helen squirted into the space in front of her first and inhaled. "It's not bad that," she mumbled. Lifting her top up, her hand disappeared underneath it. You could hear her spraying the deodorant. Helen sniffed her underarms. "I smell lovely, like a proper woman. I think I'm going to have to invest in a few bottles of this myself, what's it called again?"

Susie grabbed the bottle from her hand and flung it back in her bag as the traffic came to a standstill. Helen smiled at her and turned her head to look out of the window. She loved winding her up.

Strangeways was now in sight. The large red brick tower stood tall from all the buildings near it, like it was making a statement to everyone who walked past it. Susie pulled up in the car park and gathered her things together. Helen was already out of the car and still sniffing her new body scent. Susie smiled at her and shook her head; Helen was definitely a couple of butties short of a picnic.

Walking into the visitors' centre both women went to the main desk and booked in. Susie handed Tim's boxer shorts in and then sat at a table nearby. Helen was stood up reading all the notices on the board. Her loud voice could be heard shouting. "Ay, Susie you can extra money to come and visit Tim, yanno." Helen was pointing her finger at the billboard in front of her. "It's called "POPS" Partners of Prisoners or summit like that."

Susie scowled at her as the other visitors found her amusing. One woman at the other table spoke. "You can claim money back for your visits; all you have to do is fill a form out and get it stamped when you go into the prison. I do it all the time, but I come from quite far away. Where have you come from?"

Susie held her head in the air and blanked the woman completely. Helen was by her side. "We live in Harpurhey, it's only a stone's throw away, so it's not that far. Do you think she'll get owt for that?"

The woman hunched her shoulders, "It's worth a try, she might get something."

Helen was just about to get into a big conversation when Susie walked past her to go to the toilets. Susie patted her on the shoulder. "I won't be long, shout me if our name get called out." Helen nodded and carried on speaking to her new- found friend. She watched Susie disappear and started asking her about who she was coming to see. You could see Helen's face loving every minute of the conversation; she was a right nosey bastard.

Susie closed the toilet door behind her. You could see her nostrils flaring as she inhaled deeply. The toilets stank of piss and at one point she was heaving at its rancid stench. Sitting on the closed toilet lid she bent her body down and searched in her handbag for the parcels. Once she'd found them she stood to her feet and pushed each of the drug- bombs deep into her pants. Her crotch looked funny and it was bulging with all the goods she'd shoved down it. With one hand, she patted them down at the front of her dark coloured jeans. She was ready to leave.

After about fifteen minutes wait, the names were finally called. Helen sprang to her feet and knew it was only a matter of time before she could have something to eat; she was a greedy cow and she was always hungry. "I'm starving," she moaned at Susie.

"What's new? You're never full, you just eat and eat all day long."

Helen giggled, "I do, don't I?"

Susie looked stressed as she went through the usual procedure in the prison. Once they were searched she started to relax. Helen was doing her head in and talking to anyone who would give her a bit of attention. Even when she was being searched she was making a scene. The woman who was searching her shook her head as she listened to her. "You need two people to search me love, your little arms won't reach round my arse." Helen was laughing loudly and a few of the officers found her quite amusing. Once she was searched you could see her putting her trainers back on her feet. Helen was yanking at her sock as she let everybody know, her odd socks had holes in.

Susie snarled at her and gritted her teeth as they made their way up to the visiting room. "Why the fuck, do you have to perform everywhere we go, just keep your trap shut for one fucking minute will you."

Helen sighed and waved her hands about in front of her body. "Chill ya beans, you miserable bitch, it wouldn't do you any harm to break a smile every now and then you know." Susie ignored her, her mind was on the visit and how she'd pass the drugs over. This was the biggest drop she'd ever done and she just hoped she wouldn't fuck it up.

Jenkins seemed in a good mood today. As she walked past him he held a smirk across his face. Susie studied him for a minute and carried on walking past him. "What was he so fucking happy about?" she mumbled under her breath.

Shouting could be heard and Susie could see it was Helen again who was making a show of herself. "Yo... our kid," she ranted. Tim was sinking his head in his arms as they both got nearer. Susie and Helen sat down at the table. Tim told his sister to go and get some food before the queue got any bigger, he was hurrying her away. Struggling to get back up from her seat Helen held her hand out to Susie. "Give us some cash then, I'd get it, but I'm pot-less." A twenty pound note now lay in her hands and Susie was raising her eyes to the ceiling. She knew Helen would make sure she filled her face on her money. She shook her head at her. "Make sure I get some change, greedy balls."

Once Tim told Helen what they both wanted, she went to join the long line up of people queuing not far from them. Tim dragged Susie's hand over the table.

"What the fuck have you brought her for?"

Susie pulled her hand from his, "Why what's wrong with bringing her, she's your sister isn't she."

Tim sighed as he ran his fingers through his hair. He looked agitated. "I just wanted it to be us two, that's all." Tim's eyes were all over the place, he could just about see Jenkins leaving the room. His arse was moving about in his seat as he stood out of it a little, he looked to be trying to get Jenkins's attention. Tim plonked his body back in his chair. "Did you bring the gear?"

Susie looked chuffed with herself and nodded her head slowly. "Yeah fuck me, there's loads, Tim. I could just about get it in the front of my pants." Her face smiled from cheek to cheek. Tim tapped his fingers on the table, and his head was twisting about all the time. "What's up with you?" Susie hissed.

Taking a few moments to answer her, he stuttered his words. "Nowt, I'm just a bit pissed off that's all, fancy bringing our Helen with you."

Susie gasped "Fucking hell, Tim, I can't believe you're going on one over this, usually you're always saying why hasn't any of my family come to see me. I can't fucking do right, by doing fucking wrong, me." Two people sat at the table now in complete silence. You could have cut the atmosphere with a knife.

Helen marched over to the table carrying a red tray in her hands. The plastic tray was covered in biscuits, drinks, crisps and sandwiches. Pushing herself back into her chair she pushed the food towards Tim. "Get stuck into that lot our kid."

Helen reached over and her body was stuck into Susie's face. "Fucking hell," Susie moaned as she pushed her blubber away from her. Helen sat back down in her chair.

Peeling her cheese and onion butty open she rammed the white piece of bread into her mouth. Speaking with her mouth full she spoke to her brother. "My mam's been going mad because you haven't written to her, she said to tell you, you'd better get writing."

Tim huffed; he wasn't listening to her properly, he seemed in a world of his own. "When do you want me to pass this lot over then, it looks quiet now, should I give it to you?" Susie whispered. Tim shot his eyes about the room, she was right the time was right; he nodded his head at her. Digging her hands down the front of her jeans she clenched the large parcels of drugs. Bringing her hand back to her lap she rested it there for a moment. Her hands came over the table as she leant over to kiss him. During the kiss she passed the first of the six drops.

Jenkins was visible inside the visiting room. He looked hot and flustered. A few other screws were standing next to him. They were all whispering amongst themselves. Tim was sat at the table, he hadn't concealed the parcel yet, his eyes were all over the place he was debating his next move.

In an instant Tim's head was dragged behind him. His hands were twisted up behind his back. The screws were shouting in a loud voice for him to stop resisting. Susie stood to her feet and was ranting at the top of her voice. "Get ya fucking hands off him now, you load of pricks." Helen was joining in and they were cursing the men. Tim was dragged off the visit. All the other visitors and inmates were up in arms. They knew what must have happened but still they sided with the inmate. Tim was gone within seconds.

Susie scanned her eyes about the room, her face was snow white. Chewing on her fingernails she whispered to Helen. "Come on, it's on top, let's get the fuck out of here." Helen grabbed the left-over butty from the table and got on her toes towards the exit. Both women jogged to the door and were greeted by a gang of screws. Susie was waving her hands above her head as she was dragged away from the door. Helen stood bewildered with her hands dug deep in her coat pocket. Susie was livid.

The two women were taken to another part of the prison; Susie could see Jenkins smiling at her before she left. At that second the penny seemed to drop. "No," she yelled as her body sank to the floor. Helen was trying to bring her back to her feet but it was no good Susie was like a lead weight. The noise was deafening in the corridor, lots of bodies were all over the place. It was frantic. Susie was flung into a holding cell on her own. She could hear Helen shouting outside the room, she too was being held against her will. Standing with her back to the door, Susie listened carefully as her body folded into two. "Get ya fucking big daft hands off me? I've done fuck all wrong, what are you holding me for."

A male voice could be heard talking in a loud tone. He was telling Helen that the police were on their way. "Police," Helen cried, "What the fuck have you phoned the dibble for?"

The words Susie heard sent shivers down her spine; goose pimples were visible all over her arms. "Intent to supply drugs," the screw replied.

Helen shrugged her shoulders. "Listen, you fucking arsehole, go and check the cameras, and you'll see I haven't done anything wrong." Her hand was waving about in front of her now. "Go on Inspector fucking Clouseau, go and check the CCTV." The sound of a door slamming could be heard. Helen was kicking and punching the walls. "Susie if you can hear me, you'd better sort this shit out, I've got kids to go home to."

Susie held her hands over her ears. Tears trickled down her face and she knew she was well and truly fucked. Feeling the front of her pants she realised that she still had drugs on her body. Her eyes were all over the room. It was bare and there was nowhere to hide anything without anyone seeing it. She was screwed. Crawling to the small platform at the back of the room she cradled her arms around her body and rocked. All her eye make-up was running down her face and it seemed like she was crying black tears. Her head dipped onto her knees as she tried listening outside the room.

Tim was still down the block in the prison. Jenkins came into his cell and made sure nobody could hear him. "Job done, they're both still in the prison, they're in the holding cells waiting for the police to come."

Tim sprang to his feet, "What the fuck is gonna happen to me, they've got a parcel from me."

Jenkins smiled, "All you say is that, she passed it to you, you never tried to conceal it I've checked on the cameras. Just say she said, here get hold of that. I mean you just took it from her and we were on you, so the story fits."

Tim smirked. "Are you sure I'm gonna be alright?"

Jenkins nodded his head. "Trust me Tim, I'll sort it, I just want all this shit to end now, and to get on with my life."

Tim agreed. "How is Susie anyway?"

Paul Jenkins hung his head low. "She's a mess; she's gonna do big time for this, no matter what."

Tim paused and coughed to clear his throat. Taking a long deep breath he stared at the walls for a minute. He placed his hand on Jenkins shoulder. "It's all over for you now boss, she's an evil bitch and I'm sorry for what she's put you through. I'll never tell a soul about what we've done, just make sure I don't get a nicking for this."

Jenkins smirked as Tim continued talking with a smug look on his face. "As for Susie, let her do her roast like I've had to do for all this time, she's a wrong 'un you know, and she's got what she deserved."

Jenkins blew a laboured breath and months of stress seemed to vanish from his face, he looked relieved. "What about the other woman with her? She's kicking right off that one."

Tim chuckled. "Our Helen is innocent; like you said when they see the footage they'll see it's only Susie who was carrying drugs."

Jenkins quickly checked the door. Reaching his hand out to Tim they shook hands. "Good luck," he whispered as he left the room.

Tim bounced back onto his bed. Looping his hands behind his head he let out a menacing laugh and cackled. "Told you, you would pay bitch, didn't I? Look who's laughing now, ay." Laughter filled the room as he kicked his legs out in front of him. His clenched fist punched into the air. "Result, fucking result," he shouted.

CHAPTER TWENTY-ONE

Susie dried her eyes and sank her head into her chest as she heard the cell door opening. A male police officer walked inside, he shot her a look of disgust and pulled out a small note pad from his pocket. Taking a minute to gather his words together, he read out her legal rights. He'd arrested Susie on intent to supply drugs. Susie was handcuffed and led from the holding area; they told her they were taking her to a police station in Salford.

Walking from the room, she could now see Helen being brought out of her cell too. As soon as she saw Susie she was like a woman possessed. "You better sort this you, there is no way I'm getting slammed for fuck all." Susie dipped her head but gave no response. Helen could still be heard shouting as Susie left the building.

The pair were taken to Pendleton police station. The officers told her they were waiting for her solicitor to attend and then she would be interviewed. The legal representative was one that Tim had used in the past; she was hoping he would get her off the hook with the offences she was facing. Susie was ordered to take a bobble out of her hair and the small laces she had in the front of her boots. She was being searched. Susie looked distraught; she still had the drugs on her. She was chewing rapidly on her bottom lip. A female officer started to search her; she was patting her hands all over her body. Susie thought she was safe as her crotch was never touched; a relieved look came to her face and she thought it was all over. The female officer now brought a flat machine near to her body and asked her to hold her hands out to the side of her. The machine was slid all over her body. The sound of a buzzing noise could be heard. Susie looked at the officer and hunched her shoulders. "What does that mean?" The woman walked off and came back with two more officers. They knew she was concealing drugs without a shadow of doubt, the machine was buzzing like a bumble bee. The officer spoke.

"Miss, we know you have illegal substances on you. We need to strip search you."

Susie backed away from them and stood with her

body pressed against the wall. "Fucking not a chance in this world are you shoving your fingers up my arse, I want to see my solicitor." Her face screwed up and she looked distressed. Thinking for a few minutes, she knew it was on top and she was gasping for breath. Digging her hand deep down the front of her pants she started to yank out all the drug packages. The officers nudged each other as she placed them all on the nearby table. Her face looked hot and she looked faint. "Can I have a drink of water please," she asked. The female officer walked away and you could hear a tap running in the distance. Susie huffed, "There you go, and that's the lot. I've got fuck all else." Her hands were patting her body. "Tim made me do it; he said if I didn't, he would get me sorted out." Her face stared at the officers. "And he would you know, you don't know the half of it, he's an evil bastard when he wants to be."

Susie was strip searched, it was the procedure. They couldn't take her word on it. No more drugs were found on her body, but the amount they did uncover was enough to send her to jail for at least five years if not longer. Once her photograph and fingerprints had been taken they led her back to her cell to wait for her solicitor to attend.

Helen bounced out of her cell; it was her turn to be searched. She looked hot and clammy and she wasn't taking any of this lying down. "Do we have to go through this; I'm nothing to do with it," she moaned, "ask Susie if you don't believe me." Helen's head was spinning around to the officers, "Hasn't she already told you?" Her eyes were all over the show now, and she was waiting for some response from the dibble, there was none. Once she was body searched they waved the silver machine over her body. Bleeping noises could be heard. "What's that fucking thing going on about," Helen moaned as she swung her arms out in front of her.

"We need to strip search you, you have traces of drugs on your body," the officer snarled.

"Have I fuck, you barmy twat, I don't touch drugs," Helen raved.

The officer raised her eyes to the ceiling. She'd heard this story so many times in the past. "Sorry love, its procedure." She spoke in a loud tone and shot her eyes over to her work colleagues.

Helen stood smiling, "Well come on then, you won't find jack shit on me." The officer led her to another room, all of a sudden Helen halted, and she looked like she'd seen a ghost. Her legs turned to jelly, gripping her jacket she remembered the stash she'd nicked from Susie earlier. Her lips were dry as she slid her tongue over them. The officer urged her to carry on walking, her face was pale. Stuttering her words she gripped the door frame. "Erm... Can I just go to the toilet please?"

The police officer shook her head, "Sorry love, we need to get you searched first."

Helen's body folded into two, dragging at her hair she pulled at the officer's legs. "Right, this is no bullshit, please you've got to believe me."

The woman shook her from her leg. "Come on now, we need to get this sorted."

Helen sprang to her feet yelling. "I've got drugs on me, yes. But I wasn't going to give them to anyone in jail. Susie had it all on the table in her house, so I just nicked some from her to earn a few quid that's all."

All the officers were stood round her now. She was making the case a lot stronger for them. She was telling them more or less that they both sat down and planned the drug run together. If this was the case they knew they could bang a conspiracy charge on the both of them. Helen searched the lining of her coat. They could see it was the same packaging as the drugs Susie had given them. Helen was well and truly fucked; there was no way she was going to talk her way out of this one. Her tears fell and she kept asking them if she was going to jail. The female officer held nothing back.

"Helen, no matter what, you've taken drugs into a prison." Her eyes scanned the table as her fingers touched the drugs they'd found on her, "and looking at this lot, you're in big trouble."

Helen was taken to have her prints done. Her face was red and tears were falling down her cheeks at record speed. "I can't go to jail." she sobbed. "What about my kids?"

Nobody was listening to a word she said. To the officers she was just another criminal who'd been caught in the act. There was no doubt in their minds; this woman was getting slammed in nick, no matter what.

Susie's solicitor walked into the interview room to meet her. Susie had been brought up from her cell. The lady was well dressed and in her mid thirties. Her grey trouser-suit looked neatly pressed and the white crisp blouse from underneath her jacket looked fresh and clean. The woman introduced herself as Nicola. Quickly reading all the notes on the table as she sat down, Susie looked surprised as she had been expecting a man to represent her, but was told he was on annual leave.

Nicola reached for a pen from her bag and started to take a few details from her client. Susie was sighing all the time and shaking her head. "Am I getting out of here, or what?" she huffed.

Nicola sat back in her chair and shot her eyes towards her client. "This is serious Susie; I think you need to know that there is a prison sentence hanging over your head. The evidence they have is enough to hold you in custody, and I have no doubt they will not allow you any kind of bail."

Susie was up in arms. "Listen Nicola, don't tell me that, just get me out of this shit-hole, how can you just say I'm not getting bail without talking to anyone"

Nicola opened her eyes wide and tilted her head to the side, "Susie, I know my job and in my opinion a bail application at the moment would be wasted."

Susie punched her fist onto the table, "I don't care what you think, this is my life you're fucking about with, just get me out of here." Silence filled the room.

Before long Susie was stood at the charge desk. It was decided she was going to be held in custody and the next day she would appear at court with her co-accused Helen. Sobbing could be heard, as they led her back to her holding cell, it took two officers to get her back inside, she was punching and kicking, and she wasn't going down without a fight.

Helen lay staring at the ceiling holding her hands on her body and constantly cracking her knuckles. Tossing and turning all night long, she knew there was no way out of this terrible mess. No matter what, nobody would believe her and she would have to face her punishment. Helen told her solicitor all about her stealing the drugs from Susie. Her legal representative told her that when they went to court the following morning he would plead her case to the judge but he told her straight not to expect miracles. Helen's eyelids were flickering rapidly as she closed her eyes for sleep, her fists were clenched together and you could hear her cursing under her breath.

Tim sat on the end of his bed, holding each of Susie's photographs. Slowly he pulled his lighter from his pocket and flicked the flame. The corner of the snapshot started to curl at the edges, his fingers were moving about as the flame ate away at the last part of his girlfriend's face. The ashes fell to the floor and he sat staring at them as he repeated the process on all her other pictures.

"Burn bitch, burn bitch," he whispered.

CHAPTER TWENTY-TWO

Vicky sat watching the clock. Declan was already staying over at her sisters and this was her first night of working at 'Delia's'. Joan told her point-blank that if she didn't turn up she would come looking for her, and this time she would deal with her big time. Tim had also been in touch with her. He was angry and told the young girl straight, that she would work to pay every last penny back off she owed him. He told her that the love he thought he felt for her had disappeared and had been replaced by hate and disgust.

Standing to her feet Vicky checked her scrawny body in the mirror. Her make-up seemed dull, there was no glow on her face and all that was left was a face full of regrets. Lighting a cig she pulled open the front door and looked at the surrounding area, everywhere seemed quiet. She shivered as the night air penetrated her bones. Vicky had already drunk half a bottle of vodka to calm her nerves and you could see her body wobbling as she started walking through the council estate towards the bus stop.

Delia's front door stared at Vicky as she stepped

from the bus, her body froze and she looked like she was going to turn back. A few men were staring at her with perverted looks on their faces; she stood debating her next move. Vicky pulled her coat tighter around her body covering her red lacy top and snarled at the men. "Fucking skanks," she whispered under her breath. The young girl's legs looked long and slender and the short skirt she wore left nothing to the imagination. Stepping closer to the entrance her fingers trembled as she pressed the buzzer on the intercom. Joan told her to come inside. Her legs began to shake and every step she took looked like she was in pain, at one point she just froze and held the banister struggling for her breath. The scar on her cheek still looked red and sore. The foundation she'd spread across it didn't cover it up that well.

The reception was quiet as she pushed the door slowly open. Joan waited for her with one hand placed firmly on her hip. Walking inside she quickly grabbed her face in her hands, as she chuckled loudly. "It's healing nicely innit?" Vicky didn't reply. Joan looked proud as she examined every inch of the wound. She felt no remorse for her actions and held a cunning look in her eyes. Joan gritted her teeth as she spoke. "That's what you get when you think you can have me over, darling; let that be a lesson to you." Vicky stood with her head held low; she was afraid. The sound of the side door opening could be heard.

Pippa came to join them, her eyes shot at Vicky as she looked her up and down with a cocky look on her face. Clearing her throat she pointed a finger into Vicky's face. "My, how the mighty have fallen, I knew from the first minute I set my eyes on you, you were a wrong 'un," she turned her head to Joan. "Didn't I tell you Joan? I could feel it in my waters?"

Joan nodded and snarled at Vicky. "You sure did love, she's a cunning little slapper this one is. We'll have to keep a close eye on her."

Pippa laughed out loud and spoke, "Right, show her the room where's she's gonna be working, she can start with next punter who comes through the door." Joan told Vicky to follow her and started walking towards the corridor. Pippa sat down and lit up a cig, she was watching every movement Vicky made, she didn't trust her one little bit.

The room was dimly lit and nothing but a small lamp in the corner of the room gave off any light. A double bed sat in the middle of the room, with black silk sheets spread across it. There was a smell on the bedding that could only be described as wet dog. A few mirrors were on the wall behind the headboard. Vicky quickly turned her head from them, she couldn't stand looking at herself and the person she'd become. Joan's voice was calm and low; she reached for Vicky's hand and told her to sit down on the bed next to her. Once they were both seated Joan shook her head as she watched the nervous kid in front of her. She knew exactly how she felt and remembered the first time she'd sold her body, she gasped.

"This is all your own fault, yanno? I mean that money wasn't mine; Tim would have dealt with me if I didn't sort it out for him. You're lucky the lads didn't come looking for you, because believe me honey," she blew a hard breath and shook her head before she continued, "you would have had more than a little scratch on your face, darling. They would have raped you, shaved your hair off, you name it, and the sick twats would have done it to you, so count yourself lucky."

Joan dug deep inside her pocket and pulled out a spliff. Passing it to Vicky she stood to her feet. "Here, smoke some of that, once you're off ya head you won't give a fuck who you're shagging. It's a job that's all, don't let it get to you, because you're gonna be here for a long, long time, to pay off what you owe. Do you hear me?" Vicky looked close to tears and her lips were trembling. Joan paused and she looked ready to throw her arms around the girl but hesitated, she headed to the door shaking her head. "Fucking life is a bitch, and then you die," she mumbled under her breath.

Vicky watched the door close, she was alone now. Lighting the spliff, she sank back into the stale smelling mattress. Smoke circled over her head and you could see her eyes slowly closing. Her body seemed to be melting into the bed. Once she'd smoked the weed she dragged herself up and looked about. Dragging her coat from her body she threw it on a nearby chair. Her eyes looked glazed over, as she sat staring at the door waiting for someone to come in. She could hear someone outside the room and looked anxious. Chewing on her fingernails she watched the silver door handle slowly move down. Pippa was stood there with a middle-aged man at her side. The smirk on her face told Vicky she loved every minute of her pain. Stepping inside the room she escorted the punter inside. "This is Vicky; she's going to entertain you tonight." Pippa stood for a moment and watched the man sit on the edge of the bed. Holding her head back Pippa chuckled as she left the room. "Bitch," Vicky growled.

The punter sat looking at Vicky; he held a seedy look in his eyes as he slid his discoloured tongue over his lips. Moving closer to her he stroked his fat fingers across her neck, he stank of sweat. "You're new here, aren't you?"

Vicky nodded as he continued. "I thought you were, because I'm a regular and I've never seen you before." Standing to his feet he rolled his nylon pants down over his knees, he kicked them off his legs to the side of the room. The man left his shirt on and his black socks and climbed onto the top of the bed. Looping· his hands behind his head he smiled at Vicky. "Come on love, get up here next to me, I don't bite." He patted the bed next to him. Vicky looked like she was struggling to breathe as she stood to her feet. Swaying to the top of the bed she plonked down next to the punter. His hands gripped her tiny waist as he helped her onto the bed. "Get ya mouth round that love, I won't take long, I never do." He chuckled and grabbed her head in his hands pushing it down towards his crotch.

Vicky could see his manhood and cringed as she grabbed it in both her hands. She could already hear groans from the top of the bed and knew the man was going to be shooting his load within minutes. His penis was small and fat and looked like a coiled worm. Licking her lips she sank his penis deep into her mouth. The man started jerking his arse up and down and at one point he was nearly choking her. "Swallow it all ya dirty bitch," she heard him saying from the top of the bed. Turning her head to the side she could see his face. The man looked like he was going to burst; he looked like a pig in a fit. His face was bright red and he looked like he was in pain. More moans could be heard and Vicky slid her mouth as fast as she could around his erect member. "Yes, yes," he groaned. Vicky pulled her mouth away from him just in time; she could see him ejaculating. His toes were curling and she knew within seconds her ordeal would be over.

"Thank fuck for that," he groaned. She snarled as her

face screwed up.

Vicky watched her first punter grab his pants from the floor. She was watching him like a hawk as he started to put them on. Fastening his belt he turned his head to face her with a smile spread across his face. "The girls call me a jerk and a squirt you know. I've always been the same, I just can't control it."

Vicky was wiping her mouth on her sleeve and just wanted him to leave. "No worries," she said.

The man focused on her face. "You don't talk a lot do you?"

Vicky shrugged her shoulders and sighed. "Nar, I'm new to this game, and it's just a bit stressful that's all." The man walked to her side and his eyes were fixed on the scar on her face. Slowly he raised his hand and stroked his fingers slowly across her cheek. Vicky pulled her head away from him and looked shocked. "What the fuck do you think you're doing?"

The man backed off and looked at her as he shook his head. "I'm only showing that I care love, that looks sore. It's obvious you've had some trouble in your life and I'm just letting you know I care."

Vicky walked to the door and yanked it open. Stood looking at him she spoke in a sarcastic tone. "Listen I'm here to do a job, I don't need a fucking counselling service." The man sighed as he grabbed his coat, he looked angry. " You're a nasty little bitch you are, tell you what, if you carry on like this, no one will want to come and see you, so take a bit of advice, stop it with the attitude." Vicky dipped her head as she watched him leave. Once he was gone she rubbed at her mouth with her sleeve and slid her clothing over her tongue. She ran to the small sink and spewed her ring up.

The night went on more or less the same; all in all Vicky had four more punters. Each of them had wanted full blown sex and by the look on her face she was desperate to get home and out of this place. Pippa and Joan walked into the room after the last man had left. Joan was stood watching Vicky and nudged Pippa in the waist. "She did alright, didn't she?"

Pippa snarled and shot her eyes over to Vicky. "Yeah she done okay, we might make a woman of her yet."

The sound of laughter filled the room. Vicky grabbed her coat from the side and walked to where they both were stood. "Right I'm off home now, is that okay with you two?" her voice was sarcastic as she raised her eyes at them both.

Pippa snapped at her, "Ay, you cocky bitch, we're doing you a favour letting you work here, if it wasn't for us you'd be lying in some ditch somewhere half dead."

Vicky gritted her teeth, she was ready to explode and you could see the anger on her face. Pippa could see Vicky's fist clenching at the side of her and stepped in towards her face. "Do you want to say something love?"

Vicky backed off; she knew Pippa would rip her in two in an instant. "No I'm just tired that's all. I just wanna go home."

"I thought so," Pippa scowled.

Joan could see Pippa was ready to bang the girl out, and tried to diffuse the situation. "Right ladies, come on now; we've all had a long night. See you tomorrow Vicky." Joan opened the door and waved her past with her hand. "Get some sleep love, the worst is over now, it only gets better."

Vicky walked past her towards the exit. She could feel Pippa's eyes on her and knew she would have to watch her back in the future. "Goodnight," Vicky shouted as she left the brothel. Vicky was shivering as the midnight air gripped her body. Pulling her coat tightly around her she lit a cigarette. Her face looked distressed and a single tear fell down her face. "Bastards, dirty load of bastards," she sobbed all the way home.

CHAPTER TWENTY-THREE

Time passed and Susie and Helen had been found guilty of the crimes they'd committed. Susie sat anxiously in the courtroom waiting for sentence to be passed. Helen was at the side of her and the two of them were eager to hear what the judge had to say. Helen's family were in the courtroom and her mother kept looking at her daughter and shaking her head. Not one member of Susie's family came to the courtroom to show any support for her. They all said she could rot in jail for all they cared. Susie had always been a bitch with her family and wouldn't give them the time of day. She made out she was better than them and always made them feel like the scum of the earth. Today she looked sad and lonely.

The judge returned to the courtroom and everyone stood to their feet. As Susie stood from her chair you could see the bottom part of her stomach sticking out from underneath her clothing. Nobody knew she was pregnant yet and she was still hoping that she would be a free woman and be able to sort it out. Susie looked tired; her eyes had dark circles underneath them through lack of sleep. Helen looked like a different woman, the weight had fallen from her, and she must have lost at least two stones. The two women sat back down and the courtroom became silent, you could have heard a pin drop.

Susie's barrister summed up her case and hoped he'd done enough to keep her out of prison. He'd told Susie millions of times to expect jail but he knew she was still hoping to walk free. As he finished talking he pleaded with Judge Merdock one last time to be lenient with his client. Susie sat on the edge of her seat as she listened to Helen's barrister speak on her behalf. Helen was nudging Susie in the waist all the time and whispering into her ear. "He seems a right cunt, look at his serious face, we're definitely getting slammed."

"Will you shut the fuck up, Grim Reaper," Susie snapped, "and let me listen to what he's saying." Helen sighed and sat forward in her seat. Her head was resting into her hands and she was hanging onto every word her barrister said. Susie looked frozen and white with fear. The judge now had all he needed to sentence the two women in front of him.

Susie was asked to stand to her feet. The judge peered over his thick lens glasses as he spoke to her. Her hands were gripping a nearby chair and her knuckles were turning white, you could see her legs shaking as she tried to remain calm. The judge spoke about the crime she'd committed and heard the whispering from the public gallery. Turning his head to the usher he made sure that silence was maintained before he gave out any sentences. Susie's lips looked dry and cracked as she slowly slid her tongue over them. All eyes were on her now and she could feel her heart beating in her ears. Holding one hand to her chest she tried to calm her breathing down, she was blowing her breath slowly from her mouth. The words of the judge made her legs give way. "Five years imprisonment," was all that she heard before she fell to the floor. Helen was distraught and ran to her side, but she was pushed away as the security guards helped her co-accused back to her feet. Susie looked like death warmed up, her mouth dropped and she was struggling to speak. The judge gave the nod to the security men and she was led from the courtroom in a daze.

Helen stood to hear her fate. She held a look of sadness over her face as she looked at her mother and boyfriend inside the courtroom. The judge sentenced Helen to the same prison term. He told her that he didn't believe for one minute the story she'd given him and for that reason she was treated the same as her co-accused. Helen pummelled her fist onto the glass panel that held her inside the dock. She was yelling at the top of her voice. "Ay, ya prick, I'm innocent. I told you I was just in the wrong place at the wrong time."

The judge waved his hand at her and dismissed any words she was saying. "Take her down," he repeated to the security guards.

Helen gripped the side of the chair and held onto it with all her might. "I'm going nowhere, me mate. I've got kids, for fuck sake, who's gonna look after my children?" Helen's mother covered her face with her hands as she sobbed. Her boyfriend looked like he was going to collapse where he stood. Helen was being twisted up inside the dock and it was only a matter of minutes before she was silenced. "Get your fucking hands of me, ya wankers," she screamed as she was being carried from the courtroom.

Susie sat in her cell waiting to be moved to a prison. Her hands were rubbing at her arms and she couldn't stop shaking. Holding her stomach she cradled the lower part of it and sobbed. Banging noises could be heard and Susie could hear Helen shouting outside her door. "I'm fucking innocent. I want my solicitor here now. I'm appealing against the sentence. Fucking five years, is he having a laugh the daft cunt."

Susie stood to her feet and banged her fist onto the door. "Helen it's me Susie, what did you get?"

Helen could hear her voice and stopped fighting with the guards for a minute. "Susie, you bastard, just you wait until I get my hands on you. Five fucking years I got, what about my kids." Hysterical screams could be heard and after a few minutes you could hear a door being slammed. Susie walked back to the small platform at the back of the room and lay down. Bringing her knees up to her chest she rocked her body to and fro.

"Right come on love, you're getting shipped out to Styal prison." The warden stood at Susie's door and looked at the white piece of paper in front of her. "Come on, I haven't got all day," the officer moaned. Susie stood to her feet and trudged to the door. Her face was red and the river of tears she'd cried was more than visible on her face. She looked weak and struggled to walk. Her body was shivering and she asked the security guard could she please have something to wrap around her body to keep her warm. Susie was passed a grey coat. Shoving it on her body her lips were trembling uncontrollably. All the female prisoners were led down a corridor. Helen was in the line of six women. Susie turned her head back to her and quickly carried on walking. Helen didn't scare her one little bit and she knew by the time they'd got to the prison she would have calmed down.

All the convicts were put into the sweat boxes in the white van. Each compartment was the same, holding just a chair and a window. Susie watched the door being closed behind her and sat with her head resting on the window. Banging her head against the glass panel she cried her eyes out. Tim had so much to answer for and she knew without any doubt in her mind that he'd set her up with Jenkins. Gritting her teeth she punched into the side of the van. "Tim, I don't know how, and I don't know when, but mark my words you bastard, I'll pay you back for every day I spend in prison." The sound of the engine starting could be heard and Susie held herself. Pulling out onto the road she knew it would be a long time before she would see these Manchester roads again. Familiar landmarks were now in view and she sank her head as she passed the CIS Building in the town centre.

Helen looked dead inside and once they reached their destination she stepped from the van with a hateful look on her face. All the women were covering their eyes as they stepped into the daylight. One woman at the side of Helen was rattling for drugs and she looked ready to fall to the ground. Helen shouted the guards over and pleaded with them to help the convict. The screws came to Helen's side and laughed into her face. "Ay Samaritan, she's a drug addict roasting for drugs, she'll get sorted when we get inside the prison, so keep your nose out, alright."

Helen looked at the woman shaking at the side of her and sighed. "Well I didn't fucking know did I, God, shoot a woman for fucking caring." The female screw nodded her head at her and that was enough to let Helen know that she was treading on thin ice. All the inmates marched inside the prison. Helen was pushing past the others in the line, trying to get next to Susie.

Susie shot a look at Helen as she barged next to her. She was preparing herself for trouble and her nostrils were flaring. "Let's stick together us two, ay," she whispered behind her hand. Susie looked relieved; all the prisoners went into a small room inside the prison. "I'm fucking proper done in me Susie. Mike's never going to be able to cope with the kids while I'm in here. My mam will have to help him out, he's fucking useless," she sobbed.

Susie could see the pain in her eyes and gripped the middle of her arm as she tried to comfort her. "Helen, things will work out don't worry. I'm just sorry you've ended up in here with me that's all."

Helen accepted the arm of friendship and sank her head into her shoulder. "I don't think I'm going to make it you know. I can't do jail."

"Neither can I love," Susie huffed, "But we're just going to have to stick together and get through this, the best we can."

Helen lifted her head up and looked deep into Susie's eyes. "Thanks love; if you're here with me I'm sure it won't be half as bad."

Susie hissed and gritted her teeth. "It's your brother Tim, you have to thank for all this fucking mess."

Helen pulled away from her with an angry face. "What the fuck do you mean by that? What's our Tim got to do with us getting slammed?"

Susie nodded her head slowly and looked about to make sure nobody was listening. "He set me up love; you just got mixed up with it all. It's like you said, you were in the wrong place at the wrong time."

Helen was bouncing about, there was no way she was letting Susie disrespect her own flesh and blood. "Get a fucking grip Susie, why would Tim stitch you up, he was getting a drop, it doesn't make sense. Have a fucking think about it you daft bitch." Helen was waving her hands about in the air and the screws were watching her every movement. Seeing she was on top, she quietened her voice down and smiled at the officer. "Sorry for shouting love, I was just having a moment." She stood next to Susie and whispered. "You can tell me later when we're alone, but there's no way I'm having it that our Tim has grassed us up."

Susie smirked and nodded her head. "We'll see about that love, we'll see."

The women were escorted onto the landings. The prison looked huge inside, Susie stayed next to Helen. Each of the inmates were allocated pads and Helen had already told the screw as they were walking along the landing that she wanted to be padded up with her sister-in- law. The sound of doors being slammed shut could be heard, and in turn each of the convicts disappeared behind their prison doors. Opening a grey steel door in front of them, the warden looked at Susie and her side kick. "Here you go ladies. One double pad as ordered." Helen popped her head around the door and scanned the room quickly. Susie walked inside as Helen followed closely behind her. The door was slammed shut.

Helen placed her belongings on the bed and walked towards the small window at the back of the room. Sticking her head through the iron bars she spoke to Susie. "Fucking hell, there's no scenery out here, just loads of other windows."

Susie tried to raise a smile as she spoke in a sarcastic tone. "What did you want a fucking pool view?"

Helen pulled her head from the bars, "I'm just saying, that's all. Fuck me, if that's all I've got to look at for the next few years, I'll go off my fucking head. I'm telling you."

Susie lay on the bed and folded her pillow under her head. She knew the baby inside her body would have to be spoken about now; she couldn't keep it a secret any longer. Dragging her blouse up over her stomach she watched Helen's jaw drop. "What the fuck is that stomach all about," she shrieked.

"I'm pregnant."

Helen walked over to her bed and placed her hands on Susie's stomach. "Fucking hell, you must be at least five months gone or summat like that."

Susie shrugged her shoulders. "Maybe, I don't know."

"What do you mean you don't know?" Helen snapped.

Susie bolted up from her bed. "I've got myself into a right mess love. I think you already know who the father is don't you?"

Helen snarled and gritted her teeth, "Yeah its Ashley's, innit?" Susie nodded. "I fucking knew it." Helen was dancing about the room now. "I'm like fucking Miss Marple me. I said to our Tim you were shagging the arse off him," her hand covered her mouth as she realised what she'd just said.

Susie bolted up from her bed and ran to her face. "I fucking knew it was you, you grassing cunt." She was in her face ramming her fingers into her chest; they were both nose to nose. Neither of them were backing down. Susie clenched her fist and launched it into Helen's face, she was screaming at the top of her voice. "So all this is your fault. Tim would have been none the wiser if you'd have kept your big fucking trap shut."

Helen was giving as good, as she got, this time and twisted Susie's hair in her fat fingers. "You're a slapper, you always have been. Our Tim deserves better then you, you skanky boot."

"Oh fucking does he now?" Susie shrieked, as they

both scuffled about the cell. Susie let go of Helen's hair, her face looked white. Grabbing the bottom of her stomach she yelled out in pain.

"Helen stop it, it's the baby." Susie fell to her knees and her face screwed up as she blew a laboured breath.

"Are you alright?" Helen asked in a concerned voice.

"Just give me a minute, and I'll be fine." Susie staggered to her bed and folded up in pain as Helen watched on in disbelief.

"See, you're a daft bastard you are, fancy fighting when you're pregnant."

Susie couldn't reply. The room felt cold and Helen stood at the side of the bed watching her doubling up in pain. "I'm going to call for help," she insisted. Susie was rolling about on the bed her face looked hot.

Helen hammered her fist onto the door. "Help us please," she yelled at the top of her voice. Marching about the cell she kept running back to the door and kicking at it with force. "Bastards, open the fucking door," she ranted. Keys could be heard rattling from outside the door. Helen started shouting again at the top of her voice. The door flew open and two female screws stood there ready for action, their eyes were all over the place looking for the problem. Once Helen explained to them what was going on they immediately came to Susie's side. The officer could see something was wrong and ordered the other warden to go and get some medical help. Helen plonked on her bed and wrapped her arms around her body, she was shaking.

"I think it's the baby, I mean, it must be, mustn't it?"

The female screw looked shocked. "How far is she?"

"I don't know, the daft bitch hasn't even been to see

the doctor yet, she's only just told me she was pregnant."

More moans could be heard coming from the bed. As Susie lifted her head up you could see small droplets of sweat on her forehead. "Get me a doctor; I think I'm miscarrying."

The screw's face looked tormented and you could see a tear forming in the corner of her eyes. "Help's on its way darling, just be patient."

A medical team came into the room. Once they knew it was safe to move Susie they took her from the landing to the medical wing. The female officer stayed with her all the time holding her hand and telling her everything was going to be alright. Susie was with a doctor who was assessing her. Once he'd done a few tests, he put all Susie's pain down to a water infection. He passed her two small white tablets and told her to take them straight away. The female screw passed Susie a cold drink of water. "There you go sweetheart; I knew it was nothing to worry about." Susie gulped the water as she popped the tablets to the back of her mouth. The doctor left some tablets for Susie and told her to take the full course of the antibiotics.

Susie looked exhausted as she lay on the bed. She could see the screw at the side of her looking at her baby bump. "So, is this baby planned or what?" she asked.

Susie shook her head. "Is it fuck, it's a bad, bad, mistake. If I wasn't in here believe me, I would have got rid of it."

The woman held her hand over her mouth and grabbed Susie's hand. "Don't say that, you don't know how lucky you are. My baby died four months ago, so you should cherish every moment of being pregnant."

Susie looked at her and could see she was upset. The woman introduced herself as Jane and started to fill her in about her own heartbreak. "My son was only four months old; they said it was cot death." Susie chewed on her bottom lip as she continued. "I had postnatal depression after his birth and I blame myself every day for his death. It must have been something I'd done."

Susie watched the woman break down in tears at her side. Sitting up from the bed she tried to comfort her. "Don't be silly; cot death is just one of them things that happen. Even the doctors don't know why, so how can you blame yourself."

The woman shook her head as she dropped it into her hands. "My life was a mess, my husband was out all the time, even when he knew I wasn't well after the birth, he just seemed to be in a world of his own."

Susie reached for her hand and slowly stroked it. "Things always happen for a reason, I'm sure you'll have more children."

The distressed woman bolted up from her chair as if boiling water had been poured over her. "Me, more kids, never. I've been through enough. My husband is a lying cheating bastard who doesn't deserve me." The officer paced about the room thinking about her home life. She told Susie a bit more about herself. "This is my first month back into work, the doctor said I should have stayed off a lot longer, but I was going mad sat there on my own, each day." Susie smiled at the woman, it was quiet obvious she's been through a lot. The pair sat talking and slowly a friendship was being built. Susie was eventually moved back to the wing once she felt a little better.

Helen looked after Susie over the next few weeks. Every two minutes she was inquiring how she was feeling. Susie was spread across her bed with the grey blanket tucked underneath her neck. "I'm getting it adopted," she whispered.

Helen rolled on her side and looked Susie straight in her face. "What you going on about?" Helen lay quiet for a minute before she spoke. "Why, don't you see if Ashley wants it first? I mean he's the father after all isn't he. His parents will have it won't they? Well, until he gets out of prison at least?"

"Are you having a laugh or what, he thinks I had an abortion months ago," Susie chuckled, "he told me straight when I told him I was pregnant, that there was no way he wanted any kids."

"Yeah but once he knows you didn't have the abortion he might feel different, it's worth a try don't you think?"

"Nar," Susie hissed, "the man's a prick, he's shagging Pippa now and I couldn't stand seeing my child with that shower of shite." Helen started to make a roll- up. Susie smiled. "Make me one ay, I haven't had a cig for hours."

"You're fucking pregnant, woman, smoking should be the last thing on your mind," Helen said.

Shrugging her shoulders Susie sighed "Just fucking make me one, I don't need any big lectures."

The women lay on their beds smoking. Susie was staring at the cciling as she spoke. "If I get it adopted, no one would ever know I had a child would they?" she shot a look at Helen, "Well that's if you kept your fucking mouth shut."

"Ay, I'm no gossip, I can keep a secret me, ask anyone," Helen protested.

"Yeah right," Susie giggled. There was silence for a minute then Susie began to talk again. "No one would ever know, I would leave prison and be able to get on with my own life. Ashley would be none the wiser, or Tim for that matter."

Helen jumped in. "Would you really get your own

flesh and blood adopted."

Susie looked her directly in the face. "It's a mistake, not a kid; imagine every time I looked at it, I would just see the mess I made of my life. Tim would never have me back if I had a baby to his best mate," she took a deep breath. "No, it's for the best, it's getting adopted. I'm going to set the ball rolling tomorrow."

"Well it's your choice, and I just hope you don't live to regret it," Helen moaned

Susie yanked the blankets over her body and faced the wall. She was staring into space. Helen was fidgeting about in her bed; the rustling sound of a newspaper could be heard. Every two minutes she was trying to talk to Susie but she just ignored her pretending to be asleep. Finally she said, "Right, we need to set the record straight about our Tim setting you up, I want to hear your side of the story."

Susie yawned and stretched her legs out in front of her. "Not tonight Helen, I'm done in, all I want to do is sleep. I'll tell you tomorrow." Helen tried talking to her again, but this time she gave her no reply, her mind was elsewhere and she had to somehow sort out the mess she was in. The days in front of her were going to be long and she knew she needed a miracle to see her through her prison sentence.

CHAPTER TWENTY-FOUR

Susie took Helen's advice and wrote a letter to Ashley telling him all about the baby she was carrying. Today she was sat waiting for the post to come hoping he'd replied to her. Helen was brushing her teeth in the sink and talking to her with the toothbrush hanging from her mouth. "Why do you look so scared? What's the worst he can say? You already know he doesn't want the baby, so anything else is a bonus innit?"

Susie sat with her legs apart at the side of the bed as she rolled a cig. "I don't even know why I ever listened to you. I should have just ignored you and done what I was doing." Helen dipped her head around the silver tap and gulped some water from the running tap; swilling it around her mouth she spat it into the sink. "Like I said, you have nothing to lose." The cell door opened and the prisoner's mail was delivered. Susie gripped her letter in her hand and just looked at her name across it. She'd never had any letters before, so she knew it must be from Ashley. Helen grabbed the two letters she'd received and pushed them into her pocket. "It's from Ashley I know it," Susie yelled.

Helen parked her arse at the side of Susie on the bed. "Open it then!" Helen was rubbing her hands together with excitement; her face was hot and flustered as she watched her pad mate just staring at the letter. "Fucking hell, open it will you."

Susie slowly slid her finger along the brown envelope and pulled out the white letter from inside. Her hands were shaking as she unfolded the two pieces of paper. Her eyes scanned the words. After a few minutes she threw the letter onto the bed. "The daft cunt, why did I ever think he would be anything but a complete nob?"

Helen reached over to the letter and gripped it in her hands, as she was reading it she was cursing under her breath. Once she'd finished reading it, she lifted her head up and looked at Susie. "Well you were right, he's a cheeky fucker isn't he? He seems angry that you're still pregnant."

Susie stood up and walked towards the window. She seemed to be suffocating and squeezed her face through the bars gasping for some fresh air. Helen came behind her and rubbed her shoulders. "I'm sorry love; I thought he might have had a change of heart."

Susie turned her head back to her; tears were rolling down her face. "Fuck it Helen, the baby is getting adopted. Jane has already told me she would help me get it sorted out."

Helen watched her as she fell onto her bed. Helen screwed her face up, "Jane's all over you like a rash lately, what's the script with her? I mean a few of the girls have said there's more to her than meets the eye. What's she after? Come on tell me."

Susie smiled at Helen, "Well you know her baby died a few months back." Helen nodded her head, "Well she's after adopting mine."

Helen giggled. "What, a screw wants to adopt your baby."

Susie sat up and chuckled. "Yeah I thought it was weird at first, but ay, who gives a fuck, I don't want it, do I?"

Helen shook her head, "Just be careful love, it's not right, why would she want a prisoner's baby when she can just go through the motions and get one from the adoption agency?"

Susie smirked and twisted her hair in her fingers. "There's a waiting list, and she would have to wait years, so with me she knows she's guaranteed a baby as soon as it pops out."

Helen hunched her shoulders, "Is she paying you for it? I mean you'll want some cash won't you? Don't let her have it for fuck all."

Susie replied. "She's talking to her husband about it, apparently he wants the baby too and they're just getting the money together."

Helen heard the words money and rubbed her hands together. "How much are they giving you? I mean it's got to be at least ten grand or summit hasn't it?"

Susie shook her head as she blew a laboured breath. "Nar is it fuck that much, I've told her I want five grand and to be looked after in here." She winked at Helen. "That's priceless innit? I mean she can get me things that I need and all that, ay perhaps she might even do a few parcels for me to get started up. We could do with some cash in here couldn't we?"

Helen held a cunning look in her eyes, she knew Susie was right, none of them had a pot to piss in and this woman could be the answer to their prayers. Helen nodded her head slowly and went to lie down on her bed. Reaching into her pocket she brought out the two letters she'd received earlier. The cell was quiet and all you could hear was the rustling of Helen turning the pages of her letter. Once the first one was read she placed it at the side of her and started to open the next letter one, it was from her brother Tim.

Helen was concentrating as she read every word on the piece of paper. Her mouth was moving but no words were coming out. Bolting up from the bed she stood facing Susie with the letter held in her hand. "Our Tim said it's your fault that I'm in here. He said to ask you about Jenkins and what you did to him."

Just the mention of Tim's name sent shivers down Susie's spine, her face lost all colour as she sprang up from the bed. "Listen gob shite, I've told you before what that bastard did to me. It's his fault you're in here, not mine love."

Helen was bouncing about the room and dragging her fingers through her hair. "Nar, there's more to it, so you better start talking and sort this out."

Susie fell back onto her bed and kicked her legs out in front of her. "Tell that brother of yours that I'm saying fuck all. We both know who's full of shit, and I can tell you now, it's not me."

Helen chewed on her lips and she stood thinking for a second and piped up again. "Well I want some answers. I shouldn't be in here."

Susie bolted up from the bed, she'd heard enough. "Listen you fat twat, you was nicking drugs from Tim to start with, if you would have kept you're thieving fingers still you wouldn't be in here, so there is only yourself to blame, is that not right." Susie tilted her head to the side and gritted her teeth together.

Helen knew she was right and backed down. "I'm just saying that's all," she moaned.

Both women left their pad to go for breakfast. Susie hadn't made any effort to brush her hair or even have a wash, she looked a mess. Walking down the landing she looked at each of the inmates and shook her head. "I shouldn't be in here me, look at what I'm having to mix with, they're a load of scumbags."

Helen held her head back and laughed out loud. "Who the fuck, do you think you are? You better take your head from up your arse, and give it a shake. These women are probably like us, just out to earn a few quid. Don't judge people who you know fuck all about? I bet they are all decent women if you gave them half a chance."

Susie creased her lips and lifted her head high. "Fuck off, never in a million years am I mixing with these trollops.

I'm fed up, not hard up, who needs friends anyway?"

Helen smiled as they passed the group of women stood chatting at the top of the staircase. "Alright ladies," she chuckled as she walked past them.

The inmates smiled at Helen and nodded their head in acknowledgement of her friendship. "Yep, smashing," one prisoner shouted back.

"See," Helen whispered as she grabbed Susie's arm. "That's all it takes, we need all the friends we can get while we're in here. The last thing we need is to start making enemies."

"Well you can talk to them if you want. I'm keeping my distance, imagine seeing them when I'm out of jail, fuck that. What happens in jail stays in jail. I'm flying solo, me, love."

Helen sat eating her breakfast. Her knife and fork were clashing together as she devoured it. Susie was playing with her food and just picked at it. A hand came over her body and a fork could be seen digging into her bacon. Lifting her head up she scowled, as she watched Helen clear the remaining food from her plate. Susie screwed her face up and pushed the food to Helen's side. "Here, you fucking gannet, fucking hell, don't you have any shame?" Helen slid the plate to the side of her and emptied the remaining food onto her own pile of food. Not stopping for breath she scranned every last remaining piece of food in front of her. "Fat bastard," Susie muttered.

Once breakfast was over Susie had an appointment with the doctor. The authorities knew she was pregnant now and they were making sure she got all the medical attention she needed. Standing to her feet she could see Jane over the other side of the room, she was waving her hand at her. The sound of chair legs being scraped along the floor could be heard as most of the prisoners were setting off to face another day behind prison walls. It was bang up for those inmates who didn't work or weren't in any kind of education. Helen had started an arts course and found out that she really had a talent for drawing. She'd copied a photo of her son and even the tutor said it was amazing.

Jane was soon by Susie's side. Her voice was low. "I've had a chat with my husband," she whispered. "I need to speak to you as soon as possible."

Susie smiled; she could tell the screw had some good news for her. "Yeah I've just got to go to the medical unit first, though."

Jane looked excited. "Can I come with you? I'll just tell the staff that you don't want to go on your own. I'm your personal officer after all aren't I, so there shouldn't be any problem?"

"Come on then," Susie smiled, "I don't want to be late." Helen watched them leave and started to mingle with the other inmates. With a wave of her hand she watched Susie and Jane leave the canteen area.

Susie and the screw walked down the long corridor. When they reached the waiting area Susie told the receptionist she was there. Lots of chairs were across the back wall and other pregnant inmates were sat waiting there for their appointments too. Susie parked her arse and held her head back against the wall. A drug addict was sat next to her and her small baby bump looked deformed. Susie scanned the prisoner and turned her head to face her. "How far are you then?"

The convict smiled and rubbed the lower part of her stomach. "I'm ready to drop next week; I'm only small aren't I?"

Susie looked shocked. "Fuck me, yes you are. I thought you were about six months or summit like that."

The woman held her hand over her brown stumpy teeth, her front tooth was missing. "I can't wait until it's out of me. I've been ill for the full pregnancy." Susie sighed and watched Jane talking to another screw. She seemed to have a glow about her today. Her cheeks looked rosy and she seemed happy for a change.

Susie's name was called out to go and see the doctor. Standing to her feet she shot her eyes to Jane. "I'm going in, if you're coming." The officer said goodbye to her colleague and quickly walked to her side.

The drug addict nodded her head at Susie. "Good luck with it all." Susie was gone.

The doctor took Susie's blood samples and her blood pressure. Everything was normal and there was nothing to worry about. The last job was to feel her stomach and to check the baby was growing inside her. Rubbing his hands together he smiled at his patient. "I'm just warming my hands up."

Susie was lay on the examination table and Jane was seated at the side of her. The doctor cupped his hands and placed them on her stomach. His face looked concerned as he pressed about on her abdomen. Susie could see his concern and coughed loudly. "Is everything alright Doctor?"

He turned to Jane and smiled. "I think its twins."

Susie's face dropped and the colour seemed to drain from her face. "Are you having a fucking laugh or what," she hissed.

The doctor patted his hands about her stomach once again. "Yes, there are definitely two babies in there."

Jane stood up and her face looked red. The doctor

told Susie he was booking her in for a scan as soon as possible to confirm what he thought. Writing a few notes down in her personal file he left the room to leave her to get ready.

Susie looked distraught; she sat on the edge of the bed kicking her legs out in front of her. "Well that's me fucked innit. You don't want two babies do you?"

Jane threw her arms around her and tears streamed down her face. "Of course I do, I know it's not what we planned but Paul with be over the moon. This is just what we need, a family."

Susie hunched her shoulders and her eyes opened wide. "I don't want any more money you know, I'm just glad you want the two of them." Susie jumped down from the bed. Straightening her clothes she smiled at Jane. "What's the good news then, come on then spill the beans. I can tell by your face you're dying to tell me something."

Jane stood behind the door and checked nobody was about. Keeping her voice low she whispered. "Paul wants to come and meet you. We have worked it all out, he said we can say we're your family to start with and we'll have temporary custody of the babies until you get out."

Susie screwed her face up. "I thought you said you were adopting them."

Jane jumped in and stopped her dead in her tracks. "Yeah we are, but it's easier to do it like this first, trust me. Once you get out, all you'll have to do is sign a few papers and that's it, the babies will be ours. Nobody will be any the wiser."

The room was silent for a minute until Susie spoke. "So when is your husband coming to see me then,"

Jane chuckled. "I've booked him a visit for tomorrow

at one o'clock if that's okay."

Susie chewed on her lips. "Yeah, it's not as if I won't be here is it."

Jane giggled and pulled the door open. She escorted her prisoner back to her cell and left her almost immediately. "Speak soon," she whispered as she closed the door behind her.

Helen was sprawled on her bed munching on some crisps. Speaking with a gob full of food she waved her hands in the air. "Was everything alright with the bambino and all that?"

Susie blew her breath and flung her body onto her bed. "I'm having fucking twins the doctor said."

Helen jumped up from the bed. "No fucking way, are ya?"

Susie nodded. "Yep, two of the little bastards to get rid of now, not just one."

Helen smirked and rolled about the bed in fits of laughter. "Susie this could only happen to you. How unlucky is that."

"Okay, okay, don't rub it in then," Susie said.

Helen licked her fingers as she finished the last few crisps in the packet. "Fuck me, that's you fucked then innit. Jane won't want the two of them will she?"

Susie smiled. "Well that's where you're wrong smart arse. She came down to the antenatal with me and she knows everything. She wants them both."

"Fuck off, no way," Helen shrieked. "You're a jammy fucker you are. Well that's a result anyway."

Susie nodded her head and lay stroking her belly. "Just think in three months time my body will be my own again, and my worst nightmare will be over. I'm meeting her other half tomorrow, so it's all gravy, now baby." They chuckled as Susie reached for a bar of chocolate from the side of her bed. Susie had gained some weight over the last few weeks and all she seemed to be doing was eating. Susie rubbed her hands together as she rammed a piece of chocolate into her mouth. "I'm a survivor me love, watch this space."

CHAPTER TWENTY-FIVE

Susie sat in the visiting room waiting for her visit with Jane's husband. She'd made every effort to look presentable, she didn't want Jane's partner thinking she was a skank and a low life. Jane was on door duty today and she was helping with all the visitors. She looked nervous and kept looking at Susie with a half-hearted smile. The visiting room was quiet as all the inmates sat waiting to see their loved ones. Susie sat tapping her fingers on the table.

People started to enter the room; inmates stood from their chairs and hugged their loved ones. Susie dropped her head onto her arms and held back the tears, she felt alone and lonely and wished somebody loved her. She would have given anything at that moment for a hug and a kiss from someone who cared about her.

Susie watched the entrance with eager eyes. Sitting chewing her fingernails she could see Jane talking to a man, she was struggling to see his face. Sitting up straight in her chair she prepared herself to meet Jane's husband. Jane came walking towards her with a smile spread right across her face. "He's just going to get you a drink and some food. I've told him to get you some chocolate because I know you're craving it." Susie licked her lips; she was hungry again and could have eaten a scabby horse at that moment.

Jane stood fidgeting at the side of her; her eyes were all over the place. Seeing her other half queuing up for food she walked over to where he was stood. Covering her mouth she whispered to him. "She's at table seven, make sure you're nice to her, I don't want you ruining things. This means everything to me you know."

"Don't you worry sweetheart, I want this as much as you. I'm going to be as nice as pie to her, don't you worry your pretty little head." Jane moved from his side and headed back to work. She didn't want anyone putting two and two together. She smiled one last time at Susie and trudged back to her workmates.

Susie looked bored and held her head down on the table on her folded arms. A man's voice made her sit up. "Hello Susie, I'm Paul, Jane's husband."

Susie lifted her head slowly and nearly died when she saw the man's face for the first time. She sprang back in her chair and yanked at her t-shirt around her neck. Her face was red and she looked like she was going to burst. The man sat down and she could see the colour draining from his face too. The two of them sat in silence for a minute. Susie was shaking and her lips were trembling as she started to speak for the first time. "What the fuck are you doing here?" Jane's husband dragged at his hair and small droplets of sweat were visible on his forehead. His eyes were all over the place as he scanned the room for his wife. Susie spoke again in a distressed tone. "Is this some kind of sick joke or summat. I'll say it again, what the fuck are you doing here. Don't you think you've done enough to me, you double-crossing bastard."

Paul sighed and reached his hands over to Susie's. "Listen, I'm just as shocked as you. Jane wants this so much, please let's try and sort something out."

Susie nearly bolted up from her chair; she was half stood up as she growled into his face. "I should just tell your wife everything. You're a dirty perverted cunt and deserve everything that's coming to you."

"Please please Susie, let's talk about this." Susie gasped for breath as she took a gulp of her coffee.

"Talk about it, are you having a laugh. You and Tim have ruined my life."

The man held his head in his hands, he looked desperate. "Susie I know what I did was wrong, but come on you were blackmailing me, I was at my wits end. Tim made me do it."

Susie spat across the table at him. "I should have cottoned on to Jane's surname, what a nob-head I am. Paul Jenkins, Jane Jenkins, why didn't I see it?" Paul slammed his flat palm on the table, a few of the inmates looked at him and he knew he had to curb his anger.

Gasping for breath he snarled at her. "Listen bitch, me and my wife have been to hell and back these last few months, give us a break for Christ's sake. We lost our son you know." Paul hung his head low and tears formed in the corner of his eyes. "I feel so guilty every day I breathe. I think God took my son for the sins I committed. Do you know how that makes me feel when I watch my wife on her knees crying for our dead son?"

Susie choked her tears back. "Don't try that bullshit with me, because it doesn't wash. You were shagging brasses, end of. You should have thought about your wife before you went paying for sex, you dirty bastard."

Paul chewed on his shaking lips as they both sat staring at each other. Jane was walking over to them now and you could see the panic written all across his face. Turning his head quickly towards Susie he pleaded with her. "Please, think about this, please don't tell her, it would kill her, trust me, she's not strong enough." Susie held her head back and her nostrils were flaring. Tapping her fingernail on her front teeth a cunning look came across her face.

Jane stood at the side of the table, she was grinning at the both of them. "Hope you two are getting on?"

Paul tried to raise a smile but his eyes were fixed on Susie, waiting for her to answer. Susie struggled to speak at first but she found the words she needed to answer her. "Oh we're getting on like a house on fire, aren't we Paul? It's like we've known each other for years."

Paul raised a smile but you could see he was struggling. Jane gripped her husband's shoulder and whispered in his ear. "This is the happiest I've been in a long time, I love you so much, thanks, babes."

Paul held the tears back and Susie could see the pain in his face. Jane left them again and walked about the room checking the other visitors. Once she was well out of the way Susie snarled at him. "So... let's talk business."

"What do you mean?" he gasped.

"Well now it's a whole new ball game, isn't it," she chuckled and rubbed her palms together. Bending in towards him she kept her voice low and stared directly in his eyes. "You owe me, you bent bastard, and I'm gonna make sure you pay in full. There's things you can do for me, starting from now, do you hear me?"

Paul nodded slowly. "Anything, just as long as you don't tell my wife."

"I want Tim sorting out," she whispered.

Paul looked puzzled. "I'm not in that jail anymore Susie, so what the fuck can I do to him."

Susie gritted her teeth, "Make it your business to sort

it out; surely you must have friends in there who can pull a few strings for you. I don't want him dead, oh no." She was sat bent over the table now and they were nose to nose. "I want him down the block; I want him to feel low. And I want him to have fuck all, just like I have."

Paul cracked his knuckles as he sat thinking for a minute. "I can do that, I have friends in the jail that can plant some drugs, will that do?"

Susie smiled and nodded her head. "Yeah for now, I want some money sending in for me too. I'm on my arse and haven't got a pot to piss in. Tell Jane what she can do in here to make my life easier."

Paul sipped his drink and watched as Susie attacked the 'Mars' bar he'd bought her. His eyes never left her face and he looked dead inside. The sound of the screw shouting to end the visits could be heard. Paul looked anxious and reached over to hold Susie's hands. Looking into her eyes he spoke with a shaky voice. "Susie please don't ruin my life. I'll do all I can to help you, but please tell me we can still have the babies. It would kill Jane if you changed your mind now."

Susie stood up on her feet and stretched her arms above her head as she yawned. "You can have the babies, don't worry. Just make sure I'm not on my arse while I'm in here that's all." Paul nodded as he walked away; he looked like a broken man.

Susie went to get searched. As she turned her head she could see Paul waiting to leave the prison. She chuckled to herself and couldn't believe what had just happened. The years she had left in prison now seemed bearable. Susie had Jenkins by the short and curlies and she knew he would do anything to keep her mouth shut.

When she got back on the wing, Helen was playing

pool with another inmate. Susie could see her as she dipped her head over the metal banister. Susie cupped her hands around her mouth and shouted down to her. "Ay lard arse, you're looking more like a bloke every day. Pull your pants up, ya arse is showing."

Helen yanked her tracksuit bottoms up and rammed her fingers up in the air at her. "Fuck you," she shouted back at her as she continued to take her shot.

Susie entered her cell. Her mail was on the bed. Her face looked puzzled as she picked up the white envelope. It looked like Ashley's handwriting. Sitting on the bed she quickly opened it and sat reading. Her face looked shocked, "What the fuck," she whispered. Susie read the words over and over again. Holding the letter to her chest she shook her head. Thinking for a minute she stood to her feet and left the pad in a rush. Bending over the balcony she shouted Helen's name. Helen lifted her head up and could see Susie was upset. She was waving the letter out in front of her. "Come up here quick, I need you to read this." Helen started running up the staircase. All her blubber was shaking as she ran, her face looked red. Taking a minute at the top of the stairs she tried to regain her breath. Her body was bent over and she gripped her knees as she blew her breath between her legs.

Susie was at her side. "Quick, come in the pad and have a read of this."

"Fucking hang on, I'm having a heart attack here. I just need to stand still for a minute to get my breath back."

"Hurry up," Susie moaned as she ran back down the landing towards her cell. Helen trudged down the corridor; her face was still as red as a tomato. Walking into the pad she looked at Susie's face and knew something was wrong. "Come on then spill, what's up."

Susie threw her the letter. "Have a read of that."

Helen parked her arse on the bed, her mouth was open and she kept mumbling under her breath. Once she read the letter she looked at Susie. "Well that's a turn up for the books, innit. Write back to him and tell the wanker to get to fuck. He had his chance, and fucked it, didn't he?"

Susie touched her stomach with a flat palm and dipped her head down as she spoke to her bump. "Oh daddy wants his babies now, what a fucking shame that he'll never see you."

Helen stood up and came to her side. "Are you going to tell him there are two babies now, not just one?"

Susie held her head back and smiled. "Fucking dead right I am. I'm gonna tell him they're getting adopted and he'll never see his kids again."

Helen shot her a look, she didn't know if she believed her. Placing one hand on her hip she spoke to her again. "Are you sure Susie, I mean you could be a family and all that."

Susie shook her head from side to side, her eyes held a strange look. "He's going to feel pain, just like I have. Everyone who's took the piss out of me is getting paid back and that includes your fucking brother."

Helen huffed. She knew there was no point in arguing with her pad mate. She was on one now and best left alone. Helen grabbed her packet of tobacco from the side, "Right I'm going back to finish my game of pool. I'm like fucking Alex Higgins now, I've had a bit of practice," she giggled as she left the room.

Susie searched for a pen, once she'd found one she lay flat on her back and started to write back to her ex-boyfriend. Every now and then she would burst out laughing. "Fucking tosser, you are Ashley. Fancy even thinking you could just write to me and everything would be alright. What a plonker you really are." Reading the letter over and over she finally placed it into a white envelope that she'd nicked from Helen. Licking the edges of it she pressed it down firmly. After writing Ashley's address on the front of it, she placed it on her bedside cabinet. "Read it and weep," she chuckled under her breath as she fell back onto her bed.

Today was one of the best days Susie had had, inside the prison walls. The future was looking bright. Now Jenkins was back on her books she knew she could pay back all the people who had wronged her in the past. As she stared at the ceiling and you could see by her face she was already planning their downfall in her mind. A small smile filled her face as she pulled the blankets over her body. Her eyes closed and she drifted off to sleep.

Vicky lay on the bed after her third punter had left. She looked a mess, her eyes were dark underneath and the pretty girl she had once been, seemed gone forever. The room was eerie and she sat looking cold. Goose pimples were visible all over her skin. Lighting a cigarette she puffed away waiting for the next man to come into her room for her services. The sound of passing traffic could be heard from outside and in the distance she could hear sirens blaring. Once she'd finished her cig she squashed it out in the ashtray. The door could be heard opening. A young man stood in front of her but his baseball cap hid his face.

He walked slowly to the bed and sat down next to

her. Vicky was reaching over to the side of the bed to get a condom when a hand was placed on her wrist. Turning her head back quickly she was about to tell her client to take his fucking filthy hands off her, but her words were stuck in her throat. "Blake," she said. Vicky bolted up from the bed and sank her fingernails deep into his face. "You twat, you fucking dirty, lying bastard," she ranted.

Blake fought her off but looked sad. After she started launching objects at him from the side of the bed he tried to pacify her. "Just calm down will you. I want to talk to you."

Vicky was like a woman possessed. "Fucking calm down, are you having a laugh ya muppet?" she yelled. Reaching for the 'Anne Summer's' Rabbit from the side of the bed, she whacked him over the head with the vibrator. "You had me over! You left me Blake, why? why?" Vicky stood over him and her hands were trembling as she clenched her fists together. Her lips trembled as she spoke. "Come on then nob-head, why are you fucking here, what do you want?"

Blake looked at her, taking a few minutes he finally spoke. "I'm sorry. I still love you and I want you back."

Vicky's body melted into the floor like a chocolate fireguard. Bringing her knees to her chest she rocked her body. "I'm a mess, because of you Blake, look at my face."

Blake hung his head low and came to join her on the floor. Reaching inside his pocket he pulled out a wad of cash. "We can start afresh, I promise you, and I'll never hurt you again. There's enough money here for us to fuck off somewhere. I've got my own place now." Vicky scanned the money, he was right there was enough money for them to start again. Her head was in bits and she didn't know what to think, she looked confused.

Blake gripped her face in his hands. Tears rolled down his cheeks as he saw the scar on her cheek for the first time. "Is this what they did to you because of me?" Vicky nodded.

Blake sprang to his feet and dug his hands down the side of his jeans. Pulling out a gun he waved it about in the air. "I'm gonna pop a cap in their arses, cheeky fuckers, who the fuck do they think they are doing this to you."

Vicky chewed on her lips. Blake was her knight in shining armour and without him she knew her life was set in stone. Dragging her up from the floor he held her face with one hand. "Are you coming with me or what, I swear I'll look after you." Vicky nodded and flung her arms around him. His body felt strong and she felt safe in his arms. "Get your stuff; we're out of this shit-hole." Vicky froze.

"What about Joan and Pippa, there is no way they'll let me leave yet. I still owe them money don't I?"

Blake snarled and his face was red with anger, you could see the vein pumping at the side of his neck. "Do you think I give a fuck about them two slags, leave them to me? Just get ya shit together." Vicky quickly ran about the room, shoving all her belongings into her handbag, she was frantic.

Vicky walked into the reception area with Blake following closely behind her. Pippa was sat on the sofa smoking a cig. When she saw her she looked confused. "I thought you were working?" Vicky didn't reply as Blake came barging past her.

Running towards Pippa he pulled the black gun from his coat and rammed it into her mouth. "She's fucking coming with me ya daft slag. No more paying any money back, she's gone from here. Do you hear me?" Blake's voice was loud and Pippa looked terrified as the end of the gun was hanging from her mouth. "I said its over, do you hear me?" Blake ranted. Pulling the gun from her mouth he swung it back and launched it into the side of her head. Pippa fell back on the sofa and didn't move.

Joan heard the commotion and came into view. "What the fuck is going on here?" she yelled at the top of her voice. Seeing Pippa was hurt on the sofa her eyes shot to Vicky. "Tell me what's going on," Joan was fuming. Vicky stood tall and gritted her teeth.

Pulling the gun from Blake's hands Vicky walked towards her. Joan looked terrified. Vicky held the shooter out in front of her and her hands were shaking as she spoke. "You dirty old boot. Who the fuck do you think you are, you crack-head. I've had enough of your shit." The sound of a gunshot could be heard and Joan's body fell to the floor instantly.

Blake quickly ran to Vicky's side. "Come on let's get the fuck out of here."

Vicky stared at Joan's lifeless body on the floor and shook Blake's grip from her arm mumbling, "Is she dead?" Blake walked over to the body and quickly shook it. Lifting his head up, he nodded. Vicky walked over to where Joan lay and swung her foot back. With one almighty swing she kicked the dead body. Blake looked scared and grabbed her again. "Vicky she's dead, leave her now, we need to go."

Vicky still had the gun in her hand and ran to where Pippa lay. The sound of another gunshot could be heard. "Now there are no fucking witnesses!" she screamed. Blake pushed the sofa in front of the corridor and made sure nobody could get inside. He reached over the counter and pulled the CCTV tape from the recorder. "Hurry up Vicky it's on top." Vicky sprinted to his side as they left Delia's.

Blake and Vicky ran and ran until they were out of sight. She was white in the face and as soon as they stopped running she spewed her ring up at the side of the road. Blake was bouncing about as he stood watching her. "You're fucking mental Vicky. I only wanted to scare them, what the fuck did you shoot them for?"

Lifting her head and wiping her mouth she snarled at Blake. "They killed me months ago, so they got what they deserved."

Blake could see the hurt in her eyes and hugged her body. "Right let's go and get Declan, I'll get the car, and then we're gone from here, do you hear me, gone."

Vicky was still. Blake grabbed her again. "Vicky come on, the dibble will be here soon, we need to get on our toes." Grabbing her hand he dragged her into a side street away from any prying eyes. They both ran off, and they weren't stopping for love nor money.

Blake kept the engine running as Vicky ran in her sister's house for Declan. Once she'd got him they quickly went to her house to grab the stuff they needed. Running from the house she was carrying a few bags. Blake jumped from the car and opened the boot. Once her stuff was inside he slammed it shut and ran back to the driver's side. "Hurry up Vicky," he yelled, he was stressed. The engine started and he sped off into the night. Declan was still asleep on the back seat with a coat flung over his body.

Once they hit the motorway Blake started to relax. Reaching his hand over to Vicky he rubbed her knee. "I love you so much you know. Everything going to be sweet from now on, I've got a nice house in Liverpool and we can start our new life together. I promise you Vicky, no more shit from me. All I want is you and Declan."

Vicky's lips trembled and her shoulders were shaking up and down. "It's all I want too Blake. I just want to be happy; I've had enough of all this shit."

The signs for Liverpool could be seen on the motorway. They were safe and a million miles away from the crimes they'd committed. Vicky had a whole new life planned now and somehow Blake seemed to be telling the truth. Holding her hand as he drove he kept smiling at her telling her how much he loved her. Blake had been doing well in his life and with the money he'd stolen from her he'd built himself a new life. The days ahead looked bright for Vicky and her son and from this day onward she would never look back at the life she led. Blake made sure Vicky would never be caught for the double murder she'd committed. He'd made sure there was no evidence left at the scene of the crime. She was his world now and he would protect her from harm, he owed it to them both, after all, this was his mess.

Vicky held her stomach as they approached a service station. "I need a piss, can you pull over?"

Blake nodded. Watching her running to the toilet area he quickly pulled his mobile phone from his pocket. Dialling a number he looked anxious, a ringing tone could be heard. "Hello Susie, it's me Blake, I've got her with me now. I'm taking her to my gaff in Liverpool." Laughter could be heard on the other end of the line. "Don't worry Susie I'll keep her with me until you're out." Blake could see Vicky running back to the car, he ended the call quickly. Ramming the phone back into his pocket he sat with a smirk on his face. "Come on pissy arse," he giggled as she got back into the car. The engine started and they carried on with their journey.

CHAPTER TWENTY-SIX

Susie lay screaming at the top of her voice as she gave birth. With every pain that surged through her body she yelled like a banshee. Jane was by her side giving her all the support she needed.

Susie finally gave birth to two boys at seven thirty five on the tenth of May. She'd only asked one thing of Jane, before she took her flesh and blood away from her, she wanted to name them. Holding the two boys in her arms for the first time, she asked Jane to leave her alone while she said her goodbyes to her sons. Once she was alone she sat up straight in her bed, looking down at the infants she spoke in a low voice. "Well boys its goodbye for now. I might come back for you one day, when I sort myself out, but for now you have to go with your new family." Looking into her boys faces she stroked their cheeks with her finger. "Ashley and Tim, I love you both so much and although you might not think so at this moment, I promise you one day we will be a family."

Tears streamed down from her eyes and landed on her the infants faces. Wiping them slowly away she blew a laboured breath as Jane came back into the room, this time Paul was by her side. He looked happy and as he reached for the new babies he stroked Susie's hands. "Thank you so much, it's all we've ever wanted." Susie choked up and passed her babies over to their new parents.

Paul Jenkins had done all he could to help Susie during the intervening months. Tim got what he deserved and the word on the street was that he'd tried to take his own life on more than one occasion, he couldn't hack prison life anymore. He was a broken man. Susie's bank balance was something that made her smile every day. She too had a new life now, and knew in time she would be a free woman. She was already planning a boob job for when she was set free.

Susie was still a vindictive bitch and somehow I don't think she will ever change, she remains a dangerous woman who it is unwise to get on the wrong side of.

As she lay alone in her bed, with her babies gone – all she had left was the smell of them on her long t-shirt. Sniffing hard she inhaled the fragrance from her two sons. "Not long boys, then mummy will be back for you. I promise," she muttered under her breath. Susie closed her eyes and a single tear could be seen on her cheek. Pulling the green blanket over her body you could see her body shaking. Susie was heartbroken.

Helen ploughed through prison life with a smile on her face. She never got down and always saw the light in any situation. She too prayed for the day when she'd be a free woman. She had a couple of debts to settle herself and knew in her heart, a few people wouldn't be smiling when she was finished with them. "Every dog has its day," she whispered under her breath as she ticked another day off her calendar at the side of her bed.

"Goodnight, sleep tight," she whispered to Susie as she placed her head onto her pillow. "Make sure the bed bugs don't bite," she chuckled as she lay staring into space with a cunning look on her face.

THE END

BROKEN YOUTH

A novel by Karen Woods

"Sex , violence and fractured relationships, a kitchen sink drama that needs to be told and a fresh voice to tell it."

TERRY CHRISTIAN

When rebellious teenager Misty Sullivan falls pregnant to a local wannabe gangster, she soon becomes a prisoner in her own home. Despite the betrayal of her best friend, she eventually recovers her self-belief and plots revenge on her abusive boyfriend with spectacular consequences.

This gripping tale sees the impressive debut of Karen Woods in the first of a series of novels based on characters living on a Manchester council estate. Themes of social deprivation, self-empowerment, lust, greed and envy come to the fore in this authentic tale of modern life.

BLACK TEARS

A NOVEL BY KAREN WOODS

"MANCHESTER'S ANSWER TO MARTINA COLE"

WITH EVIL GORDON locked up in Strangeways for 5 years, the characters from Karen Woods' debut novel 'Broken Youth' come to terms with life without him.

Misty, now married to Dominic, gives birth to Gordon's child, Charlotte. Her former best friend Francesca also gives birth to one of Gordon's children, Rico, while staying with Gordon's heroin addicted brother Tom.

Meanwhile, as the clock ticks down on his sentence, Gordon broods on the injustice of his situation and plots sweet revenge on those on the outside.

BAgHEAds

"An author Manchester should be proud of"

CRISSY ROCK

Shaun was always a child who demanded more than life could give. His mother's stuggle began when she became a single parent, leaving her abusive husband behind. Unable to cope without the family unit, Shaun turns to a life of crime and drugs and eventually ends up in the care system.

NORTHERN
GIRLS ♥ GRAVY

A NOVEL BY KAREN WOODS

> *"Victoria Greybank had
> everything a woman could ever
> dream of but as she stood tall
> in the full length mirror she
> pulled at her expensive clothes
> and hated her life."*

Trapped in a loveless marriage Victoria soon discovers her husband's late nights at the office are excuses to engage in sado–masochistic sex.

Bewildered, she falls in with a lesbian overseas property developer who comes up with a big plan to make them both very rich...

Karen Woods' third novel deals is sexy, saucy and very, very naughty.